P9-CNB-924

5/03

2/15-23

DISCARD

DELECTABLE
MOUNTAINS

Berkley Prime Crime Books by Earlene Fowler

FOOL'S PUZZLE

IRISH CHAIN

KANSAS TROUBLES

GOOSE IN THE POND

DOVE IN THE WINDOW

MARINER'S COMPASS

SEVEN SISTERS

ARKANSAS TRAVELER

STEPS TO THE ALTAR

SUNSHINE AND SHADOW

BROKEN DISHES

DELECTABLE MOUNTAINS

DELECTABLE MOUNTAINS

Earlene Fowler

BERKLEY PRIME CRIME, NEW YORK

THE BERKLEY PUBLISHING GROUP
Published by the Penguin Group
Penguin Group (USA) Inc.
375 Hudson Street, New York, New York 10014, USA
Penguin Group (Canada), 10 Alcorn Avenue, Toronto, Ontario M4V 3B2, Canada
(a division of Pearson Penguin Canada Inc.)
Penguin Books Ltd., 80 Strand, London WC2R 0RL, England
Penguin Group Ireland, 25 St. Stephen's Green, Dublin 2, Ireland (a division of Penguin Books Ltd.)
Penguin Group (Australia), 250 Camberwell Road, Camberwell, Victoria 3124, Australia
(a division of Pearson Australia Group Pty. Ltd.)
Penguin Books India Pvt. Ltd., 11 Community Centre, Panchsheel Park, New Delhi—110 017, India
Penguin Group (NZ), Cnr. Airborne and Rosedale Roads, Albany, Auckland 1310, New Zealand
(a division of Pearson New Zealand Ltd.)
Penguin Books (South Africa) (Pty.) Ltd., 24 Sturdee Avenue, Rosebank, Johannesburg 2196,
South Africa

Penguin Books Ltd., Registered Offices: 80 Strand, London WC2R 0RL, England

This book is an original publication of The Berkley Publishing Group.

This is a work of fiction. Names, characters, places, and incidents either are the product of the author's imagination or are used fictitiously, and any resemblance to actual persons, living or dead, business establishments, events, or locales is entirely coincidental.

First edition: May 2005

Library of Congress Cataloging-in-Publication Data

Fowler, Earlene.
    Delectable mountains / Earlene Fowler.—1st ed.
       p.   cm.
    ISBN 0-425-20249-6
    1. Harper, Benni (Fictitious character)—Fiction.   2. Women museum curators—Fiction.
    3. Children's theater—Fiction.   4. Quiltmakers—Fiction.   I. Title.

    PS3556.O828D45   2005
    813'.54—dc22
                                                                    2004062327

PRINTED IN THE UNITED STATES OF AMERICA

10   9   8   7   6   5   4   3   2   1

For my nieces and nephews
with love,
Lance, Sarah, Jason, Jennifer,
Chris, Matt, and Samantha.
May you all safely find your
way to the Celestial City

Acknowledgments

"May the words of my mouth and the meditation of my heart be pleasing in your sight, O Lord, my Rock and my Redeemer."
Psalm 19:14

No woman is an island, especially when she is writing a book. My humble gratitude to everyone who helped me physically, emotionally, and spiritually with this particular literary endeavor.

Ellen Geiger, an agent who deserves a star named after her. Thank you for your help, your friendship, and your timely words of encouragement and wisdom.

Pastor John "Mac" McFarland, for his insights and for being the funniest minister I've ever known.

Sonja O'Donohoe, San Luis Obispo County Sheriff, for teaching me about SWAT team procedures and for letting me borrow your name.

Don Rader, Paso Robles Library, for his always enthusiastic and thorough research.

Lela Satterfield, a talented woman of God. Thank you for taking the time to listen to me, laugh with me, and remind me that God's timing is always perfect.

Christine Zika, my treasured editor, who has a magical ability to zero in on just what a book needs to make it shine that much brighter.

My faithful, insightful friends and readers: Clare Bazley, Bunny Brown, Tina Davis, Bonnie Haskell, Jo-Ann Mapson.

All the "Doves" in my church, Fountain Valley First United Methodist (you know who you are) for your prayers and your loving support.

A special thank-you to these friends whose good wishes, gifts, prayers, and humor keep my spirits high: Janice Dischner, Jo Ellen Heil, Christine Hill, Sue Kreft, Karen Meeks, Helen May, Susan McCoubrie, Carolyn Miller, Pam Munns, Karen Olson, Sally and Robbie Parker, Laurie Van Loan, Kathy Vieira, and Laura Ross-Wingfield.

My new dog, Boudin "Boo" Fowler—corgi, writing companion, and constant bundle of surprise

Allen Fowler, husband and best friend—if I could save all my time in a bottle . . . again I would spend it with you.

A Note from the Author

When I started the Benni Harper series in 1992, the first book, *Fool's Puzzle*, was written in "real time." It was 1992 in Benni's life as well as mine. Time in a long-running series is tricky. Since it often takes a book almost two years from the time the author starts writing it to the point when it is actually in the reader's hands, time sequences can become confusing. Each author deals with this dilemma in a different way. I decided from the beginning that I would age my characters more slowly than I and my readers were aging. With Dove being seventy-five in the first book, I wanted to keep her active and vital, and I also wanted to explore the early stages of Benni and Gabe's complex relationship. Keep in mind while reading that the books, as of *Delectable Mountains*, cover late 1992 to November 1996. Now, if we could only figure out a way for all of us to age like Benni and Gabe . . .

Delectable Mountains

Many quilts draw their inspiration from spiritual sources. Found as far back in quilting history as the 1840s, the Delectable Mountains pattern has a long tradition of being connected to John Bunyan's allegory *Pilgrim's Progress*. In the story, the Delectable Mountains were filled with beautiful gardens, orchards, vineyards, and fountains of water. From the mountains' heights, the searching pilgrims could see the gates of Celestial City. The pattern is often made with bias set squares turned to form a triangular design that is suggestive of mountain peaks. It is considered one of the most identifiable American quilt patterns. Similar in design to Kansas Troubles and Indian Trail, variations of it have been called World's Fair and Solomon's Temple.

PROLOGUE

I WAS SIX YEARS OLD WHEN MY MOTHER DIED. FOR A LONG TIME afterward, the sweet and earthy magnolia scent of her would permeate my dreams. No matter what I was dreaming about, good or frightening, my mother's smell would waft through my nighttime adventures, infusing them with her unseen presence, reassuring me even through their darkest moments. I never told anyone about this. I felt that, somehow, my mother had found a way to communicate with me from heaven even though I knew from the down-to-earth practicality of my Baptist Sunday School lessons that it was likely impossible. Still, I have heard it said more than once that with God, nothing is impossible. Is it so hard to imagine that He, in His infinite compassion, might have, for a moment in time, comforted a scared little girl with her mother's familiar scent?

When I was nine, one of my favorite horses had to be put down. He was a gentle, mud-colored gelding name Jonesy. While being ridden by one of my dad's more inexperienced ranch hands, Jonesy lost his footing and tumbled down an embankment. The ranch hand got away with only scratches and bruises, but Jonesy broke both his front legs. Though it happened miles from our ranch house and Daddy claims it was impossible, I swear to this day that I heard the crack from his rifle putting Jonesy out of his agony.

That night I dreamed about riding Jonesy across the thick green pasture behind our barn and for the first time in three years, the scent of my mother fled my dreams. I woke up in the black room sobbing, feeling a devastation that I have only felt one other time in my life, years later, when my first husband, Jack, was killed in an automobile accident.

My eight-year-old cousin, Emory, was visiting from Arkansas and slept in the twin bed next to me. His all-encompassing love for me overcame his fear of the monster hands lurking underneath his bed, and he dashed down our ranch house's long, spooky hallway to fetch my gramma Dove. It was a heroic feat, which, to this day when I think of it, causes a lump in my throat.

"She's gone," I wailed when Dove gathered me up in her warm, strong arms. "I can't smell her anymore." I sobbed with the chest-rattling intensity that only children seem able to truly experience.

Dove didn't ask me what I meant. I suppose she knew, having lost many people to death by that time of her life, including her beloved husband, Jake. She rocked me in her arms, her gravelly voice assuring me that my mother was not gone, that she was, by golly, sitting on heaven's front porch right this moment with her own mother and my grampa Jake, shelling pecans for a pie.

Was that how she comforted herself at night, alone in her bed, her heart and arms aching for her husband? I always thought of her as old, as timeless as the hills surrounding our ranch. Looking back now I realize she was only forty-six when she was widowed and in her early fifties when she moved to California to raise me. That was so young really, too soon to live out her life alone. I never saw her cry for

Grampa, though I'm sure she must have many times. Dove, I discovered in the years she raised me to adulthood, for all her open-hearted opinions and love, was also an intensely private person. Her sorrow was a silent, personal experience that she rarely showed the world. Was it the constant demands of me, my dad, her five other children, and their family's various stages of need that kept her from sharing her feelings? Or was it just the one thing she decided to keep to herself, a worry stone of emotion that, in her hectic, people-filled life, was hers alone?

That moment, smothered in Dove's sweet almond scent, I said my first real good-bye to my mother. Until then, in my child's mind, I thought Mama was like Christian in *Pilgrim's Progress*, or Dorothy in *The Wizard of Oz*, that she was wandering the dangerous, potholed world, trying to find her way back home. I started understanding that night that she was already home.

Eventually I went back to sleep, Emory curled next to me like an exhausted puppy, his popcorny, little-boy scent a comfort. I slept without dreaming. And though I still occasionally dream of my mother, her scent has never returned.

Scientists say that smell is the strongest of our five senses, that it is the most connected to the section of our brain that holds and retains our memories. They say that mothers can recognize their babies by smell and newborns recognize their mothers in the same mysterious way. Some researchers believe it takes the brain longer to recognize aromas and odors than to see or hear something. But they also say that a scent memory lasts longer than any other. I read somewhere that the human brain is capable of recognizing ten thousand different scents. Some, like peppermint and lemon, are said to energize us. Others, like pumpkin pie and black licorice, can arouse us. Still others, like lavender and nutmeg, calm us. Yet only a handful of scents can make us cry, and those are as individual as our fingerprints.

Though the scientists have all these fascinating facts and theories, it is always the poets who stumble upon the real truths. Marcel Proust said, "When nothing else subsists from the past, after the people are dead, after the things are broken and scattered . . . the smell and taste of things remain poised a long time, like souls . . . bearing resiliently, on tiny and almost impalpable drops of their essence, the immense edifice of memory."

I like to think that when I die, when I am crossing the river Jordan to join those I love in heaven, that before I see them coming, before they see me, that we will, in a flash of memory, smell each other again—my first husband's clove chewing gum; my mother's magnolia perfume; my father's solid scent of leather; my gramma Dove's delicate almond smell; the pungent, earthy smell of Jonesy, his legs straight and true; and, should my husband, Gabe, pass before me, his unique, gingery smell, a scent I would recognize in a rainstorm on the darkest night of the year. And in that moment of recognition, we will all smile and smile and smile, running as fast as we can toward each other, arms outstretched, through that beautiful, eternal water.

CHAPTER 1

THE PHONE'S RING STARTLED ME AWAKE. GABE, MY HUSBAND, grabbed the phone before the second ring finished. He's a police chief, so phone calls at odd hours cause him to switch instantly into command mode.

"Ortiz here." He listened for about twenty seconds. "It's for you." He passed the phone over to me. Then he instantly went back to sleep. Another ability he'd acquired in his twenty-some-odd years of being a cop.

"Help me," a ratchety old voice demanded.

I lay there comfortably smothered under flannel sheets and our heavy winter quilt thinking, isn't this déjà vu all over again?

"What's wrong now, Dove?" I mumbled to my gramma, opening one eye to look at my bedside clock. Seven A.M. I groaned dramatically. It was Saturday morning and early for us "city folks" as Dove liked to call us, but two hours into working time for country people like her and my daddy. They lived a half hour away, outside of San

Celina, a combination college/retirement/agriculture town on the Central Coast of California where Gabe is chief of police, and I am curator of the local folk art museum. Daddy has owned the Ramsey Ranch for thirty-six years, ever since I was two years old.

Next to me, Gabe grumbled and turned his broad back to me, covering his dark head with his down-filled pillow.

"Lily's daughter is having a baby," Dove said, clearing her throat. "Well, make that two." In the background I could hear the *brawk-brawk-brawk* of hungry chickens. She must be using the cordless phone. "Quit hogging the feed, girls," she yelled.

Now I was definitely awake. I sat up and rubbed the grainy sleep from my eyes. "I don't know nothin' about birthin' no babies."

"Very funny," she said. "She's having to fly back to Kentucky because her daughter sprained her ankle and can't do a thing."

"Ouch," I said.

"You know what *that* means." Her tone was ominous.

Lily Sanders was our worship leader and music director at San Celina First Baptist Church. She had a head of thick, curly auburn hair, an incredible singing voice that could clear your sinuses when she hit some high notes, and a heart for the Lord and His people that was as big as Texas and half of Oklahoma. She was so enthusiastic and loved by the congregation that she could even coerce some of the church's grumpy old coots in the second-to-last row into clapping along with her lively gospel songs. No one could say a single negative thing about her, an out-and-out miracle in a Baptist church where gossip was too often served as the favorite side dish along with fried chicken and buttermilk pie at the monthly potlucks.

"It means that we'll be back to singing "Amazing Grace" and "Just As I Am" every Sunday till the cows come home," I said.

Not that I don't love those old hymns, but before Lily came, various volunteers in the congregation took turns leading the music each

Sunday and things had fallen into a rut. People *knew* those songs, and people love to stick with what they know.

"Worse," she said. "It means there's no one to lead the children's musical."

Lily had formed both an adult choir and a children's choir and had, for the last few years, successfully produced Christmas and Easter programs featuring both groups. In the last few months, she decided to try a program outside the normal holiday offerings and present one for the church service right before the Thanksgiving weekend. Lily was a gifted writer as well as musician, and I'd heard from Dove that she'd adapted *Pilgrim's Progress* into a children's musical and was halfway into rehearsals. Since today was the first day of November, their performance was still a few weeks away.

"That's too bad," I said to her. "I'm sure the kids will be disappointed, but there's always next year." I swung my legs around and climbed out of bed. That was a sign for my dog, Scout, to crawl out of his monogrammed, Stewart-plaid doggie bed for which I spent way too much money. He padded over to greet me, and I stroked his milk chocolate–colored, half-Labrador, half–German shepherd head. Then I leaned over the bed, kissed the tattoo of a snarling Marine bulldog on my husband's smooth brown back, and tucked the quilt around him.

"I'll make coffee, Chief," I told him, pulling on a pair of gray sweatpants and one of Gabe's San Celina Police Department T-shirts.

From under his pillow came a mumble that sounded like a thank-you.

"So, why do you need my help?" I asked Dove. I started downstairs to the kitchen. "Are you going to host a surrogate baby shower for Lily's daughter?"

"Eventually. But that's not where I need your help. Actually, you don't have a choice. I already volunteered you."

I stopped at the bottom of the stairs, tempted to throw the phone into the next room.

"For what?" My voice sounded not unlike one of her Sicilian Buttercup chickens. "Let me tell you now, Dove, I am very, *very* busy. We have a new exhibit at the folk art museum. I'm already on two committees at church, and I'm a docent for the Heritage Walk on Saturday. I'm also helping set up the new folk art museum craft store downtown."

"I'm only asking for a few afternoons a week. Your afternoons aren't all that busy." Then she went straight for the big guns. "It's for the Lord, honeybun."

I took a deep breath and counted to five. She knew I wasn't about to argue with the woman who'd raised me since I was six years old when my own mother died of cancer. Not to mention letting down God. No, I wouldn't do either of those things. At least, not before my first cup of coffee.

"Okay," I said. "I'll hear you out, but I'm not committing to anything."

"I told Lily that we'd take over the musical, and she was thrilled."

"You did what?" I squeaked, my imagination already running rampant, picturing shrieking children careening around the sanctuary with water pistols and paper airplanes made from pages torn from the hymnals. I'd spent my time in Vacation Bible School as both a student and a teacher. I knew the havoc large groups of children could create.

"She said to tell you that you are an angel sent from God. Now she doesn't have a thing to worry about except her poor little daughter. Well, not so little, apparently." Dove gave a cheerful cackle, sounding a little like her chickens.

"Dove," I whined, drawing her name out to three syllables.

"Hush. We'll have a ball. You're not even in charge. I just volunteered you as my assistant. Rehearsals are on Wednesday and Saturday afternoons in the sanctuary, but this week I'm adding Mondays and Tuesdays because we need to get to know the kids. First one is to-day. See you at church. The kids are due to arrive at twelve-thirty."

She hung up before I could say another word.

"Why do I let her do this to me?" I asked Scout while pouring kibble into his metal dish and adding a spoonful of canned food. "You want to explain that to me?" Scout wagged his tail in sympathy and enthusiastically attacked his breakfast.

"Do what to you?" Gabe said, walking into our newly decorated red-and-white kitchen. We'd just had new wallpaper put up in our California Craftsman bungalow house, and the tiny, cheerful cherries made me smile every time I looked at them.

"Dove's being a rescuer again," I said, scooping coffee into the coffeemaker. "And dragging me into it."

"Who is it this time?" he said, grinning at me, his indigo-gray eyes amused. Even with his black hair spiked in disarray and wearing gray sweatpants and a rumpled white T-shirt, he was still the handsomest man I'd ever seen.

"Lily Sanders at church. You know, the lady who leads our music."

"The one with the dynamite voice."

Though he was Catholic and attended Mass at Mission Santa Celine downtown, he also came to many of First Baptist's activities, so he knew most of the regular church members. He and our pastor, Mac, a childhood friend of mine, regularly tried to give each other heart attacks by playing a series of very competitive racquetball games.

"Right. Her daughter is having twins back in Kentucky and said-daughter just sprained her ankle."

"Ouch," Gabe said, his face wrinkling in sympathy.

"My words exactly," I said, filling the carafe with water and pouring it into the coffeemaker. "Lily is in the middle of rehearsals for her children's production of *Pilgrim's Progress*, so Dove has volunteered to take her place and volunteered *me* to help her."

"That sounds like fun," he said, opening the refrigerator and standing in front of it waiting for Dove's fresh eggs to jump out and scramble themselves. He turned around, holding the plastic bowl of eggs and immediately burst out laughing. "You should see the look on your face."

"You have to be *loco* if you think putting on a play with a bunch of kids ages four to twelve is in any way fun."

He laughed again and pulled out a frying pan, wisely deciding that maybe he should prepare the eggs this morning. "I'll light a candle this week in gratitude that she didn't volunteer me."

"I'm too busy for this," I said, knowing that my carping would be in vain. Somehow, I'd find time to help Dove. There was no way in the world I'd refuse her anything. Something she knew and took advantage of on a regular basis.

"You'll work it out," he said confidently, cracking eggs into a red-and-white ceramic mixing bowl. "I'll help with security if you need it."

I went over and circled his waist with my arms, laying my head against his warm back. "Don't think I won't take you up on that. The more adults to keep the peace the better. Our first rehearsal is today at twelve-thirty."

"Sorry, I'm going in to the office for a few hours. My paperwork is starting to take my desk hostage."

"Your excuse for every chore you want to avoid."

He didn't turn around. "It works every time, because it's the truth. I promise I'll give you a hand when I can. Really, how hard can it be?"

Before I could start in on exactly how hard it could be controlling that many kids, much less getting them to learn lines and songs, the doorbell rang.

"Saved by the bell," he said, whisking the eggs with a fork.

"Postponed by the bell," I replied. "We're not done negotiating, mister."

"Whatever it is, we're not buying," Gabe called to me as I walked toward the front door.

Though I normally look out the peephole, a safety measure reiterated ad nauseam by my protective husband, this time I didn't because he was only a room away. Assuming it was a neighbor, I threw open the door.

Then I let out a startled yelp.

Standing in front of me on our deep front porch was a lanky figure dressed completely in black wearing a grinning skull mask.

"Benni?" the deep voice asked.

CHAPTER 2

$\mathcal{B}$EFORE I COULD LET OUT A SECOND YELP, GABE WAS AT MY side. Next to him Scout growled low in the back of his throat. Gabe grabbed Scout's leather collar with one hand and stepped in front of me.

The man dropped the mask. "Don't shoot," he said. His dark cheekbones were as sharply etched as a primitive woodcarving, and except for deep-set, black eyes and a slightly broader nose, he could have been Gabe's twin. "Happy *Dia de los Muertos*."

"You jackass," Gabe said, laughing, letting go of Scout and lightly patting his rib cage. "It's okay, Scout. This guy's a friend. Well, make that a relative."

"Not always the same thing, eh, *compadre*," the man answered, his gleaming white grin revealing a definite family resemblance.

It finally dawned on me who he was. "Luis! Finally I get to meet the infamous Luis Ortiz."

"The man who taught your husband everything he knows about life, *cerveza*, and women," he said, giving a little bow.

"*Pendejo loco,*" Gabe said affectionately.

"Maybe I shouldn't let you in," I said, smiling up at his cousin. "I've almost trained all that macho arrogance out of him."

Both Gabe and Luis laughed with an uncanny similarity. "I'm just starting breakfast, *compa*," Gabe said, opening the door wider. "Get in here and join us."

During our three-year marriage, Gabe had spoken often about his cousin Luis. When Gabe was sixteen, his father died of a heart attack, and Gabe went slightly out-of-control for awhile. After a few minor run-ins with the local police in Derby, Kansas, Gabe's mother, in a fit of despair, sent him to live with his father's older brother in Santa Ana, California, a town about six hours south of San Celina. Gabe lived with his uncle Tony and aunt Maria from his junior year in high school until he joined the Marines a few months after he graduated Santa Ana High School. His uncle Tony was a thirty-year veteran of the Santa Ana police department who retired a lieutenant. I'd met his aunt and uncle and their other three sons, all younger than Luis and Gabe, who were only six months apart. But the half-dozen times we'd visited his family in Santa Ana, Luis had always been on a business trip. He'd not followed his father into the police department, but with his marketing major worked at a variety of lucrative sales positions. The last we'd heard about Luis was he'd bought a house in Newport Beach. He lived there with his third wife, Paige, and their one-year-old daughter.

"Luis could sell ice to a polar bear," Gabe always said, shaking his head and smiling. "The ladies go crazy over him."

I'd given a snort of laughter at Gabe's remark. Like *he* didn't know what that was like. I could imagine what they'd been like together.

"What brings you north?" Gabe asked after Luis sat down across from him. I poured his cousin a cup of coffee.

Luis shook his head at my offer of cream and sugar. "Just taking a little vacation. Had a meeting with a client in Santa Barbara and thought I'd pop up and see how *mi primo* is doing running his town."

"I'm doing fine," Gabe said. "How do you want your eggs? Scrambled or scrambled?"

Luis leaned back in the kitchen chair and winked while I put bacon in the microwave. "You have *el hombre* cooking? *Caramba!* If his *tia* Maria could only see him now. She's probably make him an apron." His hearty laugh filled our airy kitchen.

Gabe shook his head and opened the refrigerator door looking for his favorite add-in ingredients—cheese, bacon bits, chives, garlic salt, seasoned pepper, Tapatio hot sauce.

While I set the table, I took the opportunity to quiz Luis about Gabe's life as a teenager.

"Is it true you guys once had dates with six women in one night?" I asked, sliding English muffins into the toaster. I opened the refrigerator and grabbed a pitcher of orange juice.

"Who told you that?" Luis asked.

"It's all a lie," Gabe said.

"Your mama told me," I said to Luis, setting the pitcher on the table. "She claims all her gray hairs grew during your and Gabe's last two years of high school."

"It was only five girls that time," Luis said. "Gabe's third date dumped him for the center on the basketball team."

Gabe turned around, waving a dripping spatula at his cousin. "That wasn't my date, that was yours. *I've* never been stood up in my life."

"Eh, his ego is still strong and pure," Luis said, winking at me again. "Some things never change."

"That's not true," I said, cutting up some fresh strawberries I'd bought at Farmers' Market. "I stood you up once when we were dating." I'd been assisting a heifer's particularly hard first birth and lost track of time. It was, he'd said, the only time he'd been stood up for a cow.

"Aha, the truth comes out!" Luis said, letting the legs of his chair drop with a thump on the kitchen floor. "That's why he married you, you know. He couldn't let that incident get out and ruin his playboy reputation."

"Eat your eggs, my furry friend," Gabe said, setting the red-and-white plate of eggs in front of him. "Tell me all the family gossip."

While we ate breakfast, I quietly watched Gabe and his cousin volley comments back and forth, covering everything from their jobs to their aunt Maria's arthritis to Luis's two sons from his first marriage and his one-year-old daughter, Cassie, from his third.

"I can't believe I've never seen your daughter," Gabe said, looking down at the photograph Luis had pulled from his wallet. *Muy bonita.*"

"Just like her mama," Luis said, nodding. "Though I hope she doesn't inherit Paige's love for expensive shoes."

"What're you peddling now?" Gabe asked.

"Precious metals," Luis said.

"Like gold and silver?"

"And platinum. Lots of money in metal. Only sure thing these days next to drug trafficking and welfare fraud."

"Tell me about it," Gabe said.

"Don't tell me you have problems with drugs up here in your little piece of paradise," Luis said, spreading jam on an English muffin.

"There's problems with drugs everywhere," Gabe answered, sighing. He stood up and picked up Luis's empty plate. "What do you say to a tour of the town?"

"Can I sit in a police car and try the siren?" Luis asked.

"No, but I'll let you wear the handcuffs." He rinsed off his and Luis's plates and stuck them in the dishwasher. "I'm going to get dressed. I hope you're planning on staying for a few days. It's been too long."

"That it has, *primo*," Luis said, nodding his head. "That it has."

After Gabe left to get dressed, I started clearing the rest of the table. Luis jumped up and started helping me.

"You don't have to do that," I said, putting the lid back on the butter dish. "Sit. Have another cup of coffee."

"No, I don't mind. I was just kidding Gabe. Actually, after three wives, I'm as perfectly trained as a house cat."

I smiled. "House cats are notoriously untrainable."

He grinned in reply.

After we'd cleared the table, I offered him another cup of coffee.

"Okay, you've convinced me," he said, holding out his mug.

"So," I said, sitting down across from him at the kitchen table. "How do you like your new house?"

He shrugged and sipped his coffee, his dark eyes avoiding mine. "It's a house. Paige is a professional decorator, so it's beautiful, a real showplace. It's going to be featured in *Orange Coast* magazine." He looked around our warm, bacon-scented kitchen. "Not a bit like this place."

I felt my spine stiffen. "Excuse me?"

His sharp cheekbones glowed rosy. "I'm sorry. I didn't mean that the way it came out. I mean, the house Paige decorated is beautiful, but it has no *vida*, no *corazon*. You know, life . . . heart. You and Gabe, your house . . ." He gave me an apologetic smile. "You know, it's a home."

"Yes," I said, relaxing my spine. "I do."

"Gabe always was the lucky one," he said softly, his black, thick-lashed eyes looking past me and out the kitchen window.

"I'm pretty lucky myself," I said lightly. "I'd better get dressed. I have a rehearsal at twelve-thirty."

"Are you in a play?"

"Not in it, helping to direct it. It's a children's musical at the church based on *Pilgrim's Progress*. My gramma is in charge of it, and I'm helping her."

"Sounds like fun," he said, smiling.

"You sound like Gabe. We'll see." I shook some soap powder into the dishwasher.

"I traveled a lot when my boys were small," he said, his full lips turning down slightly at the edges. "Unfortunately, I missed all that. Even missed their first communions. Now they're grown and in college and don't care if I ever show up except when they need money."

"I'm sure that's not true," I said, but remembered what I once overheard his father, Gabe's uncle Tony, say about Luis.

"Luis is a good man, takes care of his family with money," Uncle Tony had said, his voice sad and resigned. "But he keeps his time for himself."

When I asked Gabe about Uncle Tony's comments, he defended his cousin. "Uncle Tony always expected so much of Luis. Being the oldest in a Mexican family, especially when your parents weren't born here, is hard. Sure, Luis is kind of selfish, but who isn't? Uncle Tony was gone a lot at work himself when he was young. Besides, he has higher standards for Luis than for his other sons. That's unfair."

I didn't answer. It was a sensitive subject for Gabe, who still felt guilty for the many years of putting his own work and desires before his now twenty-year-old son, Sam.

I snapped back at the sound of Luis's voice, just catching the end of his sentence about his youngest son who was thinking about changing colleges.

"Tell me about your kids," I said, falling back on that reliable topic when you didn't know someone well.

"Luis Jr. is a senior this year. Long Beach State. He's going to be a math teacher. Juan is a sophomore at Fullerton and still is majoring in girls and basketball. Last week Cassie said something that sounded like *daddy*."

I smiled. "That must have been exciting for you."

Luis nodded, contemplating the surface of his coffee. "They're good kids. Their moms are doing a good job raising them in spite of the fact that I'm not around much. To be honest, I'm not sure they even notice when I'm gone."

Luckily, Gabe walked back into the kitchen, Scout trotting after him. I wasn't sure where to go with my conversation with Luis at that point.

"How long are you here for?" Gabe asked, pulling on a sweatshirt.

Luis shrugged. "Hadn't thought about it."

"Have a place to stay?"

His face was vague. "Saw some motels when I drove into town . . ."

"That's ridiculous," Gabe said, glancing at me, his eyebrows raised. I nodded in my agreement. "You'll stay here with us. We have a perfectly good guest room."

"No way, man," he said, his eyes dropping down to study the top of the kitchen table. "That's too much trouble."

"It is not," I said. "Really, Luis, we'd be glad to have you as long as you don't expect three meals on the dot. We're a catch-your-meals-on-the-run kind of couple."

"What I'm used to," he said, looking at me, then Gabe. "I appreciate and accept your offer."

"Good," Gabe said. "So why don't we get you settled, then I'll show you around my town."

Luis stood up, shaking his head. "Listen to him. His town. He sounds like Matt Dillion."

"Man, we loved *Gunsmoke* as kids, didn't we?" Gabe said.

By the time I got dressed, Gabe had already shown Luis to the downstairs guest room, and they were heading out the door.

"Don't forget I'm going to the cemetery this afternoon with Elvia and her family," I called after them. "We're decorating graves." Day of the Dead was a big celebration with my best friend Elvia's family, and I'd gone with them to decorate their family graves since I was in grade school.

"What're we doing for dinner?" Gabe called back.

"How about Liddie's at six o'clock? Luis can't not eat at Liddie's."

"Can't not?" Gabe repeated, laughing at me. He loved it when I occasionally fell into the double negatives of my Southern background.

"Go play, you big *mocoso*," I said, dismissing him with my hand.

Luis laughed and gave him a playful shove. "She has your number."

Gabe grunted and gave him a shove back that reminded me of a twelve year old. Luis shoved him again, causing Gabe to laugh and call him something demeaning in Spanish. Their voices faded away as they went down the porch steps toward Gabe's sky-blue Corvette, their easy bickering sounding like it had been only days rather than years since they'd seen each other.

Though Gabe never complained about it, it sometimes saddened me that he didn't see his family much. He'd certainly made himself a good life here in San Celina, something he'd admitted he'd never expected when he'd temporarily taken over his friend Aaron's police chief job four years ago. Though it didn't seem to bother him, his new life encompassed me, my family, and the town I'd grown up in, and I often wondered if he was ever lonely for his family back in Kansas or Santa Ana. Gabe never spoke of it one way or another, but the pure pleasure on his face with Luis in the room told me that he did miss them. It seemed a fortuitous thing that Luis showed back up in my husband's life right at this moment. I swore to myself that I would make Luis's visit so comfortable that he'd want to return often.

"Ready to go, Scout?" I asked my dog who had been patiently sitting by the front door for the last ten minutes. I decided to bring him to this first rehearsal as a kind of icebreaker. Though I knew some of the children from church, many of them were kids from the neighborhood and might be a little shy about me and Dove taking Lily's place. Scout, with his gentle personality and his perky German shepherd ear and floppy Labrador ear, was just the thing the thing kids needed to focus on rather than Lily's sudden departure.

I couldn't remember when San Celina First Baptist Church hadn't been a part of my life. One of my earliest memories was sitting in the overheated Sunday School rooms listening to flannel board stories of Noah and the Ark and Jonah and that hungry whale being told to me in the sing-song, clickity-clack voice of Miss Velma Jacobson. Now eighty-one, she had taught five- and six-year-olds at First Baptist since Kennedy was in office.

At twelve-thirty-five, only five minutes late, I pulled into the parking lot of the plain, stucco church, painted a soft, Navajo white with dark brown trim. I parked my purple Ford Ranger right next to my gramma Dove's almost identical red truck. Though Isaac, her second husband of almost two years now, bought her a tricked-out Chevy half-ton capable of pulling a two-story house, she preferred to tool around town in what she called her little "putt-putt." There were only two other cars in the lot, something that struck a chord of fear inside me. That meant that most of the parents had dropped off their children and fled.

"You stay in the truck, Scooby-Doo," I told Scout, while I pulled on my wool-lined Wrangler jacket. The November temperature, normally warm, had taken a sudden dip today. "I'll come get you during refreshment time." I rolled down both windows, filled his travel bowl with bottled water, and gave him a quick chest rub.

In front of the double door leading into the sanctuary, Walt Adams, one of the church's few full-time employees, was on his knees, trimming the rosebushes that grew underneath the church's two stained glass windows. Though the sanctuary doors were closed, I could hear the raucous sound of children.

"Hey, Walt," I said, stopping to watch his careful pruning, delaying the moment I'd actually have to enter the fray. "How are you?"

"Real fine, thank you," he said, looking up at me, his gray eyes narrowing in the midday sunlight. "You?"

"I'm good."

Today he looked older than his seventy-two years. I only knew his age because two months ago Dove and the other women in First Baptist's Women's Missionary Union threw him a surprise birthday party. Today, as usual, he wore a gray Dickies work shirt and pants and black Red Wing boots, probably not aware that he now dressed on the cutting edge of fashion.

"Sounds scary in there," I said, gesturing to the shiny brown sanctuary doors.

He stood up and nodded, smiling a closed-lipped smile. His freckled face was damp and sun-blushed. "Dove will be glad to see you."

"No doubt," I said, still lingering. "How'd you like that book I gave you?"

At his party, Walt and I had started talking about a notions box he'd made for the church talent auction, where the congregation donated their "talents" such as cakes, quilts, dog-grooming, and various other abilities, with the money going toward our homeless ministry. Walt had donated a tiny, hand-carved box made of small pieces of wood glued together to form a quiltlike pattern over the top and sides. I'd bid on it and won. It reminded me of tramp art, a type of folk art carving popular back in the thirties. A few days later, at my best friend Elvia's bookstore, Blind Harry's, I saw a book about tramp art. I left it in the church office for Walt with a note telling him this old-time folk art reminded me of his box.

"The book was real interesting," he said, his eyes lighting up. "That tramp art is something. Didn't even know what I was doing had a name."

"Isn't it interesting how tramp artists used old orange crates and cigar boxes? They were the original recyclers."

He gave a small chuckle. "Didn't call it recycling back in the thirties. Just called it making a living. Or trying to."

"No kidding. From what that book says, a lot of men fed themselves by making those pieces."

"Thank you for thinking about me."

"You're welcome," I said, smiling. "But I do have an ulterior motive. I'd love to have you join the artists' co-op and make some of those boxes to sell in our new museum store downtown." This was the second time I'd asked him to join the co-op affiliated with the folk art museum. The first time, about six months ago, he'd politely declined, saying he had too much to do around the church.

His sun-browned lips, rough as two pieces of old wood, smiled back. "Don't know if anyone would actually part with their hard-earned money for one of my boxes."

"You bet they would. Don't forget, I did."

"Well, yes, you did . . ." He shook his head, *tsking* softly under his breath, implying that perhaps I might not be completely right in the head.

"Now, stop that. I know good art when I see it."

"I'll think about it. Probably have to keep the book a little longer then, study up on this tramp art."

"Keep it as long as you like. I'd planned on donating it to the folk art museum's reference library. Please, think about joining the co-op. I bet you'd love the other woodworkers."

He turned back to the roses, obviously uncomfortable with my invitation. "I'm awfully busy here."

"Okay, just wanted you to know you are welcome any time." I looked around at the flower beds, the immaculate front lawn, the freshly painted new sign in front. "You know, this place was getting downright seedy before you came to save us."

He looked down at the ground, embarrassed. He'd worked as the church's maintenance man about ten years now, after attending the church for about a year. He was, declared Mac, our pastor, the best person we'd ever had at the job. He repaired things before anyone even knew they were broken.

"I do my best." He continued studying the scuffed toes of his black work shoes. The sugary scent of the few blooming roses wafted up, sweetening the air around us.

"All I have to say is we're darn lucky to have you," I said.

Before he could answer, a loud crash came from inside the church, bodies hitting the closed double doors. We both jumped and gaped at the doors. From inside the foyer, the faint sound of young boys laughing bounced against the dark wood.

"Yikes," I said. "I'd better get in there quick before someone damages vital body parts."

"Best put on your breastplate of righteousness," he said, picking up his small shovel.

"Not to mention taking up my sword," I replied.

I stepped inside the now-empty foyer. The swinging double doors opening to the sanctuary still moved slightly. Through the two small windows I could see the pandemonium. Feeling like Wyatt Earp entering a Wild West bar, I pushed the doors open.

At the front of the church, Dove tried to walk with two chattering kids about five years old hanging onto her chambray shirt tail. Up in the choir loft, about twenty or so other kids ranging from six to eleven pushed and shoved each other. My observation about the empty parking lot proved to be accurate. There were no other adults present. As much as Dove commanded respect, this many kids would be hard for any one person to control. Desperate times called for desperate measures.

I cupped my hands on both sides of my mouth and let out my loudest, from-the-gut, Tarzan yodel. The power of it echoing through the high church ceilings as well as the unexpectedness of it caused every child to immediately hush and stare in disbelief at a grownup who could yell louder than they could.

Mac burst out of his office, his bearded, mountain-man face shocked. He was six-foot-four with a size forty-six chest and a full beard the color of roasted almonds. Today he wore a blue-and-black-checked flannel shirt, jeans, and red-laced hiking boots. He looked more like Paul Bunyan than a minister.

"What in the world is going on?" He started down the aisle toward me, his ruddy face perplexed.

I smiled sweetly at the kids and said in a loud voice, "Now that I have everyone's attention. You all better sit down and be quiet so we can work on this play or there'll be no shopping at the Good Behavior Store."

Dove had told me about the store earlier. Depending on how well the kids behaved and followed directions, they were given tickets that they could redeem for small toys, comic books, and candy bars.

Behind me, I heard a man's deep, familiar laugh and the sound of clapping. "Very impressive, Ms. Harper."

I turned around to face the one person I never, in a thousand millenniums, expected to step over the threshold of First Baptist. Detective Ford "Hud" Hudson of the San Celina sheriff's department.

He wore a tweedy, western-style sports coat, dark blue jeans, and a tan Stetson with a rodeo crease. Next to him, gripping his hand, was a copper-haired little girl I recognized as his daughter, Maisie. If I remembered right, she was about seven now.

The words tumbled out my mouth before I thought about how ungracious they sounded. "What in the heck are *you* doing *here*?"

CHAPTER 3

*H*UD AND I HAD HISTORY. WE'D BEEN INVOLVED TOGETHER ON a few homicide cases, the last one about eight months ago. He was someone who, depending on my mood at the moment, I either really liked or wanted to strangle. He made it clear that he felt the same about me and was very candid about telling me he thought my religious beliefs were the equivalent of a load of fresh steer manure. Seeing him here with his daughter, whom I knew he adored, was the last thing I expected.

"Is that any way to greet a seeking pilgrim?" he asked. "And you such a dedicated Christian."

Dove, too far away to hear our conversation, cleared her throat and commanded in her best you-don't-want-to-mess-with-me voice for the kids to take a seat and quiet down. Wisely, they obeyed her.

"Hello, I'm MacKenzie Reid," Mac said, coming up behind me. "Mac. I'm the pastor here. Welcome to First Baptist." Mac placed one of his large hands on my shoulder and squeezed it, telling me nonverbally to let him take over. He'd obviously heard and probably disapproved of my inhospitable tone. No doubt he'd gently chide me about it later.

Now Mac is my pastor, and I respect him immensely. But he is also someone I'd known since I was a kid because he'd been raised on the ranch next to ours. I remember his wild and not-so-saintly high school days when he and Uncle Arnie, my daddy's youngest brother, were good friends. Mac and my family had a relationship that sometimes didn't fit into the typical pastor/church member realm. To put it bluntly, he and I often squabbled like brother and sister. I try to understand and honor his position and authority despite the fact I remember that he once dumped a load of goldfish in the baptismal and started a rumor among the young kids who were to be baptized that morning that they were flesh-eating piranha. Because of his position, I didn't shrug his hand off my shoulder, though I sure felt like it.

He smiled and held out his other hand to Hud. Hud's genial, boy-next-door face became wary, hesitating a moment before he took Mac's hand.

"Ford Hudson," Hud said, his dark eyes guarded. "Hud."

"Nice to meet you, Hud." Mac let go of my shoulder and stooped down so that he was eye level with Maisie, his gentleness apparent even with his grizzly bear proportions. "Hello, what's your name?"

"Maisie Hudson," she whispered, gripping her father's hand tight.

"It's really nice to meet you, Miss Hudson," he said, smiling and holding out his hand to her. She stared into his soft, pewter-colored eyes and placed her tiny hand in his.

"We're here for the play rehearsal," Hud said. "Maisie missed a few days because of the flu, but she's ready to get back into it."

Though I was dying to ask how in the world Hud's daughter ended up being in the children's play, I held my tongue.

"I think they're just getting started now," Mac said, looking over at me, his gray eyes narrowing in amusement. "Benni is one of our new and very enthusiastic leaders."

"So I heard," Hud said, laughing.

"Laugh all you want, it got their attention," I said, holding out my hand to Maisie. "C'mon, kiddo, let's leave your dad to talk with Pastor Mac. You can come back in two hours, Hud."

"Okay," she said, skipping over to me.

Hud's face grew a little panicked. For all his bravado, the possibility of being in the clutches of a Baptist minister was probably one of his worst nightmares.

Down at the front of the church, Dove had finally gotten the kids settled down and reasonably quiet. She handed me a script of Lily's original play, *Pilgrim's Progress—The Joyful Journey*.

I glanced through the tattered, photocopied script that included numerous songs. "Do we have anyone to play the piano?"

Dove picked up a black notebook and started flipping through it. "It says here Beth Cochran is our musical accompaniment. That's Burt Cochran's youngest girl. She graduated from San Celina High this year. Just started Cal Poly on a music scholarship."

"I know her. Wonder where she is?"

One of the older kids, a boy who looked to be about ten or so and whose name tag read "Salvador," piped up, "Miss Beth always comes late. She has a boyfriend. He sometimes plays guitar with her."

"His name is Jason," offered another boy with platinum hair and bright blue eyes. His name tag read "Travis." "He has a tattoo of this big old eagle all across his back." His voice lowered with respect. "It's awesome."

Dove rolled her blue eyes at me. "That's all fine and good, but until Beth and her tattooed boyfriend show up, *if* they show up, we can work on the speaking parts. I can bang away at the piano if need be." Dove's piano playing was self-taught and adequate, but we both knew we needed Beth's musical expertise.

She leaned over and whispered in my ear, "Honeybun, there's no way you and I can do this without help. We've got to recruit some volunteers or this play is not going to happen."

"I'll talk to Mac." I glanced down at the script. "It says in Lily's notes here that they have this first song pretty well down. Why don't you have them run through it a few times, then we can break off into groups and start working on the speaking parts?"

I walked back down the aisle toward Mac and Hud who, by the look on their faces, were obviously in a serious conversation. I hated to interrupt any type of spiritual discussion, but we needed help, and we needed it fast.

"He's not their first choice," Mac said, as I got closer. "But I think he's going to surprise them. I've seen him throw a pass so beautiful it would make you cry. Baylor's lucky to have him."

So much for serious spiritual conversation. They were talking about Baylor's newest quarterback. Baylor University in Texas was Mac's alma mater. He'd played defensive tackle there, was even a first-round draft pick for the pros, which he opted out of in favor of getting his master's in divinity.

"Hey, Benni," Mac said. "we've got ourselves an old Tulane Green Wave here! He was a running back." His smile was wide and genuine. Next to the Lord, football and cutting horses were Mac's passions.

Hud had taken off his tan Stetson and held it lightly with his fingers. "My football record is not as impressive as Mac's. Warmed the bench most of my three years on the team. Taught me patience, though."

"A virtue in your profession, no doubt," Mac said, nodding. They'd obviously already discussed Hud's job as a homicide detective.

"It's mandatory," Hud said.

"Hate to break up your bull session, boys," I said. "But we're in desperate straits here." I looked up at Mac. "We'll need some help if this play is going to be ready by the Sunday before Thanksgiving. That's only a few weeks away. Mac, do you know if there are any other volunteers who were involved with this? Lily was in such a tizzy when she left that Dove wasn't able to find out many details."

"We normally have a few teenagers who come to help the kids with their lines," Mac said. "Beth Cochran and Jason Meadows have been working with Lily this time."

"Well, no one showed up today. Maybe they didn't know we were having a rehearsal."

"That's entirely possible," Mac said. "Not to mention, it is Saturday afternoon." Behind us, Dove had started the kids singing a song called "City of Destruction." It was about Christian, the main character in *Pilgrim's Progress*, talking about the city he lived in at the beginning of the book.

It's the City of Destruction,
We built it on the sand.
It's the City of Destruction,
No future and no plan. It's the City of Destruction,
We scurry on our way,
But what will happen in the end,
Nobody dares to say.

They were a little off key, but did pretty well considering Dove missed half the notes. It was a jazzy song with lots of rhythm and the kids sang it with enthusiasm, not exactly realizing what the words meant.

I looked at the men and widened my eyes slightly. "Those words seem entirely appropriate right now."

Mac patted me on the back. "Don't worry, Benni. It'll all work out. God is in control of the whole cosmos as well as our little play.

Remember what Jesus said in Luke—'Who of you by worrying can add a single hour to his life? Or a single cubit to his height? If you cannot do this little thing, why do you worry about the rest?' "

"I know," I said, sighing. "Right now I'm not interested in cubits though. I just want a couple of warm bodies to listen to the kids say their lines."

Mac glanced over at Hud. "Do you have any pressing homicide investigations planned for the next two hours, Hud?"

Hud smiled and shook his head.

Mac turned back to me. "Two willing servants at your service."

"Great," I said, surprised, but grateful. "I'll tell Dove."

We separated the twenty-eight kids into four groups to rehearse in different sections of the church. Dove took her group to the choir room; Mac took his to the recreation hall; I commandeered the front part of the sanctuary; and Hud took the back pews. Once we'd broken down into small groups and distanced them from each other, it was easier to keep them from bouncing off the walls and also brought the noise level down substantially.

I had my group of six sit in a circle on the blue-gray carpet in front of the altar and say their full names and ages so I could get to know them better.

Salvador Rodriguez was cast as Christian, the play's lead actor. Being a natural leader, he started. "Salvador Jaime Rodriguez. I'm ten."

I recognized him from Vacation Bible School last summer. He was a neighborhood child whose parents owned a small Mexican restaurant in San Celina.

"Okay, Salvador, glad you're here." I said. "Next?"

"Susan Bea Ballard," said a giggly, pigtailed girl, from behind her hand. She glanced over at Salvador, obviously enamored. "I'm ten and *a half*." Her parents had been classmates of mine at San Celina High School. They'd been voted cutest couple and were still so cute it made your teeth hurt.

Salvador rolled his eyes. "Liar, I'm a month older than you."

"So?" said the girl, sticking out her tongue. "I'm still ten and a half."

"So just say you're ten," he said. "Saying a half is dumb."

"Is not," she said, reaching over to pinch him.

"Hey! Keep your cooties to yourself!" He scooted away from her fingers. Everyone in the circle started giggling.

"Okay, okay," I interrupted. "Let's keep going."

"Brian and Brianna Winner. We're twins," said an African-American girl, her fingernails painted a pale lavender. "We turned eight two days ago. But I'm two minutes older." Her brother grinned, showing two missing front teeth, content to let his sister do the talking. They were First Baptist regulars and their mother was president of the Women's Missionary Union and made beautiful African-themed quilts that she sold at the folk art museum.

"Travis Hammer," said the platinum-blond boy who'd been so impressed with Jason's tattoos. "I'm named after a character in a book."

"Travis McGee?" I guessed. I'd grown up reading John D. Mac-Donald's books. He was one of Daddy's favorite authors next to Louis L'Amour.

He shrugged, unimpressed. "Yeah, but I've never heard of him. I'm almost nine."

I recognized Travis from church. His father, Jonathan Hammer, was a local tax attorney and a somewhat new member of San Celina First Baptist. I didn't know him personally, but well enough to greet on Sunday morning. It was known throughout the church body that he was, financially, a very generous member. According to the rumor mill at First Baptist, whose motto too often was "If you can't be kind, be vague," a few years ago he'd been politely asked to leave his last congregation, the Presbyterians down the street. That probably should have warned us that he might be what Dove called a "challenge to our Christian fortitude." You had to work pretty hard to make the Presbyterians mad.

The last child was a soft-voiced Hispanic girl who looked younger

than the others. I'd noticed during the time we were introducing ourselves that she never stopped looking at her hands, clasped tightly in
her lap. Her shiny black hair was neatly French-braided, and she wore
faded, pale-yellow corduroy pants and a pink, long-sleeved shirt with
a blonde Barbie on the front.

"What's your name, sweetie?" I asked.

She looked up, her round black eyes as shiny and unreadable as a
moonlit ocean. "Angelina Portillo," she whispered. "I'm *seis*. Six."

"That's a really pretty name," I said, encouraging her. "Do you
have a middle name?"

She nodded. "Benita. After *mi madre*." She hesitated for a moment. "My mama," she corrected.

"That's almost like my name," I said, giving her a big smile. "Is
your mama called Benni, like me?"

She shook her head, her face solemn. "My *tia* Juana called her
Nita. She said my mama always called me *Benita poca* before she
went to be in heaven." Angelina paused, her tiny face struggling with
the intimacy she'd just revealed.

The other kids stared at her, barely comprehending what she was
saying. She looked so uncomfortable with everyone's eyes on her. I
felt dismay that through simply telling our names, the fact that her
mother had died came up.

"Okay," I said, squeezing her shoulder. Changing the subject
would be the best way to remedy the awkward moment. "Now that
we all know each other, let's get started and see how many lines we
can memorize today."

We took turns reading through the scenes and working on memo-
rizing the parts Lily had assigned them. Before we knew it, it was time
for refreshments. We all met back in the recreation hall where our
teenage helpers, Beth and Jason, had finally arrived.

"I need to call the costume ladies," Dove said to me. "Will you
take care of the refreshments?"

"Sure," I said. "I'll tell Beth and Jason to start a game of musical chairs or something to try to burn off some of the kids' excess energy."

"Need any help in the kitchen?" Mac asked me.

"No, thanks, I can handle it," I said. "You probably need to get back to your sermon."

"I do," he admitted.

"I'll help Benni," Hud said.

"That's great." Mac held out his hand. "Nice meeting you, Hud. Thanks for your help. Stay safe out there."

"Thanks, Mac. You too."

Hud followed me into the church's commercial-size kitchen, located at the back of the recreation hall attached to the sanctuary by a row of Sunday School rooms. "So, ranch girl, which do I hand out, loaves or fishes?"

"Try granola bars and boxed fruit juice," I said. "It's not that complicated. What we mostly have to do is make sure every child gets just one of each and that the empties don't end up on the floor or tucked in the pockets behind a pew to be found on Sunday when someone reaches for a hymnal. Otherwise Mac will never hear the end of it from Sissy . . . well, he'll never hear the end of it."

"Got it," Hud said. "The Ladies Who Sniff for Dust Society. We must protect Mac from their ever vigilant eyes and noses."

I opened the huge refrigerator and pulled out the case of boxed drinks. "How do you know about them?"

He took the box from me. "I grew up in the Catholic church. We had those ladies, too. They used to drive my mawmaw nuts back in Texas."

MawMaw, he'd told me before, was his late grandmother. Hud was part Cajun and grew up in Beaumont, Texas. His grandfather, Iry Gautreaux, whom I met earlier in the year, had moved out here to be closer to Hud, his only grandchild.

"How is Iry?" I asked, opening up the box of chocolate chip granola bars. "Just start stacking the juice there." I pointed at the countertop opening that had a sliding door to pass food through.

Outside the opening, we could hear the kids starting to line up, the girls' high, squeaky voices and the painful-sounding thumps against the wall when the boys pushed each other too hard. Dove's indulgently scolding voice quieted them down slightly.

"PawPaw's doing great," Hud said. "Did you know he has his own place now?" He'd been living with Hud the last time Hud and I ran into each other downtown.

"No, I didn't. Where is he living?"

"The Mission Palms senior apartments."

"That's a great place. A lot of my docents live there. I'm surprised I haven't heard about him. The casserole patrol is usually unnervingly current on all the new bachelors."

"Casserole patrol?" He placed the last couple of apple juice boxes in the long domino-like line.

I counted out twenty-eight bars, then set out a few extra just in case. "They compete to see who takes the best casserole to any new men in the building. Men your grandpa's age are at a premium. I'm surprised his date book isn't completely full for the next year."

"Actually, he's only been there a month. But, come to think of it, every time I call, he never seems to be home."

I nodded. "The casserole patrol." I rolled up the pass-through's cover. The noise level rose accordingly.

"Did someone say a prayer over the snack?" I yelled over the din.

"Yes, Miss Benni," one of the girls said. "Miss Dove did."

"Then have at it," I said. "No shoving and one each." I looked back at Hud. "You can bet dollars-to-doughnuts Iry's been booked up by the casserole patrol. Tell him when he has time to come by the folk art museum. I'd love to see him again, not to mention we can always use new docents."

"I'll relay the message," Hud said.

We concentrated on handing out refreshments. Then I went to get Scout and his tennis ball so that the kids could play with him on the front lawn while Beth and Jason practiced the play's music. Hud, Dove, and I patrolled the area making sure that nobody wandered off or got in Walt's way as he edged the grass along the sidewalk. With ages running from six to eleven years old, it was a challenge to keep them together and entertained, though having Scout there helped. He was certainly getting his fill of ball chasing.

During the last fifteen minutes before their parents came to pick them up, we set up the Good Behavior Store, where with tickets they received for things like being quiet when asked or throwing away trash other than their own, they could buy little prizes like pencils, plastic toys, and magic tricks. Though none of the toys were worth more than fifty cents or a dollar, next to refreshment time, this was the most popular part of the rehearsal.

By three o'clock, every child had been picked up except Angelina Portillo, the quiet little girl who'd been in my group. I sat on the top of the steps leading to the sanctuary and watched her and Maisie chase each other around the hundred-year-old valley oak in the church's front lawn.

Hud and Dove walked over to where I sat.

"Who's picking Angelina up?" Dove asked.

"I don't know," I said. "I'll go ask."

"Angelina, Maisie," I called, walking toward them. "It's time to leave."

"Okay," Maisie called back, grabbing Angelina's hand and running toward me.

When they reached me, I stooped down to their level and asked, "Who's picking you up, Angelina?"

She looked down at her pink tennis shoes. "My *tia?*" There was a definite question in her voice.

"What's her name?" I asked.

Her voice was almost inaudible. "Juana."

"She works at the dry cleaners," Maisie said. "She works until five o'clock. But it's okay. Angelina stays home by herself all the time."

Dove and Hud walked up in time to hear Maisie's comment. Dove's face had her *tsk-tsk* look on it. Hud lifted his eyebrows at me in a what-now expression. This was a common problem among too many families, something I'm sure he'd seen many times during his years in law enforcement.

"We can't let a six-year-old child go home by herself," Dove said. "Let me go get Lily's book and see where she lives."

"In the apartments by the train station," Maisie said, cheerfully. Her normal shyness had taken a backseat when she'd realized there was a child younger and more timid than herself. "She can see the train from her bedroom window!" Maisie's eyes widened with what she obviously thought was Angelina's good fortune. "She stays sometimes with Rachel who lives next door. Rachel's fifteen and has a *boyfriend*."

"Okay," I said. "Lily might have the babysitter's number listed. Maybe we can see if this girl's number is listed and if she can pick up Angelina."

"Rachel's boyfriend is named Chuy," Maisie said. "They kiss a lot." She looked over at Angelina and giggled. Angelina giggled back.

I laughed at the amazed expression on Hud's face as he listened to the words pouring out of his normally reticent daughter's mouth. "The Cajun pecan obviously doesn't fall far from the tree, Mr. Detective. Think she's learned a few interrogation techniques from papa?"

Hud gave a hesitant smile and shook his head. "What're you going to do?"

"We'd better check with Mac," Dove said. "Maybe he knows something about Angelina's aunt."

"I'll go," I said.

Mac's office door was closed, and the secretary's desk in front of it empty. Mrs. Malloy, First Baptist's church secretary for the last thirty years and four pastors, never worked on Saturdays. I rapped softly on the dark oak door.

"C'mon in," Mac's deep voice called.

I stepped inside the book-lined office. Mac was sitting on the army-green corduroy loveseat eating an apple, a thick book open in his lap.

"All the kids picked up safely?" he asked.

"All but one. Angelina Portillo. Do you—" Before I could finish my sentence, he stood up.

"I'll take her home," Mac said, an odd expression on his face.

"That's not exactly the problem," I said. "Apparently her aunt is working, and there's this girl next door . . ."

"I know," Mac said, cutting me off. "Rachel isn't always available. I'll take her to Mrs. Mesa, another neighbor who sometimes watches her when Juana is working. Mrs. Mesa doesn't drive." He picked up his leather jacket and started putting it on.

"How did Angelina get here then?" I asked, hoping she didn't come by herself.

"Rachel probably walked her here. But it's a long three blocks."

"The infamous Rachel who likes to kiss Chuy," I said, laughing.

Mac, distracted by some private thoughts, didn't smile at my comment.

"Maisie told us," I added.

Mac, still didn't react. "I'll make sure she gets home."

"Okay," I said, still confused by his distracted manner. "Problem solved. Thanks, Mac."

He followed me back out to the front of the church where Dove and Hud watched the girls running around the front lawn. Though Angelina was shy around adults, she seemed perfectly comfortable with Maisie. Watching them run around the brownish-green lawn, their black and red hair colors a blur, reminded me of Elvia and me at that age.

"Mac's going to walk her home," I told Dove and Hud. "He knows where she lives."

Hud gave Mac a curious look, but didn't say anything. I'd known Hud long enough to sense when he thought something wasn't kosher. Whatever his thoughts, he kept silent.

"Say good-bye to Angelina," he said to Maisie. "We've got to go meet your mother at Liddie's."

Maisie and Angelina waved good-bye to each other, and Maisie ran toward Hud's bright red Dodge Ram truck.

"Hey, thanks," I said to Hud. "We appreciate your help."

"No problem," he said. "Catch you later."

He was gone before I realized I never asked him exactly how Maisie ended up being in our children's play.

"If you'd tell me where she lives, I could take Angelina home," I told Mac. "I know you're working on tomorrow's sermon and are probably behind."

"No," he said abruptly. "I need a break anyway. Angelina and I are old friends. It'll give us a chance to catch up." He smiled down at the little girl. She returned his smile, revealing two missing bottom teeth.

"Okay," I said, puzzled. Was there some reason he didn't want me to see where Angelina lived?

He took Angelina's hand and walked down the street. She talked with great animation to him, probably telling him everything that had happened at rehearsal. She obviously knew him well. Maybe I was chasing imaginary rabbits. She was probably just one more neglected child whom he was trying to help maneuver through the rough roads of late-twentieth-century childhood. I went back inside the recreation hall where Dove was running a vacuum over the speckled gray commercial carpet.

"That didn't go so bad," I said, putting the Good Behavior Store prizes into a huge plastic box. "Maybe we'll be able to pull this off."

"Next time will be easier," Dove said, her voice confident. She picked up the black notebook that held Lily's original script complete with her personal notations. "We should copy this. It's the only set of Lily's notes we have. Unfortunately, the church's photocopy machine is on the blink."

"I'll take it by San Celina Printing," I said. "I'll have a couple of copies made." I took the notebook and set it down on the pew next to my purse.

"Have you ever met Angelina's aunt?" I asked, closing up the box of toys and carrying it to the office supply room next to Mac's office. "Do you know anything about how her mother died?"

"She doesn't have a mama?" Dove asked. "Poor little thing. No, I don't know anything about her or her aunt. They don't go to church here."

I retrieved an empty juice container that some kid had stuck behind a potted plant and threw it in the trash. "I'll ask Mac about her."

"What's got your interest up in this little girl?" Dove asked, pushing the vacuum toward the utility closet next to the kitchen.

I explained about Angelina's middle name and how I'd inadvertently made her tell the group her mother had died. "I feel bad about that. I kinda feel like I, of all people, should have been more sensitive."

Dove put away the vacuum, then came over and gave me a quick hug. "Honeybun, you couldn't have known. You know that everyone, not just you, assumes that all families consist of two parents, two-point-three children, and a golden retriever. Family just means a whole lot more than that, always has. Anyway, you know now and can be careful what you say."

❖

I PULLED INTO ONE OF THE EMPLOYEE PARKING SPACES BEHIND Blind Harry's bookstore just as Elvia was coming out the back door.

"I was getting ready to call you," Elvia said. "I was afraid you'd forgotten."

"No way. I love going to the graveyard with you and your family. But big things have happened since I last talked to you on Thursday," I said, climbing into her new black Cadillac Escalade, a present from her husband, my cousin Emory.

Inside the normally leather-scented interior, the smell of flowers, specifically the dusky, heavy scent of marigolds, was almost overwhelming. Elvia's family didn't have a lot of people buried in the Catholic cemetery, but those who were there got the full treatment every year on All Saints' Day.

"What things?" Elvia asked.

I told her a quick, condensed version of Lily's dilemma and Dove's impetuous decision that she and I would save the day.

"Oh, fun," Elvia said, the expression on her fine-boned, brown face saying the exact opposite.

"My feelings exactly. Can we drop off Scout before we go to the cemetery?"

"Sure."

I spread a small blanket she always carried for Scout across the backseat. He settled down, giving my hand a quick nuzzle. I scratched under his chin. "I know, it's a nice car, but don't get too used to it."

After getting him situated, I let out a long sigh and relaxed into the comforting arms of the leather passenger seat.

"So, how did the first rehearsal go?" Elvia asked, pulling out onto Lopez Street, heading for my house.

"Chaotic. Loud. But pretty fun. I think we might actually pull it off."

We dropped Scout off in the backyard. I tossed him a biscuit, and promised to be home soon. Then we headed south on Lopez toward the cemetery where her mom was already working on the family graves.

"If anyone can pull something like that off, it's you and Dove,"

Elvia said. "I still can't imagine a children's play based on *Pilgrim's Progress*. We studied it in my English lit class at Cal Poly. It's a complicated story."

"Lily simplified it a lot. She included all the major points and made sure every child has a speaking part. The funniest part is Mac. He plays Giant Despair."

She glanced over at me, her red lips smiling. "Perfect casting."

"Especially standing next to the kids. Did I mention it was also a musical?"

Her dark eyes widened. "You're kidding."

"No, I'm not. But the songs look pretty easy to learn. I listened to a tape of them on my way over here. Mac says he'll find us some help."

"I should hope so."

At the cemetery, almost her entire family was there, as well as a lot of other families doing the same thing we were, decorating the graves with marigolds, baby's breath, paper streamers, and shiny windmills, the kind a child might buy at the county fair. Señora Aragon had been there all day, no doubt, overseeing the cleaning of the gravestones. When we walked up with our arms full of flowers, she was sitting in a lawn chair chatting with another woman her age who was tending the graves next to the Aragon plot.

"*Mijas!*" she called to us. "Have you eaten yet? I made chicken *mole*." Her famous *mole* sauce, made with chilies, cinnamon, and chocolate, could make my husband groan in a way I normally only heard in our bedroom.

"*Hola*, Mama," Elvia said laying her bundle of flowers down, then bending over to kiss her mother on the cheek. "I ate at the bookstore, but I'll take some home to Emory."

"Gabe will be mad he missed it," I said.

"I'll send some home to Gabriel," Señora Aragon said when I took my turn hugging her. Elvia and I had been best friends since second grade, so Señora Aragon was like a *madre dos* to me.

"He'll be thrilled, though he'll probably have to fight his cousin, Luis, for it."

"His cousin is visiting?" Elvia said. "You didn't tell me that."

"Didn't get the time," I replied. "He showed up unexpectedly on our doorstep this morning."

"His cousin?" Señora Aragon said, settling back in her chair and folding her hands across her flowered dress. "His name is Luis? Tell me about his *familia*."

I laughed, thinking about how much alike the Southern and Mexican cultures are. That was always the first question out of Dove's mouth when she met someone new. "So, who's your family?"

"You know Gabe's family down in Santa Ana? His *tio* Tony was his dad's older brother. There's four boys, and Luis is the oldest. He's about six months older than Gabe."

"What does his *tio* do?"

"He was a Santa Ana policeman, but he's retired now. None of the boys became cops though. Manuel's a fireman. He's the second brother. And the other two, Juan and Alejandro, work in construction. Luis sells stuff."

"Stuff?" Elvia asked, looking up at me from where she was sprinkling marigold petals over the surface of the Aragon plot that held her *abuelo* and *abuela* as well as two great-aunts who never married.

I knelt down and started helping her spread out the orange and gold petals. The earthy scent of them brought back memories of the other All Saints' Days I'd come here with the Aragon family. "Right now it's precious metals."

"Like gold and silver?" she asked.

"And others. He sells them to plating and manufacturing companies. I think he said something about satellites." I shrugged. "To be honest, I didn't pay much attention when he was telling Gabe about it. Whatever it is, I guess it pays pretty well. He just bought a home in Newport Beach."

Two pathways over, I could hear her dad and two of her brothers, Rafael, a college professor in Fresno, and Miguel, a San Celina police officer, laughing with some fellow football fans about something that happened during last week's UCLA/USC football game.

"He must be doing well, then. Is his wife with him?" Elvia asked.

"No, he's alone. He was up here on business. Actually, we didn't find out that much. Like I said, he dropped in unexpectedly this morning, and Gabe asked him to stay. We're meeting for dinner tonight at Liddie's, so I'll find out more then. I do know he is on his third wife. He has a little girl with her. Two college-age sons with his first wife."

Señora gave an unapproving cluck. She was a faithful Catholic and didn't believe in divorce. "His poor mama," she said, shaking her head. "What is it with young people today? When I was a *niña* . . ."

Elvia moved closer to me and whispered, "Change of subject, please. Rafael and Sandy have separated."

"What?" I whispered back, shocked. "When?"

"We just found out this morning. I don't know the details yet." She stood up, rubbing the small of her back, and said in a loud voice, "How did play rehearsal go, Benni?"

"Great," I replied, following her lead. "The kids are just adorable."

So with that not-very-subtle move, we pointedly started discussing the play and the kids who were in it.

"A lot of the kids are neighborhood children," I told Señora Aragon while Elvia strung paper streamers from one Aragon gravestone to another. "I don't really know some of them, but there's this one little girl who almost has the same name as me."

"Albenia?" Elvia said. "I thought you were the only person in the world with that weird hybrid of a name." My given name, Albenia, was a combination of my dad's name, Ben, and my mother's name, Alice.

"No," I replied, throwing a tattered marigold at her. "Benni.

There's a little girl there with the name Angelina Benita. Her middle name was after her mother who, I found out, died. She was the reason I was late coming to your store. There was no one to pick her up. Her aunt, who apparently is her guardian, works in some dry cleaner downtown."

Señora Aragon sat up straighter in her chair and called over to me, her voice clipped. "Are you speaking of Juana Martinez?"

I shook my head. "I don't know her aunt's last name. The little girl's last name is Portillo. Why?"

Señora Aragon's face seemed to shut down. "No matter. Señora Martinez sometimes comes to church at the mission. That is all."

I knew Elvia's mother well enough to read her body language and that wasn't just all. There was something she knew about Angelina's aunt that she wasn't sharing with us. I glanced over at Elvia to gauge her reaction, but she was busy working on some tangled streamers and hadn't seen her mother's odd reaction to Juana Martinez's name.

"Tell me how Paloma is doing," Señora Aragon said, using the Spanish word for dove. "How is her chickens?"

"Dove's just fine," I said, picking up on her cue that she didn't want to talk about Juana Martinez. "Her Danish Brown Leghorns are laying more eggs than she can sell. I'll probably be bringing you a couple dozen this week."

"*Bueno, bueno,*" she said, nodding her head. Her black bun glistened in the afternoon sun. "One can never have too many *huevos.*"

"That's what we say down at the station, Mama," Miguel said, walking up just in time to catch his mother's last sentence. All of us burst into laughter at her innocent statement with the double entendre. *Huevos* was also the Spanish slang for balls.

"Hush, *mijo*," she said, waving her hand at him, laughing herself. "Have some respect for your *mama vieja.*"

He bent down and kissed her on the top of her head. "You're not old, Mama. Just well-seasoned."

We spent the rest of the afternoon there eating candy skulls and Mexican sweetbreads, talking and decorating the graves. As the sun started going down, people started lighting candles, and the cemetery, instead of looking spooky, took on a beautiful, golden-orange glow. Across the pathway from us, a man brought out a guitar and started strumming it, singing a soft, Mexican lullaby about the dying sun, the golden moon, and how each little girl and boy has a star with their name carved on it by *El Señor* Himself. I remembered Señora Aragon singing the song to me and Elvia when she used to tuck us in Elvia's pink canopy bed. We all joined in and watched the sun, just like in the song, disappear on the horizon where it went to sleep and let the moon stand guard through the night.

It was almost six o'clock when I said my good-byes holding a plastic container of chicken *mole* and making promises to visit Señora Aragon soon. Elvia drove me back to the bookstore to pick up my truck.

I was loading the container of chicken *mole* and three books on antique toys I'd ordered from Elvia onto the front seat, thinking about what I'd do after dinner with Gabe and Luis, when I realized that I'd left Lily's script and notes at the church.

"Dang it," I said to Elvia, who had walked me out to my truck. "I've got to run by the church and get that notebook. I told Dove I'd drop it by San Celina Printing and have it photocopied."

"You could use the bookstore's copier," Elvia said.

"Thanks, but I think I'm going to have a couple of copies made and have them bound. I'll let the print shop do the work." I leaned over and hugged her. "Kiss my crazy cousin for me. We all have to get together soon. I'll call you tomorrow about plans for dinner at my house. I want Luis to meet you both."

"We're free all week," she said.

The church parking lot was empty, telling me that Mac had either finished his sermon or had taken his studying back to the parsonage a half-mile away. Since I didn't have keys and didn't want to disturb Mac or drive out to the ranch and get them from Dove, it was lucky for me there was a light burning in the church's recreation hall, which had a connecting door to the sanctuary. I guessed that Walt, whom I knew lived in a duplex apartment two doors down, was probably still working. There was a little room we called "Walt's Fix-it Shop" where he kept his tools and boxes and jars of "stuff." In the many years of being our church's handyman, he'd acquired every type of screw and bolt and nail and widget you would ever need to repair anything.

I parked near the hall and went through the open door.

"Walt," I called out. "It's Benni Harper." I didn't want to give the poor man a coronary by sneaking up on him.

When I reached the closed door of his room, I knocked and called out again. Light shone underneath the door, so I knew he had to be there. Walt would never waste the church's money by leaving on an unnecessary light.

After a few more knocks, I carefully turned the doorknob. "Walt, it's Benni Harper." I opened the door to an empty room.

A small, faded blue radio played softly in the background. It was tuned to KCOW, our local country station. The DJ, a new one who called himself Buckaroo Brad, was announcing the winner of the station's "Name Our Thanksgiving Turkey" contest. The strains of the song "Turkey in the Straw" echoed in the empty room. The room was cold and smelled of wood dust and turpentine.

I glanced around and concluded that he must still be on the grounds somewhere. A black barn-shaped lunch pail, the old-fashioned kind you don't see much anymore, sat next to the radio. A coping saw sat out on one of the tables next to some thin wood cut into small, scalloped pieces.

I went back out of the room and wandered through the maze of Sunday School rooms and meeting rooms, past the front office and

Mac's office to the door that led to the sanctuary. Luckily, there were small night-lights every so often illuminating my way. Though it occurred to me later that I should have been afraid, that I should have been more cautious wandering through the dim hallways of the empty church building, at the moment I didn't even think about being in danger. This was the church I'd grown up in, its walls and windows, choir loft and baptismal as familiar and comforting to me as the barns and corrals at my dad's ranch.

When I reached the door leading to the sanctuary, I finally decided to flip on the switch that operated the light right above the pulpit where Mac preached every Sunday. Whether I found Walt or not, I thought I'd left the notebook on one of the back pews, and I'd need light to find it.

I stepped into the sanctuary, calling out Walt's name one more time. My voice echoed up to the church's vaulted ceiling, flying about the room like a trapped sparrow.

"Walt!" I called, then stopped, my voice stuck in my throat.

He lay in a crumpled gray heap in front of the altar table, right under the words chiseled in wood—"This Do In Remembrance of Me." Words Mac repeated every time the church celebrated the Lord's Supper.

I rushed over to him, my heart pounding so loud that it felt like it would explode in my ears. I knelt down next to him, trying not to gag at the smell of fresh blood. Blood trickling out from under his head and soaking into the speckled gray commercial carpet our church just purchased a few months ago. Carpet whose installation Walt supervised.

He lay on his side, one hand outstretched toward the door I just came through, the other twisted under his body. It was a head wound. Not the result of a fall, but the result of something hard coming down on the side of his head. His eye were open, staring. He appeared dead, but I had to be sure.

I forced myself to reach out, place my fingers on his neck, feeling for a pulse. The sticky texture of his blood made the chicken *mole* I'd eaten earlier rise up and burn my esophagus. I couldn't feel a pulse.

I pulled off my wool-lined Wrangler jacket. Should I cover him with it? Pull it over his staring eyes? That seemed the most humane thing to do. But Gabe's firm voice inside my head was telling me not to touch anything, keep the scene as pure as possible.

Gabe. Clutching my jacket, I ran out of the sanctuary into the church office. I threw my jacket on the counter, punched in Gabe's cell phone number, getting it wrong the first time and reaching someone named Paul.

"I'm sorry," I said, taking a deep breath and dialing slower this time. Gabe answered in seconds.

"Gabe," I said.

"Where are you?" he asked before I could continue. "I've been waiting fifteen minutes. Luis is on his way. I was getting ready to call you—"

"The church," I broke in, trying to keep my voice steady. "Gabe, there's been an . . ." I almost said accident. "Walt's hurt bad. I think he's dead. Please, hurry."

"Are you okay?" he said. In my mind I could see him stand up, ready to take charge. "Did you call nine-one-one?"

"I'm fine. I . . . No, I'll do it now."

"I'll do it." He paused for a split second. "Benni, are you safe?"

"I'm in the church office."

"Leave the building and go out to the street. Now."

"Okay," I said, glad to have someone in authority give me permission to do exactly what I wanted more than anything to do . . . flee. I burst out of office into the empty parking lot. I didn't stop until I reached the sidewalk, awash in the odd pink glow of the new street-lights. They gave the street, as familiar to me as any in San Celina, an eerie feel. I stood there, jacketless, shivering in the night air, wondering how long it would take the police to arrive, wishing I had brought Scout with me.

Call Mac, a voice inside me said. Looking around quickly at the empty parking lot, I ran over to my truck where my cell phone lay in the front seat.

"Mac, we need you at the church," I said, pressing the cell phone against my cold cheek. "Someone's hurt."

"Who?" he asked, his deep voice steady. It was a voice accustomed to emergencies, familiar with sudden death and sadness.

"Walt Adams," I said, a small sob escaping. "I think he's dead."

"I'll be right there."

When I started back toward the street to wait for the police, out of the corner of my eye a movement startled me. A pale flash of something low to the ground disappeared around the corner of the church building. My first thought was that it was an animal of some kind, maybe a possum. But it was too tall for a possum, and the color wasn't right. Should I investigate? My feet seemed frozen in place.

It occurred to me seconds later, when I saw the flashing lights of the approaching police car. The shape was that of a small child. A child who just might have seen who killed Walt Adams.

CHAPTER 4

A BLUE-AND-WHITE SAN CELINA POLICE DEPARTMENT PATROL car pulled up in front of me, and two men stepped out. Though I'd hoped it would be Miguel Aragon, one of Elvia's little brothers, someone I'd known since he was in diapers, it was a couple of officers I'd never met.

They calmly stepped out of their vehicle, slipping their nightsticks into place, their expressions fixed with the same "game face" I'd seen so many times on my own husband. The expression that many cops had a hard time leaving at work. The one that put everyone in a category—victim, criminal, or cop. One was a blond, twentyish man with a Marine jarhead haircut. The other was an African-American officer with wide-set eyes who looked to be in his thirties.

"Mrs. Ortiz?" the black officer said. "Are you okay?"

I nodded. Though I'd never officially taken Gabe's name, I didn't make an issue of correcting anyone. The chill from the early evening breeze seeped through my soft flannel shirt. I hugged myself both to keep warm and to try to keep from physically trembling.

Before he could continue, a fire department EMT vehicle rolled up. Two guys jumped out, their young faces animated and on high alert.

"Where's the patient?" the red-headed one asked, pulling out a square medical kit.

I pointed toward the church. "In the sanctuary, in front of the altar."

The paramedics trotted down the sidewalk. The officer in charge, whose name tag read S. Boyles, turned to the younger, blond officer. "I'll go check it out. Stay here with Mrs. Ortiz." He nodded at me and strode down the sidewalk after the paramedics.

The blond officer, obviously a rookie, didn't know what to say to me so he chose the route of silence, which suited me fine. I hugged myself, glancing every few seconds down the street, looking for Gabe's Corvette. Though it felt longer, it was only minutes later that he pulled up. Right behind him was Mac in his Explorer. They reached me at the same time.

Gabe wrapped his warm arms around me. "Are you okay, *querida*?"

"Yes," I said, though it wasn't true. But I could fall apart later. Right now Gabe had work to do and didn't need to worry about me.

He let go of me and looked over at Mac. "How did you—"

"I called him," I interrupted. "I figured he should be here."

Mac said, "I'll wait out here with Benni unless you need me."

Gabe nodded and walked toward the open sanctuary doors.

Another car drove up in front of the church, stopping behind the police car. It was a silver Mercedes that I recognized as Luis's. He stepped out of the car and came over to me and Mac.

"What's going on?" he asked. He wore a soft, gray cashmere sweater and gray dress slacks. His black hair was still wet, and his cologne drifted over the light breeze—Polo. The same brand Gabe used.

"Someone's been hurt," I said.

"Who?" he asked, sticking his hands deep into his tailored slacks.

I wasn't certain how much I should tell him, though it would all be public knowledge soon. I glanced up at Mac, whose face remained neutral. "Walt Adams. Our church maintenance man. I found him. Someone . . . someone hit him. I think."

"Oh, Benni, that must have been awful for you," Luis said, his dark eyes sympathetic. "Gabe called me on my cell phone, told me there'd been an accident at the church. I wanted to come see if I could help."

"How did you find it?" I asked.

"Stopped and asked," he said, giving a half-smile. "This isn't a terribly large town. And there's only one First Baptist." He held out his hand to Mac. "Luis Ortiz. I'm Gabe's cousin."

"Mac Reid," Mac said, shaking his hand. "I'm pastor of this church."

Luis looked over at the church building, getting busier now that three more squad cars and the Criminal Investigations van had arrived. "Gabe inside?"

I nodded.

He started walking toward the sanctuary. I probably should have warned him that Gabe would ask him to leave the crime scene, but I was glad for the moment alone with Mac.

"Who would hurt Walt?" I asked Mac. "He was one of the nicest people I've ever met."

Mac shook his head, his bearded face troubled. "Let's see what Gabe has to say."

I didn't press it. There must have been a million things going through his mind right then about why this happened, how he'd explain it to the congregation tomorrow morning. Not to mention that we had a problem about *where* we'd actually hold services tomorrow. We obviously couldn't use the sanctuary. I was sure the carpet would need replacing, and that couldn't be done before tomorrow morning. I shivered and hugged myself tighter.

"Here," Mac said pulling off his dark blue, zip-up sweatshirt and placing it around my shoulders. The warmth was immediate.

"Thanks. Mac, there's something . . ." I hesitated a moment, not certain I should say anything before I spoke to Gabe. Then again, Mac was the pastor of this church, he knew it and the neighborhood better than anyone. If it was a child I saw, maybe he'd know who he or she might be.

"What?" he said, laying his big hand on my shoulder.

"Mac, I think I might have seen a child."

"A child?"

"Running from the church. Right after I found Walt. Do you think—"

Before I could continue, Luis walked back toward us, a chagrined expression on his face. "He asked me to come out here and wait with you guys," he said.

"Don't take it personal," I said, wishing now I'd warned him and saved him from being embarrassed. "I've found it's better to stay out of his way when there's a possible crime scene." I walked over to one of the police cars and leaned against it. Luis joined me while Mac stood with his back toward us and stared at the commotion inside the church. A few minutes later Gabe came out.

"Does he need me?" Mac asked.

"Nothing you can do for him now," Gabe said. "He's been dead a while. Probably before Benni found him. Blunt force trauma, it looks like. I need the forensic people to do their thing without any more contamination to the area." He looked down at me.

"What do you think happened?" I asked.

Gabe shook his head, pulled at the end of his thick, black mustache. "Who knows? Could be a robbery gone bad. His wallet is gone. Whatever they hit him with is gone, or at least not in the immediate area. Maybe someone thought he had access to the church's money. Maybe just some crazy kid needing money for drugs. Looks like they got him just as he was turning around." He looked over at Mac and Luis. "Excuse us a moment."

He put his arm around my shoulders and led me a few feet away. His blue-gray eyes pierced mine, all cop now. "Tell me everything you did right before you found Mr. Adams. You know the routine. Don't leave anything out."

I closed my eyes for a moment, picturing what I'd done, seen, and heard right before I found Walt. Gabe walked me through step by step, prompting me every so often with a question.

I hesitated a moment when I came to the part where I saw the flash of light color that appeared to dart around the corner of the church building. Gabe caught my hesitation.

"What are you remembering?" he asked.

I inhaled deeply. "I think I saw a child run around the corner of the building."

Behind Gabe, I could see Mac's face. It was stoic, unreadable, but he was concentrating on me, on what I was saying to Gabe. When I caught his eyes, his face turned neutral again.

Gabe made me repeat what I saw or thought I saw three times. Though it was a little tiring, I knew why he did it. Memory is a funny thing. The more we go over something, especially when the incident is fresh, the more details we remember. He'd told me that once when I quizzed him about interrogation techniques that police use. I was hoping he could see that my curiosity about his job and how it's done was paying off now. I didn't complain when he asked me to go over it a fourth, then a fifth time. Gabe called it peeling the onion. You go through layer after layer until you find something usable.

"Hair," I said, suddenly remembering something the fifth time that I didn't the first four, proving his theory to be true.

"Hair?" he prompted.

"The child had long hair. It glinted in the moonlight." We both looked up to where I was pointing. There was a bright, three-quarters moon. "Long dark hair," I added, seeing it in my mind lie in a shadow across the pale shirt of the fleeing child.

"A little girl," Gabe said.

"Or a boy with long hair."

"Yes, you could be right." He glanced at the pink stucco apartment complex next to the church. There had to be at least a hundred apartments there, no doubt most of them housing children. "We'll do a door-to-door." He inhaled and shook his head. "With this neighborhood, it'll be tough." Besides the apartments next door, First Baptist was in a neighborhood of duplexes and single-family dwellings. At this time of early evening, that child could have come from anywhere in a half-mile radius.

"I'd better call for more detectives," Gabe said, pulling out his cell phone. "We'll need to canvass the neighborhood."

I walked over to Mac, taking off his sweatshirt and handing it back.

"Keep it," he insisted.

"I'm warm now, thanks," I said.

"Excuse me," Luis said, pulling out a package of cigarettes. He politely walked a good distance away so as not to inflict us with his smoke. We watched him go over to a pine tree, bend his head, and light his cigarette, protecting his match with a cupped hand.

On a hunch, I asked Mac, "Who do you think the child was?"

He started to speak, then stopped, obviously feeling torn by some kind of loyalty.

"If she or he did see something, they might be in danger."

"I can't tell Gabe." His blunt tone surprised me.

"What? Of course you can."

"Come over here," Mac said, taking my elbow and leading me over in front of the church sign. Known in San Celina for its clever sayings, often penned by Mac himself, this week it said, "Carrying a lot of weight on your shoulders? Try a little knee bending."

"What is it?" I asked, my palms wet with anxiety.

"If it's who I think it was, she can't be involved in this. It could cause irreparable harm to her . . . and to others."

I waited a moment, hoping my silence would encourage him to explain further. When he didn't, I said, "What kind of harm?"

"She . . . if it's who I think it is, she isn't legal. Neither is her . . . guardian."

Mac harboring illegal immigrants? Though I'd heard rumors of certain people in our local Catholic church maintaining a sort of underground railroad for people, mostly Latinos, coming illegally into our country, I never imagined Mac being involved. Then again, he and Father Mark were pretty close. Father Mark, one of Santa Celina Mission's priests, was an ex–gang member who turned to God when his wife and daughter were killed in a drive-by shooting. He was never one to do anything the conventional way, something that made him both beloved and sometimes reviled by different political and social factions in our town. Gabe, in the awkward position of being police chief, yet admiring and liking Father Mark, told me he just ignored the rumors and would until there was concrete evidence that the priest was breaking any laws.

I didn't react for a moment, not really sure what I should say. Mac's predicament was one that no one would ever find comfortable, a struggle between man's law and God's law. I was always of mixed opinion about the illegal immigrants who lived and worked among us. Though it was easy in theory to say send anyone back who isn't here legally, the truth was a lot of our agricultural labor as well as other menial work that United States citizens didn't want to do, *wouldn't do*, was provided by these people. That was especially true in San Celina County. And, though we didn't like to contemplate it, but for the grace of God and a fluke of nature, any of us could have been born on the other side of the border. Who's to say any of us wouldn't do anything we could, break any law, to get to a country where we could find jobs to feed our families, provide a better future for our children?

"What are you going to do?" I asked. "If she saw something, she could be in danger." It hit me then. I knew who it was. "It's Angelina Portillo, isn't it?" I brought my hand up to my mouth. "That poor little girl."

Mac's face looked miserable. "Benni, please, you know I would normally not ask a wife to keep something from her husband." He stopped, ran a hand over his face. "No, strike that. I'm not going to tell you what to do. That's up to you. Yes, it might be Angelina. She and her aunt, Juana Martinez, live in a duplex two blocks over, and Juana often works late. Sometimes Juana asks a neighbor girl to watch Angelina. But the girl's a typical fifteen year old and often isn't home, so Angelina's on her own. There's another older woman, Mrs. Mesa, but she works odd hours at a retirement home. When Angelina gets scared or lonely, she often comes over here and sits in the library and reads or plays with her dolls. Walt and I would watch out for her, make sure she got home safely. How could I refuse her refuge in God's house?"

"Where are her parents?"

His lips straightened into a thin line. "Her father died right around the time she was born. I'm not sure how. Her mother died of meningitis about a year ago."

"Is Juana legal?" I asked.

Mac shook his head no.

"Angelina was six years old when her mother died," I said softly. The same age I'd been. The big difference between us, though, was I was fortunate to have a large, loving family around to protect me, as well as my guaranteed citizenship in the most powerful country in the world.

"How did she end up here in San Celina?" I asked, swallowing hard.

"Angelina had no close family except Juana, who came over here with her husband about a year ago. Juana's husband was killed in a bar fight a few months ago, and Juana's been struggling to make it ever since. Father Mark helped her get a job at the dry cleaner. Angelina's mother was Juana's only sister. When she died, some friends, with the help of Father Mark, smuggled Angelina across the border in a car trunk and brought her to Juana." He looked away. "She managed to buy Angelina some papers, enough to enable her to enroll in school . . ."

His voice trailed off, letting me fill in the blanks. Angelina's papers were good enough to fool the public school system, who tended not to question citizenship as deeply as other agencies, but they would disintegrate like a dandelion puff when scrutinized by the police. Not to mention it would put Juana and Angelina both in danger of being deported back to a life that was much less kind than even their bare subsistence living here.

"Oh, Mac," I said, not able to articulate anything else.

Gabe closed his phone and started toward us, his face grim.

"You need to talk to Juana," I said quickly to Mac. "Find out what Angelina saw, if she saw anything. Maybe it wasn't her."

Mac rubbed a nervous hand up and down his chestnut-colored beard. "I'd already decided to do that. As for telling Gabe—"

I held my hand up, making a snap decision that, even as I did it, knew would hurt me eventually. "I won't. For right now, anyway."

His expression was grateful even as he said, "I feel sick about that. Encouraging you to deceive your husband."

"You are not encouraging me to do anything," I said firmly. "This is my decision, and I accept full responsibility. I'll give you time to talk to Juana and Angelina." I looked right into his gray eyes. "Then I will have to go to him. I can't wait very long."

"I'll talk to them as soon as I can," he promised.

Gabe would want to strangle me when he found out I knew about this possible lead and didn't tell him immediately. But, for not the first time, his job, and its promise to uphold the letter of the law, and my belief in what was the moral, not necessarily legal, thing to do, were in conflict. How many more incidents like this could our marriage endure?

Gabe walked up to us. I looked at the ground, trying to compose my face into a neutral expression at the same time my heart was beating double time. I took in a deep breath and looked up into his sober face.

He slipped the cell phone in the top pocket of his dark blue shirt. "Four detectives are coming out to start canvassing the neighborhood. This will probably take awhile." He looked over at Mac. "I'll need you to stay, if you can."

"Absolutely," Mac said, pulling his sweatshirt back on.

"Sweetheart," he said to me. "You can go home. I have no idea when I'll be finished here." He glanced over at his cousin, who was still standing next to the pine tree, watching the front of the church. "Luis never ate dinner."

"Okay, I'll get Luis settled in then and fix something for you both. Should I bring it down here?"

He shook his head. "I'll eat when I get home." He leaned over and kissed the top of my head. "Are you sure you're okay?"

"Yes," I said, not looking at Mac. "I'm fine."

Luis followed me home, parking his Mercedes out on the street, leaving the driveway for Gabe's Corvette.

"Are you hungry?" I asked Luis, bringing him more towels. I stood in the doorway of the guest room. Its cherry-brown Mission-style furniture had just been delivered last week. A Crown of Thorns quilt made by Dove and me in deep forest-greens and rich burgundies covered the queen-size bed.

"Starving," he said. "I have to tell you, I love this room. Paige decorated our house in some kind of froufrou French antiques. I'm afraid to sit on anything."

"Thank you," I said, warmed by his compliment. "You're the first guest to stay here. You even have your own TV." I opened the armoire across from the bed.

"You'd better watch out. I may not ever leave."

"Oh, I doubt San Celina will amuse you for long. Not much excitement here compared to Southern California." I grimaced, aware of the irony of my words. "Really, tonight is not our normal routine. Most of the time Gabe's life consists of paperwork and meatloaf."

"He looks happier than I've ever seen him." His face took on an expression that I could only describe as dispirited. For the first time it occurred to me that maybe his visit here wasn't spur of the moment. Maybe he needed to talk to Gabe about something personal. Since that was something only Gabe could do, I offered what was within my power at the moment.

"Speaking of meatloaf," I said. "Do you have any real likes or dislikes in terms of food?"

"I'm easy to please," he said, picking up his expensive-looking leather suitcase and setting it on the bed. "I'll eat anything I don't have to prepare."

That made me laugh. I'd heard Gabe say that exact same thing. "Spoken like a true Ortiz man." His melancholy expression had changed back into an easygoing manner that reminded me of Gabe's son, Sam.

After a quick dinner of grilled cheese sandwiches, a green salad, and cherry pie, Luis went to his room and shut the door. I was glad for the time alone so I could think about what had happened, what I'd found out from Mac.

How long should I hold back the information about Angelina from Gabe? This type of situation had been a strain in our marriage from the beginning. He hid things from me, and I hid things from him.

There was no doubt that it didn't help build an intimate relationship, but each time we did it, we both felt we had good reasons—he, to protect me, and me, usually trying to protect someone else. It all boiled down to what he did for a living, his promise and belief in upholding the law, usually no matter what. He often saw things more black and white than I did, as well he should. Who would want a chief of police who bent like a willow in the breeze? Then again, things like this dilemma with Angelina and her aunt would be much easier if Gabe were an architect or a busdriver rather than the chief of police.

Knowing she'd give me an earful if I didn't tell her what had happened before she heard it on the church's grapevine (sometimes known as the prayer chain), I called Dove at the ranch.

"Oh, that poor man," she said, clucking under her breath. "Lord, have mercy on us all. What is happening to our town when a person isn't even safe in their own church?"

I murmured an agreement, wondering for a brief second if I should tell her what Mac and I suspected about Angelina. Though I gave myself the prerogative to change my mind later, I decided to keep it to myself, so that she wouldn't have to also struggle with the moral dilemma of whether or not to tell Gabe.

"Are you okay, honeybun?" Dove asked. "Do you need me to come stay with you?"

"I'm a little shook up, but Luis is here, and Gabe will be home soon. It was . . ." I choked a little on my words. "Oh, Gramma, he was such a sweet, kind man, and it was such a horrible way to die."

"Yes, he was," she said. "We'll miss him mightily. And what a terrible thing for Gabe's cousin to see on his first day here. Why don't you bring him out to the ranch after church tomorrow? We'll barbecue some tri-tip and some chicken, make him feel welcome."

"That's a good idea. Guess I'll see you at church in the morning."

"Speaking of church, where *are* we going to have services?"

"I have no idea. I forgot to ask Mac. Guess we'll just have to show up with everyone else and see."

"I'll call him and see if he needs any help." There was a short pause, then she asked, "Are you really all right?"

Nothing that laying my head down in your lap and having a good cry wouldn't help, I wanted to say. "Yes," is what I actually said.

Scout had stuck to my side like superglue ever since I'd come home, sensing my troubled spirit. It still amazed me how much this dog, whom I hadn't raised from a puppy, was tuned in to my deepest feelings.

"C'mon, boy," I said, pulling his grooming brushes from the utility closet in the kitchen. "Let's give you a good brushing." He followed me, tail wagging, out to the back porch.

Like Gabe when I gave him back rubs, there was nothing Scout loved more than me preening over him like a new mother. And it was relaxing for me, a time of minor physical activity when I could think without feeling obligated to talk.

While I groomed Scout, I thought about Walt, the person who killed him, the child who possibly saw it all. I prayed for guidance on what I should do, when I should tell Gabe. But no answer came, at least not one I could discern. By the time Scout's coat gleamed like melted milk chocolate and his eyes were rolled back in ecstasy, I'd decided that my decision to wait until Mac talked to Angelina and Juana before I told Gabe was the right one, at least the best one in a situation where the choices were limited.

"Thanks," I said, scratching his broad, shiny chest. "You've been a big help." He licked my wrist in appreciation. Once we were back inside the house, he flopped down in front of the fireplace, completely relaxed.

Gabe came home at a little before midnight. Plum-colored circles under his eyes caused them to appear a deep blue in the glow of our bedroom lamps. I was in bed reading one of my books on antique toys.

"How did it go?" I asked, laying my book down. "Do you want something to eat?"

He started unbuttoning his shirt. "No, we had food brought in. My detectives were able to make contact with about three-quarters of the tenants in the apartment complex next door. How much truth we got from them is debatable. Most of them are first-generation Mexicans. They don't trust the police. And there were lots of kids." He unbuttoned his Levi's and pulled them off. "The detectives will continue canvassing tomorrow. But the longer it is . . ." He peeled off the rest of his clothes and headed for the shower, the rest of his words muffled by the start of the shower.

I finished his sentence in my head. The longer they go between the crime and questioning people, the harder it is to acquire accurate information. Guilt gnawed at my stomach, knowing that I had the power to make his life easier, not have his detectives waste time chasing rabbits.

Then again, there was no *guarantee* that Angelina was the witness. Why bring grief and trouble into her and Juana's life unless it was absolutely necessary? I'd check with Mac tomorrow and see what he'd found out. Then I would tell Gabe.

After his shower, Gabe crawled into bed and pulled me to him. His skin was still warm and damp and smelled of soap. I kissed the rough skin under his chin.

"Your cousin is nice," I said. "I made him grilled cheese for dinner. He showed me more pictures of his little girl. She's really cute. He's so proud of her. He didn't talk much about his wife. I think there might be something going on there. Trouble in their relationship."

Gabe's arms tightened around me. "I wouldn't be surprised. Frankly, she sounds like a climber to me. Luis is a really smart guy in most ways except for picking women."

"Not like you, huh?" I said, softly scratching his stomach.

"Absolutely," he said, his voice low and intimate. "Only the best for me."

I ran my hand up his chest, the hair tickling my palm, feeling more than a little guilty. "What did you guys talk about today?"

He settled down into the bed more deeply, his arms around me loosening slightly. "Just things. You know, family and jobs. Our kids."

"Does he seem a little sad to you?"

He didn't answer for a moment, then said, "No more than any of us Ortiz guys. I suppose it's a family trait."

Though I wanted to probe the subject deeper, something inside me told me to let it go, that now wasn't the time. Gabe definitely had his own melancholy side, depressed moods that snuck up on him like a skillful pickpocket, stealing away the light in his eyes and replacing it with a stoic heartsickness. His, I suspected, had much to do with his time in Vietnam, his undercover narcotics work, the many broken relationships in his past. His mind worked overtime during those moods, reliving and regretting his choices. I worried about him during those times, had early in our marriage tried to joke him out of them until I realized that doing so was impossible. I finally learned to just step back, remain a powerless, caring bystander, and let him ride them out himself.

I kissed the side of his neck, my lips cool against his damp, scratchy skin. Intermingling with the aroma of clean soap was his unique gingery scent. I was mature enough to realize that I couldn't make another person happy, that a person's happiness was a weird, unpredictable combination of attitude, genetics, and life experiences. But I was in love enough to know that I would do whatever I could to make this man happy until the day I died.

❖

AT EIGHT THE NEXT MORNING GABE WAS STILL ASLEEP. LUIS HAD also not surfaced from his room. The house was as quiet as if Scout and I were there alone. I glanced out the kitchen window and saw why everything had such a hushed quality to it. A thick fog had rolled in, muffling even the sounds of passing cars. I turned the thermostat up to take the chill off so the house would be toasty when the men finally stirred.

I left a note propped next to the coffeepot telling them there were fresh raspberry muffins in the bread box and that I'd be home from church by noon. "Be dressed and ready to go to the ranch," I added to the note. "Dove has a barbecue planned for Luis." Hopefully the fog will have burned off by then.

Though I'd had a restless night's sleep filled with troubling dreams and felt tempted to stay home from church myself, I knew I should especially attend this morning, both for my own spiritual need and to show support for Mac. I made a quick call to my cousin, Emory, who, like Dove, hated hearing things pertaining to our family through the grapevine. In his case, it would be someone from the *San Celina Tribune*, where he worked for awhile before setting up the west-coast office for his dad's smoked-chicken business.

Luckily, Emory answered so I wouldn't have to tell the story twice. He could relay the details to Elvia.

"Hi, cuz," I said. "Before you leave for church, if you're going today, I just wanted to . . ."

"I heard, you little brat. Why didn't you call me last night?"

"How did you hear so fast?"

"Connections, sweetcakes, connections. You have no idea how plugged into this town I am. Poor old guy. They said it was likely a robbery."

"Geeze Louise," I said, not willing to commit myself.

"Don't try to sweet talk me. Tell me the scoop."

"Apparently I don't need to. Why don't *you* tell me what you know?"

He gave a low chuckle. "Don't get your knickers in a knot. All I know is First Baptist's church handyman, Walt Adams, was killed in the sanctuary last night, a possible robbery victim, and that you found the body. Haven't you looked at the paper yet?"

"No," I said, struggling to put on a pair of leather loafers. I was wearing black dressy slacks and a gray sweater, appropriate for the somber tone there would be at church today. I also wanted to look as inconspicuous as possible, in case there were reporters there. Not that I had any hope of not being recognized. My position as Gabe's wife, as well as my former forays into criminal investigations, had, unfortunately, squelched that a long time ago.

"It's already front page news. I must say, I never expected to see crime scene tape and First Baptist's sanctuary in the same photograph."

"Mac must just be sick," I said, finally getting my shoes on.

"So, tell me what the papers haven't reported."

"Since I don't know what they've written . . ." I glanced over at the mantel clock. "I'm late for church. Look, I'll give you all the details I know this afternoon. Dove is having a barbecue at the ranch for Gabe's cousin, Luis. Why don't you and Elvia come out and meet him? You won't believe how much they look alike."

"Okay, I suppose I can wait."

"I suppose you'll have to. Trust me, Emory, I don't have that much to add to what you know." As much as I loved and trusted my cousin, I wasn't going to tell him about Angelina. He still had too many friends at the paper. Besides, I certainly wasn't going to tell him about it before I did Gabe.

"Wear something that will look good on the front page," he said. "The buzzards will be hovering."

He was right. I pulled up to church in my purple pickup and was immediately accosted by two reporters and a photographer. The reporters started firing questions at me. I'd been through this often enough to just keep saying, "No comment," as I walked toward the crowd standing in front of the sanctuary. The fog still hadn't lifted, giving the day a spooky feel. Yellow-and-black crime scene tape across the church's double doors didn't help reduce the *Twilight Zone* atmosphere.

A large, computer-printed sign on the doors said, "Sunday School canceled for *this Sunday only*. Church services will be temporarily held in the recreation hall at 11:00 A.M."

We drifted over to the recreation hall where men of the church were still setting up folding chairs. Dove saw me walk into the room and barreled through the crowd toward me.

"Are you sure you're all right?" she asked, pulling me into a hug.

"Yes, ma'am," I said. "Have you seen Mac?"

"He's in his office. He's working on what to tell people."

"Has Walt's family been notified?" It just occurred to me that I had no idea if Walt even had a family, where they lived, what his relationship was with them. He'd belonged to our church for ten years and though I'd sat next to him at potlucks, talked to him about aphids and ladybugs, and pulled weeds where he told me to pull them on church workdays, I didn't really know much about him.

"I'm sure Mac must have called someone," Dove said, her round, powder-soft face unusually distressed.

"Do you know anything about his family?" I asked.

She shook her head. "He kept to himself. I asked after his family one time, and he just said that he'd lost touch with them. He didn't seem to want to go any further, and I didn't push. Invited him out to the ranch for Sunday dinner a couple of times, but he said he was busy, that he would get back to me. He never did."

"That's so sad," I said softly.

"Yes, it is," she said, tucking her arm through mine. "It deeply shames me that I didn't try harder to know him."

Mac's sermon was short, but heartrending. He briefly told what happened to Walt the night before, though at that point everyone had already heard most of the details. He called for a special prayer for Walt, his family wherever they were, the police investigating the crime, and the person who killed Walt, that their heart might feel remorse, turn themselves in, face the consequences of their actions, and seek God's forgiveness. During his sermon about the meaning of grace, the room was so quiet you could hear birds chirping and the sound of someone's droning lawnmower.

In his closing prayer he asked for safety and wisdom for all those who attended today and closed the prayer with a line that likely left more than a few people bewildered. "Help us, Abba Father," he prayed, "to show mercy to those whose circumstances compel them to seek sanctuary. Help us be that sanctuary no matter what the cost. You are our shield and our protector, our ever-present help in danger. In Your Precious Son, Jesus' name, Amen."

Mac's prayer immediately made me think of Juana and Angelina. I wanted to talk to him after the service, but with all the church members crowding around him and reporters hovering, it was obvious he wouldn't be alone for quite a few hours. I decided to call him later in the afternoon. I was already picturing Gabe's disappointed look when he found out that I'd held back from him Angelina's possible involvement in this case. Then again, I thought hopefully, maybe it wasn't her and the whole problem would be moot.

"I invited Emory and Elvia to the barbecue," I told Dove out in the parking lot where the sun was now just peeking through the hovering fog.

Isaac, her husband and my much beloved step-grandpa, said in his booming voice, "There no such thing as too much company for Dove."

His voice was as big and impressive as his bear-size, white-haired frame. He wore starched jeans and a thin, expensive-looking sweater with subdued American Indian symbols on it. No earring this morning. He must have dressed in a hurry, forgetting his one piece of jewelry other than his wide, platinum wedding band.

"Hush up, old man," she said indulgently as he opened the door to their bright red Chevy pickup. "Get me home *tout suite*. Now that Emory's coming, I've got to make more potato salad."

"We've enough for a month of Sundays now," he said, giving me a broad wink. "We could feed the whole Razorback football team and half the cheerleaders."

"You have no idea how much of Dove's potato salad Emory can put away," I said, grateful for the moment of levity after a sobering morning.

When I arrived home, the guys were sitting on the front porch in wicker chairs drinking iced tea, laughing at something so hard they were bent over at the waist. Scout lay on the porch in front of them, chewing a tennis ball. It was good to see my husband relaxed and happy, enjoying himself with someone who obviously knew him well. If it hadn't been for this homicide at the church, this could have been a wonderful week for Gabe. He rarely acted this carefree and silly, except when he was alone with me.

"You guys ready to head out to the ranch?" I asked, climbing the steps and reaching down to scratch behind Scout's ears. I couldn't help staring at them sitting next to each other. Their resemblance was startling at times.

"Looking forward to it," Luis said. "Gabe, here, says he's actually done some roping and branding. Is that true?"

"He's turning out to be a pretty good ranch hand," I said, smiling. "So is Sam. Stick around, and I'll get you up on a horse and trained too."

He shook his head and sipped at his glass of tea. "Me and cows? Don't think so. Only way I like 'em is on my plate and rare enough to see hoofprints in the mashed potatoes."

"We'll see," I said, leaving the chuckling men to go inside and change clothes.

At the ranch, Emory and Elvia's Escalade was already parked in the circular driveway. When we stepped out of Luis's Mercedes, Sam and his new girlfriend, Theresa, were coming out the front door. She was a cute little Italian girl with huge, dark eyes, long ebony hair, and a glittery ruby stud in her nose. He met her when she cut his hair a month ago. He'd lived at the ranch since he moved to San Celina a few years ago and was such a good worker that Daddy said he could stay there forever.

"Hey, Sam and Theresa," I said. "Where're you off to?"

"Gather some eggs," Sam said. "Dove's making homemade ice cream." He bounded down the steps and ran over to Luis, enveloping him in a hug. "Hey, Luis, what's up?" They broke apart and gave each other the Gen X version of a handshake, the bumping of closed fists.

"Hey, kid, not much. How's it with you? Who's this gorgeous *señorita*? She couldn't possibly be with *you*."

"Ha, ha," Sam said. "Theresa, this is my dad's cousin Luis. He's a flake, but he's way cooler than my dad."

"Don't forget who still pays your college tuition," Gabe said, pretending to be annoyed.

"Ignore the old fart," Luis said.

"I try as much as humanly possible," Sam said.

"Hey, *viejo loco*," Gabe said to Luis. "No agitating the troops."

Theresa stood watching the men banter, her face a little apprehensive.

"Ignore them," I said to her. "There's enough hot air flowing around right now to float two blimps. Sam, go gather your eggs while ye may. We need to introduce Luis to everyone."

By the time we'd introduced Luis around, the tri-tip and chicken was ready, and we sat down to eat at the dining room table, made big enough for everyone by the addition of two leaves. Daddy said a quick grace, and we all started passing platters of food.

"Dove, this meal is incredible," Luis said, sitting on one side of me,

Gabe on the other. He gazed in wonder over the variety of food. "It looks like a magazine spread."

It was just one of Dove's normal Sunday dinners, but I realized to someone not used to her, it was pretty impressive. Besides the tri-tip steak and chicken, there were pink pinquito beans with salsa, corn on the cob, potato salad, mashed potatoes, tossed green salad with fresh tomatoes from Dove's garden, ambrosia salad, garlic bread, home-made baking-powder biscuits, fried okra, fresh green beans, and mac-aroni and cheese.

"There's German chocolate cake or peach cobbler with homemade ice cream for dessert," Dove said, grinning with pleasure. "Or we can make strawberry shortcake, if you like. Oh, where is my brain? I for-got the gravy. You can't have mashed potatoes without gravy."

"You sweet talker," I said to Luis, handing him the bowl of steam-ing pinquito beans. "Now I see how you make so much money selling things."

He winked at me. "*Mi madre* didn't raise no dummy."

After the meal, around three o'clock, the fog finally burned off and the sun shone bright and warm. We all retired out to the front porch to sit and let our Sunday dinner randomly contribute to our fat cells. The only people who seemed to have any energy were Sam and Theresa. We watched while he tried to show her how to rope a dummy cow in the front yard. When we could muster the energy, we called out silly instructions and opinions.

"How about a tour of the ranch?" Luis said after a while.

"Give me a few minutes," Gabe said from the lounge chair where he was dozing.

"I'll show him around," I said. "You stay there, Friday."

"Friday?" Luis said, as he followed me out to the barn.

"Hasn't he ever told you I call him that?"

He shook his head. "We don't talk as much as we used to. I travel so much, he's so busy." He stuck his hands into the pockets of his jeans. "It's a shame how little we know about each other's lives now. When we were in high school, we were inseparable."

I glanced up at him. "Did he tell you how we met?"

Again he shook his head. So I quickly told the story of my first involvement with a homicide, one of the artists at the co-op, how Gabe had been the temporary chief of police taking his friend Aaron's place before Aaron died.

"I called him Sergeant Joe Friday to make fun of him," I said. "He questioned me so matter-of-factly. And . . ." I glanced sideways at Luis. "It really irritated him, which at the time, was my intention."

He laughed. "Yes, that would definitely bug him. So, what changed?"

I shrugged. "I guess I grew on him, because we became involved, fell in love, and it sort of stuck as my nickname for him. I'm not a honey-baby-sweetie kind of girl, you know? So I call him Friday, but in a good way now." I opened the door to the barn and waved him in.

"Sergeant Joe Friday," he said. "He's always followed the rules to the letter . . ."

"Until they don't suit him," I finished. "That part of him is Serpico."

He threw back his head and gave the hearty laugh that was such an eerie duplicate of Gabe's. "You *do* understand my cousin. Good for you. Maybe this time his marriage will stick."

His candid remark caught me unaware. I held back the automatic caustic reply that came to mind. Gabe was so happy about his cousin being here, I didn't want to spoil it. For once, I thought before I spoke.

"I've met Lydia," I said carefully, looking directly in his face. "And I like her. She's a good person and a great mom to Sam."

He nodded, his cheeks flushing slightly. "I know she is. That was crass of me. I apologize. I'm not usually so tactless. Forgive me?"

"Sure," I said, embarrassed by the turn in conversation. This was the second time he'd made a cutting remark, then immediately apologized. Was this a normal trait of his? He was such a polished sales-man, I couldn't help wondering if he did it on purpose. I sensed there was some underlying antagonism he had for his cousin. Did Gabe pick up on this? All I could think to do right that moment was change the subject. "Have you ever ridden a horse?"

"No," he said, glancing over at the empty stalls. "I've tried a lot of crazy things, but riding horses isn't one of them."

"I could teach you, if you like," I offered, picking up a lead rope that had fallen to the ground and hanging it on a nail. "Sam had never been on a horse either before he came here. Now he rides like he was born to it."

He reached over and ran his hand over the rough wood of one of the stall doors. "He's young. I'm not as eager to try new things as I once was." He sighed and looked away from me, out the open barn doors to the hills behind our ranch. In the distance you could see three of our eight ranch horses. "It sure is peaceful here."

"Right now," I said, smiling. "You should be here during roundup. It's a madhouse. And the food. If you think the spread you saw today was something, you should see it then. Dove cooks for three weeks."

"When do you do this?" he asked, leaning against a stall door.

"Around Thanksgiving. My aunts, uncles, and cousins all come from their ranches in Wyoming and Nevada. But sometimes in the spring too. Depends on when we have calves that need tending and also when my aunts and uncles can get away from their own ranches." I tilted my head and looked at him. "Thanksgiving is only a few weeks away. You could come back up for it."

He didn't look at me. "Don't know what I'll be doing for the holi-days."

"You, Paige, and Cassie are welcome anytime."

"Show me some cows," he said, suddenly standing upright.

"Cows we got. More cows than you'll probably care about seeing."

I fired up Daddy's beat-up 1971 Jeep Cherokee and drove Luis out to the pasture where the horses were, then to a pasture where we kept some heifers tending to their new calves.

While we drove to the first gate, I asked him that famous old ranching question. "If you see three cowboys in a pickup truck, how can you tell which one is the greenhorn?"

He shook his head. "I have no idea. The one wearing the newest hat?"

"No," I said, laughing. "He's the one in the passenger seat nearest the door."

"Why?"

I stopped at the first gate, turned to him and said, "The combination is two, thirty-one, fifteen. Close it after you. The golden rule in ranching is always 'if it's closed, close it after you, if it's open, leave it open.' "

He looked puzzled, then it dawned on him and he laughed. "Okay, I get it. The one driving and the one in the middle never have to get out to open the gate."

I grinned. "Yep."

He seemed to enjoy himself, asking pretty standard questions about cattle—how we gathered them, did we know each one, did we ever get attached or feel bad when we sold them for slaughter.

"My first husband, Jack, was a real softie," I said. "With every batch of heifers he'd take a shine to one, and he'd baby her like she was a pet dog. I often thought he might have been happier being a vet rather than a rancher. He even liked the ones who couldn't seem to get pregnant, had a special love for them and tried everything to help them. Drove his older brother, Wade, crazy. Wade was a rancher, through and through. 'You don't name future food' he used to tell Jack."

"My second wife loved her Shih Tzus like that," Luis said. "I think she loved them more than me. For sure they ate better, because she'd actually cook for them." He laughed lightly, telling me that he didn't mean to wife bash.

I took him to the highest spot on our ranch, a place with the unimaginative name of "Big Hill," where you could see in the distance all of San Celina and even part of Cal Poly's old metal agricultural buildings. There were small stands of gold-and-red big-leaf maple trees, giving the brown-gray hills a little New England color. We climbed out of the Jeep and hiked the last quarter-mile to a cottonwood tree whose heart-shaped leaves had turned a bright yellow. I showed him the place in the tree where Gabe and I had subtly carved our initials surrounded by a heart. The cool air smelled of dry grass with a hint of mustard.

"Kind of silly, I guess," I said, suddenly embarrassed. "We were dating." It was also the spot where we'd decided to elope to Las Vegas rather than have a big wedding, though Dove managed to talk us into having another "real" wedding, officiated by Mac, when we returned.

He traced the carving of the heart, a wistful smile on his face. "You're good for him."

The sun was already starting to dip toward the hills when we drove the Jeep back into the barn and headed back to the house. A sharp, cold wind had picked up so everyone had deserted the front porch and had gone inside.

"Hope they didn't eat all the dessert," I said.

"That would be a real tragedy," Luis agreed. "I can't believe it, but I'm actually starting to feel hungry again."

On the front porch, Sam and Theresa had just finished with the hand-crank ice cream maker that Dove would never let us replace with an electric one.

"Doesn't taste the same," she insisted. To be honest, I think she was right.

Inside, they'd started cutting the cake and dishing out the peach cobbler. Daddy stood at the kitchen counter, wielding a metal ice cream scoop.

"You're back," he said, feigning disappointment. "I was getting ready to eat your share." He held out a bowl of hot peach cobbler to Luis.

"I'd've had to fight you for it, sir," Luis said, taking the bowl.

We all laughed and crowded in to sample the desserts. Gabe had taken his second bite of cake when his cell phone rang.

"Grandson, why don't you throw that thing in the chicken house for a day?" Dove complained. "You never get any rest."

"Wish I could, *abuelita*," he said, sighing and going into the other room to answer it. When he came back a few minutes later, his expression was tense.

I set down my bowl of peach cobbler and went over to him. "What's wrong? Is it something about Walt's murder?"

He shook his head. "No, that was Father Mark. You know the Aznar violin? Somebody stole it."

CHAPTER 5

"*T*HAT'S TERRIBLE!" DOVE AND I CRIED ALMOST SIMULTANE-
ously.

"When did it happen?" I asked.

Gabe looked around at us, his hands resting on his hips. "They just
discovered it missing about an hour ago. When it happened is another
question. Father Mark gave permission to one of the members of the
Mission Orchestra to play it in a special baroque concert next week.
When the violinist went to take it out of its glass case in the mission,
he discovered it was a replica. No one has any idea when it had been
replaced."

"Just how valuable is this violin?" Emory asked.

"It's priceless," I answered, setting down the knife I'd been using
to cut the cake. I'd done research on local crafts for a historical museum meeting a year or so back. "It's two hundred and three years
old and made by Rafael Aznar, a Salinan Indian. Well, part Indian.
His father was Spanish. There's no other record of a Native American–

built violin from the California Missions period. It's made with native California woods like bay laurel and valley oak. It's worth fifty or sixty thousand dollars here in the states, but in Europe it could be worth a million dollars. The California Missions period is hot for overseas collectors now."

"What kind of security was there for this violin?" Isaac asked.

"It was in a locked glass case," I said. "Other than that, it's right out there with the rest of the mission exhibits. It's a self-guided tour, but there's only one way in and one way out, right by the docent at the ticket booth."

Isaac's incredulous look made me feel a little defensive about the mission's casual security. "I know, I know, it seems incredible. But the missions have so little money for staff and security. They probably depend a little too much on people's integrity. They had to balance security with the desire to allow the public access to the missions and their art." It had become a problem in the last few years, thefts from the missions, but until now it had only been a basket here, a small icon there. The blatant theft of the Aznar violin changed everything.

Isaac, born and raised in downtown Chicago, just shook his head in wonder.

"Seems to me," Emory said, "the mission was taking a big chance with the amount of tourists who go through every day. You even have an alarm system at the folk art museum."

"We were required to get one," I said. "Otherwise the state museum and other museums wouldn't loan us their exhibits. Don't forget, Constance Sinclair paid for it. We couldn't have afforded it on our small operating budget."

"The family who donated the violin to the mission is extremely upset," Gabe said.

"I sure don't envy Father Mark having to calm them down," I said, looking at Gabe, then at the desserts. "Do we need to leave?" We could take the cake and peach cobbler with us, though we'd miss out on the ice cream.

"No need," Gabe said, picking up his piece of cake and heading for the living room sofa. "My detectives are on it and will keep me informed."

We were home by eight o'clock. After saying a quick good night, we headed for bed. It had been a long day for Gabe, with the murder of Walt Adams. With the theft of the Aznar violin, it also looked like it was going to be a stressful week.

"What is Luis going to do tomorrow?" I asked Gabe after we climbed into bed. "It seems rude to leave him alone."

"He'll be fine," Gabe said, settling the comforter around us. "I showed him around town, and he has a car. He says he needs to rest, think about some things, that we don't have to worry about entertaining him. I think you might be right about him having marriage problems."

"Did he say something to you?"

"No, just read between the lines."

"How long have they been married?"

"Two years. It's still a sore spot with my *tia* Maria. She really loved Sofia, Luis's first wife. Thought he was a fool to leave her. She'd just gotten used to his second wife, Carmen, when he left her. His latest wife, Paige, sounds like a spoiled brat. *Tia's* probably right, he should stick with his own." He punched his pillow, fluffing it up.

I felt a twinge of hurt. "You mean a Mexican girl?" Did his aunt feel that way about me? I didn't think so, but it made me wonder. Gabe was part Anglo; his own mother, a retired Kansas schoolteacher, was white as a slice of Wonder bread, but because of Gabe's skin color, the Anglo part of his heritage often seemed to take second place. I made my voice light. "Do you think your aunt thinks I'm a spoiled *gringa*?"

He reached over and stroked my cheek with the back of his hand. "She adores you, *querida*. I'm sure it's not Paige's skin color that bothers *Tia* Maria. From what I gather, Paige is fifteen years younger than Luis and comes from a wealthy Newport Beach family. My guess is she's a rich white girl who wanted a little ethnic diversion and now is tired of him and probably, after a few visits with his family, a little ashamed."

"That's sad," I said, looking up at the shifting shadows on our bedroom ceiling. Outside, the wind whispered through the limbs of the oak tree guarding our window.

"It's life," he said, his voice dropping into a sleepy murmur. "He's a big boy. He could cut his losses. Find someone who'll accept him for who he is."

"I suppose," I replied, wondering how we could help him through this rough time. Having endured some painful moments in my own marriage with Gabe, I now had more understanding for people who were in the midst of a marriage crisis. It was a type of pain that ripped at the fragile strings of your heart in a special way that was hard to explain to someone who'd never experienced it.

"Don't worry, *querida*," Gabe said, his hand reaching under the covers to stroke my thigh. "Luis has always landed on his feet. He probably just needs some time and space to figure things out."

THE NEXT MORNING, I WAS DRESSED AND HEADING OUT OF THE house at seven A.M. before Gabe and Luis had finished their first cup of coffee. Again I marveled at Gabe's complete relaxation around Luis. Gabe normally was slightly uncomfortable when we had visitors, always in that agitated, can't-wait-for-them-to-leave state. He was truly enjoying his cousin's presence.

"What's the rush?" Luis asked me, his black hair falling across his forehead in the same boyish way Gabe's did when it wasn't combed.

Except for the color of their eyes and the slightly finer chisel of Gabe's nose and mouth, they looked like brothers sitting at the breakfast table, both wearing almost identical navy sweatpants and white T-shirts. Had they ever been mistaken for twins?

"Ton of stuff to do today at the museum," I said. "We have a new exhibit arriving at ten A.M. from a sister museum in Dayton, Ohio. Plus we're still trying to get the shelves stocked on our new craft store downtown."

"What is the exhibit this time?" Gabe asked, standing up and going over to the coffeepot to refill his cup. "I know you told me . . ."

"It's antique toys and games. Some of them are pretty valuable, though nothing like the Aznar violin. Still, I want to be there and check in every piece myself. Opening night for the exhibit is a week from Friday." I looked over at Luis, who was feeding Scout a bite of scrambled eggs. "Hope you can stay long enough to come to it."

"You never know," he said, giving me a crooked smile.

I went over to Gabe, stood up on tip-toe, and kissed his cheek. "Let me know if you find out anything new about Walt, okay?"

"Sure," Gabe said, digging through the newspaper on the counter for the sports pages.

I turned away, so he wouldn't see the guilty look on my face. I had to call Mac soon and see if he'd talked to Angelina's aunt.

"Scout, let's go," I said, walking toward the front door.

At the museum, D-Daddy Boudreaux, my capable and dependable assistant, was already in the upstairs gallery doing something with some kind of electric tool.

"It's just me, D-Daddy," I yelled as I climbed the stairs.

He was bent over working on a display case, adding a lock. He turned off the electric screwdriver when I entered the gallery.

"You heard about the Aznar violin," I said, looking at the empty packages of case locks.

"Yes, ma'am, on the news this morning. I bought these awhile back and never got a chance to put them on. Figured we better not take any chances." He straightened up and stretched a little, his hands adjusting the tool belt at his waist. With his thick head of white hair and lean body, D-Daddy was still a good-looking man even in his mid-to-late seventies. He was also the major reason I always had plenty of enthusiastic female volunteer docents from the senior center.

I sighed and said, "You are a true gift from heaven, D-Daddy. I was worrying about what we were going to do about this exhibit. Some of the toys are pretty small and easy to pocket."

"Don't worry, *ange*. To get to these toys, they'll have to pick double locks, them." He swept his hand across the room.

"How early did you get here?" I asked.

"Six A.M. I'm up that time anyway."

I went over and hugged him. "You're the best. I owe you one home-cooked dinner."

"Make it your special fried chicken, and you have a deal."

"You got it." I checked my watch. "The shipment is supposed to come before eleven A.M. I'll be in my office trying to catch up on paperwork."

"Almost done here," he said, gesturing at the dozen or so display cases built by him specifically for this exhibit. "Then I'll be downstairs working on patching the museum." The museum was a Spanish hacienda over two hundred years old and made of adobe. It was a continuous task to keep the crumbly walls patched. And lately, to our dismay, free from graffiti.

The museum's downstairs gallery had a needlepoint and stitchery exhibit showing for the next month, with a fall and Thanksgiving theme. It would run through the four-day holiday and then we'd be putting up an exhibit of locally crafted menorahs and nativity scenes.

The walkway to my office in the old stables in back, which also housed the artists' workrooms, dripped sweet-smelling honeysuckle dew on me and Scout. In my office, I turned on the space heater to take the chill off the small room. Scout immediately flopped down in front of the glowing elements.

"Don't hog all the heat, Mr. Piggy," I scolded him good-naturedly. He just beat his tail on the thin, commercial carpet a few times and didn't move an inch. I pulled out my file of grant applications, a never-ending job, and sat back in my chair to read through them, making notes for my eventual letters begging for money.

Before I knew it, two hours had passed. Looking at the wooden cowboy-hat clock made for me by one of the co-op's woodworkers, I saw it was almost ten o'clock. I stood up and stretched. I knew Sylvia, our head docent this year, had opened the museum at nine-thirty sharp. With Sylvia in charge, the museum's hours of operation were as organized and predictable as meal times at a Girl Scout camp. She knew every docent's tour schedule by heart and always made certain the gift shop in the lobby was manned. In fact, she was so organized, the other docents, with real respect and humor, had taken to calling her Sarge.

I walked down the hall past the woodworkers' rooms where about a half-dozen men were busy with saws, chisels, and sanders. I waved and continued through the large room lined with locked cabinets, also made by D-Daddy, where the quilters often set up their quilt frames. It was empty today except for one quilter sorting through a stash of fabric in one of the cabinets.

"There are Fabrics Anonymous brochures in my office," I called to the quilter. Someone, as a joke, had printed up some brochures mimicking Alcoholics Anonymous' twelve-step program, but made it pertain to quilters' addiction to fabric.

"Oh, I'm a lost cause," she called back cheerfully. "But at least it's not fattening."

"Thank goodness," I agreed. "Or we'd all be in trouble."

I was coming through the museum's back door when I ran into Sylvia.

"I was just coming to get you," she said, patting her thick, silvery hair. "The toy shipment's here."

"Good timing," I said. "My eyes were starting to cross from staring at those grant applications."

Inside the museum's lobby, a UPS guy was unloading his first dolly of boxes. "Got six more boxes," he said. "These need a signature."

"That's why I'm here," I said, taking his electronic clipboard that always reminds me of *Star Trek*.

Once I checked to make sure everything had arrived and the boxes were intact, I signed his clipboard and stood among the boxes, trying to decide where to start. Knowing the tight schedules of most UPS drivers, I hadn't asked him to carry them upstairs and was now beginning to regret my altruistic decision.

"Guess I'd better fetch our dolly," I said to Sylvia, my back to the museum's double doors. "Those boxes aren't going to float upstairs."

"You're not moving those upstairs yourself!" Sylvia exclaimed. "You'll hurt your back. We should go get some of the woodworkers."

"I'm pretty strong." I held up my arm like I was Popeye. "Feel that muscle. I don't want to disturb them. They have their own work."

Her face broke into a wide smile.

Behind me a familiar male voice said, "Can I feel your muscle?"

"Detective Hudson," Sylvia said, her tone of her voice going up one octave. "How nice to see you again."

I turned around to face Hud, who had a manure-eating grin spread across his face. He was dressed in a white shirt, tie, tweed western-style sport jacket, and blue jeans. A black felt Stetson and deep-blue lizard cowboy boots completed his outfit.

"No," I said. "But I will let you use your muscles to help me move these boxes to the upstairs gallery."

"*Let* me help you?" he said.

"You're a contributor to this museum, right? Do something a little more strenuous besides write a check, city boy."

"She's mean as a baby diamondback," he complained to Sylvia, giving her a broad wink. He picked up one of the smaller boxes. "Where do they go?"

"Upstairs gallery," I said. "I'll get a dolly from D-Daddy."

"Thanks," I said to him after all the boxes were moved upstairs. I pulled out the sheet that came with the boxes. The first box was supposed to contain penny banks.

Hud rubbed the foot of one of his boots against the back of his calf. "Aren't you curious about why I dropped by?"

"Not really." I picked up the first object and carefully pulled off the bubble wrap. Monkey with tambourine wearing red jacket. I checked it off my list.

"I was in the area running down a lead and wondered what was happening with the Adams homicide. Saw your Barney-colored truck in the parking lot so I thought I'd stop in and ask."

I took out a second bubble-wrapped toy. An Uncle Sam. I checked my list. "Don't you have an inside source in the city police department?"

"Sure I do. You."

I looked up at him. He leaned against one of the cabinets with the double locks, his face genial and almost sincere. "That's your bad luck then because I probably know less than you."

"And if you did know more, you probably wouldn't tell me."

"Would you if you were in my position?" I picked up another metal toy. This one looked like a Ferris wheel. I scanned my sheet looking for a correlating name and description.

"No, but you're a nicer person than me."

"Trust me, I'm not."

His expression changed quickly from genial to concerned. "Seriously, I'm not sure Maisie should participate in the play."

I set the wrapped Ferris wheel down on a glass counter. "Oh, Hud, she plays Faithful. That's a starring role. It would break her heart.

And we need her." My mind instantly started running through the list of children, considering who might take over her part if Hud made her quit.

"I know, I know. I hate disappointing her, but of more concern to me is her safety. Until I know more details about this homicide . . ." He shrugged, his eyes taking on that cynical, trust-no-one look I knew so well from my own husband.

"Look," I said, thinking fast on my feet, wanting Maisie to stay in the play, for both her sake and ours. "I'll tell you as much as I can when I know something, but in the mean time—"

"In other words, nothing," he interrupted.

"Would you hush? I have a solution if you'd listen. We need volunteers at the rehearsals, and you want your daughter to be safe and not be disappointed. You could be a parent volunteer."

"Oh, no," he said, holding up his hands. "I'm not—"

"Concerned about your daughter's safety or happiness?" I finished.

He frowned at me. "Ms. Harper, you are a dirty fighter."

I looked back down at my list. "All the parents would probably feel safer if we said we had our own personal police protection, a *real live* sheriff's detective." I kept my tone casual. But I knew it wasn't just the parents I was thinking about. Deep inside, I was nervous about going back there with just me, Dove, and maybe Beth and her boyfriend, Jason, for protection. Because of his busy schedule, Mac wasn't always on the church property.

Hud's blondish-brown eyebrows moved together, his brown eyes narrowing slightly. "Are you scared, Benni?"

I shook my head too quickly, not fooling him for a minute.

He looked at me for a long moment. "You know, I would feel better if I was there. What time is the next rehearsal?"

"Today at three-thirty," I said. "I sent home a schedule with Maisie. You could probably check with her mom."

"I will," he said. "We'll be there. Laura Lee will be much relieved."

"Laura Lee? That's your wife's name?"

"Ex-wife. Maisie's mother."

"Oh." This was the first time I'd heard her name. I couldn't help wondering what she was like. Though I knew Hud had been married, he seemed so settled into the single life that I couldn't imagine him in a domestic relationship, even though he appeared to be an involved and caring father.

"I take it we won't be rehearsing in the chapel," he said.

"Probably not. Go around back to the recreation hall. That's where we'll work until Gabe allows us to use the sanctuary again."

"Sounds reasonable. Let's hope the detectives can solve this quickly, though I realize they arc at a huge disadvantage."

I gave him a puzzled look. "Why?"

He grinned at me and touched two fingers to his hat brim. "Why, they ain't sheriff, of course. Poor jerks."

"Get lost, Inspector Clouseau." I said, waving my hand at him and turning back to the toys.

I listened to him clomp down the stairs, then pause a few minutes at the gift counter to do what he excelled at, flirting with whatever female was present. The sound of women's laugher caused me to shake my head at his predictability.

Having him help at the play rehearsals wouldn't make my jealous husband happy, but it would relieve a lot of concerned parents' minds. I looked at my watch. It was almost noon, and I'd promised the co-op members setting up the new gift shop downtown that I'd stop by about one P.M. to help them unpack and start organizing the new store. It was opening during this week's Farmers' Market, when Lopez Street was blocked off for the weekly food, craft, and community festival that had become famous throughout California.

I still hadn't called Mac to find out if he'd talked to Angelina. I wanted to tell Gabe tonight if Angelina was the girl I'd seen at the church. The church's answering machine told me to leave a message. I'd forgotten that Monday was Mac's day off.

"Hi, Mac," I said. "Benni here. I'll try you at home."

I hung up and tried his home number and talked to another answering machine. "Hi, Mac. It's Benni. I'm trying to find you. Why don't you get a cell phone? I want to know what you found out. Please call me." I rattled off my cell phone number.

I had forty-five minutes before I was due at the new gift shop, which we'd named Local Hands—A Folk Art Store. I swung by Emory's chicken restaurant, Boone's Good Eatin' Chicken, for a quick bite. It was only three blocks from the museum's new store and two blocks from Blind Harry's. The restaurant was packed, a sight that made me happy because Emory's dad, Boone, had been concerned that smoked chicken might not go over as well in California as it did in Arkansas.

Luck was with me because I spotted Mac in a back booth eating the "Big Cluck Special"—half a smoked chicken, coleslaw, corn bread, brown-sugar baked beans, and a slice of sweet potato pie. After ordering a smoked chicken sandwich and piece of sweet potato pie to go, I inched my way through the lunch crowd to his table.

"Hey, Brother Mac," I said, sliding across from him in the green leatherette booth. "I've left messages all over town for you. You are in need of a cell phone, my friend."

He lifted his eyebrows and took a huge bite of chicken breast. Its smoky aroma wafted across the table making my stomach rumble again. He chewed thoughtfully, swallowed, then said, "I'm trying to be the last holdout. I check my messages every two hours. What's on your mind?"

"You know what. Did you talk to Angelina and her aunt?"

He nodded, took another bite.

"So?"

He took a sip of iced tea before answering. "I don't think it was her." His pewter-gray eyes were flat as tinfoil. But the almost indiscernible twitch in his jaw right about his beard line was his giveaway.

I rapped the wooden table top in front of his plate. "Hello? MacKenzie Reid? It's me, your old friend, Benni Harper. The person who's known you since before you could shave. Quit lying to me."

"I'm not lying. She said she didn't see anything, that she wasn't there."

"Okay, was *she* lying?"

He stared, unblinking, into my eyes. "I believe her."

I inhaled, then let my breath out slowly, feeling both frustrated and, if truth be told, relieved. Not having to face Gabe with keeping an important witness from him was certainly what I wanted. Still, worrier that I was, I was certain that if Angelina had witnessed the crime, she was psychologically, and possibly physically, at risk.

"Mac," I started, not quite knowing what I was going to argue, but realizing that it couldn't be left at this.

"Don't," he said, holding up his hand. "Benni, it's better if we don't speak of this again. The deeper you become involved, the more conflicted you'll be. Please, just trust me that I'm doing the right thing."

"How do you know you are?" I asked. "If she did see something, and she's the only one who can lead the police to whoever killed Walt Adams, how can we justify not finding out what she knows? Not to mention how this experience will haunt her for the rest of her life. What if she accidently says something and the killer hears it? She could be in real danger. What about that?"

He made two fists, bowed his head and rested his forehead on them. I wasn't sure if he was praying or just thinking, so I kept quiet. In the background, I heard my name being called to pick up my order.

Mac slowly lifted his head. "She really did tell me she wasn't there. Do I believe her? To be honest, I don't know. People like her aunt Juana become adept at being evasive. Even if she had seen something,

I'm not sure it would help the police find Walt's killer. As for protection, you know as well as I do how the police work. They can protect her for a few days, but what if the case isn't solved immediately? Are they going to follow her around for the next month, the next year, for the rest of her life? Not to mention, they'll start probing into her background." His voice went low. "Benni, as I told you earlier, they aren't here legally. Juana has no close family in Mexico to watch out for her and Angelina. There is nothing for them there. Do you want them sent back to Mexico where they would likely have to live on the streets?"

"You know I don't," I whispered.

"Then treat her like any other little girl and let me take responsibility for this situation." His eyes grew shiny and hard, revealing the steely nerve that probably impressed the pro football scouts back in his college days. No one would get through this man if he decided to block them.

"Okay," I said reluctantly, thinking, easy for you to say, buddy boy, you don't sleep with the chief of police. Sooner or later, I'd have to tell Gabe about this, though I didn't have a clue how or when. "We don't have to worry about security at the rehearsals," I said, wanting to switch the subject. "Hud said he'd be a permanent volunteer. He's doing it to protect his daughter, but the rest of us will benefit."

Mac nodded. "That's great. He's a good man."

"Yeah, he is. He seems to like you."

Mac held out his hands, his eyes soft and teasing now. "What's not to like?"

"Please," I said with a groan as I slid out of the booth. "You've been hanging around Gabe too long. You're supposed to rub off on him, not the other way around."

"There's a lot about your husband we'd all do well to emulate," he said, licking barbecue sauce off his thumb.

I reached over and patted the top of his hand. "Do not tell him that, please. His ego is big enough, and I'm the one who has to live with it. We'll be up at the church for a rehearsal today at three-thirty. We'll use the recreation hall."

"No problem. I'll be there for about an hour, then I have a meeting with Father Mark." He looked back down at his food.

"*Hasta luego*, Pastor," I said.

"*Vaya con Dios, mi hermana*," he replied.

I ate my sandwich while walking the three blocks to Local Hands, the folk art museum's new store, finishing the last bite as I stepped over the threshold. I gave my sweet potato pie to a deserving artist who'd been working at the store since seven A.M., then asked where I could help.

"We need those chess sets unpacked and arranged," Sylvia said.

I spent the next hour setting up three hand-carved wooden chess sets in the shapes of cowboys and Indians, as well as two ceramic ones that had pieces made up of various dog breeds. The incredible detail on the chess sets warranted the two-hundred-dollar price tags. I worked slower than I probably should have because I couldn't help stopping to admire the facial details in the various figures—Buffalo Bill's tiny beard, Chief Crazy Horse's feathered war bonnet, the pawns carved as little pugs, while the queen was a poodle and the king a Great Pyrenees. The smiling corgis as rooks was an especially whimsical touch.

At two P.M. I offered to make a run down to Blind Harry's for cookies, muffins, and coffee. After taking everyone's orders, I left Scout at the store and started down the street, perusing the extensive list, trying to decide if I'd be able to carry all of it back. I'd probably have to rope one of Elvia's clerks into helping me.

Blind Harry's bookstore was looking spiffier than ever now that Elvia owned it. My cousin Emory's wedding present of this store to her was one of the most loving gifts I'd seen. She'd recently redecorated the children's section, enlarging both the inventory and story-time area. Above the small stage was a mural of Señor Azure, the fly-ing blue turtle in a story told to Gabe by his father. I'd told the story to Elvia once and she liked it so much, she decided to make Señor Azure the official mascot of the children's section.

I climbed the stairs to her office to say hello. She was sitting behind her desk flipping through a book catalog.

"Hola, mi amiga," I said, flopping down in the padded visitor's chair in front of her country French-style desk.

"Hi," she said, glancing up. "What're you doing here?"

"That's a nice way to greet your best friend. Just stopping by to get some coffee and muffins for the crew down at the new museum store."

"How's that going?" she asked, setting aside the catalog.

I shrugged. "Everything looks great. Whether people will buy? That remains to be seen. So, what did you think of Gabe's cousin?"

Her eyes dropped back down to the catalog. "He seemed nice enough."

Her response surprised me. " 'Nice enough'? That's very noncom-mittal."

It was her turn to shrug. "I don't know. He seemed . . . well, you said he was a salesman, right?"

I nodded.

"I'm guessing he's very good at his job."

I didn't answer. It was obvious she didn't like him, which I found a bit odd. Luis was so personable, actually a more easygoing version of Gabe, whom Elvia really liked.

She waved her hand in the air, dismissing her own remark. "Don't mind me. I'm just cranky. How are things going with the play?"

"So far, so good. Hud is one of our parent helpers."

She raised one perfectly-shaped eyebrow. "How did that happen?"

"His daughter, Maisie, is in the play. It will make the parents ex-tremely happy that he's there protecting the kids."

"My question is who is protecting *you* from him?"

I grinned at her. "Dove Ramsey, of course."

"To be safe, I think she should bring her man-hating goose, Socrates."

"The only problem is Socrates doesn't like little boys either, and I want to retain that half of my cast."

"Then keep your hatpin sharp and ready, as Dove would say."

We both laughed. When Elvia and I turned sixteen, within a few months of each other, Dove had gifted us both with one of her grandmother's antique hat pins with the advice to use it whenever a boy we dated tried to get fresh with us.

I stood up and stretched. "Guess I'd better get that coffee for my hardworking artists. Come and see the store when you can."

"Put it on the store's tab," she said. "My contribution to the arts. I'll come to the grand opening."

On the way downstairs to the coffeehouse, I ran into Luis.

"Hey, cousin!" I said.

"Hey, back, *prima*. What're you doing?"

"I'm making a coffee run for the people setting up our new folk art museum gift shop up the street. Then I'm heading out to the church for another rehearsal." I cocked my head. "If you're not busy, we can always use help with the kids."

He gave an engaging smile while holding up his hands in protest. "I'm not that great with little kids. But, do you need any help carrying the coffee back to your colleagues?"

"I'll take any help I can get," I said, opening the door. "Thanks."

"So," he said, as we waited for my complicated order of nonfat lattes, double-mocha espressos, and low-foam vanilla cappucinos. "Have you heard anything from Gabe about that guy's murder?"

I shook my head. "But I haven't talked with him since this morning. He's so busy that I try not to bug him during the day."

He looked down and studied his hands. One of his thumbs was black from an old bruise. "You're a thoughtful wife."

I gave a light laugh. "He might disagree with you on that sometimes."

We talked a little longer until Luis excused himself to use the men's room. I was perusing a discarded *Reader's Digest* when I heard a voice call my name loud enough to make the lone patron in the book-lined coffeehouse look up from his own reading.

"Benni Harper, I've been looking for you all day. We have to talk."

The man's harsh tone caused Jose, the manager of the coffeehouse, to stop in the middle of making a mocha cappucino and stare at the man in the gray suit. It was Jonathan Hammer, Travis's father. He strode toward me, his face flushed with anger.

I stood up, but didn't walk toward Jonathan, forcing him to come to me. "Hello, Jonathan. What can I do—"

He shook the newspaper in his hand. "This just isn't acceptable."

Startled, I said. "Excuse me?"

"Your husband is not doing his job properly."

I let out a sigh. Okay, I understood now. Yet another citizen aggravated with how Gabe did his job. "Look," I started.

His face froze for a moment, staring at something behind me.

I turned and saw Luis coming toward us, his face still and expressionless, an eerie doppelganger of Gabe on the defensive.

"What's going on?" Luis said, coming up to stand beside me.

I have to admit, I felt more than a little relief. Sometimes you just had to appreciate good, old-fashioned, Latin machismo. I laid a hand on Luis's forearm, letting him know I had things under control.

"I'm sorry you're upset, Jonathan, but I'm sure you can appreciate that I have no control over any decisions Gabe makes."

Being the wife of the police chief had changed my life many ways here in the town where I'd grown up. The hardest adjustment for me was how much we were in the public eye. Often people assumed that the best way to Gabe was through me. At the folk art museum fundraisers, many of our politically liberal donors didn't always approve of Gabe's more conservative way of running the police department and tried to communicate their displeasure to him through me.

"He'd better get more than one lousy detective on my case." Jonathan's smooth, clean-shaven face flushed like he'd been drinking.

"What case is that?" I asked, though I knew it was a mistake to engage him. Having Luis next to me increased my bravado.

He thrust today's edition of the *San Celina Tribune* under my nose. Walt Adams's homicide made the bold, black headline.

For a moment I was confused. Was Jonathan Hammer involved with Walt Adams? "I don't understand. Are you related to Mr. Adams?"

"Not *that*. This." He jabbed at the story underneath the headline. "Priceless Violin Stolen From Mission."

"Oh," I said. "How . . ."

"My father was an important collector of California Mission antiques. He bought that violin years ago from the family of the man who originally made it. When my father died last year, he willed it to the mission, mistakenly thinking they had some kind of decent security there."

"I'm sure Gabe's detectives are doing their best to recover the violin," I said, trying to keep my own voice calm and neutral. Gabe owed me an extra-long foot rub for taking this one.

"Detective. Singular, as in one. He only has one detective working on this. Do you know this violin could be worth a million dollars? My father should have donated it to a worthy museum, one that cared about its value."

"I heard it was," I said, thinking, there's the problem. Jonathan just found out it was worth that much money and is angry at his dad for not leaving it to him. "I'm sure the department is doing their best to recover it."

"Are you deaf? Did you hear what I just said? One detective is on the case."

"I really think you should call my husband—"

"I've tried! He won't take my calls. That's why I tracked you down. You tell him—" His pointing finger almost made contact with my shoulder.

Luis pushed in front of me. "Benni is not responsible for what her husband does or doesn't do. Why don't you take your squabble with the way Gabe does his job up with him?"

"I certainly would if he'd see me! Who are you anyway? Get out of my way." He started to push around Luis.

Luis grasped his upper arm and gently pushed him toward to stairs. "You're out of here."

Jonathan jerked his arm away. "That could be classified as battery! I have witnesses." He glanced over at the single, book-reading patron, a retired firefighter who often played chess with Gabe.

"I'm legally blind," the man said, winked at me, then looked back down at his book.

When Mr. Hammer looked at Jose, he just shrugged.

"*No habla Ingles*," Jose said, almost causing me to laugh out loud. Jose was born and raised in San Celina and spoke English better than I did.

Jonathan scowled at me. "I have important friends in this town who can make your husband's life miserable." He whipped around and stormed back up the stairs.

"What an ass," Luis said, shaking his head.

I laughed nervously. "Thanks for defending my honor, Luis. There's a taste of what it means to be married to Gabriel Ortiz, chief of police."

"Tell my cousin you deserve combat pay."

I walked over to the counter and picked up the drinks and bags of muffins that Jose had packed.

"You okay, Benni?" Jose asked.

"Yes, thanks. Elvia said to put this on her tab." Over my shoulder I said to Luis, "We'll certainly have a story to tell Gabe tonight."

Luis picked up two cardboard coffee carriers. "Does that happen to you very often?"

"Enough that I'm used to it. I've learned not to try and explain Gabe and his actions to people. I just keep repeating that they need to talk to him."

Outside, the sun had dipped behind a billow of gray-white clouds, darkening the street for a moment. The air seemed to grow ten degrees cooler, seeping through my flannel shirt. It felt like winter had arrived overnight, though December twenty-first was over a month away.

"Gabe's life is different than what I expected," Luis said.

I glanced over. His eyes stared straight ahead, concentrating on dodging the people on Lopez Street's crowded sidewalk. "In what way?"

"He's, I don't know, so settled. Has a place here, a purpose. He seems . . ." He looked over at me now, his brown eyes were warm with tiny lines radiating from them. Unlike Gabe, he didn't have a five o'clock shadow. Was that part of Gabe's maternal genetics, something from his grandfather Smith?

"He seems content," Luis said. "Despite the stress of his job and all, I'd say my cousin is content."

Though the words he said pleased me, I couldn't help hearing his sad tone. "Are you doing okay, Luis? I mean, I know it's none of my business, but if there is anything I can do to help . . ."

I could feel my cheeks flush, feeling awkward for asking such a personal question to someone I didn't know that well. But he was important to Gabe. That made him important to me. Besides, without hesitation Luis had stepped up and defended me. It had touched me and made me feel proprietary about his happiness.

He looked ahead again, not breaking his stride, a stride he'd thoughtfully matched to my shorter one. "I haven't told Gabe this yet. I . . . lost my job three months ago and . . . well . . . Paige and I . . ." He stopped for a moment, his coppery face twisted with pain. "She left me, took Cassie, and moved back in with her parents. She's fighting for sole custody with limited visitation."

"Luis, I'm so sorry. Is there anything Gabe and I can do to help?"

He shook his head. "Nothing you aren't already doing. I appreciate your hospitality and just being with Gabe helps. The hardest part is only getting to see Cassie once a month. And I have to fight for that."

We reached the door of Local Hands, and two of the artists burst out, exclaiming gratitude for the coffee and muffins. Their presence cut our conversation short before I could ask why he was only seeing his daughter once a month. It seemed an awfully stingy custody arrangement.

"I'll see you tonight," Luis said, handing the coffee carriers to one of the artists.

"White enchiladas on the menu," I said. "Your mama's recipe."

He smiled at me, though it didn't reach past his mouth. "You must have really impressed my mother. She doesn't give that recipe out to many people."

"Just did what I was taught. I helped her in the kitchen before dinner, ate a lot, asked for seconds, and washed the dishes afterward."

He stuck his hands deep into the pockets of his jeans. "I only took Paige home twice, and she stayed in the living room the whole time with the men. At dinner she barely ate anything. My mother took it personal." He shook his head. "Fat grams terrify Paige. And my family." He shrugged, letting the situation speak for itself. "I'll see you tonight." Then he turned and headed back up the street back toward Blind Harry's.

CHAPTER 6

I WATCHED LUIS WALK DOWN THE STREET AND WONDERED IF I should tell Gabe about his cousin's marriage and work problems. Luis didn't ask me not tell, just said that he hadn't done so yet. I decided I wouldn't go to sleep tonight without telling Gabe about it. Keeping one important piece of information away from my husband was enough.

At three o'clock Scout and I left the folk art store and headed for the church, making it there in time to see a crowd of parents converge on Dove when she stepped out of her truck. With Scout loping along beside me, I rushed over to where a half-dozen people surrounded her, all speaking at once. Their questions were, of course, about their children's safety. Dove was trying to answer three people at once, looking more than a little annoyed and ready to snap someone's head off.

"It's taken care of," I said, pushing my way into the crowd to stand next to Dove. "We have a volunteer who is a county sheriff who has promised to come to every rehearsal."

"So where is he?" one of the mothers demanded. "I'm not leaving my daughter here until I know she's safe. You would think that at a church she'd be safe. It's just a travesty that I can't even leave her for two hours at a *church* and not have to worry about her safety. Who is this sheriff person who is going to protect our children? And where is he? I'm not leaving my daughter until we see this sheriff person." She clutched the hand of a cute brown-haired girl who played the character of Talkative in the play. Maybe we should have offered the part to her mother.

"He's Maisie Hudson's father," I said, glancing over at Dove to let her know I wasn't making this up. "I talked to him this morning." His Dodge Ram pickup pulled into the parking lot at that moment. "And here he is. But if any of you parents want to stay, we'd love to have you. We always need help with the kids learning their lines and especially during snack time—" Before I could finish, I could already see heads shaking, parents finding excuses why they couldn't stay. Good, free day care was always hard to find.

"There *is* a policeman here," they murmured among themselves, not wanting to give up whatever plans they had made for the next two hours. We weren't naive about why some people allowed their children to be part of the First Baptist children's theater.

"What's going on?" Hud asked, walking up with Maisie.

"These parents are concerned about their children's safety," I said. "But I've assured them you will be here the whole two hours."

Hud smiled at the muttering parents. "Don't worry. I'll make sure your children are well protected." With his words, the parents didn't take long to kiss their children good-bye and dash back to their cars.

"God bless them," Dove grumbled.

I grinned at her. "I'm kinda questioning the sincerity of that blessing, Gramma."

"The kids are great, but before this is over, the parents will drive me completely batty."

I glanced over at the screaming, laughing children playing on the brownish-green lawn right by the sanctuary's front doors, still criss-crossed with crime scene tape. A quick head count showed twenty-five today. Angelina's black braids darted among them. Who dropped her off this time? Who would pick her up? Mac's Explorer wasn't in the parking lot yet, though he said he'd be here.

"How did *he* get involved with this?" she asked me, hitching her thumb over at Hud, talking about him as if he wasn't there. She knew about my background with him and was naturally suspicious.

"Like I said, he's Maisie's daddy, and he agreed to help out."

She narrowed one eye at him. Not much wool was ever pulled over Dove's eyes. "Mr. Hudson, are you here just to watch out for the kids and help us out? That's it? No other shenanigans?"

"Yes, ma'am," he said, letting loose of his daughter's hand so she could run over to play with the other kids. "I'm here to help however you need it."

She looked over at me. "Gabe know about this?"

Only one time did Dove and I discuss Hud's attraction to me, and, to be honest, mine to him. It was right after she'd noticed it last March at the Broken Dishes guest ranch.

"He will tonight," I said, defensively. "It was nice of Hud to offer his help. You know we need it, and the added bonus of him being a police officer doesn't hurt. You saw how it appeased the parents. I'm sure Gabe will be glad there is someone here watching out for us."

She looked directly into my eyes, communicating what she was thinking without a spoken word. You be careful with this one. There's some kind of danger with this boy.

I narrowed my eyes, mentally sending back, I know what I'm doing.

I've heard that one before, missy, she silently replied.

"It'll be fine," I said out loud.

"Okay, then," she said, then faced Hud, whose cocky smirk wasn't advancing his case. "We'll need you to stay the whole time. Please keep in mind this is the Lord's house, and I expect you to act accordingly."

He took off his hat and said, "Yes, ma'am. I've already checked with my captain, and he's fine with me working this into my schedule. I'm working cold cases these days so none of them are a rush. I'll do my best to keep my thoughts pure under what can only be classified as a difficult situation."

Dove didn't answer him, clearly not amused by his smart mouth. She looked at me and said, "Remember, honeybun, it's best not to skinny dip with snapping turtles." She turned her back on both of us and marched toward the church.

He looked at me with raised eyebrows. "What does she mean by that?"

"Who knows? But you'd better behave because she's raised four boys and has nine grandsons. She knows how to torture men in ways you can't even imagine."

We started rounding up the children and herding them toward the recreation hall, our new practice area. I introduced Hud to the kids, told them that he was Maisie's dad, a sheriff's deputy, and was going to be one of our permanent helpers. "If you need anything or something bothers you, don't be afraid to tell Mr. Hudson, Dove, or me."

"Does he have a badge and a gun?" one of the boys called out.

Hud grinned, took out his badge and showed it to the kids. Though it was in his holster, he refused to show them his gun. "Y'all see enough guns on television," he said, putting his badge back in his pocket.

The boys let out a small groan of disappointment.

"Let's get started," I said, looking over at Dove.

"I'm going to call about the costumes while you warm them up," she said. "I'll be in the church office."

First I passed out a prize ticket to everyone, to encourage them to behave well. It was a challenge to get twenty-five kids quiet at the same time, especially when you had a couple of boys who loved to make farting noises to tease the girls, who then felt compelled to scream. Another loud and melodious fart-noise reverberated from the back row.

"Michael, that's gross!" a girl screamed, then giggled, causing a wave of giggles to run through the kids. "Miss Benni, Michael tooted."

The boys snickered and shoved each other.

"Okay," I yelled. "Next person who toots gets to take a time out and memorize three Bible verses. 'Jesus wept' doesn't count. Plus no snack."

"Whoa," Hud said behind me. "Glad I didn't have chili for lunch."

I said without turning around, "Mr. Hudson, protect us quietly, please."

"Yes, Miss Benni," he replied. The kids giggled at what I assumed was him mocking me behind my back

I picked up a roll of blue tickets. "How many people went to Sunday School this week?"

A dozen or so hands went up.

"Okay, one ticket for that. Who brought their Bibles?"

Almost all their hands waved at me.

"Great, another ticket for that. Who has two eyes and a nose?"

The kids giggled and held up their hands.

"Good, *two* tickets for that. Now, remember," I said, passing out the tickets. "Every time you do what I ask the *first time*, you'll get a ticket, and the more tickets you get, the more and better prizes you get to buy at the Good Behavior Store."

I kept a special eye on Angelina, standing next to Maisie, whispering in her ear. When I finished passing out tickets, I called my dog.

"Scout, come." He obeyed immediately. "Scout, heel." He came to my left side. "Now, let's see if you can do better than my dog. We're going to practice sitting down and standing up together."

After a few barks and whines from the boys in the back row, I managed to get them fairly quiet. "Hands to your side," I called out. "Everyone down on the ground like little seeds. Little seeds can't talk or move." Following my lead, we all put our hands on our heads and stooped down, pretending to be seeds. It was silly, but it worked in getting them to pay attention. "Okay," I said, slowly standing up. "Seeds are growing, but not talking." By the time we stood up, I had their attention. I kept my eye on Angelina, who seemed as carefree and happy as any of the other kids. If she'd been traumatized by seeing Walter killed, she was doing a good job hiding it. We practiced sitting and standing until they'd managed to do it in unison at least every other time.

After a rousing rendition of "This Little Light of Mine, I'm Going to Let It Shine," a perennial favorite, we moved to one of Lily's original songs, "I Have Hands That Go Clap, Clap, Clap." We went through the four verses that included stomping feet, snapping fingers, and the last one, "I have lips that say I love you." With the last verse, we used a modified sign language to say I love you—thumb to our chest, hands crossed over our chests, then a forefinger pointing outward. By that time, Beth had arrived with Jason, and I told the kids we could take a ten minute break.

Dove returned a few minutes later. "Let's do a quick walk through the whole play. Now that Beth's here, we can work on the opening songs. We need to talk about sets. Lily said some artists at your co-op were making them?"

"Right," I said. "JoAnn Allison. She's the art teacher over at San Celina High. It's a class project. She's incredibly dependable, so I'm not worried."

"Give me her number and I'll call her," Dove said. "We got to get this show on the road."

While Dove went to call JoAnn, the kids converged around Jason and watched him take his guitar out of its case, touching its smooth wood, and asking questions about the tattoos decorating his wiry forearms. Maisie, who was beginning to feel comfortable among the children here, pushed her way to the front while Angelina held back. Scout mingled with the children, in dog heaven with all the attention he was receiving.

I walked over to Angelina, stooped down to her level, and looked into her black eyes. I was going to take a chance at something because it just wasn't in me to sit around and do nothing. "Hi, Angelina. *Coma esta?*"

"*Muy bien,*" she whispered, looking down at her feet. She was wearing little, red Mary Janes today with white, lacy socks that peeked out from her faded, but spotless, denim pants.

"We're so glad you could be with us today," I said, taking her small hand in mine. "Do you remember how we're alike?"

Her head lifted, and she smiled shyly. "Our names." She pointed a finger at me, then at herself. "You're Benita. Like me."

I smiled back. "That's right. We can be special friends because we have the same name. You know, friends can talk to each other and tell each other things they don't tell anyone else."

She watched me intently, as if she were reading my lips.

"If something is scaring you, you can tell me," I said, hoping I was doing the right thing. "I'll do everything I can to help you, okay?"

She nodded, her shiny eyes solemn now, her thumb had slowly worked its way to her mouth. I waited a few moments, then squeezed her hand. "Okay, go on over and say hi to Beth. Maybe she'll let you play the piano."

I felt a little disappointed. What did I expect, for her to suddenly blurt out that she'd seen everything, knew who killed Walt Adams, and wanted to tell me so that person could be brought to justice? She was only six. If she saw anything, she was probably trying desperately to forget it. I shook my head, annoyed with myself. I should just heed Mac's words to stay out of it.

I followed her back over to the piano where Beth was showing some girls how to play "Heart and Soul," and all the boys were crowded around Hud who'd been coerced by his daughter into rolling up his sleeve and showing his own tattoo. It was on his upper left arm and showed the outline of Texas tinted the colors of the Texas state flag with a yellow rose laying across the top of the state and a Texas Ranger star marking Houston's location.

"Very pretty," I commented.

"Pretty!" one of the boys exclaimed. "Tattoos aren't supposed to be pretty! They're supposed to be wicked."

"Yeah," Hud said. "My tattoo isn't pretty, it's wicked."

"Beth, Jason, let's get the kids started on musical chairs while Mr. Hudson and I prepare their snack."

I pulled on Hud's upper arm. "Enough with the body art show."

"Yes, ma'am," he said, rolling his eyes at the snickering boys.

Inside the kitchen I said, "You realize everything you say and do is reported in detail at home." I started counting juice boxes.

He leaned against the yellow formica counter. "What was I doing that was so wrong?"

I sighed, lost count and started again. When I was through, I said, "Nothing, Hud. It's just that I want them to remember something about today other than the tattoos that decorate you and Jason."

"Have a little faith," he said, laughing. "I'm sure a few things you said stuck."

"Go count the Rice Krispies bars," I said, pointing to the food cupboard. Really, his and Jason's tattoos didn't matter one iota to me. I was worried about Angelina and was trying to distract myself by finding something else to harp on. Who would pick her up today? There was still no sign of Mac. Should I take her home? What if no one was there?

"Maisie sure likes coming here," he said, opening the giant box of snack bars.

"That's good," I said, distracted by my thoughts about Angelina.

"The songs you sing with them are cute."

"Yeah, they are." Mac never said how Angelina was getting home. Would he be back in time to take her?

"Maisie loves doing that one where you use sign language."

I wondered which dry cleaner her aunt worked at. Maybe I could drop her off there instead of their empty apartment. That would be safer, but would her boss allow it?

When I didn't answer, he yelled, "Hey!"

I looked up, startled.

"Why are you so interested in Maisie's friend?"

That caught me by surprise. "What?"

"The little girl with the black braids. You've watched her like a hawk since you got here. What's her name?"

"Angelina," I said, forcing myself to look into his eyes, knowing that if I floundered and looked elsewhere, I'd appear like I was hiding something. Which, of course, I was. "Angelina Portillo."

His steady cop eyes held mine. "Is she a member of your church?"

"No, a neighborhood child. About half the kids here don't go to our church. That's kind of the idea of the children's theater group, to reach out to the local kids."

His expression was cynical. "Thereby reach their parents who might attend your church someday and start adding to the church coffers."

I swept my hands around the old kitchen, part of the recreation hall that had been there for forty years and badly needed refurbishing. "Does it look like money is our biggest concern?"

"This Angelina Portillo. Does she have a particularly sad story?"

I looked back down at the lined-up snacks, carefully lining up the boxes of cherry juice. "She's a sweet little girl, Hud. Her aunt works hard, and they don't have much. I was just making sure she was feeling comfortable."

He leaned close, his lips inches from my ear. I could smell the mint from the gum he was chewing. "Ranch girl, I know you, and some-thing's worrying you about that little girl. I'm guessing it has to do with Mr. Adams's homicide. I can see it in your face, and you'd bet-ter tell me what it is because she's friends with my little girl and that makes it *my* business."

I turned abruptly away from him and headed back out to the hall without answering. Dang my expressive face.

Fortunately Dove picked that moment to walk over to me. "Have you got everything under control?" she asked. "JoAnn's outside, and I need to go over the set plans with her."

"Sure, we can run through the play once and see how it flows."

"I'll be back in a minute." She gave Hud a perfunctory frown, just to keep him in his place, and headed out the door.

"Okay, kids," I yelled out, walking down the center of the hall. "Everyone take a seat up front. We're going to start reading the play from the beginning." I told Scout to lie down in a corner. He obeyed me more quickly than the kids did. Once he was no longer a part of the play time, it was easier to get the kids settled down.

We ran through the play once, with Jason, Beth's boyfriend, stand-ing in for Mac's part, that of Giant Despair. The kids reacted with giggles and exaggerated screams when Jason tried to mimic Mac's deep voice singing,

I am Giant Despair,
Caught you in my lair.
All the folks who come my way,
In my castle have to stay,
In Doubting Castle,
In Doubting Castle.

Then I read the witch's part, which would be played by Nonie Johnston, one of our sweetest older ladies who was, ironically, known for her delicious homemade angel food cake. It's the part where she tries to talk Hopeful and Christian into killing themselves rather than wait for Giant Despair to kill and eat them.

Salvador, who played the part of John Bunyan, read, "Then did the prisoners discuss the witch's advice. Christian was half in favor of suicide, but Hopeful said she would rather suffer all hardship than kill herself. So they were in a lamentable state all day, but when night came they began to pray and sing. For Hopeful said if they had to die, they ought to do it bravely and well."

We sang the song that Christian and Hopeful sang in the prison to keep their spirits up.

For every prison, there's a door
For every door, there is a key,
And if we only had it now, we'd be free!
In every darkness, there's a light,
Piercing through the gloom of night.
In every heart, a still small voice.
There is a choice, there is a choice, there's a choice . . .

After running through the song a few times, I saw by the clock that we had about thirty minutes left. Just enough time for snack and shopping at the Good Behavior Store.

"You guys were great today," I told all of them, passing out another round of blue tickets. "I'm so proud of you. Salvador, please say a prayer for our snack, then you all can line up while I set up the Good Behavior Store."

"Thank you, Jesus, for our snack, amen," Salvador said, obviously anxious to eat.

"Amen!" all the kids echoed then pushed and jostled their way to the back of the room.

Hud sat in a folding chair, his arms crossed over his chest.

"Could you please help Beth and Jason serve the snacks while I set up the store?" I asked, ignoring his annoyed expression.

He stood up and adjusted his jacket. "We will talk about this later," he said in his most authoritative cop's voice.

I smiled at him, not a bit affected by his verbal power play. He forgot I was married to a cop. "Thanks so much for your help. After the children have their snack and shopping, can you make sure none of them leave the building? It's getting dark so I'd rather they stay inside until they are picked up."

He scowled, then did as I asked. As cops are so expert at doing, once he was around the kids he slipped out of the gruff, alpha-dog mode into that of good-natured parent. True to his word, he stayed until the last child had been collected by an adult. I paid particular interest to who picked up Angelina. It was one of the mothers at our church, Sandi Lerner, whose daughter was cast as Sincere, one of the shepherds who give the wandering pilgrims directions.

"Mac asked me to give Angelina a ride home," Sandi said when I walked over to question her. "Her aunt doesn't get home until after eight o'clock."

"She's not there alone, is she?" I asked, touching my fingertips to Angelina's shoulder. I would go with her before I'd allow that.

"No, I'm taking her to the next-door neighbor's house," Sandi said. "Mrs. Mesa apparently watches her while Angelina's aunt works. But she doesn't drive."

"I can take her," I said, nervous about letting Angelina out of my sight.

"No problem," Sandi said cheerfully. "It's on our way home. When's the next rehearsal?"

"Thursday. We'll call you if there are any changes." I looked down at Angelina. "Didn't you have a sweater?"

She nodded. "A yellow one." She turned around to look back at the piano. It was laying on the bench next to Beth's sheet music.

"Let's go get it," I said, holding out my hand.

"We'll be outside waiting," Sandi said.

When I stooped down to help Angelina put it on, buttoning the top button close to her small pointed chin, I said, "Remember what we talked about earlier? About being special friends?"

She nodded, her eyes watching my hands fasten the tiny plastic daisy-shaped buttons.

"I'm going to give you my phone number, and if you get scared and need someone to talk to, you can call me. Okay?"

"Okay." A warm, baby-powder smell came from her.

I found an old church bulletin, tore off a corner, and wrote my cell phone number on it. I stuck it in the pocket of her jeans. "When you get home, put this paper in a safe place. If I don't answer right away, you can leave a message. Do you know how to do that?"

"Yes," she said, nodding her head, her expression proud. "Rachel next door showed me how. It's easy."

I smiled. This generation was phone and computer literate at such a young age it sometimes scared me. But in this case, it was definitely a good thing. "Remember, you call me anytime if you get scared, okay?"

"Okay." She looked at me for a long moment, then leaned closer. "That's why I hid," she whispered in my ear.

My stomach started twisting. As offhandedly as possible, I said, "When did you hide, honey?"

Her face her face suddenly went blank, her black eyes wide. Well-trained by her aunt, she was already experienced at being evasive. She looked at me, her expression miserable, knowing she failed to keep the secrets her aunt told her to keep. Tears welled up in her eyes.

"Where was this, Angelina?" I asked, feeling panic start to rise inside me.

Her bottom lip trembled. "I can't . . ."

I abandoned my questions and patted her lightly on the back. "It's all right. You go on with Mrs. Lerner. I'll see you soon."

I watched her run toward Sandi Lerner and her daughter, sick that I had not found out a thing that would help Angelina and in the process had probably frightened her more.

After cleaning up the last of the juice boxes and empty snack bar wrappers tossed by Michael Jordan wannabes who fell vastly short of his shooting abilities, I helped Dove lock up the recreation hall and walked her out to her truck.

Hud, ever vigilant, despite his annoyance at me, had his daughter buckled into her car seat while he leaned against the front of it and watched Dove and me.

"I'm glad he's here," Dove said, waving at Hud, who gave a quick wave back. "But he's also trouble on a stick, Benni. You watch yourself around him."

"I can handle Detective Hudson," I said, planting a kiss on her warm, slightly damp cheek. Though she wouldn't admit it, this was hard on her physically. I needed to figure a way to take on more of the burden without her realizing it. "Give me some credit for having a little common sense."

"There's nothing commonsensical about how that man looks at you," Dove said, her voice scolding, but indulgent. "You just make sure you don't be looking back in a way that encourages him."

"Go home," I said, opening her truck door. "Get some rest. We have a big week coming up. I'll see you tomorrow at three o'clock."

"No, you'll see me tomorrow at nine A.M."

"For what?"

"Forgot to tell you. Our favorite rabble-rouser, Sissy Brownmiller, called an emergency meeting of the historical society. It seems with the theft of that fancy-pants fiddle, she thinks we should change the way we've set up the self-guided tours of the historical houses. For once, though I'd shoot myself in the foot before I'd admit it to her, she might be right."

My mind quickly ran over tomorrow's schedule. I still had most of the antique toy exhibit to unpack, not to mention arrange and type out display cards. "What time did you say the meeting was?"

"Nine A.M. You're in charge of refreshments. There'll be about twenty people." She climbed into her truck and shut the door before I could protest.

"Okay," I muttered to myself walking over to my own truck where Scout was patiently waiting for me. "Tomorrow's schedule . . . first go to Stern's Bakery, then to the historical museum, then work on the exhibit . . ."

"Benni!" Hud called, walking toward me.

"Oh, great," I said to Scout. "I don't want to spar with him right now. Do you think you can manage a distraction? Maybe lift your leg on his boot?"

Scout's tail beat up and down on the ground, but he remained sitting next to the passenger door. At that moment, Mac's Ford Explorer pulled into the church parking lot.

"Thank you, Lord," I said out loud.

When Hud reached me, I said, "I need to talk to Mac, Hud. Very important personal matter. I'll see you tomorrow at the next rehearsal!" I weaved around him and headed toward Mac who had pulled into a spot next to his office door.

"Benni Harper, I will hunt you down," Hud called after me.

I held up my hand in acknowledgment. "Good night, Inspector Clouseau."

Mac stepped out of his car, his arms full of books, papers, and his well-worn, brown leather Bible.

"Hey, Benni," he said. "How was the rehearsal?"

"Not bad. Beth and Jason showed up so we were able to run through the complete play once. The kids know the music pretty well. It's the dialogue and blocking we're struggling with."

"Good, good," he said, only half-listening to my report.

"Mac, I don't think Angelina was telling you the truth. I think she did see something the night Walt was killed."

He fumbled with the papers and books in his arms. His heavy Bible and a half-dozen papers dropped to the ground.

"Shoot," he said, his voice tight, frustrated. Silently, I bent down and helped him pick up the papers. I held his brown leather Bible to my chest, the leather worn and scratchy at the edges from use. I was accustomed to seeing him use it every Sunday for the last four years, ever since he'd been called as minister of First Baptist. He'd used this Bible to marry Gabe and me.

"Let's go to my office," Mac said.

Scout and I followed Mac into the dark building. He turned on the light and dumped his load on his neat desk. Behind his head was a hand-carved cross made of olive wood imported from Israel. I knew Walt made it because I owned one. He had sold them a couple of times a year at the Farmers' Market downtown and donated the money to the children's department at First Baptist.

"So," Mac said, sitting down heavily in his high-backed chair. "Why do you think she's not telling the truth?" Weariness, both physical and emotional, gave a gray cast to his normally ruddy complexion.

I handed him his Bible and sat in a visitor's chair across from his desk. Scout flopped down next to my feet. "I'll admit I prompted her a little."

When he started to say something, I held up my hand for him to stop. "I know, even if she had seen something, it might have been better that I didn't mention it. On the other hand, Mac, if she *did* see what happened to Walt, the knowledge might be scaring her to death. She could be carrying a huge burden with no one to help her. We have to find out for sure if she saw something and help her deal with it, even if we don't tell anyone about it. Who knows what will happen to her psychologically if we ignore the truth? I think we should go to

Gabe now. His department has the means, the people qualified to question her properly. Who knows what damage you and I are perpetuating by ignoring the fact that she probably saw something?"

He listened to my diatribe patiently, something I suppose they train you to do in seminary. I couldn't tell by the blank expression on his face whether he agreed or disagreed with me. He leaned forward, resting his elbows on the desk, his chin in one hand. It was a long moment before he spoke.

"You are right in most of what you said, Benni. This has been tearing me up inside, and I'll admit, though I've been on my knees a half-dozen times since yesterday, God still hasn't seen fit to answer my questions. I flat out don't know what to tell you." His sunburned face softened with despair in the golden light of his office. The room was so quiet, we could hear Scout's soft snoring.

I inhaled deeply. The air smelled of old books, musty and comforting, and was sweet from the large ripe apple sitting next to his nameplate. "Mac, what should we do?"

"Pray," he said. "Pray until we get an answer."

I sighed. "I need to tell Gabe." In my heart, I knew it was the right thing to do.

Mac nodded. "I understand."

I hesitated, biting my bottom lip. "He'll want to talk to Angelina."

"Yes, I know."

I picked up his nameplate and ran my fingers over the indented letters—"MacKenzie Reid, Minister of the Good News," I read out loud, setting it back down. "You have a doctorate, don't you?"

He nodded at the nameplate. "I like that title better."

Reluctant to leave his office because it meant I'd be that much closer to telling Gabe about Angelina, I asked, "When will the sanctuary be reopened?"

"This Sunday. The police left a message that they're through with the area. We're having the carpet replaced on Saturday."

"They never found any of Walt's family?"

He ran his hand over his neatly trimmed beard. "Not that they informed me. Walt told me he had none, but that's not to say he was telling the truth. Many times people who've done things they aren't proud of, lived lives they've regretted, are estranged from their families and even when they've repented and changed, don't feel they deserve to be in relationship with their families again. That's where we come in as a church. We should be their families."

"What about his things?"

Mac shrugged. "I guess the police will eventually let me have them. I'll give what is useful to charity. The church will pick up his funeral expenses. The deacon board has already approved it."

"His workshop here. Have you checked it?"

Mac gave me a puzzled look. "No."

"Did the police?"

"I'm sure they did. They had the run of the place."

"Can I look through it?" I didn't know why all of a sudden I wanted to see his workshop, except that maybe there was something there that would explain who he was, why this terrible thing had happened to him. And, to be honest, I was dragging my feet about going home and facing my husband.

"I don't see why not. I'll be here for another half hour or so."

"I just want to take a quick look," I said, standing up.

"Benni," he said.

"Yes?" I waited, looking at his stricken face. Shadowed in the soft light of his office, the lines in his face seemed deeper, making him appear older than his forty-four years.

"Don't forget, God knows how this will all play out. It's under His control."

I nodded, wishing I was as certain of that as he was.

To reach Walt's workshop, it was quicker to cut through the sanctuary, which was dimly lit with automatic security lights along one side of the room. Black-and-yellow crime scene tape was still draped around four folding chairs set up around the large dark spot on the carpet. I quickly looked away from it, feeling sick to my stomach, and stared up at the pale oak cross hanging over the baptismal behind the choir loft.

A good, old-fashioned flashing light and voice from the air like Paul got would be real helpful now, Lord, I said inwardly. Then, remembering what happened to Paul, I added quickly, but I'd like to keep my eyesight, thank you. But the air in the quiet room remained clear and wordless, smelling faintly of orange-scented wood polish.

After I entered Walt's workroom, Scout lay down in front of the open door, a comforting guardian. I could tell the police had searched Walt's workshop because of the slight disarray. They'd done a fair job of keeping things neat, but I'd been in there before and Walter was as persnickety as my Great-Aunt Garnet was about things having their place. Pegboard mounted on two of the walls had an outline of each tool etched in white paint so there would be no doubt where each tool went. About a dozen tools were thrown casually on top of the workbench, something that I knew Walt would have never allowed. Though I know I was being silly, I carefully put each tool back in its proper spot so Walt's tidy spirit could rest in peace.

I looked through every drawer and cabinet, not certain what I was searching for and knowing Gabe's homicide detectives were professionally trained at this. But, I reasoned, I saw things with a different eye. Maybe I'd spot something they didn't even know they'd missed. It had certainly crossed my mind that Gabe might be less irritated about my keeping information from him if I also found something that his officers missed.

Inside the last cabinet were his unfinished projects. There was an array of half-finished carved crosses, each just a little different from the others, and a partially finished nativity scene—he had all the animals and the baby Jesus finished. The rest of the cast was sketched on pieces of cherry wood. It was my guess he'd been making the six-inch figures as a gift for the church. It hit me suddenly how quickly our lives can be extinguished, how in the middle of things, when we least expect it, our time is over. Would we do things any different if we knew the date and time of our death?

The bottom shelf held another surprise. A type of decorative box that I immediately recognized. He'd obviously taken the book I loaned him to heart and made his own tramp art box.

I picked up the notched-wood box and carried it to his workbench so I could study it more closely. It was about the size of a bread box and had six drawers and a hinged top. I opened each drawer and the top. All of them were lined with bright red velvet. It was most likely meant as a trinket or jewelry box or maybe even a sewing box. I ran my fingers over the intricate notched carving, probably made, from what I'd read, with a small pen knife. I turned it over. There was a tiny bit of carving in the right corner.

"WA to AHO." Walt *had* made it. And he'd put both mine and Gabe's last initial. Changing my name, or rather adding it to Harper, was something Walt and I discussed a few months ago at a potluck dinner after he heard Sissy Brownmiller scold me again for not taking my new husband's name.

"Mind your own dang business," I muttered as she walked away from the dessert table. Why in the world people nitpicked at other people about the personal details in their life that don't harm anyone else was beyond me. I felt like chucking my piece of Dove's lemon chiffon pie at Sissy's chiffon-covered back.

"People sure are funny, aren't they?" Walt said, standing next to me.

"Why in the world does she care one way or the other?" I asked. "I mean, really, what is it with people? And, between you and me, I've been considering changing my name, but just hadn't gotten around to finding out how to do it. But remarks like hers make me want to dig my heels in the sand."

He gave a rare smile. "Yes, people like her can do that to you. But don't let her keep you from doing it if you want to. It's such a small thing, and it'll make that somber husband of yours smile. Who knows how long any of us has on this earth? Why deprive him of a single minute of happiness?"

"Good point," I'd said.

What an eerie coincidence. Had he sensed something was going to happen to him? I tucked the box under my arm and turned out the workshop light. Since the police had already searched this room, maybe it would be okay if I took this box, though I had no real proof he meant it for me. I would donate it to the museum. Though not incredibly valuable in terms of money, it was valuable as an art piece made by someone we cared about at this church and in this county. Walt Adams's work deserved a place in our small, but growing, permanent collection of the Josiah Sinclair Folk Art Museum.

"Scout, come," I said, walking quickly back through the sanctuary.

When I entered Mac's office, he was closing his leather briefcase.

"What have you got there?" he asked.

I held out the dark-stained box. "I found it in one of his cupboards."

Mac took it from my hands. "This is certainly different. Do you think Walt made it?"

"It's a style of carving called tramp art. I'm sure it's his work, his initials are carved underneath."

Mac set it down on his desk and opened the hinged top. "Tramp art?"

"It's a kind of folk art that became popular in our country during the Depression. The artists often used orange crates or old cigar boxes or actually any wood they could find."

Comprehension lightened Mac's face. "I get it. Hoboes made it."

"Sort of. It was mostly out-of-work people. Historians think it has origins in European ornamental wood carving. But for the American version, all you need is some cheap wood, a pen knife, maybe a few other tools, and some glue. Turn it over."

He turned the box over and saw the inscription, then looked up at me in surprise. "He made this for you?"

I nodded. "That's what it appears to me. I want to donate it to the folk art museum. What do you think?"

"I don't see why not. The police said they are through searching his possessions, and I have no idea how to reach any of his family, if he even has any. Besides, it's obvious he made it for you. He'd want you to have it."

He opened all six drawers again, his face frowning in concentration. I knew what he was doing because I'd also done it.

He looked up and gave a sad smile. "No secret clues in here that tell us who might have wanted him dead."

I lifted my shoulders. "That occurred to me. But I think we've read too many mystery novels. It's never that simple."

He gave a troubled sigh. "Nothing ever is."

I looked up into his tired face, illuminated by the parking lot's bright security lights. "I'm telling Gabe tonight. Just a warning, we might be setting up a marital counseling session with you tomorrow." I gave a quick, nervous laugh, not entirely sure I was joking.

He walked me and Scout to my truck and rested his big hand on my shoulder before I climbed in. "Benni, I trust you and whatever you decide about telling Gabe about Angelina. I'll be ready for his questions."

It was past six o'clock when I arrived home. Gabe's car was not in the driveway. Luis's silver Mercedes was parked on the street. Gabe had given him a key, and television voices filtering through the guest room door told me he was here. I set the tramp art box on the hall table and fed Scout. Then I started making the white enchiladas I'd promised Luis. Luckily, there was a pound of cooked chicken in the freezer that I thawed in the microwave and, cheating a little, used canned green chilies rather than burning my own like his aunt Maria taught me. By the time Gabe arrived home a half hour later, the enchiladas made with green chile and a white sour cream sauce were baking in the oven, and I was tossing a green salad.

"Something smells good," he said, lifting the back of my hair to kiss the nape of my neck while I mixed the salad dressing. "And it smells like you're cooking too."

"You are a wise man, Chief Ortiz," I said, laughing while his lips caressed the back of my neck.

"I love you, *querida*," he said, turning me around and kissing me firmly on the lips. It turned deeper and more intense, enveloping me in his strong, masculine, late-afternoon scent of spicy aftershave, male hormones, cotton shirt–smell, coffee, and mint. He stopped only when I pulled away, murmuring against his lips that I needed to get dinner finished.

"What's got into you, Friday?" I asked, turning back to the salad.

He slipped his arms around my waist and rested his cheek on the top of my head. "Had a good day at work, that's all. I have especially looked forward to coming home to my beautiful wife."

"Not to mention his favorite cousin," Luis said, coming into the kitchen.

Gabe laughed, let me go, and went over to playfully punch his cousin in the arm. "Hey, Louie, Louie, how was your day? Wish *I* had a kick-back job like yours where I could take off on vacation whenever I wanted."

That last comment told me that Luis hadn't seen Gabe since this morning and told him about losing his job or Paige leaving him.

"Kick-back job?" Luis said. "I saw what you do, Señor Flojo. Talk about an easy job." His deep voice rose into a falsetto. "Sign here, sign here, and oh, oh, Mr. Chief of Police, where would you like me to make reservations for lunch today?"

"What do you know about real jobs?" Gabe laughed good-naturedly. "You spend your time riding around on yachts eating lobster with rich people."

"You'd better not let Maggie hear you mimic her like that, Luis," I said, pulling dinner plates from the cupboard. "She'd kick your handsome brown butt clear back to Newport Beach."

Gabe's assistant, Maggie, was an extremely tolerant, but tough African-American lady who owned a ranch in north San Celina County. She ran Gabe's schedule with the same efficiency she ran her cattle operation.

"Don't rat me out," Luis said cheerfully, taking the plates from me, his dark eyes shiny as two marbles. "I beg of you."

Was this the same melancholy man I talked to at Blind Harry's? As he leaned over to take the silverware from me I caught a whiff of alcohol, telling me what he'd probably spent his afternoon doing. A little liquid courage to be able to tell Gabe the truth of his life? Or maybe just to get through tonight? Either way, it worried me. I'd never seen a troubling situation yet where alcohol helped the problem.

But maybe I was wrong this time. Dinner was full of jokes and laughter, and when it was over, I turned down their half-hearted offer to help me clean up. "You two haven't had enough time to visit. Go sit out on the porch and get a little fresh air. I'll bring you some coffee and peach pie."

"You want to kick this lamebrain out and let me move in?" Luis asked. "He doesn't deserve you."

"Keep your paws off my woman," Gabe said.

"Take Scout for a walk," I replied, pushing them both out of my kitchen. "Luis, tell Gabe about how you protected my honor today."

"What?" Gabe said.

"You should have seen me," Luis said. "I was amazing." Their masculine laughter echoed down the hallway.

As their voices faded away, I started cleaning up the kitchen. If my plan worked, Luis would take this opportunity to tell Gabe about losing his job and his marriage problems, thereby letting me off the hook. Now my dilemma was, do I dump the information on Gabe tonight about Angelina or wait? He'd be so concerned about Luis that it might be better if I waited until tomorrow morning. Then again, I'd waited long enough. No, I would tell him tonight.

A half hour later, I was putting the last dish in the dishwasher when the front door opened. Scout rushed into the kitchen for his evening dog treat. I gave it to him, scratched his chest for a moment, then joined the men in the living room. By their sober faces, I assumed Luis had told Gabe his bad news. Gabe sat in his leather recliner, arms crossed over his chest. Luis stood with his back to me, pretending to peruse one of the built-in bookcases that bracketed our natural stone fireplace.

"Anyone want pie and coffee?" I asked, hoping I was only imagining the chill in the room.

"Thanks, not right now," Gabe said tersely.

"No, thanks," Luis said, turning around. "I think I'll go out for a little while. I feel the need for a drink coming on." He started toward the door, grabbing his brown leather jacket from the coat rack.

"Do you think that's a good idea?" Gabe said.

"Don't hassle me, bro," Luis said, his tone more tired than angry.

"Luis . . ." Gabe started.

"Later, man. Don't wait up." He nodded at me and opened the front door. The scent of wet earth and rain blew in, lingering around us long after he closed the door behind him.

"Is he okay?" I asked Gabe.

Gabe shrugged. "He's being a jackass."

I didn't know what to say. Gabe's voice was so harsh and angry. I wanted to ask what happened between them, but also wanted him to tell me himself. So I stood there holding a dish towel, waiting for him to continue.

"He got himself fired," Gabe finally said, staring at the blackened logs in our fireplace. "And Paige left him."

"I know," I said.

His head jerked up, his mouth opened slightly with surprise.

"He told me this afternoon at Blind Harry's. I was waiting to see if he'd tell you tonight. If he didn't, I was going to tell you." I twisted the dishtowel in my hands, trying not to sound defensive.

He ran his fingers through his dark hair. "I got angry at him. I guess that's obvious."

I nodded. Scout trotted into the room, came up beside me, and sat down, leaning his bulk against my calf. I reached down and played with his floppy ear, running my fingers over his velvety fur. "What did you say?"

"That he was being an idiot. That he'd already blown two marriages, and he'd been stupid to screw this one up. That jobs aren't that easy to find at our age. That he has a family depending on him."

"There are two sides to every story," I said, remembering our own marriage struggles. This Paige didn't sound like the greatest catch in the world to me.

"Did he tell you why she left?"

I shook my head no.

"He cheated on her," Gabe said, his voice hard. "More than once. As much as he jokes about me, Luis was always the one who never could keep his pants zipped."

I hated hearing that about Luis, didn't think he was that kind of man. Then again, what did I really know about him? We'd been acquainted exactly two days while Gabe had known him his whole life.

"What about his job?" I asked, sitting down on the sofa.

Gabe sat forward in his chair, resting his elbows on his knees. "We didn't get into that too much so I don't know the circumstances. I was just so upset about him screwing around that I focused on that."

I didn't say anything. I understood why that particular subject would be sensitive to Gabe. Our marriage had recently been tested by Gabe's own tap dance around adultery. We would always bear the scars from that time. He still felt guilty about it, though I assured him over and over I was fine, *we* were fine. Then again, he'd never actually cheated. Would I be so forgiving if he'd given in to temptation and slept with his old lover?

I went over and sat on the arm of his chair and caressed the back of his neck. I ran my hand against the prickly hair, then smoothed it down. His hair was slightly shaggy, needing a trim. "Friday, there's nothing we can do about it tonight. Let's sleep on it and see how things look tomorrow."

"Nothing will change," he said, sad now.

I didn't contradict him, knowing it wouldn't help. But I knew one thing. I could never tell him about Angelina tonight. That would definitely have to wait until tomorrow morning.

CHAPTER 7

$\mathcal{T}$HE NEXT MORNING GABE WAS ALREADY SHOWERING WHEN MY alarm went off at six A.M. When I went downstairs to make coffee I glanced down the hall at the closed guest room door, then out the front window. Luis's Mercedes was parked in front. I couldn't help wondering what time he finally came in.

While I measured out coffee, I contemplated whether I should have oatmeal or endure Gabe's scolding while I ate peach pie for breakfast. How would Luis's revelations affect his visit with Gabe? What began as a wonderful, relaxing time for both of them had turned horribly complicated.

"I guess that's just how life is, Scooby-Doo," I commented to Scout, pouring out his morning ration of kibble. "You are darn lucky to be a dog." His tail wagged slowly at my words. I could always count on him to be sympathetic. I leaned over the sink and gazed out into our front yard. It was a cloudy, moody day. This conflict between Gabe and his cousin made me feel sad and helpless. The same way I felt about Angelina.

Gabe came downstairs dressed for work in his normal gray Brooks Brothers suit, a crisp white shirt, and a conservative navy-and-burgundy patterned tie. He kissed me on the temple. "What's for breakfast?"

"How about oatmeal?"

He nodded his approval and sat down at the table, unfolding the newspaper. A few minutes later, while I stirred his favorite slow-cooking Irish oatmeal, a few choice Spanish curse words burst from his mouth.

"What?" I said, whipping around, the mixing spoon flinging hot oatmeal onto the kitchen counter. Scout leaped up growling, his tail high, ready for battle.

Gabe handed me the paper, and I scanned the front page. Two lead stories updated Walt's murder and the theft of the Indian-made violin. Another article on the Chumash casino and its new buffet. "I don't get what . . ."

"Read the editorial," Gabe said in a clipped voice.

The toasty smell of the cooking oatmeal filled the warm kitchen while I stirred with one hand and held the paper with the other. The editorial was a long, vicious attack on Gabe and his department and how "interesting" it was that both the mission church, where Gabe was a member, and the church where his wife was a member, were entangled in capital crimes, that maybe Gabe was not the most competent person to be running San Celina's police department. The reporter, a Mel Chapman, went into detail about how Gabe acquired the police chief job, by taking it temporarily as a favor to his dying friend, how he was just slipped into place by the city manager, who then left for another job a mere six months later. Mr. Chapman implied that perhaps Gabe got the job simply to appease a radical and very verbal Latino political faction of San Celina County.

I threw the paper down on the table. "Bull manure. Who the heck is Mel Chapman?"

"Just took over the city desk," Gabe said. "Moved here from San Diego. We busted his son for selling Ecstasy. Needless to say, Mr. Chapman is unhappy with us."

"I wonder if Emory knows him." I set a bowl of steaming oatmeal in front of him. "Maple syrup? Raisins? Brown sugar? All three?"

"Just raisins." He took a sip of coffee, his body stiff with anger. "This is all I need today."

I hugged him from behind, resting my cheek on the top of his head, inhaling the clean, citrus scent of his hair. "He's an idiot, Friday. There's no truth in that article, and anyone who knows you knows that."

"We don't have a single clue about who took that violin."

I sat down across from him. "You've got a great detective team. They'll solve it and Walt's murder, and Mr. Chapman will have to eat worms."

He finished his cereal silently and was slipping on his jacket when his cousin wandered into the kitchen. From the looks of Luis's disheveled hair and bloodshot eyes, he'd definitely spent a good part of last night drinking.

"Now *that's* going to solve a lot of problems," Gabe snapped at his hungover cousin.

"At least it's something I'm good at," Luis said, giving Gabe a lazy grin.

Gabe glared. "Luis . . ."

Luis held up a hand. "Save the lecture for later. Nothing you say right now will penetrate this fog." He brushed past Gabe and headed for the coffeepot.

Gabe looked over at me, his face questioning.

It's okay, I mouthed to him. Luis wasn't the first hungover man I'd ever been around. I glanced up at the clock. It was seven-thirty. "I'll be leaving in an hour for an emergency historical society meeting. There's oatmeal in the pot and orange juice in the refrigerator, Luis. Help yourself."

Luis winked at me. "Coffee is all this *hombre* needs, *querida*."

Gabe opened his mouth to say something, but I rushed over and grabbed his arm.

"Let me walk you out," I said, maneuvering him out of the kitchen with my body.

Out on the porch, he snapped. "I won't have him disrespecting me in my own house."

"Gabe, he adores you. I don't think he meant anything disrespect-ful by it. My guess is he's still half-plastered and doesn't know what he's saying. Go to work, let him get sober, and you two can talk to-night. You can set some ground rules about the rest of his visit."

"Or I can throw him out on his ass," Gabe said. "And for the book, he knew *exactly* what he was saying." He abruptly kissed the top of my head and started down the stairs. "I have to go before I give into temptation and . . ." He didn't finish his sentence. I'm not sure I wanted him to.

I almost called at him to stop so I could tell him about Angelina. But I knew it would be better if I waited, let him cool off, and went to his office later this morning. He would take the news better and a few more hours wouldn't matter at this point.

In the kitchen, Luis sat at the table staring at his empty coffee cup.

"More coffee?" I asked, going over to the coffee pot.

"Thanks," he said without looking up.

I poured the coffee, staring at the top of his black, rumpled hair. It looked so much like Gabe's. The genetic connection of these two men was so obvious in their physical appearance and in their emotional makeup. That's probably why he irritated Gabe so much. No one liked seeing a reflection of their less-than-perfect personality traits.

"Sure you don't want something to eat?" I asked. "It might make you feel better."

He looked up at me, his brown eyes miserable as a sick puppy's. "He's really pissed at me, isn't he?"

I put the coffeepot back. "You guys can work this out tonight."

His red-rimmed eyes filmed over. "Maybe I should leave."

"That's up to you. But you and Gabe should talk before you go."

He brought his face close to the steaming coffee, but didn't take a drink. "I'm sorry I was out of line a minute ago. I did it because I knew he'd get mad."

"Apology accepted. Now you need to mend fences with your cousin."

"Among others," he murmured.

"It'll be okay, Luis." The minute I spoke I knew they were just empty words. Why do we compulsively spout platitudes when we actually don't have a clue whether things will work out? Like dogs howling in the night, we use mindless words to fill the void, hoping someone or something will answer us and assure us we're not alone.

By the time I showered and dressed, Luis had already left. Wherever he went, I hoped it didn't include any more of our local bars. I wrapped Walter's tramp art box in an old towel and stuck it behind my truck's front seat. I'd forgotten to show it to Gabe. But right now, it was unimportant. I'd take it to the museum, photograph it for our files, then bring it back tonight.

Outside, the air was downright cold, winter already here despite the calendar's assertion it was still fall. I went back inside and grabbed my favorite red cashmere scarf, a Christmas gift from Gabe, and wrapped its softness around my neck. I studied my reflection in the hallway mirror. Red cashmere and blue plaid flannel shirt. That'll do.

It was a quarter to nine when I stopped at Stern's Bakery to pick up refreshments for the emergency historical society meeting. While waiting for my order, I went over to say hi to the Coffee Guys, a group of men who'd been meeting three times a week at Stern's for the last twenty years. During an election year it was tradition for the *Tribune* to make a trek down to Stern's to hear what this very vocal and eclectic group had to say about the candidates. Attendance ranged in numbers between ten and thirty, depending on who was working or on vacation, with a core group of fifteen regular members. Their jobs ran the gamut of prosecuting attorney to garbage collector to insurance agent to freelance sign painter to long-haul truck driver. They were democrats, republicans, and independents. Like an informal book club, they picked a topic rather than a book, and their discussions were often loud, sometimes heated, and always ended with laughter.

"Hey, guys," I said. "What's happening?"

"Not much," said Lance, a math teacher at San Celina Community College.

"What's the topic today?" I asked.

They all looked down into their coffee cups and half-eaten doughnuts and muffins, their chagrined expressions revealing. On the table lay three newspapers, all folded to Mel Chapman's editorial.

"It's okay," I said. "I promise I won't tell Gabe he was the topic today. Otherwise, those unpaid parking tickets I know some of you ignore . . ." I smiled, just to show them I was kidding.

"We're on his side," said one of the men, Ray, a respected child psychologist. "He can't really be held responsible for that violin theft just because he attends Mass at the mission."

I picked up one of their chocolate French crullers and took a bite. "What do you guys think of the violin theft? Think it was an inside job?"

They started debating how easy it would have been to steal the unprotected instrument, what they would have done to secure it, what they thought Gabe should do to recover it. I let them ramble on, glancing every so often at the crowded bakery counter, waiting for my name to be called.

"They say that replica was almost good enough to fool an expert," said Bob Satterfield, a retired navy chaplain. "You know what I'd do, Benni?"

"No, what?" I answered automatically, only half-listening because I was mentally running through today's to-do list. It was the last few words of his reply that caused me to say, "What? Repeat what you just said."

Bob grinned, happy he'd gained my full attention. "I said you should check among those woodworkers of yours at the museum. If there was anyone capable of making a violin that would fool people, it would be one of them."

My mind went instantly to all the talented woodworkers affiliated with the museum and co-op. Was that possible? Who and why? I tried to remember if any of them had acted strangely in the last few weeks. Then again, what's the definition of strange when dealing with creative types?

"Look at her," Bob said, jabbing the guy next to him with his elbow. "She's thinking so hard, smoke is coming out of her ears."

I laughed, brushed his comment away with a casual wave. "I don't want to have anything to do with that missing violin. Like everyone else, I just think it's a crying shame."

"If you solve the case, just make sure we old farts get a mention," said Mr. Marshall of Marshalls Jewelry. His sons now ran the downtown jewelry store that ruled the corner of Lopez and Market for the last fifty years. He sold my first husband, Jack, my tiny diamond engagement ring, letting him make payments for a whole year, no interest.

"You bet, Mr. Marshall," I said. "I'll spring for coffee."

"Big spender," Lance said. "Stern's gives it to us for free."

I laughed along with them. The bakery did kick in for the coffee because the men ordered more than enough food to pay for it. "Okay, then banana-nut muffins all around."

"That's more like it," he said.

My name was finally called, and I carried the bags out to my truck where Scout waited patiently. I stroked his head, then gave him a quick hug. "I wish all the men in my life were as easy to live with as you." He licked my hand and flopped down on the front seat.

At the museum, I tied Scout's leash to a post on the front porch and headed downstairs. The meeting was already in progress. I set the pink bakery box down next to the large coffeepot and slipped into a seat in the last row. Right after I sat down and unwrapped the red scarf from around my neck, Hud sat down on the folding chair next to me.

"Hey, ranch girl," he said out of the side of his mouth. "Got any blueberry muffins? I didn't have time for breakfast."

"What're you doing here?" I whispered back while trying to discern just what Sissy Brownmiller was droning on about in front of the twenty historical society members who had attended this emergency meeting. Sissy had finally achieved her lifelong dream of being elected historical society president. She was suggesting we cancel the Heritage Walk this weekend until we could figure out how best to protect the museum's and other historical building's exhibits.

"I'm a member," he said. "This is an emergency meeting, right?"

"Don't you ever have to actually *work*?" I hissed.

"No building will be vandalized during my tenure," Sissy was saying.

"Who elected you the sheriff's department's attendance monitor?"

"Hush, I'm trying to listen," I said.

"Sissy Brownmiller repeats everything at least six times. You know that."

His bull's eye-comment did make me smile.

"Benni Harper, is there anything you or Mr. Hudson would like to share with the rest of the group?" Sissy Brownmiller called out, her long, sloped nose twitching like she smelled something bad. Her thirty years as a fourth grade Sunday School teacher served her well in her ability to intimidate. "You seem to be enjoying your own little meeting back there."

Everyone turned in their seats to stare at us.

"No, ma'am," we sang out simultaneously, causing a ripple of laughter from the others.

Dove glanced at Hud, then raised her eyebrows at me.

"Then, please, save your comments for our open forum," Sissy said.

"One demerit for you, one demerit for me," Hud whispered.

I moved over one chair and set my purse and scarf between us.

"We can't cancel it," Dove said, after finally being recognized by Sissy to speak. By the look on my gramma's face, if Sissy hadn't called on her soon, there would be fur flying in this overheated room. "We've been advertising it for months, and we need the money. We'll have to think of some way to keep all the rooms covered with docents each day. We can work double shifts."

A disgruntled murmur rippled through the members. "We could eliminate Sunday," someone suggested. "That's always a slow day."

"How will we cover each room anyway?" one man asked. "There are five buildings and some of them, like the Mackey house, have ten rooms."

"How about cutting out all of the buildings except the Padilla hacienda and the Mackey house and having a living history exhibit?" a lady in front suggested. "Like they do at Hearst Castle at Christmas."

I'd attended the living history tour last December at Hearst Castle, and it was fun. People from the community dressed up as Hearst and some of his famous guests and posed in the rooms where Hearst entertained. They moved around and chatted in low voices. We couldn't hear what they were saying, but their presence and the costumes gave the rooms more life than a sterile, roped-off room.

"That's a good idea," Dove said. "We'll be able to cover every room that way and protect everything. Some of us can be tour guides and others actors. And I think Friday and Saturday will be plenty."

"It's a wonderful idea," said Edna McClun, a longtime member. "There're no lines to learn, so all we need to do is decide who will be which famous San Celina historical figure and find costumes."

"We have plenty of old clothes," Dove said. "Let's take a quick coffee break. We'll make a list of the people who lived in each house and hand out parts today. Cast members will have to get together with their group before Friday. We have two tour buses from Fresno coming then."

Though Sissy had her nose pushed out of joint by Dove taking over the meeting, even she couldn't protest. It was the perfect solution. "Order, order!" she yelled over the chattering room. "Let's do this properly. Would someone like to make a motion . . ."

"I move we take a break and let Dove and Edna assign us parts," Anna O'Connor called out.

"I second it," Dove declared.

"Dove, you can't second it," Sissy said, pointing her gavel. "You thought up the idea. That's out of order."

"Oh, for cryin' out loud, Sissy . . ." Dove started.

"I second it," I called out.

"Motion granted," Sissy said, slamming down the gavel on the podium, the satisfied look on her face revealing this was her favorite part of the job. "And *I'll* help with assigning the parts."

Dove glanced over at me and rolled her eyes.

Within a half hour, they had assigned parts and posted the schedule. We crowded around it like a bunch of students trying to find out who made the football team or cheerleading squad.

There were groans and laughter as people saw the parts they were given. I waited until the crowd thinned and then ran my finger down the handwritten list. When I saw my name and who was to be my partner, I groaned. I was to be Sarah Mackey, wife of John Mackey, who was played by Hud.

"I didn't even have to bribe anyone," Hud said behind me, chuckling.

I ignored him and went over to Edna and Dove, who were explaining their choices to a couple of other dissatisfied members.

"My family and I are direct descendants of Sarah Mackey," one lady said. "I don't understand why I can't play that part."

Dove opened her mouth, her expression like that of a Jack Russell terrier ready to snap, but Edna, more diplomatic than my gramma, grabbed Dove's arm and said quickly, "We know that, Norma, but we don't have time before Saturday to do anything except use the costumes we have on hand."

"So?" Norma said.

"So, Benni and Hud are the youngest among us."

"Sarah lived to be ninety," said Norma, who was in her seventies. She and her family owned a local nursery for years, but recently sold the land to developers.

"Well," Edna said. "But in this particular scenario we're envisioning, they are in the parlor."

"I can sit in a parlor just as well as Benni Harper," Norma said.

I almost said, you can have it, Norma, when Edna broke in.

"Well," Edna said, looking in dismay over at Dove. "If we change Benni, then Hud won't be the right age . . ."

"For pete's sake, Norma," Dove interrupted. "Do we have to spell it out for you? Benni's the only one of us with a waist smaller than an old cedar trunk, and she can fit into the dang dress."

When Norma walked away in a huff, I said to Dove, "That wasn't one of your more diplomatic moments."

"We do not have time for people's vanity. Norma ought to be

thrilled, we made her a Spanish *señora* over at the hacienda. She gets to wear a thousand-dollar pearl mantilla."

"I have a question," I said. "I was under the impression you thought I should stay away from Hud. So what's this all about?"

"Not my call," Dove said, giving me the eye. "It was Edna and Sissy who said you and Hud should play those parts. You're the youth factor in this whole equation. We are merely utilizing your physical beauty."

I snorted at that remark.

"Just mind your p's and q's with that boy. Besides, I figured what kind of trouble could you get into sitting right out there in public wearing a corset and crinoline underpants."

"Corset?" I said to her back. "Now just a dang minute."

"Hush and go fetch your costume, honeybun."

Within the hour we were assigned our costumes and the schedule for our performances, and told to meet with our living history groups at least once to work the kinks out of the program.

"Where do you want to meet, Mrs. Mackey?" Hud said, following me up the stairs to the main floor of the museum. We were both carrying dark blue garment bags. "There are so many subjects that we could discuss as Sarah and John Mackey. Our honeymoon, for example. I'll never forget the first night we . . ."

I tuned him out, already thinking about which of the woodworkers would be the best to discreetly ask about the possibility of one of the other woodworkers making the stolen violin's replica. That wouldn't be easy.

"I smell burning brain cells," Hud said.

"See you later, Detective," I called over my shoulder while untying Scout from his post.

At the folk art museum, after taking the tramp art box to my office, I went to the woodworking room to see who was there. Five men were working with a variety of saws and sanders. The air buzzed and whined and smelled of sharp pine pitch and new wood. After looking over the group, I decided that Joe Rodale was my best bet for information. He was a retired Riverside County sheriff's detective who, more important, worked part-time as a clerk down at Farm Supply, which made him privy to much of San Celina's best gossip.

"Hey, guys," I called out, walking into the noisy room.

A chorus of greetings were called back over the noise. I walked over to Joe's bench where he was working on one of his natural-pine rocking horses complete with real horsehair manes. He made about three or four a month. Tourists bought them before the varnish dried.

"Hey, Joe," I said. "What's cookin'?"

"Not much," he said, turning off his saw and looking at me from over the top of his safety glasses. He was in his early fifties and had a perfectly trimmed white goatee. "What can I do you for?" His voice was amicable, but his eyes had that direct, slightly suspicious look cops never lose once they acquire it on the job.

"Could you come to my office? There's something I want you to take a look at."

"Sure," he said, setting down his saw and tossing his glasses on the workbench.

"Somebody's in trouble," one of the men teased. "Going to see the principal."

"Let 'em have it, Benni," another called. "Spare the rod, spoil the deputy."

Joe took the ribbing with a good-natured flip of a well-known hand gesture, causing the hoots and hollers to increase.

He apologized to me as we walked down the hallway to my office. "Sorry, Benni. Automatic reaction."

I just laughed. "I grew up around cowboys, and I'm married to a cop. I've seen a few birds flipped in my lifetime."

Once inside my office I closed the door and gestured at one of my visitors' chairs. I took the other one so we were facing each other.

"So," he said. "What's up?"

I shifted in my chair, not knowing just how to word this politely. What I would be suggesting is that one of his colleagues might be a criminal. "Well . . ." I started, then gulped once.

He leaned toward me, resting his elbows on his knees. "Benni, just take a deep breath and start at the beginning. That's what I used to tell all my suspects. I promise, nothing you say will be used against you."

I laughed, immediately put at ease. "And you're a big ole liar."

He grinned. "Yeah, but I can't tell you how many times that worked on lamebrained suspects. I sure miss the job sometimes."

"I bet you do. I can't even imagine Gabe being retired."

He leaned back in his chair. "So, what's worrying you?"

"It's about the Aznar violin." I told him the comment Bob, one of one of the Coffee Guys, made.

"That's actually a very good lead," Joe said, his expression thoughtful. "Any one of us probably has the basic talents it would take to make a half-assed replica, but it would probably depend on how good the copy actually is. Have you talked to Gabe about this?"

I shook my head. "I wanted to check with someone like you to see if it was absolutely nuts before I threw it at him."

"In any investigation, it's only a nutty theory if it doesn't pan out. If it does, then it automatically becomes brilliant."

"Okay, I'll tell Gabe then."

He stood up. "If that's all you need, I'll get back to work." He started toward the door when Walt's tramp art box caught his eye. "Wow, what's that? It's pretty cool."

"A tramp art box."

He ran his hand over the pieced top, then opened it. "I thought that's what it was. I've seen them in pictures, but never a real one."

"It's not an antique. I found it in Walt Adams's workshop at the church. You know, the man who was killed. He made it."

Joe cocked his head. "Yeah, I read about it in the *Tribune*. Too bad. He seemed like a nice guy."

"You knew him?" That surprised me.

"He and I talked a few times. He came down here one time to use one of the jigsaws for some toy he was making his grandson who—"

"Did you say grandson?" I broke in.

"That's what he said. Why?"

I tried to appear nonchalant. "He never told anyone at our church if he had family, and Gabe hasn't been able to locate anyone."

Joe shrugged. "He definitely said grandson."

"Thanks. I'll make sure Gabe gets that information."

"Let me know how this plays out, okay? You've got the old detective in me interested."

"You bet."

After he left, I closed my office door and immediately called Gabe. Now, I not only wanted to tell him about Angelina, I also had this information about Walt's possible family. Plus there was another little something that started nagging at me, something that seemed crazy, but it was too much of a coincidence. Could Walt have been somehow involved with the stolen violin? Could he have made the replica and somehow been killed for his effort? I might be chasing rabbits, but right now, it seemed as plausible as anything else.

As usual when I was desperate to talk to Gabe, he absolutely wasn't available. The poor man spent three-quarters of his life in meetings.

"When is he free?" I asked Maggie.

"He's booked until six," Maggie said, her voice apologetic. "One meeting right after the other."

I thought for a moment. None of this information was something he needed to hear during the five-minute bathroom break between meetings.

"Even lunch?" I checked my watch. It was one-thirty.

"As we speak he's meeting the sheriff for a late lunch at Daniello's."

"She's real nice. Have you met her yet?"

Sally Schuler was a down-to-earth woman who'd surprised everyone by winning the election last year and had also, to everyone's surprise, been completely accepted by the overwhelmingly male deputies. We'd recently gone out to dinner with her and her husband, Wes, a landscape architect. We spent the evening discussing dogs and ranching. She'd been raised on a Montana cattle ranch, and she and her husband bred Pembroke Welsh corgis.

"I can actually read her handwriting, bless her neat little heart. So, need to leave a message?"

"No, I'll just drop by about six. I have something to talk about with him alone."

"Yeah, heard you've got company. How's that going? Chief seemed more grumpy than usual this morning. You cutting him off the sweet grain until his cousin leaves?"

I laughed. "Nah, Gabe hasn't lived around his own family for so long, he's forgotten it isn't always fun and games. They'll quit growling at each other and be the best of friends again tonight, I'm sure." I wasn't, but hoped my optimistic words would glide through the air and influence them.

"I hope so," Maggie said, slipping into the Mississippi drawl learned from her mama. "Cause, honey, you know this ole girl won't be puttin' up with the kinda attitude he's been totin' for very long."

"Gabe knows that."

After we hung up, I decided to swing by the house and make some lunch before going to play rehearsal. As I stepped out of my truck, Luis came down the front steps gripping his black leather suitcase.

"Sneaking out without paying your bill?" I asked.

"Caught me," he said. He wore a button-down blue Oxford shirt, faded Levi's, and leather topsider loafers without socks. His black hair was wet and shiny from a recent shower. Except for the slight puffiness around his eyes, you would have never guessed he tied one on last night.

"Oh, my goodness," I said, pointing down at his shoes. "You and Gabe are two little yuppie peas in a pod. I used to tease him unmercifully about wearing his topsiders without socks. I've almost got him broken of it."

He glanced down at his shoes, then back up at me, a chagrined look on his face. "What can I say? It's a Southern California thing."

Crossing my arms over my chest, I said, "So, Señor Ortiz, where do you think you're going?"

He set his suitcase down and looked back down at his feet. "Thought after this morning it would be better if I took off. You know Gabe when he gets in one of his moods. He's—" He broke off abruptly and looked me directly in the eyes. "Forget the sugarcoating. We're pissed at each other, and it's better if we don't see each other for a while."

"I disagree. Life is too short, and you two are too old to be acting like spoiled brats." I picked up his suitcase and started for the house. "You are *not* going anywhere until you talk this out."

Before I reached the porch, he grabbed my upper arm. "Benni, please."

I turned around. The pure sadness on his face was heartbreaking.

He gently took the suitcase from my hand. "I know you mean well, but Gabe and I need to figure this out. Sometimes that's easier if there's a little space between us."

"Please don't leave San Celina. Gabe won't admit it, but he'd never forgive himself if you two parted like this."

He hesitated a moment, then said, "I'll get a motel in town for a day or so. I need the time to figure out what I'm going to do anyway."

"Okay," I said, feeling helpless. "But, promise me you won't leave town without resolving this with Gabe. He loves you, you know."

He paused a moment before answering. "I know."

CHAPTER 8

I ARRIVED EARLY AT THE CHURCH HOPING TO CATCH MAC SO I could ask his advice about this situation between Gabe and Luis. No one was there so I unlocked the recreation hall and went inside, leaving the door open so parents would know where to bring their kids. Maybe I should have been afraid, but I wasn't. It was still daylight and Scout was with me. Besides, I was convinced that whoever killed Walt Adams was not just a robber looking for a quick buck, but was somebody Walt knew. And though I had no proof, I was halfway convinced it had something to do with that missing violin.

I opened up my copy of the *Pilgrim's Progress—The Joyful Journey* script and scanned it, making notes to myself about which sections gave the kids problems. If we pulled this production off, it would be a true miracle.

I didn't even hear Angelina walk up. If Scout's tail hadn't started beating softly on the carpet, she could have shot me before I noticed.

"Hi, sweetie," I said, patting the floor next to me. "You're here early." The large black-and-white schoolhouse clock over the entrance to the kitchen read two-forty-five. "Did someone drop you off?"

"Pastor Mac picked me up." She gave me a big smile. "We had ice cream first."

"I'm jealous," I said, smiling back. "What kind?"

"Chocolate chip. My favorite is cookie dough, but they were out."

"Is he still here?"

She nodded vigorously. "He's working in his office."

I set down my script. "We have a few minutes before everyone gets here. Have you been working on your lines?"

She gave another big smile and said in a loud voice, "It's a friend, Hopeful. I've been watching you and your friend. He died bravely."

I flipped through my script and found the place where her part of Hopeful is first introduced, right after Christian's friend, Faithful, dies and Christian is thrown into prison.

I read Christian's lines, making my voice sad. "I wish I had died, too."

"But I've come to sneak you out," Angelina/Hopeful replied. "I want to go with you."

"You do?"

"Yes. In fact, I used to be a pilgrim before I started living in Vanity Fair."

"Well, being a pilgrim isn't easy, you know. Look what happened to us."

"Better that than the pleasures of sin, Christian. I mean it! With God's help, this time I'll make it all the way."

I stood up, following the stage instructions. "Oh, Hopeful, I know you will! But first get me out of here. Hurry!"

I held out my hand to Angelina, and she grabbed it. "Run, run! Giant Despair is trying to get us!" We ran across the hall to the door leading to the kitchen.

"Run!" Angelina yelled, giggling all the way.

We stopped when we reached the kitchen. "We're safe!" I grabbed her up in a big hug and swinging her around. "Giant Despair can't find us here."

She held on to me tightly, giggling into my shoulder. "Oh, Benni, Giant Despair is later. You forgot."

I set her down, then stroked the top of her head. Her black hair was as soft as dandelion fluff. "You're right, Angelina. You know this play better than anyone. You are a perfect Hopeful."

"My *tia* helps me every night," she said proudly. "She's learning the words so she can understand when she sees the play."

I stooped down and studied her delicate features. "That's wonderful. She will be so proud of you."

Her face suddenly turned solemn and her voice grew soft. "*Tia* says we might be moving soon. I told her please, not before the play." Her black eyes became glossy with tears. "I like it here. I don't want to leave. Maisie is my *amiga*. My friend."

"Did your *tia* say why?"

"She doesn't say, but I know. It's because of the bad man."

"The bad man?"

I held my breath, anticipating what came next. A part of me wanted to put my hand over her mouth, tell her I was the wrong person to be revealing this to. But I also knew that if I shut her down, she might bury it so deep that it would be years before she dealt with what she saw.

Her voice was a whisper now. "The bad man who yelled at Walt."

"The bad man yelled at Walt?" I repeated, trying to keep my voice calm and even.

She nodded. "I was hiding in the water place." She pointed to the baptismal behind the choir loft. "I wasn't playing," she quickly added. "There was no water. I was just trying out the steps."

"It's okay," I said, putting my arm around her. "No one's mad that you were playing in the baptismal. Let's sit down a minute." I sat down on the kitchen floor, crossing my legs. She copied me, her little knees touching mine. "Tell me what you saw. I promise, you won't get in trouble."

She hesitated, obviously being told by her aunt to never answer questions to any person, especially an Anglo. They might be *La Migra*, the Spanish slang for Immigration, the bogeyman every undocumented Latino child learned about almost before they can talk. *La Migra* is more scary than any imaginary monster because green-suited officers can take your parents away.

"The bad man was loud, and his voice was mad. Walt said he was sorry." She looked from side to side, obviously uncomfortable with telling me this.

"Did you see the bad man's face?" I found myself holding my breath, waiting for her answer.

She slowly shook her head. Relief flooded my body. She crooked her finger at me to come closer.

"What?" I asked, dipping my head close to hear her tiny whisper.

"He said the *F* word." Her eyes were wide and shocked. "*Tia* says people who say the *F* word, their tongues will turn black and fall out."

I raised my eyebrows but didn't answer. If that were true, the streets in this college town would be blessedly quiet for a good long while.

"Did you see anything else?" I hated pushing her, knowing that it might bring back the memory of her seeing a man killed, but at the same time, she at least wouldn't have to bear the burden alone. And I'd protect this little girl with every ounce of my physical being.

She shook her head again. "I ducked down so the bad man couldn't see me."

Thank you, Lord. She didn't actually see Walt get killed. "Did you hear anything more?"

"They yelled some more. Then I put my hands over my ears because I was scared. After a while Walt didn't sing anymore. He always sang when he cleaned the pews."

I leaned closer and took her hands in mine. "Angelina, when you climbed out of the baptismal, did you see Walt?"

Her tiny hands were ice cold. She nodded slowly, her eyes blinking rapidly. "He was bleeding," she whispered. "I told him . . . I told him . . ." A sob caught in her chest. Behind me, the refrigerator cycled and turned on, its off-key hum loud as a swarm of bees in the quiet room.

"What?" I asked softly. "What did you tell Walt?"

She swallowed and said, "I said *te amo*, then I ran home." Tears caused her round black eyes to look like shiny little stones. "I wanted to tell Pastor Mac that Walt was bleeding, but he wasn't there. I told *mi tia* when she got home, and she tried to call Pastor Mac, but he wasn't home. I wanted Walt to have Band-Aids for his bleeding."

"Oh, sweetie," I said, putting my arm around her. "You did the exact right thing, I promise. You told Walt you loved him, and that was the perfect, perfect thing. Walt is in heaven now, and he'll always remember that you told him you loved him. That was the best thing you could have done."

She trembled under my arm, her head resting against my shoulder. I'd have to immediately tell her story to Gabe. There was too much of a chance the man who killed Walt would find out Angelina had seen him and would do something to silence her. We had to protect her.

We sat there for a moment, not talking. Her voice sounded almost normal when she asked, "Can I keep it?"

"Keep what?" I asked, confused.

"The wooden stick. It's *buena suerte*." She thought for a moment. "Good luck. Señor Walt told me."

I was still confused. "What wooden stick, Angelina? Do you have it with you?"

She nodded and stood up, reaching deep into her pants pocket.

"I've had it a long time, since two weeks. I carry it always with me."
She pulled out a small piece of unfinished wood.

I took it from her and looked at it closely. When I saw what it was,
I felt half-relief and half-despair. It was an unfinished tuning peg for a
violin.

CHAPTER 9

WHEN I HEARD THE VOICES OF KIDS BEING DROPPED OFF BY their parents, I asked, "Are you okay, Angelina Benita?"

A flicker of doubt ran across her face. "My *tia* said not to tell anyone."

"Don't worry," I said, standing up and holding out my hand. "You did the right thing telling me. Pastor Mac will talk to your *tia*. Can I keep your lucky wood piece for a day? I want to show it to Pastor Mac. I'll make sure and get it right back to you."

She nodded, taking my hand with a child's complete and utter trust.

As far as she was concerned, the problem was over. For me and a lot of others, it had just begun.

Hud was outside in the parking lot sitting on the tailgate of his truck talking to some parents. Mac's Explorer was parked in its normal spot so he must have arrived during the last half hour.

I told Angelina, "Go ahead and play with the others. I need to talk to Mr. Hudson." I walked over to him. "Can you stay out here a minute and watch the kids, Hud? I need to speak to Mac for a moment."

"Sure," he said, studying my face intently. His expression told me he knew that something was up.

Mac's office door was open, and he was sitting behind his big desk, a large book opened in front of him.

"Hey, Mac," I said. "You open for business?"

He looked up at me, his eyes crinkling slightly when he smiled. "Twenty-four hours a day, including Christmas and Easter."

I stepped inside and sat down across from him. "I don't have much time because kids are arriving and Hud's watching them alone, but I wanted to tell you that Angelina talked to me. She told me what she saw that night."

He nodded, setting down the thick, black pen in his hand. Next to him sat an open box of Wheat Thins and a sixty-four-ounce travel mug with "Grand Canyon Caverns" printed on the side. "I thought she might tell you or Dove if you were ever alone with her. She seems to feel safer with women. I can understand why."

"You realize we have to tell Gabe everything right away." I considered telling him about the tuning peg that Walt had given Angelina, but decided to tell only Gabe. I closed my eyes, dreading the emotional night ahead of me.

One hand came up to massage his temple. "Yes, I came to the conclusion that if she had information that would help find this person, we should try to find it out. We'll trust that Gabe will feel compassion and look the other way about their immigration status."

"I can't believe that would be his top priority. To be honest, I'm not sure she'll be all that much help in terms of identifying the killer. From what I gathered, she didn't see the man's face, just heard his voice." Still, there was the tuning peg, a twist in the case that didn't look good for Walt's reputation.

He picked up the yellow cracker box and closed the lid. "Why don't you call Gabe and have him come over to my office this evening? I'll bring Juana and Angelina here. It would be less intimidating than if the police, or even Gabe alone, showed up at their apartment. And I want to be there during the questioning."

"I agree. After rehearsal, I'll go by his office. I have some other troubling things I need to talk to him about."

"Anything I can help with?"

I hesitated, then said, "Not right now, but we may need your counseling expertise at some point. It has to do with his cousin, Luis."

Mac nodded, his expression completely serious. "We met the night Walt died. He and Gabe look a lot alike."

I ran my fingers across the top of Mac's name plate. "They *act* a lot alike. That's probably why they're snorting around each other like a couple of cranky bulls."

"About anything in particular?"

"Luis is going through some job and marriage problems that hit a little too close to home for Gabe. He's not happy with how his cousin is handling things. Luis is drinking too much. I imagine you've heard this same story a million times."

Mac scratched the side of his beard with the back of his knuckles. "Yes, it's more common than people know, even right here in the church. Maybe especially in the church. Let me know if you need intercession, but let's give them a chance to work it out themselves."

"You're right, but I'll keep your number on speed dial."

Dove finally arrived, late because of a flat tire that she insisted on changing herself instead of calling AAA. "They're too slow," she said.

We managed to run through the complete play without stopping. I made a point not to pay any more attention to Angelina than any of the other children, hoping that Hud wouldn't figure out that something significant was about to happen. But he knew me too well. Anxiety was obviously written all over my face. He caught me as I was heading for my truck.

"Wait a Texas minute there," he said.

"You'll stay until all the kids are picked up and my gramma leaves, right? Thanks, I appreciate it. I'm late for an appointment. Gotta go." I opened the truck's passenger door to let Scout jump in. I pushed past Hud and started around the front of the truck. By the time I reached the driver's door, he'd beat me there. When I went to open the door, he flattened his hand against the frame, keeping it closed.

"I don't have time for games, Hud," I said, yanking on the door.

"Neither do I. If you'd stand still for longer than two seconds, I've got something to tell you about Angelina."

I looked over at the children playing in the bright security lights that we'd turned on earlier than usual. Dusk was turning the sky a misty blue-purple, and the thick, humid air muted the sounds of children's laughter. I spotted Angelina on the grassy area in front of the sanctuary, her head bent toward Maisie's as they whispered little-girl secrets. Just like Elvia and I had.

I turned my eyes back to Hud. On his set jawline, there was a slash of dark red from where he cut himself shaving. "What?"

"Angelina told Maisie she saw something Saturday afternoon."

I didn't react for a moment. "What did she say?"

"She told her that a bad man hit Walt. That she was hiding in the baptismal."

I leaned against the truck and looked over Hud's shoulder. "I know."

"How long have you known?"

"Don't worry. Mac, Gabe, and I have it under control." Not exactly true, but it sounded good.

"I didn't want my daughter involved in this, but since she obviously is involved now, I need to know what y'all know."

"No." I hadn't told Gabe yet, so I sure wasn't going to tell Hud.

"I figured that's what you'd say. So I did a little probing of my own, but I'm not going to tell you anything I've found out."

"That'll help your daughter," I said, throwing up my hands in frustration.

Before we could continue, Maisie interrupted us. "Let's go, Daddy." She came up to him and leaned against his blue-jeaned leg. "Everyone's gone home, and I'm hungry."

Hud and I glanced over at the lawn. All the kids were gone, and Dove was getting into her truck.

"Where's Angelina?" I asked, looking over at the empty lawn. While Hud and I talked, she'd disappeared.

"Her aunt came and picked her up," Maisie said. "They're having burritos tonight. Daddy, can we have burritos tonight?"

"Sure," Hud said.

"See you tomorrow, kids," Dove called. "Same crazy time, same crazy channel."

"Yes, ma'am," I called back.

"Daddy, I'm hungry," Maisie whined.

"Get in the car, pumpkin," he said. "We'll leave in a minute. Right after I discuss something with Miss Benni."

She waved good-bye to me and skipped over to his Dodge truck, her coppery braids bouncing up and down.

"Hud, if you know something that could help find out who killed Walt Adams it would be dereliction of duty for you to keep it from me . . . uh, Gabe."

"Dereliction of duty? Fancy words."

"I mean it."

"Trade you." His face was stubborn.

"You are an immature brat."

"That's rich coming from you."

We glared at each other in a visual standoff.

He broke away first, turned, and walked toward his truck. "Jonathan Hammer," he called over his shoulder.

"Travis's dad? What about him?"

"Your turn," he said, opening his truck door. He mimed holding a phone to his ear. "Call me."

I watched him put his truck into gear and back up slowly.

"Jerk," I said out loud.

Jonathan Hammer? The attorney whose family donated the violin to the mission? The one who was so mad at Gabe? My hunch was that there was a connection between Walt Adams and the missing violin. Was it the reason he was killed? How was Jonathan Hammer involved other than being the person who donated the violin? Did Gabe know any of this? Surely if Hud did, Gabe did. I headed toward the police station. My husband and I were overdue for a long talk.

At the station, the front reception office was already closed so I called Gabe on my cell phone.

"Come around," he said. "The back gates are still open."

I went around to the maintenance yard where I waved to a couple of mechanics working on a patrol car and headed for the back door to the police station. It led into the lunch room, which was empty this time of early evening. In the next half hour or so it would be shift change, and things would become livelier, at least until everyone left in their patrol cars.

Gabe was sitting in his tall-back leather chair, his tie loose and top collar button open. The slight puffiness under his eyes told me he'd had a rough day. Unfortunately, now I was going to make it a little rougher.

"Hi," he said, not getting up.

I went over to him, sat down in his lap, and gave him a long kiss.

"Whoa," he said, after a few minutes. "You'd better stop or I won't be able to walk out of here without breaking some kind of indecent exposure law."

I laughed softly and stood up. "Have a bad day?"

He shrugged. "Not any worse than usual. How was yours?"

I leaned back against his desk, facing him. "Interesting. We just finished play rehearsal. I have some stuff to tell you."

His amiable expression didn't change. "Okay, what's going on?"

"Keep in mind I made a judgment call about when I should tell you all this. I was not deliberately holding back to annoy or one-up you. I am on your side. Remember that, okay?" I went around his desk and sat in one of his blue fabric visitors' chairs.

His face went from amiable to suspicious in a nanosecond. "What's this about, Benni?"

I started from the beginning and told him everything about Angelina's possible involvement, Mac protecting them, our suspicions, our fears, and as much as I could remember word-for-word of Angelina's conversation with me this afternoon. To his credit, he sat back, arms across his chest and listened to every word without interrupting once. I left out the comment Hud made about Jonathan Hammer. Bringing Hud's name into this right now didn't seem a wise thing to do. I'd try to work it into the conversation later. I ended with telling him my theory about one of my woodworkers being involved, and how it occurred to me that Walt might possibly be involved in the violin theft. I pulled the half-carved tuning peg out of my pocket and gave it to him. When I was finished, I waited while his eyes studied the wooden peg, his expression tense. I steeled myself for his explosion.

He just sat and stared at the peg until I thought I'd scream. Finally he said, "When are you going to start coming to me *first* with information like this?" His voice held no anger, no accusation.

I stared up into his cool eyes. "Truth?"

He gave a sharp nod. "Truth."

I inhaled deeply. "When you are no longer a cop and feel your first loyalty is to the letter of the law. I told you, it was a judgment call."

He pressed his lips together. "Fair enough. Why didn't you tell me last night? Or this morning?"

"Well," I said carefully. "Last night was a little tense, wouldn't you agree? And you rushed out so fast this morning that I couldn't. I've tried to get to you all day. I can't help it if you are so busy."

"No excuse. You could have told me you needed to talk about something important."

"Like I said, it was a judgment call. I didn't say it was necessarily the right one." Should I apologize? No, I decided. It truly was something I thought was the right thing to do at the time. I'd do it again, so apologizing would be phony. But I could try to ease the situation. "Friday, I'm sorry we don't see these things the same way. Really, I am."

Gabe sighed. "I need to talk to this little girl immediately."

"Mac said he'll bring Angelina and her aunt to his office this evening so you can talk to them. But only with him present."

Gabe's bottom lip stiffened. He resented being told what to do in his area of expertise, especially by another man, even if that man was his friend. This whole thing was getting a little too tree-marking, alpha-male for me.

"Can't we agree that the most important thing is keeping Angelina safe?" I said. "I don't want Angelina frightened any more than she already is."

He held my gaze. "As hard as this might be for you to believe, neither do I, Benni."

"Okay, let's just get it over with so we can go home." To what, I didn't know. I didn't have the heart to tell Gabe right at that moment that his cousin had left, but I'd definitely have to tell him before we headed home.

He called Mac and made arrangements to meet at Mac's office in an hour. While Gabe called the head detective to tell him all the things I'd revealed, I drove home, dropped Scout off, and fed him. I arrived at the church minutes before Gabe. Mac still wasn't there so we sat in our separate cars, both being stubbornly juvenile until he finally gave in and came over to my truck, sliding into the passenger side beside me. We sat there for a minute without speaking.

"I'm pretty aggravated at you," he finally said.

"Well," I said, staring straight ahead. "I don't know what to say except I'm sorry we're so different."

"But in the spirit of compromise, I'm going to tell you what we've found out about Walt Adams. We may not even need the little girl's testimony. We might already have another lead."

I turned and gaped at him. "You've known this for the last few hours and didn't tell me! That's cold."

His expression was triumphant and a tad superior. "It hurts when someone you love holds out on you, doesn't it?"

Touché. "Okay, so we're even now. Why won't you need Angelina's testimony?"

"I said may not. It depends on how this lead turns out."

"So what is it?"

"Walt Adams has a son," he said. No, he practically crowed it.

I couldn't believe the one thing I had actually *forgotten* to tell him would end up being my trump card. I hated doing it . . . well, no actually I didn't. I *liked* winning. "I know," I said smugly.

Chapter 10

"*Y*OU'RE JUST SAYING THAT TO ANNOY ME," GABE SAID.

"I am not! Joe Rodale told me. Well, he actually said that Walt said he was making a toy for his grandson. I didn't actually know he had a son, but if he has a grandson, then I'm assuming he had a son . . . or a daughter. But I have no idea who they are or where they live."

"Something I know that you don't. How nice considering *I'm* the chief of police."

"No need to get sarcastic. C'mon, Mac will be here any minute."

"Walt's son is named Kevin Adams. We found a letter from him in Walt's apartment. They were apparently estranged, though Walt was attempting to change that."

"Thus the toys for the grandson."

"Maybe. At any rate, according to our interview this afternoon with Kevin, Walt deserted him and his mother when Kevin was ten years old, and he's not had any contact with him since. That was a lie because in that letter he was asking Walt for money. The letter was dated six months ago. We also found receipts in Walt's apartment for money orders made out to Kevin Adams. One for eight hundred dollars, one for five hundred."

"Why would Kevin Adams lie about seeing Walt?"

"Who knows? He has a minor record. Arrested once for drunk driving, once for possession of an illegal substance. In his case, two ounces of marijuana. When the detectives pressed him on why he lied, he just said that his dad was a selfish jerk who deserved what he got."

"Nice," I murmured. "Do you think this devoted son could have killed his father?"

"There's no proof he was involved with his father's murder, but we're keeping an eye on him, trying to dig deeper. He has an alibi for the time the medical examiner said Walt Adams was probably killed."

"What was it?"

"He was at Trigger's drinking with his buddies. Two of them say he was there all night. Of course, they'd probably lie for him, so I'm not convinced yet he's in the clear."

My blood felt like frozen slush in my veins. Trigger's. A roughneck cowboy bar over by the bus station. It was the last place my first husband, Jack, had been seen before the auto accident that killed him three years ago.

"Trigger's has reopened?" My voice sounded raspy in the truck's chilly cab. The bar had closed a while back, shortly after Jack's death, something I privately cheered at the time. It was also a place that held a few memories for me and Gabe, though not especially happy ones.

Gabe nodded, watching me closely.

"When?" I asked, staring straight ahead. A wind had come up, and the top of the elm tree next to the church sign waved like hands at a parade. I was surprised I hadn't heard about Trigger's, that someone hadn't told me.

"A couple of months ago. I didn't tell you because . . ." He reached over and caressed my shoulder.

"That's okay," I said, turning back to him and laying my cheek on his cool hand. The hair on the top of his hand scratched my cheek. I closed my eyes and rubbed my cheek across his hand like a cat marking territory. "Is that all?"

"No," Gabe said, his voice sounding relieved. "There's one other thing. He also has an alibi with the bartender there, a Sheila Murray. But, like his friends, we're not sure we can trust it. She's Kevin's current girlfriend. She has a seven-year-old son, so maybe that's who Walt was making the toys for. As far as we can tell, Kevin has no children of his own. We found no records of any marriages."

I opened my eyes and straightened up. "So, what do you think?"

Gabe leaned back in the seat. "We don't know what to think yet. Those are just the facts we've come up with. I might find out more when I talk to this little girl."

"You said you might not need her."

"That's not definite. I'll know more after I talk to her."

Mac's Explorer pulled into the parking lot right then. We could see Juana and Angelina in his car. Gabe opened the truck door and stepped out into the cold night air.

"Friday," I said, putting my hand on his arm. "About their immigration status . . ."

A sharp wind blew into the cab, whipping my curly hair around my head. Gabe reached over, grabbed a handful, and held it out of my face. Then he leaned across the seat and kissed me gently on the lips. "Trust me, *querida*. I have no desire to hurt these people. I'm not with the INS. I just want to solve this murder. If you or Mac had come to me right when you suspected she was involved, I could have told you both that."

Feeling both relieved and ashamed for not trusting him, I climbed out of the truck and followed him to Mac's office.

"Great, we're all here," Mac said, nodding at Gabe as he unlocked his office. "Let's get out of this cold wind."

Once inside his office, Mac directed each of us to where he wanted us to sit. Gabe and me on the two visitors' chairs, Juana and Angelina on the loveseat next to the window. He pulled his own chair out from behind his desk so we all sat in a semi-circle facing him. I glanced over at Gabe and could tell he didn't like how Mac was directing this meeting, but we were on Mac's turf, so he didn't really have a choice.

Juana, a slender, copper-skinned woman with long, elegant hands and a braided bun, sat on the edge of her chair, as nervous as a sparrow. She glanced at Angelina every few seconds, her expression one of sheer terror. Angelina, on the other hand, knew all of us except Gabe, so she was probably the least nervous one in the room.

"Let's open in prayer," Mac said. He prayed quickly, part of it in passable Spanish. Juana crossed herself right after Mac said amen.

"Okay, let's get started," Gabe said. He looked at Mac, his voice neutral. "I think it might be better if I did this in Spanish."

"No problem," Mac said.

The questioning didn't last long, and Gabe's tone was gentle and nonthreatening when he talked to Juana and Angelina. But it was obvious by the woman's agitated demeanor that she was aware of Gabe's ability to take away their freedom.

From the moment Gabe spoke, Angelina stared at him. The aunt's obvious discomfort and fear of Gabe's position had not been missed by her niece. Angelina answered Gabe's questions with a frightened voice that often went so soft that he had to ask her to repeat her answers. She was only six, but she seemed to know that this man could change her life with one word.

"I think I have enough," Gabe said, standing up. "Mac, could I speak with you privately?"

They left the office, and I was alone with Juana and Angelina. I smiled at both of them. Juana shyly smiled back. Angelina, relieved now that Gabe had left the room, played quietly in the corner with the basket of toys that Mac always kept in his office. Except for Angelina's humming as she sang to herself, the only sound was the ticking of Mac's desk clock. Juana sat as still as a marble angel, her hands clasped tight in her lap.

Neither Gabe nor Mac was smiling when they came back a few minutes later, but I knew both these men and could tell neither was angry either.

"Ready to go, Benni?" Gabe said, holding out his hand.

"*Adios, señora,*" I said to Juana. "See you at practice, Angelina."

Juana nodded, and Angelina stared at Gabe a moment, her dark eyes unreadable, before she looked over at me and waved good-bye. Would she always be afraid of the police? I wanted to hug her and assure her that Gabe would never hurt her or her aunt, but did I really know what he would do?

At my truck, I finally couldn't hold out any longer. "What happened? What did you and Mac decide to do?"

Gabe opened the driver's door for me. "Angelina told me everything she told you. Mac and I decided that, for now, we're just going to keep what we know under our hats. I'll inform the lead detective, but until we have some idea who might have done this, we don't want it to get out that she was even there."

Dove's lifelong belief that a secret is a secret until two people know it came to mind. "Do you think that's possible?"

"Right now the only people who know are you, Mac, Juana, Angelina, and me. And they are very good at keeping quiet."

I hesitated, hating to bring Hud and his daughter into the equation. "A couple of other people know."

His eyebrows moved together into a frown. "Who?"

Reluctantly, I told him about Hud and Maisie. "You can't really get angry, because Angelina was just being a little girl, and actually Maisie did the right thing telling Hud."

Gabe inhaled deeply. "Why is it every time I turn around that guy is hanging around?"

"What's that got to do with protecting Angelina?" I was diverting, I knew, but it was also the truth.

"Nothing, it's just an observation." He looked up at the sky, black now and full of stars. The moon was a half-crescent, as pale as new butter. "I guess I'd better give him a call."

"You might want to ask him about Jonathan Hammer." There, I did the right thing and told Gabe something right away. Hud would kill me because I knew he was expecting me to track him down to find out what he meant.

He looked perplexed. "The guy who donated the violin to the mission?"

I nodded. "The one Luis protected me from the other day."

"What about him?"

"I don't know. Hud was taunting me with his name this afternoon, implying he knew something. I didn't feel like sparring with him to find out what it was. It might just be his usual baloney, but who knows?" I shrugged and slipped into the driver's seat.

"I'll call him when we get home."

"Okay." I closed the door, then rolled down the window. I had one more thing to tell Gabe that he wasn't going to like. "About Luis."

He leaned inside the window, resting his arms on the frame. "What about him?"

I curled my fingers around the cold steering wheel. "He left."

"Left? When?"

"This afternoon. I don't know where he went, though he promised he wouldn't leave town until he talked to you."

Gabe straightened up, cursing under his breath. "That's always been his M.O., running away when things don't work out his way."

I didn't say what I was thinking, that I actually understood why Luis left. Gabe was the type of man who inspired great passion and emotion in people. Wanting his approval or fearing his disapproval could often be an overwhelming experience. I'd seen it in his relationship with his son and his officers, and I'd felt it myself. When Gabe was angry, you received mixed messages making you feel like appeasing him and fleeing at the same time. There were times when I felt driven to move out of the cyclone of his emotion so it wouldn't consume me, buying myself some time and space to figure out how to love and live with this man. I understood why Luis might need the same before talking to his cousin.

"Well," I said, filling the empty air with meaningless words. "I'm sure everything will work out between you."

"Or not," he said, trying to hide his emotions.

"I'll see you at home, Friday," I said softly. "Drive safe."

He nodded and walked toward his car.

I arrived home minutes before Gabe. The answering machine was blinking with one message. It was from Luis.

"Hey, kids," he said, his voice a fake cheery tone. "I'm staying at the Almond Tree Inn on Marsh Street. Room 3112." Then there was a long pause. "Hey, I'm sorry for any . . . uh . . . hey, *primo*, call me, okay? We can grab a beer . . . uh . . . or a steak or something. That's it, I guess. Bye."

When Gabe walked in, I pointed to the answering machine. His face didn't change expression as he listened to Luis's message.

"Well?" I asked, watching him push the erase button.

He took off his jacket and started upstairs.

I followed him, Scout at my heels. "You're going to call him, aren't you? He seemed really sad when he left. He knows he screwed up. He wants to make things right with you."

He tossed his jacket onto a chair in our bedroom. "What makes you think that?"

I went over and picked it up, slipping it onto a wooden hanger. "Because I talked to him this afternoon. He apologized to me for calling me *querida*. He knew he made you mad, and he felt bad."

"He never apologized to me."

"Maybe that's why he wants to have dinner with you." I took off my boots and tossed them on the floor, annoyed at his reaction. "For pete's sake, he wants to make things right with you. You just got mad at him a few minutes ago for running away. You're not being logical. What he did and said doesn't merit the level of anger you're giving it. Why are you being so unforgiving?"

His back was to me while he unbuttoned his shirt cuffs. His words came out clipped and unemotional. "Because he slept with my wife."

CHAPTER 11

*T*HAT SHUT ME UP FOR A GOOD THIRTY SECONDS.

Gabe continued to unbutton his shirt, peeled it off, and tossed it in the clothes hamper.

It was disconcerting hearing the words "my wife" come from his mouth when he wasn't speaking about me. "What? He and Lydia? . . ." I couldn't say it.

He didn't answer while he took off his slacks. I stared at the large spider-web scar on his taut, runner's thigh, partially hidden by his black leg hair. A permanent souvenir from Vietnam. A French kiss from a Bouncing Betty, he would say wryly whenever I ran my fingers over it after we made love, the only time he would ever talk about his time in Vietnam.

"Lydia and I were separated, but not divorced," he said. "Granted, I was no angel myself, but at least I didn't sleep with family members. When he called you *querida* . . ." His voice faltered slightly. When he turned to look at me, his expression showed his pain. "It was like he was saying he could do it again."

I opened my mouth to protest, but he held up his hand.

"I know you wouldn't, sweetheart. It was just his implication, his reminder that he'd slept with my . . . with Lydia. . . . I know you've always thought it was my fault that Lydia and I split up. I let you think that. But it takes two, Benni. She did it to spite me and so did he."

"Why would he do that?" I whispered. "He's your family."

His mouth straightened out, his bottom lip hidden by his thick black mustache, a sign that he was very angry. "Who knows? He and I always had a competitive relationship. Because I became a cop like his dad, and Uncle Tony always sort of laughed at what Luis did for a living." He shrugged. "It's complicated."

Like family always is. I took a deep breath and said, "You never thought to share that information with me before he stayed here?"

His face went absolutely still. "Why would I? What purpose would it serve?"

"How about intimacy? How about the truthfulness you're always preaching that we should have with each other? There's also that little issue of trust that keeps cropping up."

"I need to shower," he said, his expression shutting down, his cue that he didn't intend on talking about this anymore. He walked into the bathroom, and I heard the shower start. When he got like that, there was no use wasting my time trying to force him to talk.

"Fine," I said to the empty room. "That's just fine."

I went downstairs while he showered, thoroughly annoyed, yet also feeling sad about what was happening between him and Luis. So, in the spirit of "performing the action of love and waiting for the feeling to follow" as Mac so often preached, I fixed his favorite Mexican cocoa, sweet and hot and strong with cinnamon and a touch of cayenne pepper, just like his papa used to make. When the shower turned off, I took a mug upstairs and set it on his night-stand.

"Thanks," he said, coming out of the bathroom, toweling his hair dry. "I think I'm going to read in bed."

I wanted to ask him if he was going to call Luis, but this wasn't the right time to continue the conversation. Maybe I'd stop by Mac's office tomorrow and ask him what he thought I should do. Maybe another man could give me insight into this emotional quagmire.

I puttered downstairs in the kitchen, allowing Gabe the space he needed right now. When I went up with another mug of hot chocolate, he was already asleep. I took off his glasses, kissed his forehead, and turned out the light. He murmured his thanks and turned over on his side.

It was only nine-thirty, and I was wide awake as a barn owl. After trolling the television stations and not finding anything interesting, I decided to go to bed early myself. I was locking the front door when my cell phone sang out from my purse. I caught it on the second "Happy Trails to You."

"Hello?" I said in a low voice.

"Hey, ranch girl," Hud said.

"How did you get this number?" I knew I never gave it to him.

"I'm a detective," he said, chuckling. In the background, high-pitched, Cajun music played. "I was wondering if you were wondering about Jonathan Hammer."

"I can't believe you are calling just to taunt me," I said, turning off the Tiffany floor lamp next to the front window. Before I closed the blinds, I looked across the street. My elderly neighbors, Beebs and Millee, were waltzing to some music I couldn't hear. Millee wore a hot pink feather boa. Beebs wore a flowery hat. I wished I was dancing with them.

"It's my life's mission. Did you tell Mr. Wonderful about Jonathan Hammer?"

"As a matter of fact, I did. He was going to call you tonight, but something came up. He'll call you tomorrow, I'm sure."

"Want to know what I know?"

Before Gabe knows was his implication. I groaned inwardly. He absolutely knew how to manipulate me. I should say no. This was wrong, and I'd have to tell Gabe that Hud called and that he told me the information before he told Gabe.

"Just tell me," I said, hating myself for giving in to temptation, understanding completely the old cliché about curiosity killing the cat. That darn cat just flat out couldn't help itself.

"I just love it when I have you over a barrel," he said, his laugh sounded tinny and faraway.

"I'm hanging up unless you tell me what you've found out about Jonathan Hammer."

"He has a child with Sheila Murray."

"So?"

"She's a bartender at Trigger's. It's a lowlife bar over by the bus station."

"I know where it is," I snapped.

He was silent a moment. "Did I hit a nerve?"

I sat down on our leather sofa, realizing the connection now. "She's dating Kevin Adams."

"Give the girl a kewpie doll."

I thought for a moment. Something else hit me. Travis Hammer was probably the "grandson" Walt had been making the toy for.

"I bet Gabe knows this already, but I'll tell him in case she managed to keep her relationship with Kevin from the detectives. They'll probably want to talk to her again."

"Doubt they'll get much. My sources say she's a tough one."

"Gabe's problem, not yours. I switched the cell phone to my other ear. "Look, you did your due diligence, now let Gabe's department take over."

"Due diligence? You're starting to sound like a real professional. But don't forget, I still have a stake in this. My daughter is involved."

"Only in a peripheral way. Just make sure she doesn't tell anyone about what Angelina told her. No one knows what Angelina saw except you two, Gabe's detectives, Gabe, Mac, and me. Gabe wants to keep it as quiet as possible to protect Angelina and, of course, Maisie."

He paused a moment, and I could almost make out the French words from the Cajun music. "You're right. I'll back off."

I almost fell off the sofa. "Excuse me, but unprotested cooperation? Being reasonable? Sir, what have you done with Detective Ford Hudson? You couldn't possibly be my crazy Cajun friend."

There was a long silence. "That's nice," he finally said, his voice uncharacteristically subdued.

"What?"

"It's the first time you've called me your friend."

There was another awkward silence. "Hud, I gotta go. Thanks for the information. I'll tell Gabe tomorrow morning."

"Sure thing, *catin. Tracasse toi pas.*"

"What?"

"Don't worry."

"You too." I pressed the cell phone's red END button and sat for a moment, staring at the floor, thinking about the turn our conversation had taken. Just when I wanted to strangle him, he said or did something that revealed his vulnerability.

I tucked the phone back into my purse and went up to bed, feeling so exhausted I wanted to sleep for a week. There were moments when I longed for my younger years when things were less complicated. But when I crawled into bed next to Gabe, his warm night-smell enveloping me, the cocky Marine bulldog tattoo on his back peeking out from under the quilt, I also remembered the passionate moments, the times of laughter, the joy and comfort of having this particular human being sleep beside me at night, and I was thankful that my life was exactly where it was at this moment in time.

NEITHER OF US BROUGHT UP LUIS AT BREAKFAST THE NEXT MORN-ing. When I saw Mac today I would mention what happened. Maybe he could talk to Gabe, help him sort out the situation with Luis. I had to admit, hearing that Luis had slept with Lydia when she and Gabe were separated changed a little about how I saw Gabe's cousin, but the Biblical story of the woman caught in adultery kept coming back to me. One of Jesus' best lines, I always thought, because who among us really could cast that first condemning stone?

"Are you and Mac okay?" I casually asked Gabe, refilling his coffee cup.

He looked up from the paper. "Sure, why?"

I set the carafe back in the coffeemaker. "Just wondering. I know he didn't handle the situation with Angelina the way you would have preferred."

A tiny muscle flickered at the top of his jaw. "No, he didn't. But he couldn't know that their immigration status wouldn't be a top priority with me. He thought he was protecting them." He ran his hand down his burgundy tie, smoothing it out. "Mac and I are cool."

"Good," I said, turning back to the stove to turn his egg-white and mushroom omelette. Maybe Mac could mediate between Gabe and Luis.

"What's going on with you today?" he asked.

"Same old thing. Going to the museum. Oh, I have to pick up a part of my costume at the historical museum. My corset is missing. I'll never fit into that dress without it."

Gabe's eyes lit up and he grinned. "Corset? The mental image of that is very intriguing."

"Words that can be spoken only by someone who *doesn't have to wear one.*" I tossed a red-checked tea towel at him. "If you're good, I'll let you tie my corset strings."

"I'd rather untie them," he said.

"Then you'd better be *really* good." I turned back to the omelette, not wanting him to see my face when I told him about Hud's call. "By the way, Detective Hudson called last night. He left some information for you." It was a pale ivory lie, but one, I justified, told in the interest of marital harmony.

"I didn't hear the phone ring," Gabe said.

"It was my cell phone. You were sleeping so peacefully. I didn't think it was important enough to wake you."

"What did he have to say?" His voice wasn't suspicious, so I obviously pulled off my little deception.

"Apparently Jonathan Hammer had a child with Sheila Murray, that bartender over at Trigger's who gave Kevin Adams an alibi. Did you all know she's his current girlfriend?"

"Yes. That's also why Kevin Adams's alibi is a little shaky." His face grew thoughtful. "I didn't know about her and Jonathan Hammer, though."

"It supports my theory that Walt's death might have something to do with the violin theft." I slipped the omelette onto a plate and set it in front of Gabe.

"We'll see," Gabe said, not as impressed as I thought he should be.

I buttered my sourdough toast. "It makes more sense than someone just breaking into the church and killing him."

Gabe cut a bite of omelette and gestured at me with his fork before putting it into his mouth. "Don't forget, sweetheart, his wallet was stolen."

"I know, but that could be a setup." As selfish as it was, I almost hoped that his murder was more than just a robbery gone bad. If Walt was involved in something shady, then it was just another robbery.

That meant any of us at church could have been the victim. None of us were safe.

"Sometimes," Gabe said, chewing thoughtfully. "Things are just what they are. I'll have a detective check out the connection, but we're also looking at local drug addicts and petty thieves."

After he left for work, I quickly dressed and headed for the folk art museum. Scout stood at the door waiting, his golden eyes begging me when I told him to go lie down. "Sorry, but I've got a million things to do today. You'd be spending your whole day in the truck and that won't be much fun." I gave him an extra dog biscuit and a quick noogie behind both ears.

On the way to the museum, I decided to swing by the new gift shop and see how preparations for the grand opening were coming along. Balloons, I added to my growing list of things to do today. I needed to order them and check on the cake I'd asked Stern's to make.

"Everything looks fantastic," I said a few minutes later, walking into the store. Almost all the arts and crafts were in place and Babs, the woman who'd volunteered to train the artists who will be working in the store, was giving a group of them a crash course on the electronic cash register. Each co-op artist would work five hours a week as their part in keeping the store running.

"Thanks," Babs said, obviously proud of her work. She'd been the key person in getting Local Hands organized because she once owned an art gallery in Scottsdale, Arizona. "I think we're as ready as we'll ever be. Look what your sweet cousin sent." She pointed over to a sinfully large bouquet of red and white, long-stemmed roses in a silver ice bucket. "He also sent over a case of very good champagne." She handed me a thick, ecru-colored envelope with my name written with a flourish across the front. The matching notepaper read, "Break a leg, sweetcakes. Put me down for one of your prettiest baby quilts (here's hoping). Love you, Emory."

"I'll have to drop by his office and give him a big hug," I said, smiling. That was just like Emory. "We can serve the champagne at the opening." Mentally I added ice and a plastic washtub to my list.

I was admiring a display of hand-sculpted, clay circus animals when I heard my stepson Sam's voice.

"Hey, Sam, what's up?" He was handing Babs a bright yellow flyer.

"We're already being asked to post fliers," Babs said. "Your stepmom's got the final say on who we support, Sam." She passed it over to me. "Think I should allow this one?"

"Ah, c'mon," Sam wheedled. "It's a good cause, and Elvia's posted one. You know how picky she is." In a college town, businesses had to be choosy about how many fliers they posted for "worthwhile causes," otherwise no one would be able to see through their front windows.

"I don't know. What's it for?" I asked, teasing him.

"The Amaizing Corn Maze over at the Reynolds Farm. The ag department at Cal Poly designed and made it, and the psychology and sociology students are running it. The food services and culinary departments are in charge of the snack bar. All the proceeds are being donated to Head Start afterschool programs." In an effort to convince me, he flashed the devastating smile he inherited from his father.

"Save the dazzling ivories for someone more susceptible, stepson," I said, taking the flier and laughing. "I've read about these. It sounds like fun."

"This one is so cool," Sam said, enthusiastically. "It's five and a half acres and has six miles of paths. It's five bucks a person, three dollars for kids, and we're even having Moonlight in the Maize on Friday and Saturday nights."

"What's that?"

"The maze is open until ten P.M. Bring your own flashlight."

"Sounds like a recipe for trouble to me," I said.

"Man, you sound like Dad," he said, rolling his dark brown eyes.

"Please, not that! Okay, we'll post it. Is there plenty of security at night?" I *was* beginning to sound like Gabe.

"Yep," he said, whipping a roll of Scotch tape out of his leather backpack. "As a matter of fact, I'm in charge of security."

"Sam, that's wonderful. Your dad will be proud."

"Don't tell him," Sam said, making a face. "He'll try to give me a bunch of stupid advice. I've got it under control. I've arranged to have some off-duty sheriff's deputies there, so I have it covered."

"Yes, sir," I said, saluting him sharply. "I'll keep all information concerning Corn Maze security on a strict need-to-know basis."

He gave me a halfhearted smile.

Gabe would likely be impressed that Sam was taking responsibility, though it might hurt him slightly that Sam went to the sheriff rather than Gabe's department. I could understand why his son would do so. Sam was trying to find his own way in a world where his dad was not only very prominent, but also too eager to give detailed advice.

"Why don't you come try it out?" Sam said.

"I'd love to, but my life is jampacked already. Give me another flyer, and I'll post it on the community board at the folk art museum."

"Great, thanks! See you later, *madrastra*." He barreled out the door with his handful of fliers.

After being assured by Babs and her trainees that my help wasn't needed, I started for my truck, then decided to take a detour and go by Emory's office to thank him in person for the flowers and champagne. His office was located on the second floor of one of the county's oldest brick buildings, and downstairs was now the Ross Discount Department Store. Boone's Chicken reception area, decorated in mission style, was quiet and empty except for the receptionist, a tough, sixtyish lady named Jolene who had upswept, red-orange hair the color of a smog-infused, Southern California sunset. Her protective, pitbull attitude toward Emory made me laugh, and my cousin sometimes flinch.

"She's great with solicitors," he'd said to me the first week she worked for him. "They *never* come back a second time." He grimaced. "But sometimes clients don't either."

"Guess a subscription to *Southern Lady* magazine wouldn't be a good Christmas present," I said.

"More like *Guns and Ammo,*" he said, chuckling.

He'd met her while writing a human interest story for the *Tribune* on women doing short time in the county jail. In self defense, she'd stabbed her drunk, abusive husband with a nail file, puncturing one of his lungs. An inexperienced public defender netted her some jail time, and when she got out, she remembered the respectful way Emory had treated her. She called him up asking for help finding a job. He hired her himself. She was born and raised in Blevins, Arkansas, and was a diehard Razorback fan, which, of course, completely and utterly endeared her to my cousin. They were, I would guess, the only two Razorback fans in San Celina.

"Hey, Jolene," I said. "Is the prince seeing any subjects today?"

"He's acting like someone peed in his grits," she said, raising one painted-on eyebrow. "If he don't straighten up, I'm taking away his hog hat."

"I'll warn him," I said.

"Go on back. Would you remind him he's got a conference call at two o'clock with his daddy and some fancy-pants banker from New York?" She turned back to her computer, where she had a serious game of poker going on with some scary-looking, artificial opponents.

"Sure thing."

I knocked softly on Emory's door, then walked in. His office was also decorated in cherry-stained mission-style furniture, but his obvious Arkansas roots were displayed through his extensive collection of Razorback paraphernalia, including his beloved custom-made hog hat with the flashing red eyes. Right now it was perched on the hat rack next to the door. He was leaning back in his chair, his eyes closed, hands in back of his blond head. He wore a pair of charcoal-colored dress slacks, a purple-and-gray tie, and a pale lavender shirt. His suit coat hung on the rack next to his hog hat and if I knew Emory, the suit was probably Hugo Boss or Armani and tailored to fit his lean body to the last quarter inch. He could have posed for a *GQ* ad.

"Hey, get your lazy butt to work," I said, sitting down in one of the visitors' chairs in front of his wide desk. The desktop was messy with files and papers. A can of Diet Coke sat next to his phone.

He opened his eyes and sat forward. "Hey, sweetcakes."

"How's things in the land of chicken parts?"

He groaned dramatically. "Who cares? I always swore I'd never go into Daddy's business, and here I am."

I looped my purse over the chair arm and grimaced at him. "The things we do for love. I have to go to cocktail parties and wear dresses. You have to peddle drumsticks."

His green eyes crinkled in amusement, and he took a sip of Coke. "It's worth it, though, isn't it?"

"Depends on what day you're asking me."

"Today?"

"Today, I'd say it's a toss-up."

"Trouble in the henhouse?"

I told him about Gabe and Luis's fight. Emory and I were as close as brother and sister, so I didn't hesitate telling him about Luis and his past relationship with Lydia.

"Sticky stuff," Emory said, his face serious now.

"Yes, and you'll be proud of me, I'm staying out of it."

"For the moment."

"Oh, shut up. I'll only get involved if they start screwing things up."

"Of course," he said, not even trying to keep a straight face.

I pointed a finger at him. "I wasn't asking your opinion, just telling you what was going on. I'm actually here for another reason."

"What's that?"

"First to say thank you for the beautiful flowers and the cham-pagne. In these days of women paying our own way and opening our own doors, you are still a Southern mama's dream."

He dipped his head in acknowledgment. "You're most welcome. What else?"

The second thing came to me when I saw Jolene. My cousin, in his short tenure at the *Tribune*, had acquired an amazing array of con-nections. It occurred to me that he might know a few interesting bits of information about Jonathan Hammer and his whole convoluted mess of relationships. Because of Emory's association with the paper and Gabe's intense animosity to journalists, Gabe didn't utilize Emory as much as he could. They liked each other and put family above their careers as much as possible, which meant when Emory was a journalist they never talked about their jobs at family functions. They continued that practice even after Emory stopped working for the paper.

"What do you know about Jonathan Hammer?" I asked.

"Why?"

"Tell me what you know first so I don't color your opinion with anything. Then I'll tell you why. Just trust me on this."

"Fair enough. He's a tax attorney whom I would never use because he tippy-toes a little too close to the governmental bonfire for my taste."

"How so?"

"He's just barely legal in his dealings with the IRS. He's always be-ing investigated, though he's never been charged. His clients know what they're getting when they hire him, someone who'll make sure they pay as few taxes as possible, but with the understanding that they could possibly be red flagged or audited. My guess is that he's probably always done shady things. He just hasn't been caught yet."

"He's also a jerk."

"There's that too. He could definitely use some pointers from Miss Manners. Sounds like you speak from personal experience."

I told him about the confrontation Jonathan, Luis, and I had at Blind Harry's.

"Good for Luis," said Emory, who would like anyone who stood up for me.

"That's all you know about him?" I said, disappointment in my voice.

"Let me see," he said, leaning back in his chair. It squeaked in the quiet room. "I've heard he's had some child custody problems."

"How would you know something like that?"

"His boy's mama is drinking buddies with Jolene. They used to tend bar together before Jolene was convicted. Sheila's come by the office a few times with her son. Jolene asked me some questions about custody rights. I put two and two together."

"Jolene is friends with Sheila Murray?"

"You know her name. Sounds like you've already been doing a little snooping. Does Chief Ortiz know?"

"As a matter of fact, he does," I said.

Emory threw back his head and laughed. "Liar."

"We're working together on this one. Sort of."

"Sort of?"

"I can't help but be involved, Emory. I found Walt, for cryin' out loud. And the little girl who—" I stopped, realizing too late I'd said too much.

"The little girl who what?" He pulled his chair close to his desk. "Sweetcakes, you're holding back on me. Give me the full scoop right now."

I groaned out loud. "I'm not supposed to tell anyone. You have to promise me you will not tell a soul besides Elvia about this. A little girl's life might be at stake."

His face became serious. "Benni, it's me, your cousin. No note pad or tape recorder."

"Yes, I know."

"Wow," he said when I finished. "Is there any way I can help?"

I stood up, hitched my purse over my shoulder. "Not really. I don't know why I'm even asking about Jonathan Hammer except there's just too much of a coincidence with all these people being connected."

"Agreed, but it's also, and don't smack me for saying this, it's Gabe's job to find out how."

I sighed, running my fingers through my tangled hair. "You're right, of course. Maybe that's why I came to see you. I needed to hear that from someone other than Gabe."

"On the other hand," he said, flashing me that mischievous smile that usually landed us in trouble when we were kids. "What if Mr. Hammer's ex-lover told more to a friend of a friend than she did a cop? If she's one of Jolene's pals, I'll bet law enforcement officers are not her favorite people. She might not be altogether truthful about every little thing."

"Emory Littleton! Are you encouraging me to question Sheila Murray without my husband's approval? Circumventing his investigation? Going behind his back?"

"No, I'm just saying what if?" The journalistic gleam of snagging the story first glowed in his green eyes. "I'll go with you."

"Go where?"

"Trigger's."

I drew in a sharp breath. It hadn't occurred to me to go to Trigger's to talk to this Sheila. I wasn't sure it was something I *could* do.

"What's wrong?" Emory asked, tilting his head.

"That's where . . . you know . . . Jack . . ."

He frowned, visibly annoyed at himself. "Sorry, forgot about that. Scratch that little field trip. You ought to just let it go."

"Yeah, I should."

He came around the desk and put his arm around me, his voice gentle. "I'm sorry, sweetcakes. You must be reminded of that day all the time. I didn't mean to do it again."

"I know." I lay my cheek against his shoulder. "Come by the grand opening tomorrow night. I'll save you a corner piece of the cake." The part with the most frosting was always his favorite as a kid.

❖

MINUTES LATER, I WAVED GOOD-BYE TO JOLENE, TRYING NOT TO think about her connection with Jonathan Hammer's ex-lover. But the nagging sensation that I should go talk to this Sheila followed me all the way down the steps to the street. Before I realized it, I had pulled into Trigger's gravel parking lot, a million emotions flooding through me at once, feelings I didn't like and couldn't control.

I sat in my truck and stared at the flat-roofed, cinder block building. Samuel Adams and Bud Lite neon signs glowed green, red, and yellow in the darkened windows. The parking lot was three-quarters full, the lunch crowd still lingering over their midday coffee or beer. They used to sell the juiciest beef dip sandwiches in town. It was the only reason I ever agreed to come here with Jack and his brother, Wade. Once upon a time, this bar was where all the county's young ranch hands and blue-collar workers met to watch a football game or rodeo broadcast, grab a beer, or play some pool with their friends. By the look of the beat-up trucks and cars surrounding me, it still attracted the same crowd, but there was also a sprinkling of brand-new SUVs and shiny Lexuses that told me, like the rest of San Celina, the upper-middle-class, ex-big-city crowd was moving in here, just like they had everywhere else. Soon, Trigger's would be a sports bar with only two country songs on the jukebox and twenty-three kinds of foreign beer on tap. But right now, it was still a place where cowboys gathered for a Coors, truck drivers met for a pastrami sandwich, and a dollar in the old jukebox bought you songs by George Jones, Dwight Yoakam, and Johnny Cash.

And it was still the last place my husband had ever been seen alive.

Listen to you, I scolded myself. You're as bad as Gabe. Jack was no longer my husband. Jack was dead. Gabe was no longer married to Lydia. He was married to me.

But our pasts really don't ever completely retreat from our memories, not even if bars close down, not even if ex-wives move away or remarry, not even if spouses die. Our pasts stick to us like dust mites, clinging to every tiny unseen hair on our skin. Our pasts stare at us everyday in the bathroom mirror, as real and tangible as the spider-shaped, Bouncing Betty scar on Gabe's thigh.

I stared at the unpretentious building, its past so wound up with mine. I was irresistibly compelled to go inside one last time. I wasn't exactly sure why. There were hundreds of places on the Ramsey Ranch where I could conjure up Jack, places more beautiful, places that meant more to us. No, it was more of a compulsion to be in the last place I knew for a fact he had lived and breathed. I'd never actually sought out the spot where they'd found his overturned Jeep out on old Highway One. Maybe I should. I understood why people built roadside shrines where their loved ones last drew breath. Trigger's was that for me, and I wanted to see it one more time.

I climbed out of the truck and weaved my way through the cars and trucks parked haphazardly in the newly paved lot. When I reached the door, it burst open and three UPS guys came out, laughing uproariously at some joke.

"Excuse me," the shortest one said, his black hair gleaming in the early afternoon sun. He held the door open for me.

"Thanks," I said, and stepped inside the dim, vinegar-scented room.

I stood there a moment, gazing out over the initial-scarred wooden booths, the crowded pool table, the yellow-and-red neon jukebox. My mind flashed back to a memory as strong as if I were watching it on the big-screen TV over by the tiny parquet wood dance floor.

The bartender, Floyd, interrupted me. "You got a visitor."

"What?"

"Cop." He spit into a white mug and gave me an annoyed look. "Had to tell him where you were. Told you I didn't want no trouble."

"Thanks for nothing." I turned and searched the noisy room for Ryan's stomach or Cleary's calm, dark face. How did they find me? No one could possibly have known where I'd been going.

"Okay, I give up," I said. "Where are they?"

"He." Floyd jerked his head toward a corner booth where a dark-haired man wearing a conservative gray suit, a crisp white shirt, and a furious expression stood up and crooked his finger at me.

The epithet I muttered caused the skinny cowboy standing next to me to burst out laughing. I was, obviously, going to be given the privilege of explaining myself earlier than I'd anticipated.

Walking slowly toward the man in the gray suit, I decided on the casual approach.

"Chief Ortiz," I said. "I hardly recognized you in your grownup clothes."

His facial impersonation of a mannequin impressed me, though I decided not to share that particular thought. He pointed to the seat across from him. "Sit down."

So much for the casual approach. I slid across the slick brown vinyl, avoiding eye contact. After he sat down, we played more of the silence game. While he worked at intimidating me, I occupied myself with studying his hands, which were tapping a soft cadence on his thick white coffee mug. They were huge, strong-looking, with short, neat nails, and though clean, stained black in rough crevices no soap can reach. A mechanic's hands. I looked up at him in surprise.

The expression on his face was unreadable. I refused to give in and look down, hoping my face didn't show the dog-caught-in-the-garbage-can look I suspected it held.

Finally he spoke . . .

"Are you all right?" A low, guttural woman's voice snapped me back into the present. She moved around me, touching me lightly on the shoulder as she did. She was short, like me, but had a curvier figure that she showed to its best advantage in skintight red Wranglers and a white, low-cut, lacy tank top. Her hair, a flat, deep brown had chunky streaks of bright gold color and was piled on top of her head in a deliberately messy topknot. "If you're looking for someone, honey, maybe I can help," she said in a friendly tone. "I've worked here for about a year now. I know all the regulars."

"No," I said, stuttering slightly. "I'm not looking for anyone. It's just this place holds some old memories for me."

She gave me a knowing smile. "Good or bad?"

I considered her question before answering. "Both, I suppose."

She nodded, gestured at me to follow her over to the bar. "That's the way life is, isn't it? How about I buy you a drink? You can sit and remember as long as you like. I'll make sure no one bothers you."

Following her over to the bar, I realized in a flash that there was a good chance I was talking to Sheila Murray. Though her physical appearance had never been described to me, I could imagine her and Jolene being friends. She had Jolene's same kind of seen-it-all persona.

"What would you like?" she asked, coming around the bar, tying on a clean white apron.

"Coke is fine," I said, slipping onto one of the swivel stools at the bar. I sat to the left of the bar taps. Two stools down, a gray-haired man wearing a faded "Built Ford Tough" T-shirt winked at me.

"Leroy, keep your eyes to yourself," the woman said. She half-filled a glass with ice and squirted Coke into it, rolling her eyes. She slid the drink in front of me.

"Thanks." I picked up the glass and took a sip, then decided to just go for it. "You're Sheila Murray, aren't you?"

"Yeah, I'm Sheila. How do you know my name?" She was still friendly, but her black-lined silver-gray eyes became wary.

"I'm—"

Before I could introduce myself, she interrupted me, snapping her fingers. "I know who you are! You're the police chief's wife! I've seen you in the newspapers. You're always finding dead bodies."

"Well," I said, feeling awkward. "I occasionally do other things too."

"Why are you *here*?" she asked pointedly. Her expression became guarded. "Did your husband send you to question me?"

I laughed out loud at that one, my hands nervously gripping my cold glass. "Not hardly. He'd find that hilarious."

She picked up a clean glass and started polishing it, something to occupy her hands while we talked. "I've seen you in the society pages at a few fancy-pants shindigs You always look like you're wearing shoes that are pinching the shit out of your feet."

I smiled at her, tracing a finger down the wet side of my glass. "I usually am. I hate that part of being a police chief's wife."

"So what parts do you like?"

I thought about that for a moment. "Not many, I guess."

She gave me an interested look, surprised at my candor. "So, out of curiosity, why did you marry him?"

That was complicated, so I fell back on making a joke. "He's not exactly ugly."

She nodded, touched her forefinger to her tongue, then to her Wrangler-clad hip, making a sizzling sound as she did. "Tell me, is he as good in bed as he looks like he might be?" Then she laughed at herself. "Shoot, listen to me. Asking the police chief's wife if he's hot in bed. I truly beg your pardon." Her wide grin said she wasn't begging anything from anyone.

I propped my elbows on the counter and said, "He's better."

"Hot dog," she said. "I'm glad to hear that. Sometimes the pretty ones are so busy admiring their own asses, they don't have time to look at ours. And, honey, your husband has himself a fine-looking one."

I just laughed. What could I say? He did.

I sipped my Coke while she walked down the bar asking the three patrons sitting there if they wanted refills. After pouring two more beers and a shot of whiskey, she came back to stand in front of me.

"Okay," I said. "I'm going to be straight with you. Would you mind if I asked you a few questions? I can't promise I won't tell Gabe what you tell me, but I swear I'm not out to mess anyone up. If you read the paper you know I found Walt Adams's body. I think he might have a bit of a connection with your ex . . . uh . . ." I faltered. "Jonathan Hammer. I just . . ." I thought for a moment, trying to word it right. "I want to see if I'm chasing my tail."

She slowly wiped the clean counter in front of me with a white bar towel. In the background, Elvis was singing about a rainy night in Georgia. The crack of cue balls sounded like tiny, sporadic gun shots.

"No skin off my nose," she finally said, rubbing a circle on the counter in front of me. "I already answered all the detectives' questions. I don't have anything to hide. Trust me, the same can't be said for my son's dear old dad."

"What do you mean?"

"Honey, he's a tax attorney. Enough said."

"Travis is in our play at First Baptist, isn't he?"

She nodded. "I don't go there, but his best friend, Salvador, does. It's nice for Travis to be with other kids. Nice kids. He's a good boy. He's turning nine this weekend. We're taking him and a bunch of his friends out for pizza and to the Corn Maze on Saturday night."

"I saw an advertisement. Looks like fun."

"Would be more fun if Jonathan wasn't going, but he's paying." She shrugged, her expression cynical. "Travis likes it when me and his dad do things together with him." She exhaled sharply, her hand rubbing the formica counter so hard I was afraid she'd wear a hole right through to the wood. "The things we do for our kids." She folded the towel and stashed it under the counter. "So, what else do you want to know?"

I sat there for a moment, flummoxed. Here was my opportunity, and I wasn't prepared. I actually had no idea what I wanted to ask. That, Gabe's smug little voice whispered, is why you should leave things like this to trained professionals.

"You're dating Kevin Adams, right?" I said.

She nodded. "So?"

"Walt Adams is . . . was his dad."

"Only by blood and nothing else according to Kevin. He hated the old man. Which was kind of sad, if you ask me. I understand Kevin being upset because his old man wasn't there when he was growing up, but at least the old guy was trying to make it up to him. Kevin's a decent enough guy, but he's kind of stuck sometimes."

"Stuck?"

"He gets some notion in his head and nothing, I mean, *nothing*, can change it. The old man tried to make things right, loaned Kevin money a couple of times, even made some toys for Travis. He acted kind of like a real grandpa, which is more than Jonathan's dad has ever done. He won't even acknowledge that Travis is his grandson except to call him Jonathan's little tax deduction. But Kevin wouldn't let Travis keep the toys. Said he didn't want Travis getting attached to some flake who'd probably up and disappear. I didn't think the old man would do that. Kevin was thinking about his dad when he was young and still drinking. But, I don't push it. I have enough problems of my own. Besides, Kevin can have a real temper, sometimes. You don't always know what's going to set him off."

The expression on my face must have changed with her last statement because her expression immediately closed down.

"He didn't have anything to do with his dad's murder," she said sharply. She pulled out the bar towel again and started polishing the chrome beer taps.

"I never said he did," I answered.

"Not in words." Her mouth turned down in a scowl. "Look, I told you Kevin's an okay guy. So he pops off once in a while. What man doesn't? He might cuss and yell, but at least he doesn't use me as his whipping boy."

"Like Jonathan did?"

"This conversation is over." She turned her back on me and started wiping the stainless steel sink.

"I'm sorry," I said, trying desperately to think of a way to turn our conversation back to its easygoing tone from a moment before. "I didn't mean to sound . . ." I couldn't think of the right word, so I let my sentence trail off.

"Look, all I'm saying is if you're looking for someone who'd beat an old man without thinking twice about it, check out Jonathan. Beating up on people weaker than him is right up his alley."

"But why would he kill Walt?" That was something that had never occurred to me.

She lifted a hand, unable or unwilling to explain further.

It didn't make sense to me. If Walt was the one who built the fake violin, why would Jonathan even have anything to do with it? Unless, it dawned on me, the violin was insured for a lot of money and Jonathan Hammer was the beneficiary. He could have paid Walt to make the fake. When Walt had a change of heart and wanted to confess his transgression to Mac, Jonathan killed him to hide the fact that he was involved. It wasn't a completely unbelievable scenario. It sort of fit with what Angelina heard.

Sheila leaned on the bar, resting her elbows on the counter. "I know the cops would rather blame it on someone like Kevin rather than a rich guy like Jonathan. If they start coming down on Kevin, then I'll talk to them."

"I'm sure that's not true." But even as I said the words, I knew there was some validity in what she claimed. I wasn't naive and had been around law enforcement long enough to know that, yes, prosecuting someone like Kevin Adams, a working-class man with no political connections and a checkered past, would be a much easier than going after someone with the money and political clout that Jonathan Hammer no doubt possessed.

"I may only be a bartender," she said, "but I'm not stupid. People from your side of the track are always wanting to pin stuff on people from my side."

My side, her side? How in the course of a few minutes had we gone from easy-talking girl buddies to adversaries from opposite sides of some imaginary train track? It made me uncomfortable and embarrassed that being the police chief's wife had somehow put me in this position, someone who would more than likely be the guest at a party where Sheila was hired to tend bar. I wanted to tell her that my first and only job before folk art museum curator was waiting tables at a truckstop cafe. Even that sounded like someone who was trying too hard to convince someone that they'd paid their dues.

I stood up, pulled out my wallet and put down a five dollar bill, not wanting her to feel like I was trying to get a freebie just because of who I was married to.

"I told you, it's on me," she said, pushing my money back at me.

"Look . . ." I started to speak, then stopped, unsure of what I could say that would ease this moment. "Thanks," I finally said, pocketing the bill. "For the drink and for your opinion. For the record, my husband is a man of integrity. He'll make sure that the investigation is unbiased."

Her black-lined eyes replied that she had a beach house in Tucson she'd like to sell me.

Though I knew it would probably annoy her even more, I felt compelled to ask one more thing. "I'm curious. How in the world did you end up having a child with a jerk like Jonathan Hammer?"

She gave a quick, staccato laugh. Her chunks of dyed hair gleamed under the bar's gold-tinged lights. "There ought to be a warning label on rum bottles. 'Danger—Overindulgence could result in unwanted pregnancy.'" Her face softened. "Don't get me wrong. I love my boy. I just wish he had a different father." She shrugged one shoulder, then walked down the bar to check on the other patrons.

When I stepped out of the dimly lit bar into the crisp autumn afternoon, the sun seemed particularly bright. The parking lot gravel crunched under the heels of my boots like rice cereal—snap, crackle, pop. Even this parking lot held memories for me. The first time I'd seen Gabe's gentle side was here. I closed my eyes and remembered the feel of his strong hand on my upper arm, keeping me steady when memories of Jack had flooded back and overwhelmed me. So many memories of Jack were now layered with memories of Gabe.

I was so lost in my thoughts that I didn't realize the man passing by me in the parking lot was speaking to me.

"Mrs. Harper?" he said.

I glanced up, startled. "Yes?"

The man, an average-looking guy with shaggy blond hair, wore a white T-shirt, blue jeans, and black motorcycle boots. His red baseball cap advertised Coca-Cola. He looked like any construction worker or truck driver from anywhere.

"I know you from the newspaper," he said.

I felt my face start to warm. How was I supposed to answer that?

"You found Walt Adams's body."

"I'm sorry, I'm late for an appointment," I said, starting toward my truck. I wasn't in any mood to talk to a nosy bystander.

"He was my father," the man said. "Or that's what he liked to think."

That stopped me. I turned slowly around. "You're Kevin Adams."

He nodded. "What're you doing here?"

There was an awkward pause.

"Crap," he said, his mobile face starting to grow angry. "You were talking to Sheila, weren't you? Look, I've talked to the cops and told them I had nothing to do with Walt Adams's murder. Did your husband send you out to do a little snooping behind my back?"

I gave a small laugh. "Hardly."

"Then why are you here?"

I looked into his pale blue eyes. "I didn't come here to question Sheila. I . . . my first husband used to come here. I drove by on a whim. Your girlfriend happened to be here, and I asked a couple of questions. No big deal."

"It's a big deal to me," he said. "And I don't believe you."

I shrugged. "Sorry, but it's the truth."

He stood there for a moment looking at me, struggling with what to say or do. "I have an alibi. I told the cops that. I had nothing to do with Walt's death."

"You mean your father." The minute I said it, I knew it was a mistake.

He pointed a calloused finger at me. "He was nothing to me. Nothing."

I thought of Walt, his kindness and gentleness. At least the Walt we at First Baptist knew. How could he have inspired this kind of anger? Can a person really change that much or was the Walt we saw just an act? It all boiled down to whether you believed people could change or not. I believed they could. But the consequences of our sins follow us, even after we've repented and changed. That was reality. That was what might have killed Walt Adams.

"I'm sorry," I said softly. And I was. For Kevin and for Walt.

My apology seemed to deflate his balloon of anger. "Just stay out of it," he said. "Please. We have enough problems." Then he moved passed me and went into Trigger's.

Driving to the church for rehearsal I thought about what I'd learned from Sheila Murray. I would tell it all to Gabe the minute I saw him tonight. With what was going on between him and Luis, we didn't need any more secrets that would cause conflict between us. He'd be annoyed that I went to Trigger's and questioned Sheila, even more annoyed when he heard about my encounter with Kevin Adams. That I could handle.

Still, I might have learned something they didn't know, Jonathan Hammer's physical abuse of Sheila and her assertion that he was capable of killing. It did show a pattern of violence.

I glanced at my watch. Three P.M. Great, I was due right this moment at the church for play rehearsal. Dove was going to wring my neck.

It was fifteen minutes after three when I arrived at church. Except for Mac's blue Explorer, the church parking lot was empty. Where was everyone? My heart beat faster. For the first time I realized how nervous Walt's death had made me, how it had changed the way I felt about the church grounds.

Wishing I had Scout with me, I hesitantly walked around the side of the church building to the outside door of Mac's office and knocked softly. No answer. After a minute or so, I knocked louder. Finally, he opened the door.

"I'm sorry," he said, his eyes squinting in the afternoon light. "I didn't hear your knock at first. I was in the church praying."

"Oh, I'm sorry," I said, embarrassed to have caught him at such a private time.

He rubbed his eyes, his big chest inhaling deeply. "It's okay. What can I do for you?"

"I thought there was a play rehearsal today, but no one's here. Is everything okay?"

He opened the door wider and stepped out onto the sidewalk. "Dove forgot she had a mammogram appointment. She called all the parents late this morning. She said she contacted you."

"Shoot, it's probably on my cell phone." I dug through my purse and sure enough, there was her message. "She must have called when I was out of range." I slipped the phone back into my purse. "Sorry to interrupt you."

"No problem. I have someone coming at three-thirty anyway."

"Okay, then I'll get going."

Mac went back inside his office, and I walked over to my truck. I sat there for a moment and listened to Dove's message, which had been recorded at ten-twenty this morning. I called her back and verified when our next rehearsal would be.

"How was the mammogram?" I asked.

"Like someone drove over my bosom with a dump truck full of gravel," she grumbled.

After sympathizing for a few minutes, I hung up. I was buckling my seat belt when a car pulled into the parking lot. Mac's appointment. It was a black sedan, and the driver pulled up on the other side of Mac's car. A blond, middle-aged man stepped out. He was dressed in dark slacks and a pale yellow dress shirt. He walked toward Mac's office, favoring his left leg. He glanced briefly at me and his agitation showed in the tightness of his jaw.

When I drove by the man's car, I glanced at the license plate. The frame advertised "Lyle Roberts Ford Dealership, Bakersfield, California." Obviously not a local. Everyone who bought a Ford in San Celina went to Bellamy's Ford dealership next to the Snak 'n Chat diner on Madonna Road. It was obviously Mac's counseling appointment. I didn't envy Mac his job. It reminded me a lot of Gabe's career as a law enforcement officer, he so often saw people at their worst. How did Mac manage to stay so easygoing?

I arrived home before Gabe and decided on making one of his favorite home-cooked meals to soften him up before I told him about my afternoon conversation with Sheila Murray. It was such a cliché to manipulate a man by appealing to his stomach. Nevertheless, it always worked.

When he sat down to a hot steaming plate of shepherd's pie made with fluffy mashed potatoes and all his favorite vegetables, he was, thankfully, clueless. He just ate his dinner with a weary expression on his face. Had he talked to Luis today? That was something else we needed to discuss tonight.

"Great dinner, sweetheart," he said, clearing the table afterwards.

"Thanks. I had time to cook because play rehearsal was canceled. Dove forgot she had a mammogram appointment, and you know how hard those are to reschedule. We'll be meeting for an extra-long rehearsal on Monday because it's a holiday."

"Holiday?" he asked, opening the dishwasher.

"Veterans Day, remember? Before you know it, it'll be Thanksgiving, then Christmas."

"Where has this year gone?" Gabe said, shaking his head and scraping a plate off into the sink.

"I have no idea." I leaned against the edge of the sink. "Have you and Luis talked?"

He kept scraping the already clean plate. "No."

"Don't you think you should?"

"Don't start with me, Benni. I'll call him when I'm ready. Let me handle my cousin. I know him better than you do."

I didn't answer, turning around to look out the kitchen window. Anything I said would start a fight.

Gabe came up behind me and circled me with his arms in silent apology. I rested my chin on his muscled forearm, the coarse arm hair tickling my skin. We were silent for a moment, the warmth of our bodies melding into each other.

"I didn't mean to snap at you," he said, burying his face into my hair. "It's just complicated, the relationship between me and Luis. I'll talk to him soon. I promise."

I turned around and burrowed into his arms, laying the side of my face against his chest, listening to the steady thump of his heart. "I know I don't understand everything that has happened between you two, but I do know one thing. You love him like a brother, and it's hurting you by not forgiving him."

"I'll take care of it," he said, taking my face in his hands.

I nodded, accepting the kiss he gave me sealing his promise. The groan deep in his throat when we kissed hinted that we might be going to bed early tonight. Though that was definitely appealing to me, I also knew that I had to tell him what happened at Trigger's today, and that waiting would only make him angrier. It would likely squelch any romantic plans he was contemplating. Should I wait until after we made love? That seemed even worse than waiting until tomorrow.

He stopped in the middle of our kiss and said, "Somehow, I get the feeling you are thinking about something other than kissing me."

"Before we get too involved, I need to talk with you about something."

He dropped his hands from my face to my shoulders, holding me at arm's length so he could look directly into my face. "What did you do that is going to make me angry?"

"Sit," I said, moving out of his grasp and pointing to a kitchen chair.

Pacing the kitchen floor, I told him about my compulsion to drive by Trigger's, my conversation with Sheila, and my encounter with Kevin Adams. When I finished, he sat for a moment, staring at his hands, which he'd folded when I'd started talking and never moved an inch the whole twenty minutes it took me to tell my story.

"Well?" I prodded him.

He looked up from his hands to my face, his expression unreadable. "Well, what?"

"Aren't you going to say anything?"

He sat back in his chair and folded his arms across his chest. "You already know what I think."

"Yes."

"Then there's no use saying it again."

That made me nervous. "What do you think about Jonathan Hammer abusing Sheila?"

"I'll inform the detectives."

"What about Kevin Adams?"

"We're already investigating him. I don't like the idea that you're asking his girlfriend questions, that you are involved in this in any way, but you can't seem to help yourself. I'll do my best to protect you, but . . ." He held up his palms, his face apparently unconcerned.

I sat there for a moment, confused. I'd grown to expect his dramatic emotional outbursts. What did this mean? Didn't he care as much as he used to? Was he doing this to make me squirm? Reverse psychology? If it was the last one, I hated to admit it, but it was working.

"Enough about these people and their problems," he said, standing up and holding out his hand. "Let's go to bed."

"Okay," I said.

Upstairs, under the down comforter, we faced each other. He ran his hand down the side of my body, his fingers lingering on my thigh, then moved down to caress the damp small of my back. His hands pulled me closer, the hard and soft lengths of our bodies touched, and I closed my eyes, wanting to just give in to his touch. He started kissing my neck, moving lower, his lips and breath warm, but as tempting as they were, I couldn't stop thinking about how he reacted, how out of character it was.

"Gabe, I can't do this," I whispered, running my hands down his smooth back.

"Sure you can," he murmured against my chest.

"No." I struggled out of his arms and sat up. "Why are you acting so nonchalant? You're acting like you don't care if I get hurt."

He rolled over on his back, bringing his hands behind his head and stared at the ceiling. "Truth?" he asked after a minute or so.

"Of course," I said, exasperated.

"I would love to lock you in our bedroom and wear the key on a chain around my neck. But . . ." He sat up and looked over at me, resting his elbows on his bent knees. Though his features were indistinct in the dim moonlight filtering through our curtains, I knew every line and plane of his face. "I also want to make love to you tonight. If we kept talking about this whole mess, I would get angry and yell. You would yell back, and we would fight, and then maybe we would have sex, but we wouldn't make love. I want to make love."

"Oh," I said, feeling embarrassed.

He reached over through the darkness and drew one finger down the length of my jaw, down my neck, and over my left breast. "So, can we fight about this tomorrow?"

"Yes," I said, closing my eyes, his touch mesmerizing me, his husky voice seducing me like a familiar song—"*tu eres mi amor, te amo, te adoro, te amare para siempre, mi vida, mi vida, mi vida . . .*" Eventually, he rolled on top, pinning me under him, his strong thighs holding me captive.

Afterward, we lay there watching the shadows the tree made against our bedroom wall. It was windy tonight, and the pattern of the tree limbs changed every few seconds.

"So," he said, twirling a strand of my hair around his finger. "How was it?"

I gave a low laugh. "On a scale of one to what? It was an eleven out of ten, okay?"

"No," he replied. "I mean Trigger's."

I was silent for a moment. Like Vietnam for him, Jack was a subject I rarely talked about to Gabe. I don't know why, partly because

of worry that he would be jealous, as he definitely was early in our relationship, partly because I just didn't like remembering how Jack
died, but also because they were memories that were mine alone, and
I didn't want to share them, not even with Gabe. The last time we
talked about Jack was when I found his journal, and we discovered a
weird connection between him and Gabe. It was so emotional that we
never spoke of it again.

"It was okay," I said. "I . . . it did bring back memories. Trigger's
looks a lot the same inside."

His hand let loose of my hair and stroked my cheek. "I'm so sorry,
querida."

"For what?"

"That you had to have such sadness in your life. It pains me to
think of you . . ." His voice grew hoarse. "I remember how you
looked in the parking lot of Trigger's back when we first met. I remember thinking I'd never seen anyone look so sad. And that I wished
there were someone who felt like that about me."

I took his hand and touched my lips to his warm palm. "There is,
Friday."

CHAPTER 12

"So what do you think I should do now?" I asked the next morning while eating a bowl of Lucky Charms.

"Stay out of it?" he suggested, spreading fat-free cream cheese on his raisin bagel.

I smiled at him. "You look so handsome this morning. And so relaxed."

He sighed. "Tell me everything. Be careful. Try to stay out of trouble."

"Trouble? Me?" I feigned astonishment as I took my empty bowl over to the dishwasher. "Not a chance. *I'm* a good girl."

"If I had half a brain," he said, his voice good-natured. "I'd have slapped cuffs on you a long time ago."

"Ummm," I said, sitting down on his lap. "Big strong policeman. Can I see your nightstick?"

"Don't push your luck, *chica,*" he replied.

"The new museum store has its grand opening tonight at Farmers' Market. Can you stop by?"

"I'll try," he said. "But don't count on it. I'm swamped at work."

"I'll save you a piece of cake anyway. Only because you're such a darn good kisser."

I WALKED DOWNTOWN AND SPENT THE BULK OF THE DAY HELPING Local Hands get ready for the grand opening. At a quarter to five, right before the doors opened, Gabe called me on my cell phone. I could barely hear him through the exuberant chattering and laughter from the number of co-op members, their families, and friends crowded into the small store.

"What?" I yelled into the phone, finally stepping outside in an attempt to avoid the noise. The cacophony from Farmers' Market wasn't much better.

His voice was indistinct and fuzzy. "I'm sorry, sweetheart, but I can't get away. Something's come up. I won't be home until about nine or so."

"That's okay," I said loudly, resisting the urge to ask if it had anything to do with Walt's murder or his cousin.

"I'll see you later," he said and clicked off.

After a spirited series of grand-opening speeches, Local Hands officially opened its doors. For the first two hours we were swamped with customers. Though we couldn't expect it to always be this crowded, it was a good sign this shop wasn't a foolish venture. After I sold my second log cabin quilt, Babs came by and said, "Why don't you take a breather?"

"I'm taking you up on that offer," I said. "You can do the same when I get back."

"Me?" she said, grinning. "Are you kidding? I love this. Haven't felt this energized since I closed my gallery."

I walked onto crowded Lopez Street, which was cordoned off for six blocks for Farmers' Market. Because of the Central Coast's temperate climate, the vendors carried most fruits and vegetables all year round, but there were always seasonal specials. This cool evening in November featured piles of winter squash, cucumbers, peaches, walnuts, and zucchini. Tomatoes and strawberries were available, though not in the quantity or size available during the hot summer months. I lingered at a stall selling peaches, their ripe, perfumed scent seducing me. I inhaled the heady scent, reminded of lazy afternoon barbecues and the sensuous feel of sun on my bare shoulders. Unable to resist, I bought the whole bag and bit into one, imagining hot peach cobbler topped with half-melted, homemade vanilla ice cream.

"The color of your hair," Hud said behind me.

I jumped, startled by the sound of his voice. "What? Oh, hi." I took another bite of my peach. "What did you say?"

"That peach. It's the same color as your hair."

I studied my half-eaten peach's fuzzy, red-gold skin.

"What's going on with the Adams homicide?" he asked, grabbing a peach from my bag.

"Not much. How's Maisie?"

Hud took a bite out of his peach. "She's fine. What's happening on the Adams case?"

I almost replied nothing again, then changed my mind, gesturing at him to follow me. I really had no reason to hide anything from him since Gabe knew everything now and, frankly, an unbiased but trained opinion was something we could always use. I led him to a less crowded side street, where we weren't likely to be overheard. Then I told him what happened between me and Sheila Murray, Kevin Adams, as well as my suspicion that the stolen violin was somehow involved.

He listened without interrupting. When I finished, he said, "So, what does Mr. Wonderful think?"

"Gabe said he'll tell his investigators."

"Great, we can all sleep safer in our beds tonight."

I pressed my lips together, angry at his sarcasm. "I gotta go, Hud. I just told you what was happening because you're so worried about Maisie." I started to walk away, but was stopped short by his hand gripping my upper arm. "Hey!"

"Wait, I'm sorry," he said. "I'm being a jerk. Thanks for telling me what's going on. It does make me feel better to know."

"Daddy!" Maisie's voice rose above the insect buzz of Farmers' Market. "We've been looking for you! Mama said you were lost!" She ran up, her tiny freckled face painted on one side with green and gold sparkly stars. Angelina was behind her, her face painted in a similar fashion, but in reds and oranges.

"I'm not lost," he said, laughing when she threw herself at him, hugging him around the thighs. "You're lost. I'm right here with Benni."

"I'm not lost, *you're* lost!" Maisie repeated, giggling.

"Hey, Maisie, hey, Angelina," I said. "You all having fun?"

"Yes!" Maisie yelled out confidently. Angelina nodded, her face beaming. She held a peanut-covered caramel apple with one small bite in it.

"Girls, I told y'all not to run too far ahead of me," a woman's voice called out in a soft Texas twang.

"We found Daddy," Maisie called back. "He said he wasn't lost, but I said he was, but he said he was with Benni, but I still think he was lost."

"What was that?" the woman said, laughing, appearing from behind a man holding a huge bouquet of colorful Mylar balloons.

"We found him, Mama! We found him!" Maisie jumped up and down. Angelina silently mimicked her, gripping her caramel apple tight in her small hand, her smile white and carefree. I was glad to see her relaxed for a moment, able to be just another little girl at Farmers'

Market, not someone who had to worry about *La Migra*, going on the run, hearing someone murdered.

"So you did," said Maisie's mother, walking up to us.

I stared at her, then glanced over at Hud, surprised. He smiled at me, his face relaxed and uncomprehending.

The physical resemblance between us was remarkable. She was my height, though more delicate-boned, had reddish-blonde, curly hair, and toffee-colored eyes. She dressed more uptown than I did, expensive, black tailored slacks, a sage-green cashmere sweater, and black leather flats.

"Hey, y'all," she said, smiling at me and Hud. She held out her hand. A gold charm bracelet tinkled. "I'm Laura Lee Hudson. Maisie's mom."

"Hi," I said, taking her hand. "Benni Harper."

"It's so nice to finally meet you," she exclaimed, her handshake firm and confident. "I've heard so much about you from Hud and, of course, from Maisie. That's quite a task you and your grandmother have taken on, keeping *Pilgrim's Progress*, well, progressing." She gave a low, pleasant laugh. "I used to be a third grade teacher. Y'all are brave women."

"Maisie's doing a great job," I said, immediately liking this woman. "It's been fun, most of the time."

She touched a manicured hand to her cheek. "I think it's good for the kids to keep going despite . . ." She paused, glanced over at Hud, who'd been uncharacteristically quiet. "Despite the difficulties."

"Mama, can we buy a balloon?" Maisie asked, pulling on her mom's sweater.

"Sure, baby," she said, opening her compact black purse.

"I've got it, Laura Lee," Hud said, pulling a ten dollar bill from his jeans and handing it to Maisie. "Get one for Angelina too, pumpkin. And stay where we can see you."

"Okey-doke." She grabbed Angelina's hand and pulled her over to the balloon man a few feet away.

"Benni was just telling me what was going on with the investigation," Hud said.

"Anything new?" Laura Lee asked, her light brown eyes widening.

"No, not much," I said, wishing he hadn't said anything. "But Gabe has his best investigators working on it. I'm sure the kids are safe."

She pushed up the sleeves of her sweater, her charm bracelet tinkling again. "I'm confident they are. Though I, along with most of the parents, am relieved to have Hud at the rehearsals." She smiled at her ex-husband.

"Yes, me too."

There was an awkward silence between the three of us until Maisie and Angelina came running back. Maisie held a Mickey Mouse balloon and Angelina had chosen one that looked like a daisy.

"Here, Daddy," Maisie said, handing him the change.

"Thank you, Mr. Hudson," Angelina said softly.

He stooped down until he was eye level with her. "You're welcome, Angelina. Are you hungry? How about a barbecued turkey leg?"

Her eyes grew wide, and I hated to think that food, something I took for granted, could seem so wonderful to her.

"I'll take them, Hud," Laura Lee said, glancing over at me. "You finish your conversation with Benni." She smiled at me again. "It really was a pleasure to finally meet you."

"Nice meeting you too." I held up my hand in good-bye.

"She's nice," I said after his ex-wife was out of hearing range.

"Yeah, she's a real lady," he said, sticking his hands in the back pockets of his jeans. "Too good for me, without a doubt."

I didn't answer, not wanting to tread upon the choppy waters of old marital rifts. A change of subject was definitely in order. "It's kind of you both to include Angelina. She looked like she was having a good time."

"Mac found out she'd be home alone tonight, so he asked me to keep an eye on her. He had a couple of hospital visits to make."

I stared at him a moment, surprised. "Oh, I didn't realize you and Mac, uh . . . talked."

"You don't know everything that's going on, *chere*. Mac's a good guy."

"Yes," I agreed. "He is."

Subtle frown lines creased the skin between his dark eyebrows. "Don't be getting any ideas. He's a good guy in spite of what he does for a living."

"He could say the same about you."

His face smoothed out, and he laughed. "Yeah, I guess he could."

"Angelina seems real comfortable around you."

He kicked the ground, acting like a hayseed. "Shucks, little missy, I've always been good with kids."

"No, Hud, I'm serious. It's weird."

"Why? I'm a nice guy."

"It's not that." I shook my head, remembering how fearful she'd been around Gabe the other night. "Usually kids like her are nervous around any kind of law enforcement."

He shrugged. "I guess to her I'm Maisie's daddy before I'm a cop."

"Maybe so." I glanced at my watch. "I need to get going. I'm on break from the new museum store."

Despite the amount of people outside at Farmers' Market, Blind Harry's was relatively uncrowded.

"Is Elvia here?" I asked one of the clerks. She'd been at the opening of Local Hands, but she'd left early.

"You just missed her. She left about ten minutes ago. Meeting Emory for dinner."

"Thanks." I went downstairs, ordered a turkey sandwich and a lemonade, and sat at a table in the back perusing the latest issue of the *San Celina Free Press*. There was an exposé on a local ice cream parlor that put more butterfat in their ice cream than advertised. Not the crime of the century, but interesting enough to read while eating my solitary meal. I'd almost finished the article when Luis came down the stairs.

"Hey, Luis," I called when he reached the bottom step.

He came over to my table. "Hi, Benni. What're you doing here?"

I pointed down to my empty plate. "Having dinner and taking a break from working at the new folk art museum store. It's our opening night."

He stood looking at me, his hands deep in the pockets of his tan chinos. He was wearing an expensive-looking nubby brown sweater and appeared every inch the successful, middle-aged businessman. Had Elvia been here, they could have posed for a magazine spread portraying the perfect, upwardly mobile Latino couple.

"That's great," he said. "You must be excited." His words were polite, but the tone of his voice told me his thoughts were elsewhere.

"Why don't you join me? I'm going to sit here a few minutes."

He hesitated a moment, then said, "I think I will."

After ordering a double espresso, he sat down on the straight-back library chair across from me. His troubled expression was eerily reminiscent of what I'd seen on Gabe's face so many times.

"Have you seen Gabe today?" I asked bluntly.

He shook his head. "He called me at the hotel. We're meeting for a late dinner."

"Oh, that's good."

His expression remained troubled. He stared at his hands wrapped around his espresso cup. They were large like Gabe's, but the knuckles soft, unscarred. He obviously didn't share Gabe's love for working on cars.

"It is, isn't it, Luis?" I prodded.

His head came up, and his dark brown eyes looked directly into mine. "I don't know. Did he tell you about what happened between me and Lydia?"

"As far as I'm concerned that's water under the bridge."

He shrugged, sipped his espresso. "Not for him. He holds grudges. All Ortiz men do. My dad, for example, has never forgiven me for not becoming a cop."

For once I held my tongue and didn't say the automatic, "I'm sure that's not true." It probably was true, and it would have been naive of me to pretend otherwise.

After a few moments, I said, "I'm sure your dad is proud of you. You have two great sons and a beautiful daughter. That's nothing to sneeze at."

He shrugged again. "I talked to Paige this morning. She asked for a divorce. That makes lucky-number-three for me. Dad's really going to hit the roof." He gave me a sad, crooked smile.

"I'm so sorry," I said. "Is there anything I can do?"

He gave a short, bitter laugh. "Tell Gabe for me?"

I ran my finger down my lemonade glass, painting in the condensation.

He reached across the table and tentatively touched my hand. "I was just kidding. I'll tell him tonight." He drained his coffee and set the cup carefully in the saucer, twisting it around so the handle was in perfect line with the table edge. "She says she'll fight me for custody of Cassie. She actually doesn't want me to see her at all."

"That's not right. Why would she do that?"

He ran his finger around the rim of the cup, staring down into the silty remains of his drink. In the background, a CD played sad, Spanish guitar music that seemed entirely too coincidental. "I have no idea."

He wouldn't lift his head to look at me, his body language telling me he might have an inkling why. But whatever she held over him, he wasn't going to share with me. I could respect that. A marriage is such a delicate thing, an entity that is really only known by the two people inside it. I would be the first to admit, things weren't always what they appeared on the surface. Though he seemed a distant father, I couldn't imagine Luis wanting anything but the best for the little girl who caused his face to light up every time he said her name. Then again, I couldn't imagine he and Lydia having an affair.

"I have to go," Luis said, standing up. "I have an appointment before I see Gabe."

"Where are you going for dinner?" I asked.

"Daniello's? It's an Italian place around here somewhere."

"Two blocks north of here. They have incredible gnocchi."

"I'll keep that in mind."

Be kind to him, Friday, I thought, attempting to send my husband a telepathic message. We aren't so perfect ourselves, you know.

I took my empty plate back to the counter and ordered a coffee to go. I had a feeling it was going to be a long night.

As I started up the stairs, a man was coming slowly down the last one. I moved to the far right to give him room, carefully balancing my hot coffee.

"Ms. Harper?" the man said, taking the last step with an audible grunt. He wore a plaid shirt and khaki slacks. His face wore the tenseness of someone who kept a tight rein on his emotions.

His use of my name startled me since I was fairly sure I didn't know him. Then again, his face looked vaguely familiar. That was part of the problem with being Gabe's wife and having to attend so many functions that had nothing to do with the agriculture community. Everyone was beginning to look familiar to me now.

"Do you have a few minutes?" he asked, grasping the wooden railing with one hand.

He probably wanted to complain about Gabe. I wasn't in the mood for *that* right now. I glanced at the stairs, wondering how rude it would be just to push past him. Dove's voice telling me to treat every-one as I'd like to be treated kept me from it.

"If this is concerning my husband . . ." I started.

His face grew confused. "Your husband?"

I cocked my head. "Gabe Ortiz. The police chief?"

He held up his free hand in protest. "Oh, no, it's about Mr. Adams."

That got my attention. "Walt Adams?" I repeated, buying myself time. Then I recognized the man. "You were at the church yesterday. In the Bakersfield car."

His face became perplexed. "I do live in Bakersfield."

"Your license plate holder," I said, feeling my face turn red. "I'm a cop's wife. It's become a habit now for me to look at things more closely."

"Can we sit down and talk?" he asked, gesturing over at an empty table.

I glanced around. Except for a couple with their heads bent toward each other and the guy behind the counter, the coffeehouse was empty. But I was relatively safe here. Jose was within yelling distance.

"Sure," I replied.

His face grimaced in pain as he limped toward the closest table.

"Would you like something to drink?" I asked.

He waved his hand in refusal. "I'm fine. I just wanted to talk to you. The newspaper article said you were the one who found Mr. Adams's body."

I clasped my hands together and rested them on the table top. "Yes, I did," I said carefully, wondering how he found me. "How are you involved?"

He pressed his lips together so tightly, I swear I could hear his teeth clicking. "He killed my mother."

CHAPTER 13

"*H*E WHAT?"

He folded his own hands and stared down at them. "I suppose I should introduce myself. My name is Brian Gates. I own a small appliance store in Bakersfield. My father started it in nineteen-thirty-eight. Ten years ago, only six months after my dad died, my mother married Walt Adams. She met him at a dance at the senior center near our house."

Another complication from Walt's past.

"She called him the love of her life," he said. "Forget my father who worked himself into an early grave building a business that took care of her. Walt Adams, according to her, was the only man she ever loved, who ever loved her." Brian's voice grew bitter. "He loved her so much that he abandoned her without a backward glance."

I glanced around, trying to think of something I could say or do to excuse myself from this uncomfortable situation. Why was Brian Gates telling *me* this? Whatever Walt Adams did to this man's mother was not something that involved me. Before I could say so, Brian continued his story.

"He was a drunk and a con man. When he ran out on her, he also left her with a twenty-thousand-dollar charge card bill, and he cleaned out her personal savings. He stole fifteen thousand dollars from her!"

"Why are you telling me this, Mr. Gates?" I asked as gently as I could.

"He came back a month or so ago," he continued, looking over my shoulder, refusing to meet my eyes. "How do you like that? After ten years, he just waltzes back into our lives. Said he wanted to pay her back the money he took from her. Gave her a thousand dollars and said he'd be getting the rest to her soon. You'd think he was Prince Charming, the way she acted. She told him that she forgave him and was proud that he was trying to make amends."

"I'm sorry." It seemed like that was all I could say to anyone anymore.

He finally looked at me, tears in his pale brown eyes. "She had a stroke and died a week after he came to visit her. I wasn't going to even tell him she'd died, but I decided after a month that I wanted to confront him, tell him that he killed her as sure as if he'd shot her with a gun. I went to the address he gave her, and the neighbors told me what happened. I looked up an old newspaper at the library, and that's why I went to the church to talk to the reverend. And why I looked for you. You found him. The paper said so."

"I don't know what to tell you," I said, holding out my palms. "I liked Walt. He went to our church for a long time, but I didn't know him well. I was the one who found him, but that's all I can tell you."

"Yes, Mr. Reid said he also liked Walt, that he was a beloved member of the congregation. How nice for him. Don't any of you care that he killed my mother?"

I pushed my chair back slightly, indicating this conversation was over. There was nothing I could do to help this man and his grief, especially since he'd already talked to Mac. If anyone could have helped him, it would have been Mac. "Mr. Gates, I really have to go."

"You found him. The paper said so."

My stomach churned at the memory of Walt's bloody face. "I already told you I did."

"Was he alive when you found him? Did he say anything? Like about the money he promised my mother?"

I stared at him, shocked. No matter what I or anyone else here felt about Walt or what he did before he came here, the fact was that he was brutally murdered.

I looked him directly in the eyes. "I think it would be best if you went back to Bakersfield, forgot about Walt Adams, and got on with your life."

He slapped a hand down on the table. "You think that's easy! He devastated her when he left ten years ago, and it was all up to me to help her through it. If nothing else, I deserve whatever it is he has that is worth anything."

That's when I stood up. "This conversation is over. I'm sorry for what happened to your mother, but there's nothing I can tell you. If that isn't good enough, I suggest you talk to the police."

A fine sheen of perspiration made his tanned forehead shiny. "You know something, don't you?"

"Good-bye, Mr. Gates." I started for the staircase.

"This isn't over," he said, his voice more resigned than hostile.

I forced myself to ignore him and went upstairs. At the counter, I asked the clerk if Elvia was in her office. Right now, I needed to talk to my friend about silly stuff like whether the new flared pants called bootcut are actually bellbottoms, did pink eyeshadow actually look good on *anyone*, and what new tactics her mother had dreamed up to convince Elvia that she should get pregnant *now*. Anything except the subject of Walt Adams or Luis Ortiz.

"She left early," the clerk said. "She wasn't feeling well. I think she has a migraine."

"Okay," I said, contemplating whether I wanted to go out to the ranch since Gabe wasn't going to be home until late. Right now, seeing Dove and helping her feed the chickens or muck some stalls would be just the perfect thing to clear my mind. But I was also tired, too tired to even drive to the ranch. Instead I walked home where I found, to my delight, my purple truck, restored to its original color.

After calling the store and telling Babs that I decided to call it a night, then feeding Scout, I made myself a bowl of tomato soup and some toast. I ate it while cruising the sitcoms on television and tried not to think about Brian Gates, Kevin Adams, Jonathan Hammer, or anything to do with Walt Adams's death.

At nine-forty-five P.M. I started getting worried about Gabe. Just as I was dialing his cell phone number, Scout trotted over to the front door. Sixty seconds later, Gabe's key opened the lock.

It was obvious from the grim expression on his face that his dinner with Luis hadn't gone well.

"How are you?" I asked.

"Fine. I'm going to take a shower."

I watched him walk up the stairs, his broad back stiff under his jacket. He was still dressed in one of his Brooks Brothers suits. This one was a rich, dark gray wool, and he projected even more authority than usual. It was probably not the most friendly choice of attire for an emotional heart-to-heart talk with his cousin.

I decided to shower downstairs and was already reading in bed when he came out of the steamy master bathroom. He lifted the covers and crawled in, sighing as deeply as Scout did after his evening meal.

"Is everything okay between you and Luis?" I couldn't help asking. There was no way I could go to sleep without hearing something of what happened between them tonight.

He turned over, the Marine bulldog tattooed on his back growling at me. "I don't feel like talking about it."

I poked the dog right between his eyes. "Tough luck, soldier. You're going to talk about it or I'll never let you sleep." I tried to make my voice light, teasing, but he got the point.

He turned over to stare at me. "There's nothing to tell. Luis is Luis. Same old crap as always."

"Are you two at least speaking?"

"Look, Benni, you don't understand. This is more complicated than it appears. Just let me handle it."

"How about explaining it to me then?" Though his words hurt, I was trying to keep my voice calm.

"It's too complicated to explain to you."

"What does *that* mean? That I'm too stupid to understand the complex emotions of you and your cousin?" I sat up and rested my elbows on my knees.

"That's not what I meant."

"So, what did you mean?"

"I told you, I don't feel like talking about it."

"That's not fair, Gabe. I have a right to know a little about what's going on. Why do you have to make everything such a big deal?"

He sat up, his back against our headboard. In the moonlight, the harsh shadows on his face made him look like a stranger. "Why do you have to know about every little thing that happens in my life? You know, sometimes it would be nice just to have someone to come home to who wasn't trying to turn me inside out or cause any more complications in my life."

I felt my face freeze. "I'm sure there's plenty of women out there like that who'd be glad to sit at home and wait for you."

He closed his eyes a moment. "That's not what I meant."

"Actually, now I don't feel like talking about it. Good night." I turned my back to him, giving him a taste of his own medicine.

After a few minutes, I felt him climb out of bed and go downstairs. A few seconds later, the guest bedroom door slammed shut.

Scout came over to me and nosed my hand, whining quietly.

I reached out and stroked his big brown head. "Yes, I know. I should swallow my pride and go down there. But this time it's his turn."

Scout rumbled his distress from deep in his chest.

"Okay, I guess it doesn't matter whose turn it is. I'll apologize in the morning," I promised him.

Right before I fell asleep I realized I never told Gabe about Brian Gates. Well, it wasn't that important. It wasn't like he threatened me or anything. He was just a sad man trying to make sense of his mother's death. I'll tell Gabe about him tomorrow morning, I thought. Right after we made up.

❖

OF COURSE, THE CONCEPT OF MAKING UP THE NEXT MORNING was much easier than the actual act. I could tell ten seconds after Gabe walked into the kitchen that we were not likely to mend many marital fences this morning. Dark circles hollowed his eyes, and he looked like he'd been fighting demons all night. Though I was still irritated at his stubborn refusal to confide in me, I also felt a stab of pity.

Why was he was so determined to go through the bad things in his life alone? Why didn't he get that one of the greatest things about marriage was having someone there to talk to, someone who had you and your welfare at heart. That was the ideal, I guess. Maybe he didn't feel I really cared. If so, that was my failure. Pity turned to guilt, and I decided to be the mature one this time, the one to wave the white flag.

"Would you like some eggs?" I asked in a gesture of reconciliation. "Or I can make waffles. I have some fresh strawberries." I held out a carton of eggs. Strawberry waffles were one of his favorite breakfasts.

He picked up the newspaper, refusing to meet my eyes. "No, thank you. I'm going into work early this morning. I'll pick up something on the way." His voice was cool, unengaged. I'd read him right when he walked into the kitchen. He'd pulled his head back into his shell and nothing was going to draw him out. He poured coffee into a commuter cup and started for the door. "Have a good day."

"You too," I said, resisting the urge to throw one of the raw eggs at the back of his navy suit coat. I hated it when he was like this. It felt like he was wearing a suit of armor with no spot open or vulnerable.

"I tried," I said to a worried-looking Scout. "The next step is up to him."

I ate a chocolate Pop-Tart and threw on jeans and a sweatshirt. My costume for the historical walk today was hanging on the back of the bedroom door. I'd picked up the corset yesterday, viewing it with distaste. Maybe I could fit into the dress without wearing it. Hopefully, there would be someone at the Mackey house who could help me with it if I needed to wear it.

"You gotta stay home for this one, my boy," I said when Scout followed me to the door.

The Mackey house, down at the south end of Lopez Street, was one of the most beautiful old houses in San Celina. A three-story, gray-and-white Victorian, it was originally the home of Judge John Mackey and his wife, Sarah, who were devout Methodists and ardent patrons of the arts back in the early 1900s. Mrs. Mackey had been known for her love of the Chumash and Salinan Indians native to the Central Coast, and tried to help them maintain their cultural ties by encouraging their basketweaving art and recording their oral histories and stories. Her friendship with many of the Indians was reflected in the Victorian's library where gifts of baskets and pottery decorated the ornate bookshelves.

I went around to the house's back door where I spotted Dove dressed in a long, plain gray Victorian dress covered with a pristine white apron. She was sitting at the table talking a mile a minute on her red cell phone, a yellow legal pad with a list of names in front of her. When she saw me, she held up one finger telling me she'd be with me momentarily.

"Okay, okay," she said. "You can relieve them at two P.M. I'm sure Benni won't mind." Dove rolled her eyes at me and circled her temple with her index finger. "Yes, yes, Norma, I understand. I'm sure Benni doesn't mind giving up Saturday." She punched the END button on her cell phone. "When the good Lord poured in that woman's brains someone must have jiggled His arm."

In spite of my sour mood, I smiled. "What won't I mind?"

"Norma Radcliff is determined to play Sarah Mackey. So determined that she had special clothes sent down for her and her husband from some costume store in Santa Barbara. I told them they could relieve you and Hud at two P.M. And she wants both shifts Saturday."

"Hallelujah! Let her have it, please. The less time I have to spend in that corset, the better. I'm going to try to wear the dress without it. I've actually lost a few pounds, I think."

"Good luck," Dove said, eyeing my waistline. "You can change in there." She pointed to a fairly spacious room off the kitchen that once served as a walk-in pantry and the historical society was using as a place to store people's purses, clothes, and personal effects. With Dove sitting right there at the kitchen table, everything would be safe. "You and Hud will be on from ten A.M. to two P.M."

Before I went into the room to change, I said, "Do you have a few minutes to talk?" I hadn't updated her on everything that had happened with Angelina, Walt's murder, and all its convolutions. And I wanted her advice about what I should do about Gabe and his cousin.

Dove cocked her head. "What's wrong, honeybun?"

I sat down across from her at the table and, as I had so many times in the past, poured out my heart's puzzling contents for her to show me how to fit them together.

"Child, I told you it wouldn't be easy being married to Gabe. Not to mention you knew nothing of his family before you ran off and got hitched. You know when you marry the man, you marry his kin."

"You didn't actually tell me it wouldn't be easy until after I was already married to him," I pointed out. "It was at our second wedding at the ranch if I remember correctly."

"That's because you didn't ask me beforehand," she countered, lifting her white eyebrows.

She had me there. "What should I do?"

She shook her head. "Not much you can do. Like so many things with men, you just gotta let loose of the reins a little and hope and pray they find their way home." She smiled at me and winked. "I promise, the good ones eventually do, and the ones that don't, it's best to leave them in the back field anyway. At least until they wise up."

"Does a training whip come into play anywhere in this theory of yours?" I asked, only half-kidding.

She chuckled. "Only in self defense, honeybun." She patted my hand. "Now got get changed and let me finish my phone calls."

I went over and hugged her. "Thanks, Gramma. I don't know what I'd do without you."

"Spend too much money on psychiatrists, no doubt," she said. "I'll send you my bill in the morning."

I went into the pantry, shut the door, and tried the dress on without the corset, but no matter how much I sucked in my gut, it wasn't going to fit.

"Dove!" I called in desperation.

She came into the room, shaking her head. "Told you eating Pop-Tarts for breakfast would eventually catch up with you." She helped me into the corset, pulled the corset strings, and got revenge on me for every irritating thing I put her through as an adolescent.

"Ow, ow, ow," I yelped.

"Oh, cowgirl up," she replied.

"What in the world did these women do when they had to pee?" I grumbled once I was in the dress. I put my hair up in a messy bun with a few tendrils hanging down. It looked more eighties' senior prom than Victorian era, but it would have to do.

"I don't even want to think about it," Dove said. "My advice is that you don't, either, or that's all you'll be thinking about for the next four hours."

I walked carefully to the parlor and sat down on the end of the pale blue brocade sofa. I picked up a half-finished needlepoint canvas. "Do I actually have to work on this?"

"I've been stitching on it for two years," Dove said. "I'm sick of it. Thought you could make some headway since you'll just be sitting there doing nothing. Kill two birds with one stone."

I held up the canvas. It was the picture of a Volkswagen Beetle with peace signs and daisies bordering it. "Not too Victorian."

"It's for your cousin, Emily. You know she loves that sixties' stuff. Just hold it so no one can see the pattern."

"Yes, ma'am," I said, giving a small sigh. Emily, my aunt Kate's oldest daughter, was doing her master's thesis on the cultural implications of the Vietnam War. That reminded me of Gabe and how we'd left each other this morning.

Her eagle eye caught my sign. "What's wrong now?"

"Nothing." I looked down at the needlepoint, pretending to study the pattern.

Her voice softened. "I told you, Gabe and his cousin will work things out. They're just being men. Buttin' heads 'cause that's all they know to do."

I looked up at her sympathetic face. "I hate fighting."

She shrugged. "You fight, you love, you fight, you love. That's life."

"Wiser words never spoken, Mrs. Lyons," said Hud, who'd walked up behind her.

She turned and pointed a finger at him. "You watch yourself, young man. I've got my eye on you."

"Just one?" He grinned, gave a small bow, and tipped his bowler hat.

"You behave," she said, shaking her head and walking back toward the kitchen. "And keep your voices low. The visitors aren't supposed to actually hear you talking."

"I think I'm winning her over," he said, sitting down in the wingback chair across from me. He looked different in his late-nineteenth-century wool suit, younger and less cynical.

"I think you're nuts," I said.

"That, dear girl," he said, placing his hat on the arm of his chair, "has already been well documented and established by those much more experienced at spotting these things than you."

"Hush," I said, putting my finger over my lips. "People are starting to come in."

We lowered our voices as the first group of patrons walked past the parlor, cordoned off by a red velvet rope, and gawked at me and Hud.

"I feel like a lion in the zoo," he said in a voice low enough for only me to hear.

"A monkey is more like it," I said, giving him a fake smile.

"How long do I have to put up with listening to you insult me?" he asked, fake smiling back.

"Only four hours. Thank goodness Norma got her way. She and her husband are taking over at two P.M. She had special costumes made. And we're off the hook for Saturday."

"John and Sarah, the senior years," he joked.

"So," I said, trying to make conversation. "I've been meaning to ask how Maisie came to be in First Baptist's children's play."

He sat forward in his chair and picked up an old newspaper, pretending to read it. "Laura Lee's idea," he said looking over his paper. "She grew up Baptist even though she and Maisie attend the Methodist church on Spring Street now. She heard about your musical director's work with children, and she wanted Maisie to be a part of it."

"Lily's great. Sure wish she was back."

"Hey, I think we're doing a pretty good job."

"We'll see in a few weeks." I was still worried that we wouldn't be able to pull it off.

I glanced up at the next group of people who were standing behind the rope watching us. I smiled at them, then felt a cold chill run down my back.

Standing at the back of the group of twelve or so people was Brian Gates, his face as expressionless as a mannequin's.

A startled "Oh" slipped out of me.

"What?" Hud said, instantly on alert. He glanced over to where I was looking, but Mr. Gates was already gone.

Hud looked back at me. "Benni, what is it?"

"Nothing." I looked back down at my needlepoint and stabbed my needle into one of the neon yellow peace signs decorating the blue Beetle.

"I just saw someone I . . . I didn't expect to see here."

"Who?" he demanded.

"I'll tell you after our shift," I said, though I had no intention of doing so. What I was going to do was change as quickly as I could, then try to find Gabe to tell him about Mr. Gates.

That satisfied Hud, and we went back to making idle chitchat, though he gave me more than one curious glance during our four-hour stint.

Norma and her husband arrived fifteen minutes early, but I was more than willing to give up the time. I'd done my part to help the historical society, now I needed to find my husband and tell him there's a possibility that Brian Gates might be stalking me. I'd been stalked in the not-too-distant past and maybe I was hypersensitive to it, but seeing him unexpectedly in that group of tourists set off every warning signal in my body. But what reason would he have to follow me? I told him everything I knew.

"You can change first, if you like," I said to Hud as we walked down the hallway toward the pantry.

"Don't need to," he said when we reached the kitchen. Dove was nowhere to be seen. "I wore the clothes from home. Mine aren't quite as intricate as yours."

"Okay, then see you around."

"Wait, you said you were going to tell me—"

I shut the pantry door on his open mouth. Maybe if I stayed in here long enough, he'd give up and go away. When I came out of the pantry fifteen minutes later, he was gone. Good, I thought.

"Are you okay?" Dove asked when I came out. "That detective fellow said you were upset about something."

"I just need to find Gabe and talk to him," I said, hitching my leather backpack over my shoulder.

She nodded. "Just don't give up on him, honeybun. He's worth it."

I kissed her soft cheek. "I know, Gramma. We'll get things right between us eventually."

"Yes," she said, patting me on the back. "When you're about eighty."

Outside, Hud was leaning against the door of my newly painted truck. "You never told me what upset you in the parlor."

"It was nothing. An old boyfriend. Please move. I'm late."

He stepped aside without protest, surprising me.

"I know when you're scared, *chere*," he said, his voice soft. "Does your husband know about who frightened you in there?"

"I'm not scared," I said.

He reached over and touched my cheek. The tips of his fingers were rough and cold. "Yes, you are. Why?"

I guess it was his gentleness, his kind concern compared with Gabe's distance this morning that caused me to relent and tell Hud about Brian Gates. Though I felt disloyal telling him before Gabe, I was also afraid enough that I figured someone should know right away, just in case.

"Why didn't you tell Gabe this last night?" he asked.

I gave a nonchalant shrug. "It wasn't that big of a deal last night." I wasn't about to tell him Gabe and I were fighting.

"I would say it's a big deal. We don't know what this guy is up to."

"Gabe has important things to worry about right now." Even as I said it, I realized that made Gabe sound self-centered and uninvolved.

"So important he didn't notice his wife was scared?"

I looked away. "I'm a good actress."

"Not that good. I noticed."

I swallowed, my mouth dry. None of this was Hud's business, and I was starting to become angry. Angry at Hud for pointing out Gabe's flaw, angry at Gabe for having it, and most of all, angry at myself because surely I could have found a way to avoid all this.

"I have to go," I said, opening my truck door.

"Tell him right away," Hud said, right before I closed the door. "Promise me."

I looked through the window at him, his country boy face filled with emotion, though I wasn't sure what kind. I nodded at him, and his face relaxed.

When I arrived at the police station, Gabe's parking space was empty. I called home and got our answering machine. When I dialed his cell phone, his voice mail replied. "Gabe, call me. Maybe I'm just being silly, but I think I'm being followed." That sounded so dramatic, like television dialog. "I'm okay, really. Just call me."

I watched my rearview mirror, looking for Brian Gates's black sedan, but so far hadn't spotted it. This purple truck was beginning to look like a big mistake. It was way too easy to follow. I went by the house and made a quick sandwich, perusing the two books I'd bought at Blind Harry's on tramp art. Everything had been so tense these last few days that I hadn't had a chance to show Gabe the box I thought Walt made for me. It was sitting in our downstairs closet, still wrapped in an old towel. To be honest, I wasn't sure I wanted him to see the box right now, not with Walt putting my possibly future initials on the bottom. We'd not talked about me changing my last name to his in a long time and right now didn't seem the wise moment to revisit that conflict. I was ready to change, ready to take his name or at least add it to Harper. But I didn't want it to happen when we were mad at each other.

Reading the tramp art books was giving me an idea for a future exhibit. We could put the word out and ask people to bring functional or environmentally sensitive art, art using "found" materials. Walt's tramp art box could be the center of the exhibit. Who knows, maybe there were other examples of tramp art languishing in people's garages or attics.

The tramp art books Elvia had sold me did a thorough job documenting tramp art in photographs and in tracing its history. Before long I was lost in this art of another era, when people had time, though not always voluntarily, to painstakingly create such beautiful objects from discarded scraps. It reminded me of quilting before the seventies, when quilting came back into vogue. Before then, quilts were mostly for everyday use or considered folk art, art made by working people with the leftover scraps of fabric from clothing beyond repair. Their clever and striking designs were merely supplemented by purchased fabric. And they were made to be used. Dove still shakes her head at how many quilts were hung on the walls these days rather than put on a bed to keep someone warm. Utilitarian objects that achieve the status of art. That was the whole idea of folk art. What happened, I couldn't help wondering, when they no longer became utilitarian? Was it no longer folk art? Even the fashion of calling it "Outsider Art" was something dreamed up by the upper class. No matter how beautiful a piece of folk art was, there was that class distinction, the implication that there was an inside and an outside art world and, like Angelina and her aunt, it had to do with where you were born, how affluent you were, and how much education you had. The idea of an exhibit where this was discussed excited me.

In one of the books, a quote jumped out at me. "A hidden latch on the side of this unique tramp art jewelry box reveals a secret compartment."

A secret compartment? I jumped up to go get the box from the downstairs coat closet. After twenty minutes of enthusiastic and hopeful searching I found nothing.

Disappointed, I put the box up on a bookshelf and sat back down in my chair. What was I hoping? That a secret drawer would hold the key to Walt Adams's death? The whereabouts of the Aznar violin? There was still no overwhelming proof that they were connected. It was appearing that Walt's death was likely just the result of the mistakes made in his life before coming to San Celina and joining First Baptist.

I glanced over at the clock. It was three P.M. now, and I tried calling Gabe again. After leaving messages on his voice mail, Maggie's voice mail, and his cell phone's voice mail, my good intentions and patience had flown out of the chicken coop as quickly as one of Dove's skittish Brown Leghorns. He was obviously ignoring my attempts to contact him.

I finally left a terse message on his cell phone. "Just ignore my earlier messages. I'm sure I was being paranoid. I'm going out to the ranch for dinner. Don't know when I'll be home."

After I hung up, I immediately felt guilty for my irritated tone. But, doggone it, why was he ignoring my earlier frantic messages? Granted, I could just be paranoid, but why didn't he even call and hear me out, see if I was okay? I definitely needed some perspective. I would drive myself crazy sitting here brooding about it. The ranch never failed to calm my nerves and soothe my troubled spirit. I decided to take Walt's box out with me to show to Dove. I wanted to run the idea of the utilitarian art exhibit by her. "Finding Art" was a tentative name I was considering for the exhibit.

On my way out the front door with Scout, I ran into Luis.

"Hey," I said, coming down the porch steps. "How are you?"

"Okay," he said. "I was looking for Gabe."

"Join the club," I said, trying not to look peeved.

"Think he might be avoiding the both of us?"

"Maybe," I said, remembering how Gabe had accused Luis of running away when things got too emotionally sticky. What did Gabe think he was doing right now? "He'll show up eventually."

"I know." He stuck his hands into the pockets of his gray dress slacks. "What have you got there?" He nodded at Walt's box under my arm.

"You know that man who was killed at the church a few days ago?"

He nodded, his face politely interested.

"He made me this box. He worked quite a bit in wood. It's called a tramp art box."

He took his hands out of his pockets and asked, "May I look at it?"

I handed it to him and watched him inspect Walt's painstaking work.

"This is incredible," Luis said.

"To be honest, I think Walt's talents were wasted as our handyman, even though he was a wonderful one."

"How's it going on finding out who killed him?" Luis asked, turning the box around to look at all its intricate sides.

I shrugged, not wanting to reveal that Gabe didn't discuss his work with me. Then, my annoyance at my husband overcame me for a moment, and I blurted out, "He probably wouldn't tell me even if he knew something. He's so dang—" I stopped in the middle of my sentence, ashamed I'd criticized Gabe to his cousin. No matter how frustrated I was, complaining about him to one of his family members was tacky and immature.

Luis gave a knowing nod. "Gabe can be real independent. *Anda tu camino sin ayuda de vecino.* He and my dad take that saying to heart."

I cocked my head, indicating I needed translation.

"Walk your own road and bear your own load," Luis said, handing the box back to me. "He never did like asking for help."

"That's Gabe, all right."

"If you see him, could you tell him I'm looking for him?"

"Sure," I said.

THE MINUTE I DROVE UNDER THE WROUGHT IRON RAMSEY RANCH sign, my grumpy mood started to improve. November was not considered a pretty time of year on the Central Coast. Unless we had early rains, the hills tended to be brown and gold rather than green. But I loved this land in all its phases, and late fall–early winter, had its own variegated, unique beauty—the hills were stark and ponderous and a million shades of sorrel, umber, gold, and tan.

When I pulled up, Isaac was coming down the front porch steps, his favorite old Nikon 35mm hanging around his huge neck.

"Hey, Pops," I said, going over to hug him. Isaac Lyons was aptly named. He was like a wise, old lion, sitting on a hill surveying his kingdom. He'd brought a mountaintop of joy to Dove, this late-in-life love of hers. For that I'd always be grateful to him.

"Hey, kiddo," he said, returning my hug.

I pulled on his long white braid, almost as long as Dove's. "Where are you headed off to?"

He nodded over at the Jeep. "Up to the north pasture to take some pictures of that new colt that was born last month."

"He's a doll," I agreed. "Dove wants me to think of a good name for him. I've promised to train him for her."

"What are you and Gabe planning for your exciting Saturday night?"

I looked away, pretending to study the faded old Jeep. "Gabe's working. Thought I'd see what Dove was making for dinner."

He was quiet a moment, his bear paw–sized hand resting easily on the little black Nikon. "Want to talk about it?"

I wasn't certain if I did. Though if anyone was an easy person to talk to, it was Isaac. He was one of the most accepting people I knew. He's also been married five times. Six, actually, counting my gramma. I didn't imagine there was any imaginable marriage conflict he hadn't experienced.

I kept staring at the Jeep. When we were teenagers, Jack and I used to drive it all over the ranch's narrow, dangerous cattle roads, taking the crazy chances you do when you're young and foolish and think you won't ever die.

"Gabe's just being Gabe. He and his cousin are having problems." I paused for a moment. "Mostly I'm irritated because, yet again, he refuses to share his feelings. He won't let me help him get through this thing with his cousin." I kicked at the dirt and a rock went flying, causing Scout to lift his head. I could see him consider chasing it, then changing his mind and resting his head on his paws.

Isaac's face, an intricate road map of his seventy-something years, looked sympathetic. I felt his hand rest on my shoulder, a comforting gesture that almost caused me to start crying. This man who had changed my gramma's life already meant so much to me. How much time would we have left together? I realized that was also something that was bugging me. Gabe's apparent disregard for time.

"He doesn't realize what he gives up when he won't share things with me," I said. "We don't know how much time we'll have in this life, so when he makes it so hard to communicate, we're losing time we'll never get back."

"You're right," Isaac said.

I looked up into his sunburned face, feeling desperate. "Why can't he see that?"

"Because he's not ready to," Isaac said. "He might not ever be. You may have to accept that. But remember, the time you spend trying to change something in someone that is purely up to them to change is also wasted. If I've learned nothing else in my years on earth, it's that you have to love people where they are right at the moment, not where you want them to be."

I held his gaze for a long moment. Around us, an early afternoon breeze kicked up, making the falling leaves dance and twirl, the gritty scent of oak and the throat-itching scent of eucalyptus swirl around us.

"You are one wise old guy," I said, putting my arm around his waist. "I am so thankful God brought you into my gramma's life. For her sake and mine."

He smiled down at me. "You weren't so sure the first time we met."

I laughed, remembering how suspicious I'd been of his intentions toward Dove. "You were a globe-trotting celebrity. What was I supposed to think?"

"I've never been happier," he said, kissing the top of my head. "And I'm thankful for you too."

"Go take your pictures. Thanks for the free advice."

"Who said it was free?" he said, winking at me. "I'm expecting not only a pecan pie, but a Yankee cake at the Thanksgiving roundup."

"You got it, Pops. I'll bake you a pie all for your own self."

"Tell Dove I'll be back by five-thirty. She said that's when the pot roast would be done."

"Oh, good. I love her pot roast."

"Call your husband, kiddo. Just tell him you love him. He needs to hear that. Especially right now. Let the other stuff take care of itself."

"I will."

I watched him walk toward the Jeep. When he was out of sight, before I went into the house to find Dove, I called Gabe one more time.

No answer at work. No answer on his cell phone. I left a message on both voice mails.

"Hi, Friday. I love you. Just want you to remember that."

Feeling good that I'd taken Isaac's advice, I was in a lighter mood when I went into the steamy kitchen. Heavenly scents of baking bread, roasting meat, and fresh strawberries greeted me along with Dove's quick hello.

"Grab a knife and start hulling," she said, nodding over at the strawberries. "When is Gabriel coming?"

"Don't know if he is," I said, sitting down at the round kitchen table with a paring knife and a ceramic bowl of strawberries. "I've tried to call him all day, but he's been busy."

She looked over at me, her expression suspicious, but she didn't press for any more details. "You can take home some of these strawberries."

"I have a ton at home."

"Then take him some roast beef. In case he needs a snack tonight when he gets home." She turned her back to me to stir the gravy on the stove.

I just smiled and shook my head. Though I was thirty-eight years old and well into my second marriage, my gramma still wasn't convinced I could take care of another human being properly. Watching her white braid switch back and forth as she fixed dinner, my heart ached with love for her, with gratitude that she gave up her life once her own children were raised to start over and raise me. The swiftness of time again struck me like a thump on the chest. I wanted to go over and hug her, something that I know would cause her to bat me away because she was busy cooking. I wanted to find my husband and hug him, tell him it was okay if he never changed one bit, that I'd still love him, just as he was.

"Mac's coming for dinner," Dove said, breaking into my thoughts.

"Really? Why?"

"No reason. Just figured the boy needed a home-cooked meal, what with all he's going through these days. What he really needs is a wife."

"I hope that's not going to be the topic of conversation this evening," I said wryly. "Maybe I should call Mac and warn him."

"Pshaw," she said, bending over to check the roast. "I don't have any prospects if that's what you're worried about. I am going to suggest that he maybe try one of those new Internet dating services."

"Yuck," I said. "Who knows who he'd end up with."

She pulled the roast out of the oven and set it on the counter. "That's the wrong attitude. I have a feeling those things are going to be the way to go in the next ten years."

"What's going to be the way to go?" Daddy asked, walking into the kitchen with Mac right behind him. "Look who I found wandering around outside in the brush."

"Mac!" Dove said, going over to hug him. "I'm so glad you could come to dinner. Benni just dropped by looking for a handout, so I guess we'll have to feed her." Her eyes warned me not to say anything about what we'd been talking about.

I raised my eyebrows in reply—*Not on your life.*

"What's the next big thing?" Mac asked.

That stumped Dove for a moment.

I smirked at her. Ha, caught in her own trap. Would she lie to her minister?

When she faltered a moment, I nobly jumped in and lied for her. "Tramp art. It's really becoming hot in art circles back East."

Dove looked at me like I'd gone nuts.

"Tramp art?" Daddy said.

"You mean like that box that Walt Adams made for you?" Mac asked.

"Yes, I was reading up on it so I could compose a display card."

At that moment Isaac walked in and the conversation turned to the new colt and what Daddy planned on using him for.

"Soup's on," Dove said a few minutes later after I'd set the table.

Mac said a quick grace, and we started eating. I was on my second helping of roast beef when the phone rang. Dove started to rise, and I waved her back down.

"I'll get it. You've been working all day," I said.

It was Ric Sanderson, our part-time youth pastor.

"Benni, is Mac there?" he asked, his voice sounding out of breath. "He said he was having dinner with Dove and Ben tonight."

"Sure, he's right here." I handed Mac the phone. "It's Ric."

Mac took the phone, stood up, and walked toward the living room. We continued with our conversation and eating, trying not to eavesdrop. After what had happened with Walt, I think we were all a little jumpy.

A few minutes later Mac returned, an amused look on his face. "Not to worry, folks. An entirely solvable emergency." He looked over at me and smiled. "Especially since I have Benni here, and we all know what an enthusiastic, spontaneous person she is."

"Good try, *padre*," I said, spooning more corn onto my plate. "The answer is already no."

"Ric and Shelly are stuck in Santa Barbara. Apparently, their car broke down and the part they need is being sent up from L.A. They're going to have to spend the night there."

"Oh, big tragedy," I joked. "A romantic evening in Santa Barbara."

Mac grinned. "Actually it's probably God's providence. Shelly had been complaining they never get time alone."

"So, what's the problem?" Dove asked.

"The problem is about thirty teenagers due at the church in," he glanced at his watch, "sixty minutes with the expectation that Ric and Shelly would drive them in the church bus to the Amaizing Corn Maze."

"That crazy thing they got over there at the Reynolds place?" Daddy asked.

"That's the one." He gave a cajoling smile. "Ms. Harper, are you up to being a chaperone for an evening of a-mazing fun?"

"Ha, ha," I said, taking a bite of home-baked bread. "Sure, if you promise no more corn-y jokes."

Everyone groaned and laughed.

"Better you than me," Daddy said, wiping his mouth. "Guess y'all better get your dessert eaten. You kids will have to leave soon."

Mac and I offered to clean off the table while Dove fixed the strawberry shortcake.

"Thanks for doing this," Mac said. "You've saved me from having to call around and beg people to change their Saturday night plans."

"It's okay," I said. "Actually, I've been kind of curious about the maze ever since Sam told me about it. He's in charge of security, you know."

"Really? Gabe must have been proud to hear that, his son following in his footsteps."

"I didn't tell him," I admitted. "Sam asked me not to. He was afraid Gabe would interfere."

Mac stacked dinner plates while I gathered up silverware. "I think he underestimates how proud his father is of him. Gabe would know to stay out of it."

I pondered his words. "You know, you're right. I'll tell Gabe the next time we talk." I was tempted to say, whenever that might be, but it would only open up a discussion with Mac that I didn't feel like having right now. Let Gabe be who he is, I told myself. The advice Isaac gave me was good and wise, and I was determined to heed it as best I could.

We'd finished our dessert, and Mac and I were putting on our jackets when the phone rang again.

"It's for you," Dove said, holding out the phone. "Some man." Her face was expressionless.

"Hello?" I said tentatively.

"I love you more than my own life, *querida*," Gabe said. "I'm sorry for acting like a jerk."

"I'm glad you called," I said, taking the phone out to the front porch for some privacy. "I'm sorry. I just want everything to be okay between us."

"What's this about someone following you?"

I quickly explained about Brian Gates.

"So what's your take on him?" Gabe asked. "Did he threaten you?"

"No, not at all," I said. "That's why I told you in my other message that I think I was just being paranoid."

"You said you saw him outside Mac's office?"

"Yes. Mac's actually here right now. Want to talk to him?"

"Put him on."

I went and got Mac, told him briefly about Brian tracking me down, and handed him my cell phone. "I think Gabe wants your feelings about him."

I watched Mac's face as he talked to Gabe. "No," he said. "I don't think he's any danger, but I can't guarantee it. Okay, here she is." He handed the phone back to me.

"Are you going straight home?" Gabe asked.

I glanced up at Mac. "Actually, no. Mac asked me to fill in for the youth minister and his wife chaperoning a bunch of kids to the corn maze over at the Reynolds farm. They're stuck in Santa Barbara tonight. Car problems."

"Okay, just make sure you stay with the crowd."

"Count on it, Friday. Tell me, are you really okay?"

His voice dropped down an octave. "This thing with Luis has just got me rattled. He's gotten himself into some big trouble, and though

I want to help him, I won't in the way he wants me to. We're having dinner at Liddie's to talk more about it."

Good, I thought. Luis found him. I was silent, determined not to force him to tell anything he didn't want to tell me.

"I'll tell you everything tonight," Gabe said. "When will you be home?"

"Probably after ten. Since we're meeting the kids at the church at seven-thirty, I'm assuming we'll be doing Moonlight in the Maize."

"What?"

I explained how it worked.

"Have they got enough security there?" Gabe said, his law enforcement persona instantly sniffing out potential problems.

"There's a bunch of college students and some sheriff's deputies who've volunteered." I paused a moment, then decided to believe what Mac said about Gabe. "This is a joint effort of a lot of departments at the college, and your son is very involved."

"He is?"

"As a matter of fact, he's head of security. He set it up and organized it with the sheriff's department, but he was afraid to tell you."

There was a momentary silence. Then he said, "I'm stunned."

"But proud?" I encouraged.

He laughed. "Yes."

"Then don't forget to tell him so."

"I won't."

I let out a tiny sigh of relief. "I love you, Sergeant Friday. You're the best."

"*Te querido, mi corazon,*" he replied. "Forever and ever."

After we hung up, I went back inside. "Ready to go, Brother Mac?"

"As ready as I'll ever be. You do have a flashlight, don't you?"

"In my truck. I'll meet you at church."

We all said our good-byes, and I gave Isaac an especially long hug.

"Thanks, Pops," I whispered. "As always, your advice hit the bull's-eye."

He ruffled my hair. "Be careful in the corn, kiddo. Don't get lost."

❖

BY SEVEN-FORTY-FIVE WE'D LOADED ALL THE KIDS ON THE BUS and with Mac driving, traveled the back roads outside of San Celina to the Reynolds farm. A half hour later we'd pulled past the Reynolds farmhouse into a field that the family, with the help of Sam and his friends, had turned into a temporary parking lot. It was already filled with at least seventy-five cars and buses.

We herded the kids toward the ticket booths and snack bar, which the college departments had outdone themselves in decorating. The theme was western, emphasis on primary colors, and all the ticket takers and snack bar attendants wore red-checked western shirts and Wranglers. They even had a children's area where there were games, a cowboy performing rope tricks, a clown making balloon animals, a children's maze of waist-high hay bales, and a whole craft section where they could color, play with wooden toys, and feed the rabbits and ducks in the petting zoo.

"This is quite a shindig," I said to Mac.

"Yes, the kids have done themselves proud," Mac said. "I'm glad to see college students getting so enthusiastic about a project where all the money goes to charity."

"What do we do now?" I asked, surveying our group. If we ended up going home with the same number and the same kids we came with; that would be tonight's true miracle.

"I've paid for them already," Mac said. "We just need everyone's hands stamped, watch a short video explaining how the maze game works, then we let them go." He grinned down at me. "And pray like crazy."

"Double amen," I said.

When we got the kids lined up and hands stamped, we found out how this thing worked. Apparently, it wasn't just a matter of running around the maze like a bunch of fools. There were checkpoints that held clues to the riddles needed to find the next checkpoint. At each checkpoint was a stamp proving you'd been there. The participants eventually made their way through the whole maze . . . or not. Those who made it through the maze and had all ten squares stamped received a special prize. The teenagers were practically pawing the ground during the five-minute video that explained the rules and told how to hold up a flag if they became lost or scared so a security officer standing on one of the three wooden bridges strategically placed in the maze could yell instructions to the nearest exit.

"Stay in groups of at least three or four," Mac instructed the kids. "Remember the rules. No smoking, no running, no cutting through the corn, no eating the corn, and no bad language. We have two and a half hours before we need to start loading up the bus. Everyone have flashlights? Any questions?"

Questions? Not in a million years. They were too anxious to break away from us. An electric current of excitement rippled through them like racehorses at the starting gate.

"Okay, let's say a prayer for your safety and then get out of here." He bowed his head. "Father, please keep everyone safe. Let us have fun, but let us also remember we are here as representatives of You. In Christ's name, amen." Mac looked up and yelled, "First group back with all their stamps wins a free ice cream sandwich from the snack bar."

We laughed when they took off, spurred by the thought of free anything, even a two-dollar ice cream bar.

"Are you going to try it?" I asked Mac, gesturing at the entrance to the maze. In the corn's rustling darkness I could see the strobelike twinkling of hundreds of flashlights, hear the distant, muffled sound of high-pitched girlish laughter and the guttural shouts of teenage boys.

"I think I'll stay here and have a cup of coffee. I'm not sure my heart can take roaming around ten acres of corn after that huge meal Dove made us."

We read over the large posted menu, which did the culinary department proud—handmade ice cream sandwiches with a choice of coffee, chocolate chip, or mint chip ice cream; a full espresso bar donated by Peet's coffee; roasted corn on the cob; hot chocolate with boot-shaped marshmallows; peanut butter and chocolate chip cookies the size of rodeo belt buckles; fresh, sweet kettle-corn; orange-iced cinnamon rolls; and five varieties of caramel apples.

"Wow," I said. "That all looks good. I'm almost hungry again. Think I'll join you for coffee, then try to find my stepson and see how he's doing."

We'd just sat down when one of the girls in our group, a quiet young woman named Amy, came over to us, her face panicked.

"What's wrong, Amy?" Mac asked.

"I was in the restroom and everyone's left. I don't want to go through the maze alone." Her soft-cheeked face looked ready to burst into tears. "I was going to go with Brittney and Teena."

"They just left," I said, then turned to Mac. "I'll help her catch up with the them."

"Thanks, Benni," he said, his face grateful.

"Have you got a flashlight?" I asked Amy.

She nodded and held up a red-and-blue Roy Rogers flashlight.

"Cool," I said, going over to the box of flag poles and selecting one with a bright purple flag. "You take the flag, and I'll carry the flashlight."

"Are we going to be able to find them?" she asked worriedly.

"Sure, we will. We'll just walk fast."

We hurried through the first three stamp-and-clue spots and finally caught up with Brittany, Teena, and their crowd ten minutes later at the fourth checkpoint.

"See, here they are," I said to Amy, who was almost giddy with relief that she wasn't going to miss out on going through the maze with her friends.

"Where were you?" Brittany and Teena squealed, running over to hug their friend.

"Okay, I'll see you guys later. I have a cup of coffee waiting for me back at the snack bar." Probably cold by now, but I'd harass Mac into buying me a fresh one. I held up Amy's flashlight. "I'll need this to get back, okay?"

She nodded, a big smile on her face. Teenage disaster averted. "Thanks, Mrs. Harper."

After solving that little crisis, I started backtracking through the maze, trying to retrace the twists and turns we'd taken. After getting hopelessly lost, I made my way over to the wooden security bridge to see if Sam was there. He was, holding a police flashlight and a pair of binoculars.

"Hey, Sam," I called, walking up the steps.

"Hey, Benni," he said. "Did you go through the maze?"

"Part of it," I said. "One of the kids we brought from church missed her group so I helped her catch up. Mac and I had to bring them because the youth pastor had car trouble down in Santa Barbara."

"It's cool, huh? I can't believe how many people have come already. We've made so much money, we're thinking about giving half of it to the homeless shelter. There's more than enough to run the Head Start programs."

"That's great. Do you think someone can walk me out?"

"I'll do it," he said. "I know this maze by heart." On the way back we talked about how he'd organized all the shifts and helped people who were in trouble.

"We've only had three lost kids," he said proudly. "We reunited them with their parents within fifteen minutes."

"You're doing a fantastic job," I said, hooking my arm through his, thankful for his presence as we walked through the maze. "Your dad will be proud."

Even in the shadows made by his large flashlight, I could see Sam's face flush with pleasure. "Ah, who cares what the old fart thinks?"

But it was obvious he did. He was enjoying this security assignment. Wouldn't it be something if Gabe's son followed in his law enforcement footsteps someday?

Once out of the maze, I said good-bye to Sam and started back through the crowd to the snack bar. I was walking past the hay-bale maze near the children's petting zoo when I heard a familiar voice, one that didn't make me happy.

"Why did you bring *him?*" Jonathan Hammer said. "I'm paying for an evening with my son, and I don't want to have to look at that guy's ugly mug all night." He was standing in front of Sheila Murray, his face inches from hers. I stepped back behind a hay bale so I could hear them without being seen.

"Look," Jonathan said, his voice going down an octave. I had to strain to hear him. "We're finished, okay? The less he and I see each other, the better."

"My thoughts exactly," Sheila said, her voice tired. "This is a big mess."

Before he could answer, I heard Kevin's voice say, "Hey, what's going on here?"

"Nothing, sweetie," Sheila said. "We're just talking about Travis. Where is he?"

Their voices faded away and a few seconds later I stepped out from behind the hay bale. What was that all about? Jonathan had said "We're finished." Did he mean he and Sheila or he and Kevin? Were he and Kevin involved with the violin theft? Would Kevin kill his own father to conceal that? I definitely needed to tell Gabe about this conversation even though he'd probably discount it.

At the snack bar, Mac was talking to Father Mark, who was finishing up a caramel apple.

"Problem resolved?" Mac asked.

"Yes," I said. "I found Sam. All is well with security." I smiled at Father Mark. "Hey, Father, what's up?"

He smiled back at me, his smile white against his dark, rough complexion. He was dressed in jeans and a Loyola Marymount sweatshirt. "Not much, Benni. Just here like you and Mac, supervising some kids."

I looked up at Mac. "Have you updated him on everything?"

Mac nodded, but before he could go further one of the kids we brought ran up to him. "Pastor, Michael's feeling sick. I think he's throwing up."

"I'll check it out," Mac said to us. "Be right back."

"Buy you a cup of coffee?" Father Mark asked, nodding over at the snack bar.

"That sounds great," I said.

When he brought the coffee back, we sat across from each other at one of the wooden picnic tables.

"How are things in the Harper-Ortiz household?" he asked, his hands wrapped around the white coffee mug. On his knuckles were pinkish scars from where he'd had gang tattoos removed. In his twenties, before he became a priest, he'd belonged to one of East L.A's toughest Latino gangs.

I stared down into my own coffee. Lying to a priest was definitely something I wasn't going to do. "Not so good these days."

He nodded. "I know, Gabe called me today. We had a long talk about his cousin."

I looked up into Father Mark's dark brown eyes. "I'm glad, I guess."

"You guess?"

I gave him a half-smile. "Well, isn't being jealous of a priest kinda like being jealous of God?"

He gave a deep, melodious laugh. "Not even close, but I know what you're trying to say. Give it time, Benni. We Latino men are a hard bunch of nuts to crack, but once you do, we're yours for life."

"I know you can't tell me what he said, but just answer me this. Is Gabe okay?"

He reached over and patted my hand. "He's doing fine. This thing between him and his cousin is old baggage they need to resolve. Nothing to do with you. Gabe just needs you to be there for him while it all works its way out."

"You're not the first man to tell me that today," I said, remembering Isaac's words. "Thank you. Is everything all right with Angelina and Juana?"

His face grew sad. "We just got them settled, and then this happened. I've been working on getting both of them papers. It isn't easy. There are so many who need help."

"They are lucky to have you," I said. "All of the people you help are."

He shook his head. "No, it's the other way around. *I'm* lucky to have them. They are God's blessing to me. I would be dead without them."

We were silent for a moment thinking about what he meant. His story of becoming a priest was common knowledge. Twenty years ago his wife and baby daughter were killed in a drive-by shooting where he was the target. He left the gang life shortly after that and a few years later became a priest.

"I'm curious about something," I said.

"What's that?"

"Helping people like Juana and Angelina. It's breaking the law. I've always believed God's law was higher than man's, but sometimes

I don't know how to justify it. What do you tell people when they challenge you on that?"

He rested his chin in his hand. "If they don't believe what the Bible teaches, I can't justify it. It *is* legally wrong and perhaps even foolish sometimes. But if they are believers, I quote Matthew twenty-five to them, Jesus' own words answering those who claim to have served in His name—'Lord, when did we see you hungry or thirsty or a stranger or needing clothes or sick, or in prison and did not help you?' He replies to them, 'I tell you the truth, whatever you did not do for one of the least of these, you did not do for me.' That's my best explanation."

"So how do you know which ones to do that for?" I asked. "When there are so many?"

"The ones who cross my path, *hermana*. It's as simple as that."

CHAPTER 14

$\mathcal{G}$ABE WAS ALREADY IN BED WHEN I GOT HOME. I TOOK A QUICK shower and sat crosslegged at the foot of the bed brushing my hair.

"I tracked down your Mr. Gates," Gabe said. "I don't think he's any real threat, but he knows we're watching him now. I suggested he just go back to his life in Bakersfield, let us handle Walt Adams's death."

"Why was he following me?"

Gabe closed his eyes and settled down into his pillow. "Just didn't know what else to do, he says. I told him if you saw him again, I'd bring him in."

"Can you do that?"

"Not really, but he doesn't know that. I think we've seen the last of Brian Gates."

I stopped brushing. "I hope so. I overheard something weird at the corn maze."

"What's that?"

I replayed the short conversation between Jonathan Hammer and Sheila Murray. "What do you think?"

He didn't even open his eyes. "Sounds like to me they were just talking about their screwed-up relationship."

"You think that's the mess they were talking about?"

"We're looking into both Kevin Adams and Jonathan Hammer's backgrounds. I'll tell my detectives what you heard."

"Okay," I said, just satisfied that I told him, that I wasn't hiding anything from him. If these people were involved with Walt's death, his detective team would find out. "So, what's going on with you and Luis?"

"We're okay." His voice was drowsy, fading away.

I jiggled his foot. "No falling asleep yet. What happened between you two?"

"We're good. As good as it can be."

"Details. I want details." I crawled across our king-size bed and slipped under the covers.

He yawned, shifted to his side. "He's gotten himself into some money troubles, but he says he has it under control. He didn't offer specifics, and I didn't ask. He did tell me about losing his job and the custody battle with his wife. We talked about the past, agreed we were both to blame, and decided to move on."

"I'm glad."

"Me too," Gabe mumbled, then promptly fell asleep.

"Dream sweet, Friday," I whispered and kissed his bare shoulder.

❖

"WHAT ARE YOU DOING TODAY?" I ASKED GABE THE NEXT MORNING.

He folded the Saturday paper and set it next to his plate. "Luis and I are going for a drive up the coast. He said he'd like to see Big Sur. We'll take the Corvette."

The calm, happy look on his face revealed volumes. I was relieved they'd worked out their differences. "Take him to that great place we ate at a few months ago. With the incredible French fries."

"Oh, yeah," he said. "By the river, south of Big Sur. What was the name of the place, Amy's something or other?"

"Emily's Delight. Should I plan something for dinner?"

"No, we can go out when we get back. We don't want to be on a time schedule."

I buttered an English muffin. "I'm jealous. I'll be slaving down at the folk art museum while you two are driving up the coast with the wind in your hair."

While he was upstairs dressing, the phone rang.

"Don't forget the rehearsal today," Dove said. "Noon."

"How could I forget when I didn't even know about it?" I said, quickly revising the tentative schedule in my head. I could work a few hours at the museum, go to rehearsal, then back to the museum.

"Well, you know now. Bring snacks."

"Drive safely," I told Gabe a few minutes later. "Tell Luis 'hey' for me. Maybe we should go out for Chinese tonight."

"I'll see if he likes it," Gabe said, waving good-bye.

On the way to the folk art museum, I stopped by the market and picked up granola bars and small cans of orange juice, feeling virtuous for my resistance to buying Hostess Sno Balls and Coca-Cola, which would have been my preferred snack.

The museum was busy with both tourists and artists. A local quilt guild was hosting a "Quilt Top in a Day" class and there were two separate museum tours going on, a Girl Scout troop and a group of senior citizens from Lompoc. After an hour of greeting and chitchat, Scout and I escaped behind the closed door of my office. Hopefully, things would be a little less busy in the afternoon and I could go to the upstairs gallery, closed now, and finish arranging the toy exhibit. Inside my office, I tried to find a place for Walt's box on my one crowded bookshelf. I stood on my tip-toes and squeezed it into a spot just above my head where it would be out of harm's way, but where I could contemplate it from the vantage point of my desk.

I went through the paperwork that had mysteriously filled my in box to see if there was anything that had to be taken care of immediately. In the pile was an article from the Internet left by Joe, the ex–sheriff's deputy.

"Don't know if you saw this," he'd scrawled across the top of the front page. "Thought it might help in your investigation."

It was an article on the illicit traffic of cultural property. It had become in the last two decades an especially horrendous problem worldwide for museums, archaeological sites, churches, and even villages where religious icons were suddenly disappearing. Thousands of items had been stolen and were itemized on a list by Interpol. The Aznar violin was, no doubt, a recent addition.

I skimmed the rest of the five-page article, noting the sections where it advised those who were responsible for these art objects how to best protect them, suggesting certain precautions in the display and movement of the objects. It noted that many thefts were actually done during working hours, making it not necessarily a problem of break-ins, but one of policing the public as they viewed the artifacts. Staffing was always a problem in museums. That would have been the best way to prevent thefts. Now many museums were considering a system of warning tags, much like those in mall clothing stores, where an alarm went off when a piece was removed from the premises. The problem with this, as with most security measures, was the lack of money to fund the security improvements.

Though nothing we had here in the museum was as valuable in the illicit art world, it was something that I needed to know. I'd pass this along to the historical society, who had many more valuable pieces to protect than we did. A second article he'd printed was specifically about the Aznar violin.

"The violin," I read, "made of native California woods, was made with simple tools and hand labor by Rafael Aznar, a Salinan Indian. As a boy, he wished for a violin like the one owned by the padre, but could not afford one. He wanted to play in the Mission Santa Celine orchestra. In time, he slowly copied the padre's violin, detail by detail, creating a unique finished instrument that played as beautifully as any Italian-made violin. This youth, from a culture that had never seen any Western stringed instrument, figured out how to make this one-of-a-kind violin." Nothing I didn't already know from my research for the historical society a year ago.

It showed a picture of the violin, though it was fuzzy and indistinct. I wondered what it looked like in person. Though I'd toured the mission as a child, a common fourth grade field trip in California, I don't recall the violin as being a particularly outstanding artifact. Then again, I was only a fourth grader. I was probably more interested in the fact that we got to eat our sack lunches outside in the mission's gardens than in an old violin.

I set the article aside. It was interesting, and I would thank Joe for printing them off for me, but I couldn't see how it would help. Seeing the printed picture of the violin, though, made me want to see the real one again. I'd probably walked by the real one a dozen times in my life and never took notice of it. Now, I might never see it again.

I spent the next hour running off labels for our next mailing announcing the antique toy exhibit. Our list was growing nicely, and we now had over a thousand names. After the play rehearsal, I'd take the postcards home and work on them there. I'd started out the door with the labels and a box of postcards with the folk art museum pictured on the front when my eye caught Walt's tramp box. Something compelled me to search it one more time, looking for that secret drawer. I set the labels and postcards down and pulled the box off the shelf. As I was pulling it off the shelf, a few of the Girl Scouts, obviously on their way to the bathroom, rushed past my door in a flurry of laughter, startling me. The box slipped out of my hands onto the office floor, hitting it with a dull thump.

"Oh, no," I moaned, bending down quickly to survey the damage. Fortunately, my office floor had recently been covered with an inexpensive brown commercial carpet. It had just enough padding to keep the box from breaking badly. A good-sized piece of wood was knocked off one corner, but other than that, it was unharmed. Maybe one of the woodworkers could glue it back on. I took the broken box into the woodworking studio. The only one present was Joe. He was working on one of his rocking horses, attaching tufts of gray and black horsehair.

"Hey, Joe. Where is everyone?"

"They all decided to go out for a pizza. I'm trying to lose a few, so I passed." He patted a stomach that was only about an inch from complete flatness.

"Good for you," I said. "Bad for Big Top Pizza."

"Do you need something?" he asked.

"Actually, I do. Your expertise. I dropped this box and chipped a piece off the corner. Can you glue it back on?"

He put down a handful of coarse horsehair. "Sure." After looking closely at the chip, he chose a thin wood glue to reattach it. "Tramp art?" he asked.

"Yes," I said from my perch on one of the woodworkers' high metal stools. "Walt made it for me. His initials and mine are on the bottom."

He turned it over and inspected the bottom. "I love this tramp art stuff. Have thought about doing it myself if I ever get the time."

"There's some books on it in the co-op library," I said. "Just put them in there myself."

"I like the idea of using scrap wood to make something. Especially our native woods like this box."

"In all the books they said tramp artists used old orange crates or cigar boxes."

He shook his head. "This isn't made of orange crates. This is good wood that he found somewhere. That piece I just glued on is bay laurel. You can tell by the color."

"Bay laurel?" I stared at him a moment. Bay laurel was a local wood. He nodded. "Yes, why?"

"That's what part of the Aznar violin was made with."

"Whoa," he said. "Walt and the violin? That's a huge jump."

"Maybe," I said. "Maybe not." Joe didn't know about the half-finished tuning peg Walt gave Angelina. I slipped down off the stool. "I'd better run this by Gabe."

"Good idea," he said.

❖

I BEAT MOST OF THE KIDS TO REHEARSAL THIS TIME. WHEN HUD drove up with Maisie, he seemed a little distracted.

"Everything okay?" I asked, watching her run into the recreation hall to find Angelina, who'd arrived a few minutes earlier.

"Have a suspect I need to run down today," he said. "My sources say he is in town, and I need to barhop to find him. I've got someone who's volunteered to do it for me, but I'd rather talk to him myself."

"Likely story," I said, smiling. "You're just trying to escape having to sing these songs one more time." I could understand. No offense to Lily, but I was getting sick of this music, especially since the tunes were so catchy that like the song "It's a Small World" in Disneyland, you couldn't get them out of your head.

"It's true," he protested.

"I'm just kidding. Let me check and see if Mac will be here, then you're free. Besides, there's lots of people here today. The kids will be safe." New carpet was being placed in the sanctuary. It looked like we'd have church services as normal tomorrow.

Mac assured Hud that since he was Giant Despair and needed to start rehearsing himself, he'd be here the whole two hours. Rehearsals went smoothly for a change. We actually were able to run through the play completely and practice a few songs we'd sing at church tomorrow. While we were in the recreation hall, carpet layers were replacing the carpet in the sanctuary.

"How was the maze?" Dove asked when we set up the snacks.

"Fine," I said. "Tiring."

"Talk to me about tired when you're almost seventy-eight and putting on a children's play. Next rehearsal is tomorrow afternoon. I know it's Sunday, but I thought we could work in some extra time with the leads."

"I agree." I'd been worrying about whether the kids had been practicing their lines at home.

"What about Angelina?" I asked. "Will she be here?"

"I called her aunt, but she doesn't speak very good English. So she gave the phone to Angelina, and she said she'd be there. That child is growing up too fast." Dove shook her head in pity.

"I know." It was true, not just for Angelina, but for lots of first-generation immigrant families. The children often learned the language first, and because of that were put in the position of being the spokesperson for the family and having to deal with more mature situations than they should have to.

"I think I'll bake some of my chocolate-coconut surprise cupcakes for them," Dove said.

"They'd love that," I said. "So will I."

"For you I'm bringing carrot sticks," she said, not entirely joking.

At home, I puttered around waiting for Gabe and Luis to come home, my thoughts going over and over the possibility that I was right about Walt Adams making the violin replica. How hard would it have been? Did one need special tools? I was sure you did, but then again, Rafael Aznar didn't have them. He used the crude tools avail-

able in the late eighteenth century. But surely if Walt had made the violin he'd have to have known the rudimentary aspects of building a
stringed instrument. Where would he find that out? The Internet, like
Joe did this information? I couldn't imagine Walt being a computer
buff.

Maybe he checked a book out from the library. That would be my
next guess since Gabe never mentioned that his detectives found a
book in his possession about violin making. I glanced at the clock
over our fireplace. Four o'clock. It would still be open. If I was lucky,
someone I knew would be working the reference desk.

San Celina's still fairly new library sat on a bluff overlooking La-
guna Lake. Its stark, gray architecture had won many awards, but not
much love from the locals. It had never seemed like a library to me,
but then my fond childhood memories were of the old brick Carnegie
Library before it became the historical museum.

It took me ten minutes to find a parking space. There was some
kind of pet fair filling one side of the parking lot. I skirted hysterical
terriers and squalling cats and went inside the library where it was
cool and a bit quieter. I ran up the stairs to the reference department.
Luck was with me that day. Catalina Vieira was working the reference desk. Cat and I hung around the same group in college, both
having minored in agriculture. In our junior year, she switched her
major from history to library science. We'd recently renewed our relationship when I'd bought Dove some new chickens at Vieira Ranch
and Feed in Atascadero, a store her family had owned for three gen-
erations. They specialized in poultry.

"Hey, Cat," I said, walking up to her. She was helping a young
teenager look up the value of his car in the Kelly blue book. She nodded at me and said to him, "This is all online now too. Just Google it."

"I like Dogpile better," the young man said.

"Whatever," Cat answered. "I'll keep your driver's license while
you look through the book."

I stepped up to the desk. "Dove loves her Brown Leghorns, though they keep her plenty busy."

Cat nodded. "Great layers, but those birds are as flighty as . . . well, you know. They bounce off the walls sometimes."

"I know. Dove says she has to dodge airborne chickens every time she gathers eggs. But she said she couldn't resist the striped chicks when she saw them at your store."

She tapped her shiny red pencil on the countertop, glancing over at the young man who had the Kelly blue book, making sure he hadn't stuck it in his backpack.

"So, what can I do for you?" she asked, sticking the pencil behind her ear. Her auburn hair, streaked with gray, was pulled back in a long braid. Her smoky green eyes peered at me over square, wire-rim eyeglasses.

"I don't know if this is illegal . . ."

She grinned and leaned closer. "Now, we're talking. I'm bored stiff. Let's do something bad."

I laughed, remembering that Cat was the one in college who thought up the most outrageous stunts to pull on other colleges' ag students when we went to conventions. She'd always sweet talk some goofy-eyed guy from our college to take the real risk, though. Easy for her to do with her thick, auburn hair and a figure that still, in her late thirties, caused men to turn their heads. Not your clichéd picture of a reference librarian.

"It's not that bad, considering some of the things you've done," I said. "I want to look up someone's check-out history."

"Whoa, that's badder than you think," she said. "You're talking privacy laws."

"What if the person is dead?"

"Now, there's a good question. I imagine the privacy issue is the same."

"But you're not sure."

"I think it's something still being debated. Traditionally, we've never allowed access unless the police demanded it. To be honest, in my fifteen years as a librarian, no one's ever asked."

I leaned my elbows on the desk. "So?"

"The guy killed in your church, right?"

I nodded.

She glanced to both sides, making sure no one overheard us. "I don't know, Benni. I don't want to get in trouble. It's a hot button with libraries now. What does Gabe say?"

"I just thought of it, and he's off with his cousin so I can't ask." I gave her a beseeching look. "I'm dying to find out if something I suspect is true. Are you sure you can't help me?"

She thought for a moment. "Okay, just ask me one question. I'll probably get fired for this if they ever find out, but I'm getting sick of kids and their last-minute term papers anyway. I think I'll go back to selling chickens. Less stress."

"Did Walter Adams check out any books on violins?"

"That's it?"

I nodded.

"Let me see." She started typing on her computer, leaving it three times in ten minutes to help patrons. Finally, she was able to pull up his check-out record. "Five months ago." She stared at me, her mouth opened slightly. "You mean . . ."

"I think so," I said quickly. "But don't say anything until I give the information to Gabe. I just wanted it verified, and you did that."

"No problem. Let me know what happens. Tell Dove we've got some real nice Sicilian Buttercups coming in next month."

"Shoot, she'll buy those chickens just because of the name."

She grinned. "That's what I was hoping."

It was past five o'clock by the time I got home. There was still no message from Gabe. I tried his cell phone and got voice mail. He'd never said exactly when they'd be home, but we had talked about Chinese food for dinner.

"Call me as soon as you get this message," I left on his cell phone's voice mail. I was dying to tell him what I found out about Walt.

About seven o'clock, I was starting to get worried, when our home phone rang. It was Luis.

"Is Gabe home yet?" he asked.

"Isn't he with you?" I asked, suddenly afraid.

"Have you talked to him in the last hour?" he asked.

"No," I said, confused. "Why?"

"You'd better talk to him," he said, his voice subdued.

"Why? What happened? Where are you?"

"I'm at my hotel. Just ask him," he said, sighing. "So, how was your day?"

It was an obvious ploy to change the subject so I tried to be sensitive and go with it. "Fine. Worked at the folk art museum. Had another rehearsal with the kids. Went to the library."

"That's nice." His tone was polite.

"Luis, cut the bull. Tell me what happened between you two. Maybe I can help."

"Ask Gabe."

"I'm asking you, Luis."

He was silent for a moment. "He can explain. I think I'll be leaving town tomorrow morning. I just wanted to call and say good-bye and thank you for being so welcoming."

"Oh, Luis." I didn't know what else to say. They'd obviously argued again. Watching those two men relate was like watching a tennis match.

The minute Gabe walked in the door I told him his cousin had called.

"What happened?" I asked.

"Let's go in the living room," he said, his shoulders slumped, his whole demeanor that of a very weary man. "It's complicated."

This time he told me every detail. After their lunch in Big Sur, they drove back down the coast, taking their time, having a relaxing day. By the end of the day Gabe had talked Luis into coming back to stay with us. An hour ago, while he waited for Luis to check out of his hotel room, Luis received a phone call, one that shook him up, and after some probing, Gabe got the story out of him—the uncontrollable gambling, the debt to a Las Vegas loanshark he couldn't pay, their verbal threats, how he'd borrowed against his house without telling Paige and now was five months behind in their six-thousand-dollar mortgage payments.

"It was the reason he came to visit us," Gabe said, his voice disgusted. "Not to see me. He was hiding and eventually hoping to convince me to loan him the twenty thousand dollars he needs to get these lowlifes off his back."

"Twenty thousand dollars! What will happen if he doesn't pay?"

"Not my problem," Gabe said. "I told him to stay away from us. Just because he's thrown his life down the toilet, he has no right to drag me with him."

"That's why Paige doesn't want him to be around Cassie."

"No doubt," Gabe said, his blue eyes staring straight ahead. The tiny muscle in the hinge of his jaw twitched.

"Friday, I'm so sorry." I rubbed my hand up and down his forearm.

"Not as sorry as I am for believing he'd ever changed. He's always been a user. He didn't care one bit if he was putting me or the people I love in danger. These people he owes have no scruples. They'd hurt his family without a thought just to teach him a lesson."

A chill ran through me. That meant, if those men had followed Luis here, we had been in danger all this time.

We didn't talk about Luis for the rest of the night. While we watched television, I would occasionally glance over at Gabe, whose eyes, though glued to the flickering screen, were really somewhere else.

As we were getting ready for bed, I decided to tell him that I'd talked a friend into looking up Walt's record at the library.

Gabe just sighed. "I'll tell the detectives," he said, not even lecturing me about possibly breaking a law or about leaving the investigation to him. "That's a good lead."

"Luis called right before you came home," I said. "I wanted you to know that. He told me he was leaving tomorrow."

"Good," Gabe said. "That's the best thing for everyone."

CHAPTER 15

$\mathcal{T}$HE NEXT MORNING CHURCH WAS HELD IN THE SANCTUARY now that the new carpet had been installed. The mood was subdued as we sang "Blessed Assurance, Jesus is mine, Oh, what a foretaste of glory divine." When we reached the stanza that read, "Born of his spirit, washed in his blood," I imagined I heard a slight hesitation in the congregation's singing. Then again, not many of them knew how much blood there'd been when Walt Adams died.

After lunch at home, Gabe decided to go into the office to catch up on some paperwork.

"I won't have phone calls interrupting me every five minutes," he said.

It was also a place where Luis couldn't easily reach him or maybe wouldn't even try. I suspected Gabe would eventually forgive his cousin. *Familia* was important to Gabe, and he took the bonds seriously. But it would take time. It probably would be best if Luis did go away for awhile and solved his personal problems before contacting Gabe again.

"I'll be up at the church from two to four," I said. "Dove and I are working with the leads in the play."

"How about dinner in Morro Bay tonight?" he asked.

"Sure," I said, kissing him good-bye, wishing I could do something to change the melancholy look on his face.

Scout waited for me at the door.

"Sorry, but you gotta stay home today. We need to have the kids concentrate, and you are, as they say, a very attractive nuisance." I stroked his head and promised him a long game of catch when I came home.

❖

WHEN I DROVE INTO THE CHURCH PARKING LOT, THE FIRST THING I saw was Jonathan Hammer and Sheila Murray standing beside his dark green Mercedes arguing while Travis stood a few feet away and beat the side of an oak tree with a stick. No one else had arrived yet.

"Great," I said out loud. "Hud, where are you when I need you?" A domestic situation was not how I wanted to start out this rehearsal.

I parked on the opposite side of the parking lot and took my time getting out of my truck, hoping they'd resolve their differences before I was forced to walk by them. They obviously had a lot to say to each other, most of it loudly, with dramatic hand gestures. I glanced at my watch. Dove and the children would be arriving any time. I didn't want this to be going on when parents dropped off their kids.

They didn't skip a beat in their argument when I walked up.

"If you don't keep that scum away from my son, I'll sue you for full custody," Jonathan said, his finger inches from Sheila's nose.

She slapped it away. "That's rich. You've canceled the last two weekends you were supposed to have Travis so you could go to one of your fancy golf tournaments. That should impress the judge. You don't want your son full time. You can't even spend an hour with him without turning on a video or buying him another Gameboy cartridge."

"What was last night?" he said. "I went through that whole freakin' corn maze with him."

"Father of the year," she said sarcastically. She whipped out a package of cigarettes and shook one out of the pack.

I glanced over at Travis, who was still rhythmically beating the trunk of an oak tree with a stick. His face was neutral, like he'd emotionally vacated the premises.

"Hey," I said, walking up to them. "Why don't you two discuss this somewhere else?" I tried to make my voice pleasant and non-judgmental.

Jonathan turned to me, his face flushed with anger, and told me to do something to myself that was, truth be told, physically impossible.

"Oh, nice," Sheila said, taking a drag on her cigarette. "Classy thing to say in a church parking lot, you freak. I hope God strikes you dead."

"Look," I said. "Kids will be arriving in a few minutes, and I need to have a calm atmosphere for them to rehearse in."

"Then tell the jerk to get out of here," Sheila said.

"Not until you promise me that asshole Adams isn't going to be hanging around my son anymore. I'm telling you, he's trouble."

"Who my friends are has nothing to do with you," she retorted.

"They do when they affect my son."

"That's it," I said. "I don't care what you two say to each other, but it's not going to be right here, right now. Come back at four o'clock to pick up Travis."

I walked over to Travis and held out my hand. He took it without looking at either of his parents. At that moment, Hud's red truck drove up. I was never so glad to see someone in my life.

"Look," I said. "There's Detective Hudson. I'm sure he'd be glad to mediate your domestic differences." I looked down at Travis. "Go get Maisie and then wait for me near the front door." Maisie waved at Travis from inside the truck. He let loose of my hand and ran over to the passenger side.

Jonathan Hammer glanced over at Hud's truck, then back at me. His face was livid, but he was obviously not willing to deal with the police. He opened the door of his Mercedes. "I mean it, Sheila. Keep that jerk away from my son or I'll see you in court."

"Kiss my—" Sheila started, then stopped, obviously remembering where she was. "Just go away, Jonathan," she said, her voice weary.

He glared at her one last time, then stepped into the car, slamming the door behind him.

She looked at me, embarrassed. "I'm sorry, I wish you hadn't witnessed that."

"Aren't you more concerned about Travis witnessing it?"

She shrugged. "He's used to it."

I sighed inwardly, knowing that there was nothing I could do to resolve this situation. "We should be done around four."

"It's Jonathan's turn to pick him up." She turned her back to me and walked to her car.

"What's going on?" Hud asked, walking up to me as I struggled with opening the double front doors of the sanctuary.

"Nothing, why?" I wiggled the key and finally managed to release the lock.

"I can spot a domestic from a football field away."

"It was just that. Two parents supposedly squabbling over their kid, but really it was a power play between the two of them." I opened the doors and pushed them so they stayed open.

"Poor kid," he said, looking over at Travis and Maisie.

"Yeah," I said.

In the next few minutes Dove and the rest of the kids arrived, including Angelina. This time she was brought by her aunt.

"*Buenos tardes, señora,*" I said to Juana.

"*Buenos tardes,*" she replied, ducking her head.

"Tell your aunt we'll be done at four o'clock," I told Angelina. "And that we'll make sure you have a snack."

After she rattled off my information, Juana smiled at me.

"*Gracias, señora.*" she said, then touched Angelina's cheek briefly before leaving.

"*De nada,*" I replied.

We rounded up the kids and did a head count. Travis, Maisie, Angelina, Salvador, Brian, and Brianna, our lead actors.

"Let's do a quick run-through," I said. "We'll skip the music and just concentrate on your dialog."

While I helped the kids go through the script, Dove looked over the plans for the scenery, making changes to tell JoAnn. By the time the kids and I had gone through the complete script twice, they were getting hungry and antsy.

"We'll have lunch in the recreation hall," Dove said. "Play some games while I go set it up."

She looked over at Hud, who was sitting in the last pew, his head nodding, ready to fall asleep. "Hey, Detective," she yelled, causing him to jerk awake. "Make yourself useful and come help me in the kitchen."

He grinned sheepishly at me as he walked up the center aisle to follow Dove through a side door. "Sorry. Late night."

"Please," I said, shaking my head and laughing, "spare us the gruesome details."

"It was work!" he protested.

"Tell it to the judge," I replied, still laughing. After all the sad things I'd heard about in the last day or so, it felt good to joke with Hud about something silly.

I was in the process of sitting the kids down in a circle to start a game of "telephone" when the church's swing doors opened. I turned to see Luis standing at the start of the center aisle. The kids watched curiously as I walked down to see what he needed.

"Hi, Luis," I said. "What're you doing here?"

"I was driving by on my way out of town and saw your truck. I wanted to say good-bye."

I could smell the alcohol on his breath even though we stood a couple of feet apart. "Oh, Luis, maybe you should go get something to eat before you drive." I looked up into his eyes. They were as shiny as black marbles. Was he on something besides alcohol?

"Luis, let's go outside," I said in a low voice. "The kids."

"What?" he demanded, his voice unnaturally loud. "I'm not good enough to be around kids. Is that what you're saying?"

"No, no," I said, wishing that Hud hadn't left. "It's just they're getting ready to have lunch, and they're tired and, you know, I'm sorry about you and Gabe, but I think—"

I abruptly stopped talking, realizing I was babbling.

"I need to talk to Gabe," he said. "He won't answer his cell phone. I went by the house, and he's not there. Where is he? I need to talk to Gabe."

Though I certainly didn't want Luis to find Gabe when he was in the condition he was in, I also didn't want to subject the kids to it.

"I'll call him for you," I said. "But we need to do it outside. What's going on between you and Gabe shouldn't involve these kids."

"I'm good with kids," Luis said, his words slurring. "I raised two sons, you know. They're good boys, and I helped raise them. People forget that, you know. They forget I helped raise them. I'm paying their way through college even though the little assholes won't even talk to me half the time. Isn't that a good father, Benni? I ask you, isn't that a good father?"

"Yes," I said, trying to placate him. "They are good kids, Luis. You have a lot to be proud of. Let's go outside and call Gabe."

"I almost had it all worked out," Luis said. "But in the end, it wasn't enough. It's never enough. That could be my life's motto. Luis, what you do is never enough."

"Hey, *niños*," he called over my shoulder. "What do you think? Think that a father who busts his ass for his kids is a good father? Do any of your fathers bust their asses like I do? I bet they don't."

"Luis!" I said. "Watch your mouth."

Nervous giggles tittered behind me. I turned to shush them and instruct them to go over to the recreation hall so they could be spared Luis's erratic behavior and rough language.

Angelina's terrified face stopped my words. Her tiny mouth opened slightly, like a hungry bird. But it was the expression on her face that really frightened me. Terror. And recognition. There could be only one thing, one man that could terrify her that way. In that moment I understood why Gabe's voice had frightened her silent, why she'd been afraid of him and not Hud. It wasn't that he was a cop. He sounded like the man she'd heard in the church.

But why would Luis kill Walt?

I turned back to look at my husband's cousin, who hadn't noticed Angelina's reaction. He pulled a silver flask from inside his jacket, unscrewed the cap, and took a drink.

"Luis," I said firmly, trying to keep my voice steady. "This is really inappropriate. You need to leave."

"No, what I need is to talk to Gabe."

"I'll call him for you, but only if you come outside with me."

It happened in one of those terrifying dream moments when everything that is normal suddenly becomes bizarre. A gun appeared in his hand. He pointed it at me. I stared at the barrel, shocked silent. "Go lock all the doors," he said. "Tell those kids they'd better not make one sound."

Like a robot, I turned to the kids and said in my calmest voice, "Okay, kids, go sit up in the choir loft right now. No talking, just do as I say." Wide-eyed, realizing that this wasn't a joke, they went up into the choir loft right behind the pulpit and took seats. I turned back to face Luis, who still had his gun pointed at me. "Luis, this isn't going to solve anything. Let me get Gabe on the phone for you."

"Go lock the doors," Luis said. "It's too late. Too late for anything."

While he watched, I went around and locked the three sets of doors; the front double doors and the two emergency exit doors, one to the outside, one to the other buildings. The kids watched me with uncertain eyes. I smiled at them, trying to reassure them. The whole time my mind was racing, trying to figure out how to keep them safe, get them out of here, keep Luis calm, and keep him talking. That thought kept running through my head, like a cliché scene in a television show. As long as I kept him talking, then no one would get hurt.

"Luis, what are you planning to do?" I asked, once I'd locked all the doors. "You know the minute Hud realizes what's happened there'll be a hundred cops here. This is going to break your parents' hearts."

He looked at me through narrowed eyes. "Break my dad's heart? According to him, I did that years ago."

I swallowed hard and walked over to him, both hands outstretched. I kept my eyes focused on the space between his eyes. Don't look at the gun, I kept telling myself. *Don't look at the gun.*

"Luis, all of that is water under the bridge. Families disappoint each other, that's just life. But I know Uncle Tony loves you. You're his firstborn son. He'd do anything for you."

Luis's voice was harsh. "Anything but let me be who I am."

"Then that's his problem, not yours. He—" Before I could go on, the side door rattled and Hud's voice called out.

"Hey, why're these locked? Benni? What's going on?"

I glanced nervously at Luis, who still held his gun on me. "I have to say something, Luis. He'll bust it down if I don't."

He waved the gun at me, telling me to take care of it. "But don't open the door," he said. "Or I start shooting."

I went over to the door and yelled through it. "Hud, I can't open the door."

"Why not?" he yelled back. "Is it stuck?"

"No." I turned to look at Luis, holding my hand palm up.

Luis thought for a moment.

Hud pounded on the door. "Benni, what's wrong? Benni, answer me!"

Luis said, "Tell him I'll only talk to Gabe."

I yelled through the door, "Hud, get Gabe. His cousin Luis wants to talk to him. It's important."

Hud was silent for a moment, the realization of what had happened right under his nose hitting him. "Benni, is he armed?" His voice sounded very far away.

"Yes."

"Maisie . . ." I could hear the agony in his voice.

"She's fine. We're all fine."

"Sit tight. I'll be right—"

"That's enough," Luis said, coming over and pulling me away from the door. He called out to Hud. "Tell my cousin to call Benni's cell phone."

"Don't—" I heard Hud start.

Luis interrupted. "No more talking."

He gestured at me to join the kids in the choir loft. I went up there, gathering the kids close to me, touching them, patting their hands, shoulders, faces, hugging them, trying to assure them that everything would be okay.

"I want to go home," Brianna whimpered.

"You will, sweetie," I said, making my voice sound calm.

Angelina had grabbed my hand and would not let go. I sat down on the padded pew and pulled her into my lap.

"Come here, kids," I said in a low voice as I watched Luis pace up and down the middle aisle of the church. It was obvious he was on something besides just alcohol. "I want you to listen to me real close now. Everything's going to be okay. You just need to watch me and do everything I tell you to do. No questions asked, okay? If I tell you to hit the floor, that means I want you to lay down fast and cover your heads with your hands. Okay?"

They all watched me with wide, solemn eyes.

"Like in the movies?" Travis said.

"Exactly," I replied. "It's just like with the play. I'm the director, and you need to do what I say. Only this time it's real important that you don't argue and do what I say really, really fast. Okay?"

They all nodded. I felt Angelina tremble in my lap. "Now, let's all say a quick prayer to Jesus to protect us and then let's be very quiet while I try to talk to Mr. Ortiz, okay?"

They all nodded.

Then Travis said, "I'm not afraid. I'll pray."

"That would be wonderful, Travis."

We all bowed our heads and Travis said, "Dear Jesus, please save us from the bad man and help us not be scared. Amen. Oh, and to be able to run fast if we have to. Amen again."

"Amen," I said softly, then smiled at Travis. "That was perfect. Remember, I want you all to be quiet as little mice while I talk to Mr. Ortiz."

I reluctantly let go of Angelina and said, "I'll be right back, *mija*." She clung to my neck for a moment.

I walked down the steps from the altar and slowly approached Luis, who was now standing at the back of the church staring at the double doors.

"Luis," I said softly, afraid to startle him. He held the gun tightly, with his finger on the trigger. It was an automatic that looked similar to the one Gabe carried.

He whipped around so suddenly, I took a step back and gasped.

"What?" he asked. The look of desperation and fear on his face only frightened me more. It made what he might do that much more unpredictable.

"Luis . . ." The words froze in my throat. What could I say that would convince him to let the kids go? That was all I could think about at that moment, helping the kids escape before something unthinkable happened.

I could only imagine what was taking place this moment as Hud called Gabe and things started happening. Gabe's officers trained for moments like this, his SWAT team was continually preparing itself for hostage situations. Hostage. Just the sound of the word was terrifying. The children's parents would be . . . I couldn't even think of a word descriptive enough of the agony they'd feel when they heard. I had to talk him into letting the kids free. *Help*, I prayed.

"Luis," I said. "I understand that you are feeling bad now. But you have to let those kids go. I'll stay here with you, but they're scared and hungry. Please let them go."

"No," he said, looking past me up at the kids, who were staring at us, watching our every move. "I have to think. I have to decide what to do."

I inhaled deeply and tried again. "I understand. But you can do that with just me here. You can—"

Just at that moment, my phone rang. "Happy Trails" sounded tinny and faraway and so incongruent with what was happening.

"What was that?" He jerked his head back and forth, his breathing fast and shallow.

"It's my cell phone," I said. "It's probably Gabe. Should I answer it?"

He nodded, waved his gun at me to go ahead. I reluctantly turned my back on him and walked up the aisle toward my purse sitting on the front pew. Did he have the gun pointed at my back? I'd never felt so vulnerable in my life. Please, I pleaded, don't let him kill me in front of these kids. I smiled at them as I walked toward my purse.

"It's okay," I said to them. "It's probably my husband on the phone. You all remember him, don't you? He's a policeman."

"Like my daddy," Maisie offered, her eyes blinking rapidly.

"That's right, Maisie," I said, reaching into my purse. "Just like your daddy."

I fumbled around until I found my phone, searching at the same time for the pepper spray I always carried.

"What's taking so long?" Luis demanded, running up the aisle. "Answer the phone."

I flipped open the phone, glancing down at my purse. The pepper spray was right there in full view.

"Hello," I said.

"Benni!" Gabe exclaimed. "What's going on? What's Luis doing?"

Before I could answer, Luis looked down at my purse, grabbed the pepper spray, and threw it across the church.

Behind me, one of the children let out a small cry.

"We're fine," I said to Gabe and smiled reassuringly at the children.

Luis grabbed the phone out of my hand. "Gabe? It's your loving cousin here. How's things going, *primo*?"

He listened for a moment, then said, "Well, I'm sorry you feel that way. I'm actually going to make you famous. Or at least get your name in the paper. You'll like that, won't you? Dad will, anyway. He'll be able to cut it out, show it to all his cop buddies. Oh, maybe not. There's the part about his son being a screwup. Then again, maybe he could cut those parts out. *Hasta luego*, Chief Ortiz." He flipped the phone shut and threw it down on the pew.

Seconds later it rang again.

"Don't answer it," Luis commanded.

"That'll just make things worse. Please, stop this before it gets out of control."

He stared at me, his eyes so dark the pupils had disappeared. "Too late for that. My life is totally of control."

"No," I said, reaching out my hand. "It's not—"

"Shut up!" He waved the gun at me. "Go up and sit with the kids and shut up. I need to think."

Doing what he said, I joined the kids, pulling them close around me, trying to touch each one.

"Close your eyes," I whispered to them. "And think of the prettiest place you've ever been to. Pretend you're there right now."

"Disneyland," Brianna whispered.

"The beach," her brother, Brian, said.

"Mama," I heard Angelina murmur.

❖

DURING THE NEXT HOUR, WITH LUIS PACING UP AND DOWN THE aisle, and the phone ringing every five minutes, I whispered encouragement to the kids. I told them this was like the play that they'd been practicing, that like Christian, this was a journey, that we were going through the wilderness, but that the Delectable Mountains were not far away and how from the top of those beautiful mountains, we would be able to see the Celestial City.

"He's Giant Despair," Salvador said, looking over at Luis, who'd stopped pacing and was now sitting in a back pew, staring in our direction. He'd not said a word to us for the last half hour.

"Yes," I said, though it made my heart sick. "And we have to stay strong and not give up hope."

"I have to go to the bathroom," Brianna said, her dark eyes starting to panic.

"Me too," Travis admitted, looking shamefaced.

"Okay," I said, standing up. He had children. Maybe this would touch Luis. "Let me go ask Mr. Ortiz."

I walked down the aisle toward him. "Luis," I called, keeping my voice soft, trying to keep it from sounding fearful.

Out of the corner of my eye, I caught a dark movement next to one of the long, gold-frosted windows. Of course, the SWAT team would have surrounded us by now. Behind me, the phone rang again.

"Luis," I said again.

He looked up at me, his eyes blank and glassy.

"The kids have to go to the bathroom."

He stared at me, uncomprehending, it seemed. What had he been taking? Had it so completely overtaken his senses that he couldn't see that this was a situation that he wouldn't win?

Behind me, my cell phone rang again. "Please, let me answer it."

He didn't say anything.

"Luis, please."

He looked down at his gun, then back up at me. "Okay."

I forced myself not to run up the aisle. On the fourth ring, I answered.

"Hello?" inquired a man. His accent was southern, soft, comforting. "Mr. Ortiz?"

"No, it's Benni," I replied, hearing the catch in my voice and hoping the kids didn't hear it.

"Hello, Benni. This is Detective Luther Washington. We met a few months ago."

I tried to put a face to his name. I vaguely remembered a gangly, handsome black man. He'd had short, salt-and-pepper hair and freckles across the bridge of his light brown nose. "Yes, Detective Washington. I think I remember you."

"Are you and the kids okay?"

"Yes, we're fine. Scared. The kids have to go to the bathroom."

He laughed. It was a gentle, easy laugh. "I imagine they do. Are there facilities inside there?"

"They're near the front door. I'm not sure he'll let us use—"

At that moment, Luis must have realized that leaving me to talk at length to anyone on the outside would put him at a disadvantage. "What are you saying?" he asked.

"I can hear him," Detective Washington said. "Do you think he'll speak to me?"

I remembered this man now. Gabe had hired him from the Orange County sheriff's department because of his hostage negotiating experience.

"Ask him," he instructed me.

I held the phone out to Luis. "He wants to talk to you."

He looked at the phone, disgust obvious on his face. "Tell my cousin I said all I had to say."

"It's not Gabe," I said.

He looked at me, then at the outstretched phone. After a moment's hesitation, he grabbed the phone. "What?"

He listened, and I watched his face. Behind me, I could hear the kids getting antsy.

After a minute, he thrust the phone back at me. "Tell him I'll think about it."

I put the phone up to my ear.

"Detective Washington?"

"Benni, stay calm. We have the area around the church evacuated, and SWAT is ready to go when we give the signal. But that's going to be our very last resort. We want to get the kids, you, and Mr. Ortiz out of there with no incident. Try to talk him into that. He sounds as if he is at least listening. Is he intoxicated?"

"I think so."

"Does he seem nervous, licking his lips? Like he's on meth?"

"No . . . no . . . I think it's the first."

"Does he seem angry? Depressed?"

"The first, mostly."

"I asked him if he needed anything, and he said he'd think about it. If you can, find out what he wants. Keep him talking. I told him I'd call back in ten minutes."

"Okay," I said.

"Hang in there," he said. "We'll get you out."

"Thank you. Tell Gabe—" A wet thickness in my throat choked off my words.

"I will, Benni. He knows."

I turned off the cell phone and walked over to Luis. "The kids have to go to the bathroom," I said in a low voice. "We can't just let them suffer. Think if it was Cassie up there."

I thought I saw a flicker in his dark eyes. Had that reached him?

"Okay," he said. "Let them . . ." He looked around. "Are there bathrooms? No, I can't . . . it's too dangerous . . . I . . ." He began to get agitated, causing my stomach to drop.

I stepped closer, within a foot of him, whispering so the kids couldn't hear us. "Luis, please let the kids go. I'll stay here with you. I am just as good, no . . . a *better* . . . hostage. You know they won't do anything as long as you have the police chief's wife. The kids are just a burden. Let's just let them go so we don't have to worry about them."

His face seemed to collapse. Was he thinking about Cassie? Should I bring her up again or would that make him angry? I felt like every word I said was like a jewel, so important, capable of turning his emotions one way or the other.

"How?" he finally asked.

Thank you, Lord, I said inside.

"When the detective calls back, we'll make a deal. You can hold the gun on me and that will keep them from rushing in. Stand to the side while we open the front door. The kids can leave, and I'll shut the door. How about that?"

I watched his face trying to comprehend my plan. How *much* had he had to drink? Would he be able to follow any sort of plan or would he just panic when the door opened? That thought chilled me. I knew SWAT would have a sharpshooter stationed, ready to fire. As horrible as this was, I didn't want him to die for it.

"Okay," he said.

"Thank you, Luis," I said, relief flooding my body. I walked back down the long aisle to where the kids sat. "I want you all to stand up and quietly come down here and form a line. Mr. Ortiz is going to let you go see your parents." I forced my voice to be upbeat.

On the front pew, my cell phone rang. I glanced over at Luis, asking permission. He gave an almost imperceptible nod.

"Hello?" I asked, grasping the phone tightly.

"Benni," Detective Washington said. Already his voice felt familiar to me, a lifeline. It felt that as long as I was talking to him, nothing bad could happen.

"He's agreed to let the children go," I said.

"Thank God," he said. "What's the plan?"

"I'm walking them down to the front doors. He has his gun on me, but he'll let them go. Please, Detective." I didn't know what it was I was exactly pleading for.

"Don't worry, Benni. We have it under control. Trust us."

"Yes, sir." I didn't have any other choice.

"You've done a good job. Getting the kids out will be the hardest part."

"I know."

"Let me talk to him," Luis said, grabbing the phone. "If I see one cop—just one—Benni gets a bullet in the head. Got it?" He closed the phone and stuck it in his pants pocket.

His voice, so similar to Gabe's, sent a chill down my spine. I glanced over at the children, whose eyes were wide and terrified now.

"It's okay," I said to them. "Don't worry. You're all going to be fine."

Angelina started crying. I bent down and pulled her to me. "Don't cry. It's going to be okay. I promise."

"Yeah," Maisie said, coming over and patting Angelina on the shoulder. "My daddy's a policeman, and he'll save us."

"That's right," I said. "Everyone's going to be okay."

We walked down the aisle toward the foyer, the kids following me. When we stepped inside the foyer and reached the double doors, Luis moved to the side.

"Just crack the door," he said.

Before I did, I bent over and pulled all the kids close. "Now, listen. I'm going to open this door, and I want you to walk outside. Don't be scared and don't run. There will be police officers outside waiting for you. Go with them, and they'll take you to your parents."

I looked over at Luis, who slowly nodded his head. I cracked one of the front doors and said, "Okay, kids, go on out. One at a time. Pretend like you're heading to the Delectable Mountains. When you get to the top of them, do you remember what you'll see?"

They were quiet for a moment, then Salvador said, "The Celestial City."

"Right." I smiled at them. Their figures were blurry through the tears I willed myself not to shed. "I'll see you all at the next rehearsal. Dove will make her special chocolate chip cookies."

When the last one had gone through the door, Luis gestured at me to close and lock it. Though I was still afraid, it was like a huge burden had been lifted off my back.

"Back inside," he said, gesturing with the gun.

I walked back down the aisle until we reached the front.

"Sit down," he said.

I took a seat on the front pew and stared up at the oak cross above the baptismal. A thought struck me at that moment. What if this were the place where I would die? Right here in the same church where I'd been saved, baptized, and married twice?

I thought about Dove, the first time I saw her at the train station when I was six and she was coming to take care of Mama, Daddy, and me. She smelled like almonds even then. She wore blue jeans and a pink gingham shirt. She brought me a tin of pralines. When we got to the ranch, I remember showing her my room and the Crown of Thorns quilt on my bed.

"My gramma made that quilt," I'd told her proudly, repeating what Mama and Daddy had told me since I was three, not really comprehending yet who Dove was, why she was there. "She lives in Arkansas."

"Not any more she doesn't, honeybun," she said, laughing. It was the first time she called me honeybun.

I thought about striped chicks, the tire swing in the cottonwood tree behind the house, the sound of coyotes on a cool spring night, the smell of the night-blooming jasmine that grew under the kitchen window. I thought of my husband's muscled thighs, the glassy sheen of his black hair, the taste and smell of him, a spicy, intoxicating smell that made me understand why animals want to roll in scents that appeal to them. I thought about Jack's grave. Would I be buried next to him? Would Daddy make that decision? Dove? Gabe? *Gabe*. The guilt he'll feel will sear his soul. It's okay, I wish I could tell him. It's not your fault.

Luis sat down at the other end of the pew, close to the organ. My phone rang and rang in his pocket, but it was as if he didn't hear it. It took every ounce of restraint I possessed not to rush over there and grab it from him. But he just sat there, and so did I. Maybe I should be trying to talk to him, convince him to give himself up. But suddenly I was so weary. All I wanted to do was lie down on the soft padded pew and go to sleep.

Finally, when it started ringing for the fourth time in what had to be an hour, Luis answered it.

"What?" he asked.

I turned to watch him as he listened to Detective Washington. What did hostage negotiators learn in school? I knew they had special training and that it took a unique kind of person to do that job. How did they get those assignments? Did they apply for them? What made a person want to be a hostage negotiator?

"Hamburger, I guess," I heard Luis say. "Fries. Coke."

He was ordering food?

"No, you can't talk to her. Tell my cousin I'm taking real good care of his wife." Then he turned off the phone.

"They're getting us hamburgers," Luis said.

"Sure," I said, though the thought of eating anything made me feel like throwing up.

Twenty minutes later, the phone rang again. Luis answered it.

"Set it by the door. I'll have her covered so don't try anything." He stood up. "Go to the door and get the food. Don't try anything."

"Okay," I said, walking ahead of him.

After I picked up the food, he told me to take it back to the front of the church. "Open the bag," he said.

I tentatively opened the white, grease-stained bag, as apprehensive as he obviously was. But it contained nothing but two hamburgers, two orders of fries, and two Cokes.

I pulled out a Coke. "I'll just have this. I'm not that hungry."

He shrugged. "Suit yourself."

He set the gun down next to him. Though I'd thought about it briefly, I knew it would be impossible to try to get it away from him.

He ate without talking. I sipped my Coke, my stomach roiling at the smell of greasy fries and melted cheese.

"So," he finally said, the food obviously making him a bit more sociable. "What do you think Gabe is doing right now?"

Up until that moment, I'd felt a lot of things—fear, despair, panic, pity. But anger flared with that remark. "Luis, how could you do this to Gabe? He loves you."

His laugh was deep and sarcastic. "Oh, yeah, he loves me all right. So much he's willing to let those guys beat the crap out of me and possibly kill me. All because he won't loan me a few lousy dollars."

"Twenty thousand is a bit more than a few lousy dollars."

He glanced over at me, licking his chapped lips. "He told you."

"Yes, he did. Do you really think Gabe should give you money to pay off your gambling debt?"

"Loan. All I asked for was a loan." He leaned back against the pew, turning his head to stare at one of the frosty side windows. It was dark, which told me it was past five o'clock. How long had we been here? Three, four hours? Longer? I'd lost track of time and for once, I wasn't wearing a watch. How long could Luis hold out?

"Doesn't matter anyway," he said. "I'm a dead man no matter how you look at it. Paige left me. My sons will hate me when I tell them they'll have to drop out of college. I have nothing left."

"Don't say that. If you'd just give up now, you'll have a chance. No one's been hurt yet."

He turned to look at me, his expression haunted. "Wrong, Benni."

Angelina's terrified face when she heard Luis's voice came back to me. The voice she'd heard while hiding in the baptismal. I was right, he had killed Walt. "Why, Luis? Why would you kill him?"

He shook his head regretfully. "It wasn't supposed to happen like that. I wouldn't have had to ask Gabe for the money if things had worked out how we'd planned."

If he killed Walt because he was going to confess to Mac about making the duplicate violin, that meant Luis was involved with the violin's theft. "Do you know what happened to the Aznar violin?"

"Good question," he said. "That was going to be my ticket out of trouble. Jonathan swore to me that violin was worth a million dollars overseas."

"Jonathan Hammer?" Now I was really confused. "But you and he . . . in the bookstore . . ."

He shrugged. "We almost blew it that day. I didn't expect to see him there or put on that phony act about being upset about Gabe slacking off on investigating the theft. Jonathan had the violin all along. I know because I gave it to him. He was supposed to pay me the twenty thousand right away so I could get those Vegas jerks off my back, but he kept putting me off, saying he couldn't move the violin right now, it was too hot."

"How do you know Jonathan?" I asked, trying to do what Detective Washington had said, keep Luis talking. The longer he talked, the better the chance the police had of getting me out of this. That was what I hoped, anyway.

"We met at a poker game in Vegas about a month ago. Both of us losers. Got to drinking and talking and found out we had San Celina in common. He owed money too and came up with this idea of stealing this violin his dad donated to the mission. He even had the replica already. I thought it was all bullshit talk. You know, make a quick buck. I kind of said if he needed a partner, let me know, I would do anything. I needed some cash fast. We exchanged cards and that was it, I thought."

"Why Walt Adams? How did Jonathan get him to make the replica?"

"Through Kevin, that guy dating his son's mother. He saw a wooden toy that Walt made his son, heard from the mother that Kevin's father was trying like crazy to make things up with Kevin. Jonathan convinced this woman, Sharon, or something—"

"Sheila."

"Whatever. Anyway, he convinced her to talk Kevin into asking his dad to do it. That stupid old man didn't even realize what he was doing. He was just glad to do something for his son. One day, when he saw that the real violin had been replaced with the one he made, he called Kevin to find out what had happened. Walt then said he had to confess to Mac, that he couldn't be a part of something like that, not even to make Kevin happy. Kevin called Jonathan, who remembered my comment in Vegas. He called me and said he just needed someone to persuade this old man to not go to the authorities. He said if I could do it, he'd pay me twenty thousand dollars. I figured, how hard could it be? I didn't think the old man would be so stubborn." He looked down at his feet. "I didn't mean to kill him. He just wouldn't back down. I just . . . panicked."

I was silent for a moment. Somewhere I thought I heard rustling. Mice? Police officers? Maybe it was just my pounding heart. "What happened to the violin?"

He shrugged. "Ask Jonathan."

I was confused. "Why ask Gabe for money to pay your gambling debt?"

"He heard me talking to one of the Vegas guys who managed to track me down. What could I do? Gabe is good at getting information out of a person. I'm sure you know that. I figured asking him would get him so angry it would put him off the real trail."

He was right. Gabe hadn't suspected his cousin for one moment. The cell phone rang again and I looked at him.

He lifted his head and reached for the gun. "Go ahead."

I hit the TALK button. "Hello?"

"Hey, Benni." Detective Washington's voice was as smooth and comforting as warm pudding. "How are you doing?"

"Fine," I said. "We're just talking."

"Good, keep him talking. The longer he talks, the more apt we are to get through this successfully."

"Yes," I said.

"Let me talk to him," Luis said, gesturing with his free hand to pass him the phone. "I need a car. And money. That's all I want. I'll drop Benni off in a safe spot, and we'll call it even. That's my deal."

I didn't hear what Detective Washington said, but I knew one thing that Luis didn't. Cops don't make deals in hostage situations. No matter what you see on television, I knew this to be a fact. They'd wait as long as it took then eventually send in SWAT. But they'd never make a deal. Not even for the police chief's wife.

"Okay, fine. Call me back when you get an answer." He tossed the phone on the pew. "He says he has to talk to his boss. I guess that means Gabe. What do you think my perfect cousin is doing right now? Think he'll make a deal for you?"

"He'll do whatever is the right thing to do. I trust Gabe's judgement."

He cocked his head. "You really do love the guy, don't you?"

"Yes," I said. Then, taking a chance, "You could turn yourself in. There's still a way to make this right."

"I'm not going to prison, Benni," he said, his voice dead-sounding. "I'd rather die."

"No," I said, feeling myself panic. "You don't mean that."

"Forget it," he said, standing up, pacing in front of the altar table. He glanced at his watch. "How long can it take to get a car and some money?"

I watched him pace back and forth, wondering if I should try to get the gun away from him. He was at least sixty pounds heavier than me and high on something. Chances are I would get shot, probably killed. But was it better to die trying to save yourself or wait and see how things played out?

I remember reading once that, when you got down to brass tacks, there were only two prayers that people actually prayed—help and thank you. I looked up at the pale wooden cross.

Help.

Luis stopped pacing in front of me, his broad shoulders blocking my view. He looked me right in the eyes. "It would break my mother's heart."

"She loves you, Luis. She will no matter what happens."

He shook his head, his face sad now. "I don't know. This time . . ." He looked up at the ceiling. "This time I've really messed up. Not even Gabe can get me out of this one."

"He'll help you. It's not hopeless."

He looked back at me, his eyes glossy. "I'm in too deep."

"No one is ever too deep. Not for God."

Our eyes locked for a long moment, then he looked away. "If I could get to Mexico, I could start a new life. That's all I need, to just start over."

"You can. But you don't have to go to Mexico."

He turned and pointed the gun at me. "Shut up. Just *shut up*."

I froze, staring at the barrel.

O Lord, have mercy.

He slowly lowered the gun. "What am I going to do?"

The phone rang again. He let it ring four times before answering. "Don't call back," he screamed into it. Then he threw it across the church. It hit a quilted banner that said "Christ is King."

It was like watching the last lifeboat push away from a sinking ship. *Help. Please.*

He stared at the broken phone. Then he looked up at me. "Do you miss your mother, Benni?"

I nodded, unable to speak.

"Gabe said she died when you were six. Do you ever think about her?"

"Every day," I whispered.

"My mother is the only person who ever loved me." His voice broke.

"Your boys love you. Cassie loves you." Gabe loves you, I wanted to say.

He shook his head. "No, no. *Mami*, she loves me. Only she does." He took the barrel of the gun and scratched the side of his cheek. His cheekbones were shaped exactly like Gabe's. Gabe's evening whiskers always reddened my cheeks and neck. When he was in a good mood, he rubbed them against me to tease me, laughing at my feigned protests.

"What do you remember about your mother?" he asked.

"I don't know," I said, swallowing over the hard lump filling my throat. "The things she said to me, what I can remember anyway. How she used to braid my hair before I went to school. What she smelled like."

"What she smelled like?" He gave a startled laugh.

"Yes," I said. "She wore this kind of perfume, I don't even know the name, but it smelled like magnolias. Every time I smell magnolias . . ." I couldn't finish the sentence.

He looked at me thoughtfully. "I never thought about what my mother smelled like. Maybe she doesn't smell like anything."

"If you thought about it, I bet you'd remember."

He didn't answer. His attention suddenly seemed to be somewhere else. We sat there silently for ten or fifteen minutes as darkness slowly settled around the room. The only light came from an automatic night-light plugged into the wall next to the piano. We both sat on the front pew, staring straight ahead, separated by enough space for five people, a whole family.

Please. It was all I could pray.

"Luis?" I finally asked.

He turned at the sound of my voice, his face almost surprised, as if I'd just walked into the room.

"Get down," he said, standing up.

"What?"

"On the floor. Lay down on the floor. On your stomach."

"Luis, what—"

"Do it now!" His voice was harsh, certain.

I did as he said and laid down on the carpet in front of the steps that led to the altar. Three steps below where Walt Adams died. I turned my head so my cheek lay against the new carpet. It was scratchy against my skin and smelled clean and unsoiled.

"Forgive me," I heard Luis whisper.

I squeezed my eyes shut and tensed up. How long would it hurt before it's over? Memories flashed through my mind—Daddy's laugh,

Dove's voice calling the chickens, the smell of wild mustard, Jonesy running across the back pasture, Gabe's beautiful eyes.

I'm afraid.

Fear Not.

Thank you.

Footsteps on the carpet. So soft. Walking away.

"Luis?" I called. Then louder, "Luis?"

His voice came from behind me, sounding far away. "I know what my mother smells like, Benni. Vanilla. She smells like vanilla."

I lifted my head and screamed. "Luis! No!"

Then he pushed the double doors open and started shooting.

Chapter 16

Aᴼᴼᴼ ᴛʜᴇ ꜱʜᴏᴛꜱ, ᴛʜᴇʀᴇ ᴡᴀꜱ ᴀɴ ᴀᴠᴀʟᴀɴᴄʜᴇ ᴏꜰ ꜱᴏᴜɴᴅꜱ— shouts, doors opening, people running. I lay on the floor of the sanctuary, face down, listening, hoping, that it wasn't what I thought. It felt like hours later when a familiar voice called to me, "Benni, are you okay? It's Sonja."

I slowly lifted my head to look up at the dark vision stooping down in front of me. The figure was blurry, and it was only then that I realized I'd been crying.

"Sonja?" I repeated, my head fuzzy, like mosquitos were swarming in my brain. I narrowed my eyes to peer at her under her black helmet.

"Yes, Sonja O'Donohue. Remember me? From the department picnic? We shared that last piece of German chocolate cake. I'm still working on my Log Cabin quilt. C'mon, let me help you sit up."

"Sonja?" I asked again, allowing her to help me into a sitting position. "You haven't finished that quilt yet?" My brain felt like a short-circuited electrical board, images and sounds darting around like silverfish. Sonja was one of Gabe's officers. I met her at a department picnic. She was a beginning quilter. She was his only female SWAT team member.

SWAT team. The sound of gunfire. *Luis.*

"Where's Luis?" I asked, though in my heart, I knew. I looked into her blue eyes, the black pupils dilated with adrenaline-fused excitement. She was wearing some kind of shiny, pale blue eyeshadow.

"I couldn't see his pupils," I said to her, hearing my own voice as if it were someone else talking. "His eyes were too dark."

"I know," she said, her voice soothing. "It's okay. You're okay."

A memory crackled in my brain. Sonja had a beautiful, detailed tattoo on her ankle of a little Dutch girl. Because she was Dutch.

"How's your tattoo?" I gave a small disembodied laugh. Why did that seem so funny to me? "Gabe has a tattoo. I want a tattoo." That seemed like such a good idea right now. I looked into her face. "I like your eyeshadow. I'm not making any sense, am I?"

"Don't get up too fast," she said, her voice soothing and indulgent as she helped me up. "I've got you."

Her firm grip on my arm was the only thing that kept me from collapsing. The floor looked so tempting, the carpet new and clean, no blood stains, hard concrete underneath. When I was lying there, it felt so solid, so secure.

Can blood soak into concrete? I looked at the cross hanging above the baptismal. *Nothing but the blood of Jesus.* I'd sung that song since I was a child. So many songs in the Baptist hymnal are about blood. Why had they never scared me as a child? *Luis. It didn't have to end that way.*

"Can you walk?" Sonja asked, still gripping my arm. Her rifle was slung across her back like a soldier's.

A thought occurred to me. They were soldiers, these officers. Soldiers fighting crime. Fighting an enemy that never stopped advancing.

"I can walk," I said, turning to look into her eyes. My head was still murky, but I was alive. "I need to see Gabe."

"I know you do," she said. "I'll take you to him."

"Thank you." I stopped, suddenly afraid to leave this spot, this place where I was spared.

"What is it?" she asked, her voice gentle, kind. "Do you need to use the bathroom?"

I thought for a moment, the question seemed monumental. Why was everything taking me so long to figure out? "No," I finally decided. "I'm fine."

"Then we need to go." She pointed toward one of the side doors. "We'll go out this way."

I looked down the church's middle aisle, toward the double front doors. They were half-open and I could see people, legs and boots, the flashing lights of a cop car, an ambulance. Someone moved aside and for a moment, I glimpsed Luis's body.

Vanilla, he'd said. *My mother smells like vanilla.*

Outside, it was dark and cold and there was a car. Its tailpipe spewed a white cloud. What time was it? There was no moon. The stars seemed so bright, salt crystals spilled across a dark cosmic tablecloth.

Sonja, her strong hand still gripping my arm, helped me into the unmarked police car. "You take care, Benni," she said, before closing the door.

"Thank you," I said. "Finish that quilt. I'll hang it in the museum."

"Yes, ma'am," she said, touching two fingers to her helmet. "I'll call you the minute I do. We'll have a drink to celebrate."

Within minutes the car whisked me to a trailer, and I was taken inside. Someone gave me a glass of water. Someone else helped me sit down. Then Gabe was there, and I was in his arms.

"Oh, God, oh, God," he kept repeating. A prayer. "Oh, God." He hugged me so tight, I gave a small groan.

"I'm sorry," he said, his hands coming up to cup my face. His face was stricken with an expression I'd never seen. An expression of fear and despair, relief and happiness, all at the same time.

"Luis," I said and started to cry. "I tried . . ."

"I know," he said, holding my face, rubbing his thumbs over my wet cheeks. "It's not your fault, *querida*."

"Chief," an apologetic voice said behind him. "We need to talk to her now."

I felt his hesitation. "I can do it," I told him, saving him from making the decision about whether I was in any shape to be questioned or not.

He held my face in his hands a few seconds longer, then bent his head and kissed me gently on the lips. "You can stop anytime. We can do it later."

"Your uncle. They should hear about Luis from you."

"Yes," he said.

He said to the man who just spoke to him, "Bring her to my office when you're through."

Gabe turned back to me. "Benni, this is Detective Luther Washington. He was your negotiator. He'll debrief you."

"Yes, sir," said the man, looking down at me from behind round tortoiseshell glasses. His easy smile made his round face look even more innocuous than it appeared. He looked more like a forgetful history professor than a hostage negotiator.

I smiled back at him. "Thank you." His skill had saved the kids from the worse part of the situation. It had saved me.

"My pleasure, ma'am," he said and rubbed the side of his freckled nose.

"You're from Alabama," I replied.

"Why, you're right as rain," he said, smiling wide. "Selma, as a matter of fact."

"Beautiful state."

"I plan on retiring there someday." He stood aside and gestured toward a room in the trailer. "Raise me some Catahoula leopard hounds. This won't take long, I promise."

I looked up at Gabe. His expression shouted that he didn't want to let me out of his sight. "I'll be fine, Friday. Go call your uncle. You and I have the rest of our lives to talk."

"Yes," he said and kissed me again.

After Detective Washington took me through the incident twice, gently pulling out of me everything I could remember about what happened, what Luis said, what his mood was, he told me that was enough for now. They'd already pulled Kevin Adams in for questioning because of what Gabe had found in Walt's apartment. He'd already lawyered up, but now they had more information. After what I told them about Jonathan Hammer, Detective Washington said he'd be picked up right away.

"I have a feeling there'll be quite a bit of fingerpointing between those two." He smiled at me. "But that's not your problem. We might need to have you go over all of this again at a later date though."

"You know where to find me."

He smiled at me and patted my hand. "Thank you for being patient. I'm sure you're very tired."

"I want to see my gramma and my dad. They're probably frantic."

"I'm pretty sure they're over at Gabe's office. I'll find out."

After a quick phone call, he said, "Yes, they are all over there waiting for you. I'll have an officer drive you."

Apparently the newspapers hadn't found out the whole story yet because they managed to sneak me into an unmarked police car and drive me past the cameras without incident. That wouldn't last, I knew. Once the press found out my part in this, Gabe and I would be harassed for a week. Then the story would be replaced by something else. I'd learned early how fleeting the public's interest was, even with tragic incidents like this.

When I arrived, everyone was crowded in Gabe's office—Dove, Daddy, Isaac, Emory, Elvia, and her brother, Miguel, dressed in his police uniform, getting ready to go on morning shift.

"Lord Jesus, thank you," Dove said, rushing over to hug me when I walked in. "Thank you, thank you," she kept repeating. I just held her and inhaled her sweet almond scent over and over.

"Where's Gabe?" I asked.

"I don't know," Emory said, his green eyes red-rimmed. He stood with Elvia pulled close under his arm, but watching me like I was an apparition that would disappear any moment. "He was here for a few minutes before you arrived. Then he just disappeared."

I nodded. His uncle. He went to find a quiet place to call his uncle.

"Oh," Emory said, realizing what Gabe was probably doing. "Luis's parents."

I contemplated going through the office looking for him, but decided that he would come back when he'd done what he had to do.

About a half hour later, a uniformed officer knocked on the door. Emory opened it. "Yes?"

"Uh . . . there's someone to see Mrs. Ortiz. He's he's very insistent. I wouldn't have let him in except, well—" Before he could finish, Hud pushed past him.

"Thanks, officer," Hud said, striding across the room to where I was standing between Dove and Daddy.

He marched right up to me, put his arms around me, and hugged me hard. "Thank you," he whispered. "Thank you for keeping my baby girl safe."

"You're welcome," I answered. "You'd better get back to her. She was very brave, but it was pretty intense in there."

"I will," he said, letting me go.

"You all need to go home," I said, looking over at Dove, whose face was paler than I'd ever seen it. She looked ready to collapse. "Get some sleep."

"I don't want to leave you," Dove said.

"I'll be fine. I want to wait for Gabe. He needs me right now."

After more hugs and some protest, I managed to convince everyone to leave. "I'll call all of you tomorrow. I promise."

When I was finally alone, I went over and sat down in Gabe's chair, curling my legs under me and turning my head to lay my cheek against the leather back. It smelled faintly of the citrus-scented hair gel he used, some kind of special product he ordered from a store in L.A. He wouldn't use anything else, swore every other product made his hair sticky.

The clock on the credenza behind his desk ticked, and outside his window, dawn started seeping in around the edges of his ivory miniblinds. Somewhere in the department yard, where they serviced the police cars, I heard a man's deep laughter, then silence, then the unexpected trill of a mockingbird. I was sitting in that position when Gabe came back.

"Benni?" he asked, his voice ragged.

I was out of the chair in an instant and in his arms before he could say another word. We held each other for a long time without speaking. The long night was over. Morning was here.

"What . . . what happened?" I finally asked, my ear pressed to his chest, counting his heartbeats. "Uncle Tony? . . ."

"It was hard," he said. "The hardest thing I've ever done in my life." His lips caressed the top of my head, brushing back and forth, back and forth, the heat from his breath warming my scalp. "Let's go home."

So we drove through the quiet early streets of our town, toward home. Outside our house, a patrol car was parked. I looked at Gabe in question.

"To keep the reporters away. Just until we can get some rest."

Inside, I hugged Scout, who licked the dried salt on my cheeks.

"Go take a shower," Gabe said, nodding at the stairs. "I'll make you some warm milk."

Though I knew he needed comforting as much as me, I sensed he also needed to be doing something concrete and methodical, something he could control. After my shower, I climbed into bed, and he brought me the milk, sitting next to me as I sipped it. The clock read six A.M.

"You should take a shower," I said. "It'll relax you. Then we should try to get some sleep. It's going to be a long day."

"Yes, it will," he said.

I'd almost fallen asleep when a sound jolted me awake. I bolted up in bed, listening. Scout sat next to the bed, whining like a puppy.

"What is it?" I asked.

Then I heard it again. I climbed out of bed and went over to the bathroom door, pressing my ear against the cool painted wood. Our shower head, an environmentally incorrect one that spewed water like Niagara Falls, was one of our shared secret vices. We both like the feel of the needle-sharp spray and couldn't care less how much water we wasted. I teased Gabe that what he really liked was how loud the water was, how it drowned out his shower-stall renditions of Willie Nelson and Frank Sinatra.

I pressed my ear harder against the door. There. I could hear better now. Sobbing. The sound of sobbing. I tried the brass knob. Locked.

I sank down to the floor. "Oh, Gabe," I whispered. "Oh, Friday."

So I sat there, my hand flat on the door, Scout's head in my lap, wishing I had a key to this door. I sat there until the shower went off and the sobbing finally stopped.

CHAPTER 17

THE NEXT DAY THE *TRIBUNE* RAN THE FIRST OF A HALF-DOZEN articles about Luis's death, citing the rise across the nation in police-assisted suicides, which is what the powers who decide these things called what happened to Luis. I suppose they were right. The articles, with all the requisite quotes from prominent psychologists and FBI analysts and examples of other suicide-by-cop situations, only told half the story, the part that could be researched and recorded. They could never see into the human heart, the place where it all begins, where it all goes wrong. Then, before the ink was barely dry on the newspapers, it was over, replaced on the *Tribune*'s front page by a scandal in Los Osos concerning their new sewer system.

That first day the phone rang continuously. Gabe answered every call, saying it was just best to deal with it now, that eventually we'd be yesterday's news. I'd already talked to a half-dozen friends who'd called, when Gabe answered the phone one more time, as he had been doing since we got up. He listened for a moment, then he handed it to me.

"Your friend wants to make sure you're all right," he said, without a bit of sarcasm.

"Hello?" I asked, not knowing who it was.

"Benni." Hud's voice was jagged with relief. "I've been trying to call for hours. How are you today?"

"I'm doing okay. How's Maisie?"

"Doing better than us adults, actually. I spent the night with her and Laura Lee. They were both real shook up."

"Understandable," I said.

Because there was nothing new we could really say about what happened, I turned the conversation to the upcoming play, the new Cajun restaurant that was opening downtown, his grandfather's new apartment. We eventually ran out of chitchat and he was quiet for a moment.

Then he blurted out, "I'm sorry. For not being there. I should have never left—"

"It *wasn't* your fault," I interrupted, repeating what Gabe had said to me. "There's no way you could have known. It wasn't anyone's fault."

"I should have known." His voice was blunt, unforgiving.

"Cut yourself some slack, Clouseau," I said softly. "Everything turned out all right." Almost everything.

I DIDN'T KNOW IF WE COULD DO IT, ACTUALLY PUT THE PLAY ON IN less than two weeks, but the human spirit is more resilient than most people realize. It took a few extra rehearsal days, but in spite of some fearful parents pulling their kids out of the play, *Pilgrim's Progress— The Joyful Journey* came off with only a few minor mistakes. Then again, mistakes are what makes children's performances so refreshing, original, and downright fun. It's always the fumbled line or unscripted giggling sheep or townspeople in the background that we remember rather than a perfect performance. To be honest, I think the distraction was good for everyone.

When Mac came out on stage as Giant Despair, he was so convincing that I think he even startled some of the adults in the audience. From the sidelines, where I stood with a script in case anyone needed prompting, I watched people become transfixed when his deep voice bellowed, "You can't escape *me*. I am Giant Despair." The kids tried to act afraid, but they'd been through too many rehearsals with Mac, knew his gentle personality too well. Most of them grinned, a few giggled behind their hands, and a couple of the "townspeople" actually laughed out loud. Mac didn't help things any by making funny faces at them when his back was turned to the audience.

At the cookie-and-punch reception after the play, no one spoke of either Walt's murder or Luis's death, which was as it should be. This was the children's night and, giddy from their performance and high on sugar and adrenaline, they ran around laughing and playing, even those who'd been held captive. The resilience of children is truly one of God's most merciful gifts.

Angelina was there with her aunt, who, though still shy, seemed a little more comfortable.

"*Gracias, señora,*" she said, pressing a tissue-wrapped package in my hands. They were twin pillowcases with *El Señor es mi Pastor* embroidered on the ends.

"The Lord is my Shepherd," I repeated in English.

"*Si,*" she replied.

"*Muchas gracias,*" I said. "They are beautiful."

During the reception, Mac came over to me, still dressed in his Giant Despair outfit, and placed a gentle hand on my shoulder.

"How are you and Gabe holding up?" he asked.

I looked up into his kind, exhausted face. "We're hanging in there, Mac. We'll get through this."

"I know," he said, squeezing my shoulder. "I pray for you both daily."

Hud actually seemed to enjoy the play and the reception. He'd arranged to have a professional videographer there to record the play and promised a copy to every child. He also bought two dozen long-stemmed red roses and had the kids present them to Dove at the end of the performance. If anything had ever tempted me to kiss that man, that would have been it.

"Thanks for sending Dove the roses," I said. "Maisie did a wonderful job."

"Yes, I'm pretty proud," he said, grinning. "Not that anyone can tell. And you're welcome." His dark eyes studied me. "Are you really okay?" he asked once again.

"I promise, Hud. I'm really okay."

He dropped by to see me again at the folk art museum later on in the week, on the day before Thanksgiving. I was standing out front watering the whiskey-barrel pots filled with native wildflowers, mentally reliving my conversation with Luis yet again, changing a word here, adding a word there, trying to figure out if, somehow, I could have talked him out of it, comforted him, saved him. Every time the scene ends in my head just exactly how it happened, with the *rat-tat-tat* of his gun, the single silent reply of the SWAT team sharpshooter.

Hud asked me what happened to Angelina and her aunt. Maisie tried to call her friend and found the phone had been disconnected. I told him how I'd found out two days before that Angelina and her aunt had disappeared. I'd gone over to their apartment to take Angelina some books. None of the neighbors knew where they had gone or, at least, that's what everyone said.

"Father Mark says he doesn't know where they are," I said, trying not to sound bitter. "Mac says he doesn't either." I was certain they were not telling me the exact truth. "They said they'll be fine. I have to trust them, I guess."

I suspected the whole situation had been too much for them, the publicity daunting and frightening. Perhaps it was best that Angelina and her aunt make a new start somewhere else.

"I'm sorry," he'd replied, pushing his dark brown Stetson back so he could see me better.

"It kills me, not knowing how she'll turn out." I watched the water arch into the whiskey barrel, blinking back tears. "Whether she'll be happy."

His face was kind. "I know."

I stood there watering that stupid whiskey barrel, tears streaming down my face, not certain what I was crying about . . . Angelina and her aunt, Luis, Aunt Maria and Uncle Tony, Gabe, me, this whole insane world. When the barrel started overflowing, Hud gently took the hose from my hands, turned off the water, and tossed it aside. He led me over to his pickup and opened the passenger door, gesturing at me to get inside. Then he handed me one of the white, monogrammed, Egyptian cotton handkerchiefs that he always carried. To pick up heartbroken women in bars he once told me. He left me there to cry while he sat on the bench in front of the folk art museum and waited. When I'd cried myself out, I got out of the truck and walked back over to him.

"Thanks," I said, shoving the handkerchief into the back pocket of my jeans.

"My pleasure," he'd said.

Later that day, I was sitting on the front porch in our wooden swing watching Gabe play keep-away with Scout. Thanksgiving was tomorrow and, as usual, my family had a huge celebration planned at the ranch with my aunts and uncles and cousins coming from all over the West to eat, play poker, and give thanks. This year, I had more to be thankful for than usual. Though a few nightmares had plagued me, ones where I was running in the dark pursued by something that had no face, it was Gabe's voice that woke me every time. He would hold me until I stopped trembling.

I was perusing my *Southern Living* cookbook trying to decide on a different dessert to make besides my usual pecan pie, banana pudding, and Yankee cake. A chocolate bread pudding with bourbon sauce was looking particularly interesting and easy to quadruple.

"I'm going for a run," Gabe said, tossing the ball one last time for Scout. "Try to work off some of those calories I'm going to be eating."

"Take Scout with you," I said, swinging gently back and forth. "He needs to get in shape to wrestle with Daddy's new puppy." Daddy had recently bought a corgi puppy from Sally Schuler, the sheriff. He'd named the dog Spud, after a dog he'd owned as a boy.

"Okay," he said, bending down to kiss my temple before going inside to change into shorts and a sweatshirt.

Gabe had been more quiet than usual since Luis died. The funeral was held a week after his death down in Santa Ana in the old Catholic church on Main Street where Luis had been baptized and confirmed. It was a small gathering with just his family and a few longtime friends. Aunt Maria and Uncle Tony looked ten years older than the last time I'd seen them. When Aunt Maria saw me, she hugged me so long that Uncle Tony had to pry her away. The shoulder of my dress was dark with her tears. I suppose since I'd been the last one to see and talk to Luis, she just wanted to hold onto whatever essence of him might remain. He was right. She smelled like vanilla. I'd never noticed that before.

"Lo siento, lo siento," I just kept saying over and over while she cried.

Gabe was a pallbearer, along with Luis's sons and brothers. He also gave the eulogy, where he talked about how easily Luis accepted him as a brother when Gabe was sixteen and missing his own family, how Luis had loved his sons and his daughter, how he had loved his parents. He talked about Luis's kind heart, ironic maybe to some people when the facts about what happened to Walt Adams came to light, but as the priest said during his funeral sermon, who among us has not sinned, who among us was without blemish? "Forgive me," I'd heard Luis say before opening the church doors. If he meant it, God would. I believed that with all my heart.

When Gabe came out dressed for his run, I glanced up at my husband's stoic face, wondering how he felt about his cousin right this moment, what complex and troubling memories would live in that place his heart reserved for Luis. He never spoke of it to me or anyone else that I knew of. Maybe Father Mark, though that was between him and his priest.

When he finally came to bed the night I heard him crying, I pretended to be asleep though I longed to roll over and comfort him. I knew that it was still too raw for him to share. Still, I couldn't help reaching over and touching his shoulder, a feather-light caress of my finger tips. I was prepared for him to ignore it, pretend like it hadn't happened. Instead, his fingertips touched mine, a whisper of acknowledgment. Then he turned over and went to sleep. I lay awake for an hour after that, staring at the ceiling, knowing that when I least expected it, he would come to me and talk. As I told him in the command-post trailer the night of Luis's death, we had the rest of our lives. I could wait. But this incident had caused me to decide something. I'd spent all of yesterday doing it and was waiting for the right moment to tell him.

He stood on the bottom step of our porch and looked up at me sitting on our green-and-white porch swing. "How are you?" he asked. I'd had another nightmare last night. Worry tightened the skin around his eyes.

"Fine. You?"

He nodded. "Yes."

"Okay."

I watched him jog down our walkway to the street, Scout loping along beside him.

"Let's go out for a Mexican food after I get back," he called over his shoulder. "I'm craving some *mole*."

"Sounds good. I have a present for you when you get back."

He turned around and ran backwards, grinning at me. "Oh, yeah?"

I laughed. "Not that. Well, okay, that and something else."

"You've got me curious," he said, turning back around. "I'll cut my run short."

I'd gone to the DMV first, then spent the rest of the day changing everything else. My official name was now Albenia Louise Harper Ortiz. No dash, but I'd kept Harper. It might be cumbersome, but it was also a part of who I was. I put all the paperwork in the tramp box that Walt had made me. In all the hullabaloo, I'd forgotten to show it to Gabe. This seemed an appropriate way. Life was unpredictable, Walt had said. You never know when your last day will be. He was right, and whatever days I had left on this earth, I wanted to live as Mrs. Albenia Harper Ortiz.

I'd reached the candy section of the cookbook and was contemplating English toffee when Maisie Hudson rode up our driveway on a glittery pink-and-white two-wheel bicycle with training wheels.

"Hey, Benni!" she said. "Look at my new bike!"

Laura Lee Hudson strolled behind her, walking a small, obviously willful, apricot-colored poodle. He strained against his jeweled leather leash.

"It's very cool," I said to Maisie, standing up and setting the cookbook down on the swing. "You sure can ride it well."

"I'm almost off the training wheels," she said confidently. "I want to take them off now, but my daddy won't let me."

"Your daddy's just trying to protect you," I told her, smiling at her mom when she reached the porch. "Hey, Laura Lee. How are you?"

"Real good," she replied. "Are you free for a few minutes?"

"Sure," I said, moving the cookbook off the swing. "Have a seat."

"Thank you."

She came up the steps and sat down next to me. I could smell her delicate perfume, a flowery scent that reminded me of my mother. She was dressed in brown wool slacks and a butterscotch-colored cashmere sweater set. Burnished, gold-tinged pearls circled her smooth neck.

"Cute dog," I said, reaching my hand out for the dog to sniff. When he'd deemed me worthy, he stretched his neck out and allowed me to scratch under his curly chin.

"And he knows it," she said, giving a tinkly, pleasant laugh.

I could see why Hud had been attracted to this woman. There was something so gentle and comforting about her. I bet she was a great mom.

"His name is Charles," she said. "Not Charlie, not Chuck. Charles." Her Texas twang reminded me of my first husband, Jack's, mother. Is that what happens as you age, everything eventually reminds you of something in your past?

"As in Prince?" I said, smiling.

"Exactly." She gave another laugh.

We sat for a moment not speaking, watching Maisie ride up and down my concrete driveway. Finally, to make conversation, I said, "How's Maisie doing?"

"Fine," she said, touching her blushing cheek briefly. "She talks about it some. Mostly right before she goes to bed."

"That's good. That she can talk about it, I mean."

Laura Lee nodded and continued to watch her daughter.

I was confused as to why she'd dropped by, though I was certain there was a reason. I'd seen her only three days ago at the reception after the *Pilgrim's Progress* performance. I'd asked her then how Maisie was feeling after her frightening ordeal, and she'd said she was fine, a few scary dreams, but Laura Lee didn't think it was serious.

"I guess you're wondering why I came by," Laura Lee eventually said. We both instinctively started rocking the swing.

I nodded and kept rocking.

"I just wanted to thank you."

I looked at her, confused. "Why?"

"I want to thank you . . . oh, that doesn't sound right . . . I want to say how happy I am that you are Hud's friend."

I sat back in the swing, surprised. "What?"

"Hud is . . ." She looked down at her pink-nailed hands, ringless and tanned a golden brown even in November. She fiddled with her charm bracelet, making all the charms lie in the same direction. She looked over at me, her light brown eyes round and calm. "He's a complicated man."

I nodded, running my hand up the chain that held the swing to the porch. "That's an understatement."

"He really cares about you, you know."

Now I was really puzzled. I felt my cheeks start to grow warm. This was, by far, one of the most awkward conversations I'd ever had with another woman.

"Oh, I don't mean he's in love with you," she amended quickly. "Though I think he is. But, you have to realize, Hud falls in love easily. That's one of the reasons our marriage broke up. He's an incredible flirt and, well, there were other things. I just couldn't live with it anymore . . ."

She let her voice trail off, her eyes turning to track her daughter, who was riding her bike up and down my smooth driveway. At the top of her lungs, Maisie sang one of the songs from the play.

In every darkness there's a light,
Piercing through the gloom of night.
In every heart a still, small voice,
There is a choice,
There is a choice,
There's a choice . . .

Laura Lee and I looked at each other.

"Out of the mouths of babes," I said softly.

She nodded. "I know this is weird, me coming to talk to you about Hud, but for some reason I felt compelled to tell you what you mean to him. We never know . . ." She left it open, knowing I could fill in her thought.

She was right. We never knew.

"He's a good man, Laura Lee," I said. "But he knows where he stands with me. I agree, he's infatuated. By this time next year, there'll be someone else. I'm just a novelty to him."

"No, that's what I'm trying to say. You're different. You're his friend. You don't realize how significant that is. Hud doesn't have friends. His grandfather. Maybe me, only because I know him so well, because of our history." She glanced over at Maisie. "But I can tell by the way he talks about you that he *trusts* you. For him, that is a huge thing. And he's a better person for it. A better father."

Her pale cheeks flushed a rosy pink. This was embarrassing for her too. I really liked this woman, dang it, and admired her determination to tell me something she thought I should hear despite the fact it was awkward for her. Hud, you numbskull, what were you thinking when you let this one get away?

"I'm sorry if I embarrassed you," she said, folding her hands primly in her lap, her face troubled.

"Oh, no," I said, leaning over and touching the top of her hands. "I mean, I *am* embarrassed, but in a good way. Thank you. I do care about Hud. He's . . . well, you're right. He's my friend."

"I know," she said.

"But," I said, smiling at her. "He can be a Texas-sized pain in the backside sometimes."

"Oh, yes, he can," she agreed, her delightful laugh ringing out, causing Maisie to stop riding her bike, look up at her mom, and start laughing too.

She stood up and held out her hand. "Guess I'll probably see you around town."

I took it. Her bracelet tinkled as we shook. "Don't think I'll be going anywhere soon."

I watched them walk back down the street. Just before they turned the corner, Laura Lee looked back and waved at me. I held my hand up in reply. Somehow, I had the feeling that she and Hud weren't completely over yet, that maybe, when all was said and done, they'd end up back together.

Gabe, of course, would call me a hopeless romantic. If it didn't work the first time between them, I could imagine him saying, why would it a second?

People change, Friday, is what I'd counter. They grow up. And we'd argue about it good-naturedly as we baked brownies, then hug and kiss, and finally agree that the human heart is a crazy, unpredictable thing. Truly the craziest of all of God's creations. What was He thinking, entrusting mankind with that miraculous organ, we'd say to each other and laugh. What in the world was He thinking?

Those were the thoughts that drifted through my mind as I sat on the front porch of my house, watching the sun turn the sky the color of ripe cantaloupes and plums, smelling the thousands of scents that colored the air, sharp and sweet, bitter and salty, all the scents of human life, all the scents created for our pleasure, our safety, and for our fickle, fickle hearts. Those were the thoughts that swirled around me, like a grace-filled breeze, as I sat on my front porch swing waiting for my husband to come home.

A Note from the Author

Pilgrim's Progress: The Joyful Journey by Lela A. Satterfield (arranged by Lela A. Satterfield and Candace L. Velarde—copyright 1993 by Lela A. Satterfield) is an actual musical play for children. The playwright was worship and music director at Fountain Valley United Methodist Church for eleven years. She is currently the worship and music director at First Baptist Church in Oceanside, California. My thanks to her for generously letting me quote from her play and lyrics. If your school or church is interested in putting on this play, you can contact her at lelasatterfield@hotmail.com.